The Blackpox Threat

A Rene Natan Novel

An Old Line Publishing Book

If you have purchased this book without a cover you should be aware that this book may have been stolen property and was reported as "unsold and destroyed" to the publisher. In such case neither the author nor the publisher has received any compensation for this book.

Copyright © 2010 by Irene Gargantini

All rights reserved. No part of this book may be reproduced or transmitted in any form or by any means, electronic or mechanical, including photocopying, recording, or by any information storage and retrieval system, without permission in writing from the publisher.

Printed in the United States of America

ISBN-13: 978-0-9845704-5-4

ISBN-10: 0-9845704-5-4

This book is a work of fiction. Any references to real people, events, establishments, organizations, or locales are intended solely to provide a sense of authenticity and are used fictitiously. All other characters, incidents, and dialogue are drawn from the author's imagination and are not to be construed as real.

Old Line Publishing, LLC
P.O. Box 624
Hampstead, MD 21074
Toll-Free Phone: 1-877-866-8820
Toll-Free Fax: 1-877-778-3756
Email: oldlinepublishing@comcast.net
Website: www.oldlinepublishingllc.com

Dedication

To my parents, Maria and Italo Gargantini

In memoriam

Acknowledgements

The author gratefully acknowledges those who helped with the research for this novel. They include Luisa Gargantini, philologist and lawyer, Colin Macaulay, Ph.D., (Director of Research and Development at Viron Therapeutics Inc., London, Ontario), Maryann Shemansky, Toronto writer and sleuth, and Isabelle Scott of the Canadian Security Intelligence Service Media Relations Program.

Special thanks to the editor Sharon Crawford.

The Blackpox Threat

Characters

Peggy Alberton-Dog trainer
Milena Romano-Dale Romano's wife
Armand Belfleur-Receptionist at the 'Pamper Yourself' spa
Gordon-Dianne's new boyfriend
Lesley-Lodge owner
Samuel-Employee of Thomas Sarcin
Jacob-Employee of Thomas Sarcin
Ron Brennen-Ex-officer of RCMP
Duncan Brown-Specialist in surveillance techniques
Stephanie Demoins-Ex-model of Versace
Stan Glover-Sophia's friend
Justin Devry-Tamara's friend
Michael Devry-Justin's father
Tony Esposito-A friend of Michael Devry
Mark Farin-CSIS officer
Barbara Fattori-Professor and artist
Catherine Ferreiro-Tamara's friend
Larry-Tamara's old boyfriend
Bill Hartwart-Detective, London Police Service
Michaëlle Jean-Governor General
Alan Johnson-Agent from Public Safety
Frank Milton-Biochemist
Zaccaria McKenzie-A customer of Michael Devry
Charles Modano-Owner of Modano Company
Heather Motta-Sergeant Major, OPP
Serge Patton-Sniper
Harry Pearson-Owner of the 'Pamper Yourself' spa
Vassilli Petrovic-Ukrainian diplomat
Claude Price-Pilot of The Sea King
Bev Roland-Sophia's neighbour
Mario Rossi-Employee of the Modano Company
Dale Romano-Head of the CSIS task force
Rossiters-Sophia's neighbours
Thomas Sarcin-Businessman
Tamara Smith-Protagonist
Catherine & Joseph Smith-Tamara's parents
Peter Stalovic-Boris Youkenoff's neighbour
Dianne Templeton-Charles Modano's assistant
Brad Wilson-CSIS agent
Boris Youkenoff-Scientist
Sophia Tadlova-Vassilli's old friend

The Blackpox Threat

Chapter 1

Rideau Hall, Ottawa
May 2007

"God is the greatest murderer of all. He kills the lame and the healthy, the good and the bad. He kills individually and en masse. He kills everything on earth, at times in the most cruel and terrifying ways. Nothing survives His fury." The man in the impeccably tailored tuxedo stopped his soliloquy for a moment and lifted his head high. *"And I'm made in His image. Therefore, I can kill."*

Feeling proud of his Cartesian reasoning, the man approached Rideau Hall, the residence of the Governor General. He ambled toward the ornate entrance of the Large Drawing Room and presented his invitation to the usher. Without waiting to be gestured inside, he headed in and began mingling with the crowd, stopping to shake hands and exchanging a few words with each of the guests he knew. The Governor General, Michaëlle Jean, had thrown a party to promote new and old business in the capital. It was hosted in a room displaying the splendour of the olden days; walls were tapestried with portraits of viceregal consorts of former governor generals and chandeliers reflected light in all directions.

The man in the tuxedo stopped in front of a gilded mirror and adjusted his bowtie. He accepted a glass of champagne that a waiter offered him, moved close to the refreshments table, and began to look around. He had come to choose his first target, a female victim whose disfiguration and consequent death would make waves around the world. The Governor General would be the ideal target because her vitality and personal flare would be missed on the national scene and beyond. Regretfully, he dismissed the party hostess as an option. He knew that the security around her was tight — definitely too tight for his liking. His person of choice had to be easily accessible.

People around him turned toward the main entrance when a tall woman crossed the doorway. Her short outfit, draped across the chest, was locked in place by a yellow clip on each shoulder. She had spiky blond hair and blue eyes. Her off-white dress parted at the knee as she walked to the centre of the hall, her arm linked with the commercial attaché of the Ukrainian embassy, Vassilli Petrovic.

As if waiting for them, a middle-aged man glided toward the couple, clearly showing pleasure in meeting them. Extending his hand to both, he gestured toward a corner of the room, where a huge terracotta vase full of palm leaves and canes provided a partial screen from the crowd. The woman could be a candidate for his operation, the man in the tuxedo surmised, as he sipped his drink. Vassilli knew only important people.

He set his glass down and approached the master of ceremony. "Would you know the name of the lady who just came in?"

"Tamara Smith. She's representing the company, *Ship Me*

Safely, owned by Mr. Charles Modano. There are pamphlets on the table over there, sir, if you want to know more." The muscles of his face hardly moved as he spoke, and now his white-gloved hand pointed to the entrance. Clad in 1800s livery, with white trousers and a red jacket festooned with gold trim, he could be mistaken for one of the statues on display at Madame Tussauds Wax Museum.

The man in the tuxedo nodded his thanks and then resumed his search. In the centre of the hall, three young men surrounded another woman. Their nondescript, dark suits offered an excellent background for her shiny outfit, whose fabric interwove glittering threads with green beads. She laughed at a joke one of the men told, and flirtatiously leaned toward another. Was she important enough to deserve to be his first target? She was surely beautiful; her disfigured face would raise horror in the world and remain in the news for weeks.

Fortunately, he knew the third man close to the woman. He was Justin Devry, the son of Michael Devry, owner of the most famous private art collection in the country. He wondered why Justin had been invited — he was just a young man with no trade. Maybe he was the woman's date.

"And who is that charming lady in the green gown?" he again asked the master of ceremonies.

"Stephanie Demoins. She's planning to open a haute couture shop here in town. The one in London has been very successful, I hear. She's a former model of Versace, they say."

With condescension he acknowledged his appreciation for the information as Stephanie and Justin moved to the refreshments table and helped themselves to a few canapés. He walked toward them and tapped the man on the shoulder.

"Hi Justin, I didn't expect to see you here," he said. "Is your family planning to open a gallery in Ottawa?"

"Oh no, no. Nothing of the sort. I'm just escorting Stephanie for the evening." He turned toward his companion and said, "Let me make the introductions."

****

A constraint in her chest made Tamara Smith leave the hall as soon as Vassilli Petrovic and Brad Wilson inched away from her. The nerve they both had to approach her at the Governor General's party, where she represented her boss's company and was supposed to attract more business for him! And it had been the third time in two weeks that they had pestered her!

Gasping for air, Tamara Smith climbed into her Subaru and zeroed toward the exit of the parking lot. The words of Vassilli Petrovic resounded in her ears. "My country — or should I say the world — will be indebted to you forever," followed by the no less dramatic parting words of Brad Wilson, an agent of CSIS, the Canadian Security and Intelligence Service. "You can't fail, Tamara, the stakes are too high." Tamara zoomed into the traffic, cutting in front of a car. She ignored the blasting horn behind her and sped up. In no time she was on Highway 31, aiming for the westbound 401.

She wasn't really upset with Vassilli, a longtime friend of the family who had helped her after her parents' death. Clearly he had just passed crucial information to the Canadian Government and CSIS had brought Vassilli into play as he knew her well. He hadn't pressured her to become involved in what appeared to be a covert operation. But that Brad Wilson! He kept arguing; he kept showing up wherever she went, making her feel that she had no choice but to do what they had planned for her — that she work at the Charles Modano outfit and spy on him and his business. None of this was to her liking. When Charles Modano had asked her to join his company as a PR person, she thought she was going to settle down. The agreement was that she would help at the antique shop two days a week, and accompany Charles to social gatherings. Contacting potential buyers of antiques was easier done at parties than at auctions or art events.

She loved her job, which allowed her to meet a carefree, shallow crowd often loaded with money. Occasionally, she would take a trip to acquire special items, often in Quebec, where old mansions were being dismantled, and antiques offered for sale at a low price. Raised and educated in France, she was fluent in both English and French. Her Russian lineage showed in the fine, blond hair and clear eyes. From her mother she had inherited long, well-shaped legs and the athletic look of Ukrainian women. At 32, without a solid financial status, she felt the need for a stable occupation, and that was one of the reasons she had agreed to work for the Modano Company.

Tamara banged on the steering wheel. Now that she was in a position to set roots — maybe have a family — ghosts from her past had reappeared and tried to lure her into a mission! Why her? Why not Dianne Templeton, Charles' assistant, who had been with his company for more than five years? She surely knew more about Charles' business than Tamara would ever find out. She felt helpless, tied to a past that only vaguely concerned her. It was worse than that — she felt trapped. Didn't governments have trained agents to carry out their dirty work?

The drive from Ottawa to London took over eight hours. When she turned the key in the lock of her house she was exhausted. She took a shower and dove under the bed sheets. Maybe she should take off and go skiing on the Swiss glaciers. Nothing appeased her more than sliding down the slopes, immersed in the majestic vision of high peaks.

And with that sweet thought Tamara fell asleep.

****

The bell resounded in her ears as if it was coming from a distance. She reached for a pillow and buried her head under it. She dozed off for a few minutes, then the bell rang again, followed by a vigorous rap on the door. It was for real, she realized, as she stretched up to look at the alarm clock on the nightstand. It was noon. She rose, put on a satin robe and approached the door. She wondered who had been able to get through the security of the condominium compound. The superintendent was an extremely careful man; he would call her and open the gate only if she okayed the visitor. Tamara looked thorough the pinhole. It was Brad Wilson. The expletive that General Cambronne was said to have pronounced after the defeat at Waterloo pursed her lips. How did Brad manage to come to the door? His badge, of course. Probably it functioned as a universal passkey, almost anywhere, anytime.

The temptation to detach the battery from the bell case and go back to bed was overwhelming. She needed time to collect her thoughts and slowly come to terms with what was happening.

Brad's voice resounded crisp and clear. "It's me. Tamara, please open up."

Reluctantly, Tamara complied and stepped aside to let the man in.

"Good morning, Tamara. Thank you for seeing me. I have something important to tell you."

Tamara sighed and tightened the belt on her robe. "Good morning," she replied with a low voice. "Must tell you right up front. I just got up and I can't function without a cup of coffee."

She gestured toward a big room. "Wait in the living room."

Brad Wilson closed the door behind him and said, "Oh no, no. I'll make coffee for you. What kind?"

Tamara shot him a curious look. "Perked. The coffeemaker is on the counter."

Brad deposited a hefty briefcase beside the bearskin that covered the entrance floor and moved into the kitchen as if he knew exactly where it was located. He is probably acquainted with the blueprint of the entire condominium, Tamara mused.

"I'll go clean up and get dressed." She walked back to her bedroom and slid into the shower. She indulged in soaping under the soothing warm water. Ten minutes later she emerged, still upset about Brad's unannounced and unwanted visit. Had it not been for the wonderful aroma, which insistently teased her nostrils, she would have stalled and taken an hour to put on a pair of jeans and a sweatshirt. But the smell of fresh coffee was irresistible. After another fifteen minutes she joined Brad Wilson in the kitchen.

In the breakfast nook stood an oval table with four chairs, each seat topped by a pillow that matched the bright green on the long curtains. As Tamara approached the bay window and parted the drapes, a dozen sparrows scattered away from the birdfeeder hanging from a post in the backyard. She sat on a chair, watching Brad deposit on the table a small tray with a mug full of coffee, creamer and sugar.

"I didn't know agents were trained to be perfect butlers." As cross as she was, she couldn't avoid smiling. "So what happened between late last night and this morning?"

Brad sat opposite her, his expression grave. "We've reason to believe that a shipment is ready to be made and could be on Canadian soil very soon."

Tamara's hand, which held the creamer, stopped in midair. She stared at Brad. "How soon?"

"It could very well be a week. We don't know."

When she recovered from the shock, Tamara poured a bit of cream into her coffee, spilling some on the table. She drained her mug, her eyes fixed on Brad. She thought she had time to think, time to ponder the situation, maybe time to convince CSIS to look for an alternate mole. Not only didn't she like what she had to do, but she also felt inadequate to the task. For the first time she observed her interlocutor with attention. His face was tight, his eyelids were baggy and he was in need of a shave. Of dark complexion, with a husky build, curly grey hair and quicksilver eyes, the man normally exuded an annoying vitality. Now he looked downcast, distraught. He was tugging at the knot of his tie, as if trying to get more breathing space. She had no idea what words would suit the circumstances.

"Coffee?" she finally managed to say.

"Glad you asked."

He rose and filled a mug for himself, then returned to his seat, and sipped his drink.

Ambivalent feelings washed over Tamara. She felt trapped in a game much bigger than she was, yet she knew that she had no choice but to accept the challenge. However, the agency owed her some answers before she embarked on a covert operation.

"Why has CSIS singled me out?" She stared at Brad.

Brad linked his fingers together and stretched his hands on the table.

"Three concurrent factors. You're working for the Modano Company, which we suspect is handling the shipment, yet you aren't tied down to a desk — you're free to come and go, often taking trips for work or a vacation. This makes it possible for you to follow a special lead — should such a lead present itself." He finished his coffee and held it out toward Tamara. "Another cup?"

Tamara assented and followed Brad to the kitchen. The stainless-steel appliances of the new purple variety matched the venation of the granite countertop. Tamara looked at her wristwatch.

"We should get something to eat," she said. "But first I'd like to hear the third reason." Brad kept silent. "Well?" She frowned.

"My boss thinks you owe it to us."

Tamara banged her empty mug onto the counter and winced as it broke. "I suspected so, and that made me angry, so angry I wanted to refuse. You people think I have the duty to serve? Just because of my father and mother?"

The answer came quick and to the point. "Yes."

Tamara turned to face Brad and locked her eyes with his. "It was British intelligence, SIS — which in the movies is referred to as MI6 — that thought my Russian father had important information, information so vital that they offered him asylum. One hand gave, the other received."

"Maybe so, but both the British and the Canadian governments managed to get you and your mother out of the Soviet Union, in what is remembered as a very critical yet successful operation." Brad paused for effect. "A little girl was very sick and had to be snatched out of a Russian infirmary. She was the reason the mother hadn't boarded the plane with her husband." He paused again. "I don't have to elaborate on what would have happened if mother and child had stayed in the USSR."

No, he didn't. Those were the times when the KGB had a free hand. They would have held them as hostages, forcing her father to return to his motherland, and then they would have been tortured one in front of the other. Death would be the welcome ending. Tamara shivered at the thought, forgot about a second cup of coffee or lunch and went back to the table. She slumped into a chair.

"Now, I'm guilty because I was sick," she said. "That's preposterous! I went a long way to forget about the past. My parents, afraid of retaliation, sent and kept me abroad — you can't believe how lonely I felt those years. And then, then… when they finally felt that the past was definitely buried — I was 18 — they allowed me to join them in Canada." Tamara could feel tears coming and her voice turning into a tremble. "Do you know what happened then?"

From behind, Brad took hold of her shoulders and whispered, "Yes. I know."

Tamara turned to look at him. "You know everything about me, right?"

Brad pointed to the briefcase that was still on the hall floor. "Your life is in there, Tamara. After what happened to your parents we kept an eye on you. If it's any consolation, their death is still being investigated."

He went around the table and sat in his chair. "We have a psychologist in our group. Her opinion is that the operation we want you involved in could be a form of catharsis for you. It's known that you have been a restless young woman. Maybe it'll help you cure the wounds of the past and find peace."

Tamara banged both fists on the table. "Yeah. Eternal peace! Healing my old wounds by exposing me to new dangers! I hope your psychologist is not in charge of operations! By the way, how dangerous is all this going to be?"

"We don't know yet. But we could find ourselves dealing with criminals who would stop at nothing to reach their goals."

Tamara emitted a long-suffering sigh. "I gathered that." Vassilli Petrovic had been candid on the subject.

Brad continued. "In the fortunate case that we get close to the target, we'll shadow you but, I assure you, you won't feel any interference." His tone was convincing.

"Even when I go on vacation?"

"Not if you don't want to, provided you let us know exactly where you're going, with whom, and for how long. Any other questions?" Tamara shook her head. "Then we should slot some time for a bit of training. A few seminars. They might come in handy."

"Training? Seminars?" At 32 she felt a bit old to go back to school.

Brad's lip corners bent in what could be interpreted as a smile. "Not really. We'd like you to attend a few information sessions. Make you aware of simple methods to help your mind remember things, faces and facts, and to catalogue them —"

"Cataloguing?"

"Well, kind of labelling them with a marker for later recognition, mentally of course, as things happen; later you'll type them down for us and for you to remember." He paused. "We'll show you how to do it. It takes practice, but then it becomes natural. In short, we'd like you to profile the people you meet, and for that, you have to observe them and collect their salient characteristics: age, appearance, way of speaking, body language…"

"I don't know if I can do that," Tamara said. She was accustomed to accepting people as they were, without casting them into fixed moulds.

"You may not, not now, but I'm sure you can learn. A few… hmm…hmm, lessons and you'll be a pro."

Tamara felt as if she was swimming in rough waters and was desperately trying to reach for safety.

"But Brad, I'd be a poor spy. I have an accent, they tell me."

The Blackpox Threat

Brad waved off her objection. "With your upbringing in Russia, your schooling in France and your 14 years in this country it's almost impossible to pinpoint your accent. I know I couldn't. Yours is a charming drawl." He let a little laugh out. "In any case, we're asking you to listen into people's conversation, not to hand out speeches."

Tamara didn't react, and Brad continued. "So we'd like you to become aware of the latest communication techniques and devices, photo and audio recording."

"You mean wiretapping?"

"Well, let's call them effective surveillance techniques. We know that you frequent a health club and jog regularly — five kilometres twice a week. So we have no concerns about your physical fitness. We also know that you have a permit for firearms." He paused. "At the moment we're very much interested in the inbound shipments that take place at the Modano Company." He paused again. "Okay so far?"

She nodded. "Who will be my controller?"

Brad gave out a quick laugh and for the first time he relaxed his shoulders against the back of the chair. "We don't call them controllers anymore. I'll be your main contact."

"I see."

"Oh, one more thing. Vassilli is your friend and he's been instrumental in providing us with information. He still is." He cleared his throat. "He likes to be in charge; that's his personality. He may try to pump you for information. Tell him to give me a call. It's better if everything is channelled through one person: me, to be exact."

For a moment Tamara remained silent. Vassilli was a close friend she could confide in with no reservation. Brad's request made her feel uncomfortable.

"Will I meet with the CSIS group that works on this case?"

"Not at the moment. Maybe later, as the operation unfolds." He extracted a card from the inside pocket of his coat and handed it to Tamara. "If I'm not available or you need anything urgently, you can contact this number. It belongs to our liaison office in London."

Tamara sighed. She was in — and for good. "What's the operation called?"

"Bullfrog."

Chapter 2

Strenuous physical exercise always helped Tamara get over the troubles that so frequently occurred in her life. But even after two hours spent at the gym, she hadn't recovered her emotional stability. She lingered in the house, finding things to do in the hope of putting her mind at ease. She rearranged the furniture of the living room, dragged the black leather chesterfield close to the bay window, and set the two companion chairs, of a soft orange colour, one on each side of the chesterfield. She opened the entry closet and unwrapped the two winter scene pictures that belonged to the Modano shop. She hung them on the wall opposite the sitting area, over the Louis XV console that Charles Modano had temporarily lent her. She had moved into that condo six months ago, and she had furnished one room at a time. Her house had to be suitable for receiving clients, Charles had told her, and invited her to take a few items and display them in her parlour and living room.

"Seeing a décor piece in a furnished environment makes more impact than in a shop window, all by itself," Charles had added, and encouraged her to exchange those items with new ones quite often.

Exhausted, Tamara slumped into a chair. Hours had gone by but her mood hadn't changed. She felt haunted by the ghosts of her past; they paraded in front of her, their presence incorporeal, their influence stifling. Then the disconnected visions she had been having disappeared to give way to the tragic scene that was carved in her memory.

She was 19, back from a party with her date, Larry. They had danced, laughed and flirted, totally oblivious of the late hour.

Larry had parked his car a distance from her parents' house and turned off the ignition and lights. He had just turned to face her and pulled her close, when sudden thumping steps startled them. A tall man had sprung out of her parents' house, heading for a car parked close by. The vehicle had quickly disappeared into darkness.

Tamara lost no time. She jumped out of the car, kicked the still open house door forward and ran upstairs, fearing the worst.

She almost tripped over her father's body sprawled on the bedroom doorway in a pool of blood.

Her mother lay in bed, her throat slashed.

Blood was on the bed, on the small rug beside the bed, on the night table, on the parquet floor and even on the long, chintz drapes.

Perspiration covered her entire body when the intercom rang, brusquely taking her back to reality. Like a robot Tamara pressed the button to hear what the condo's superintendent had to say.

He wanted to know if he should open the gate to Mr. Vassilli Petrovic.

The Blackpox Threat

"Let him in," Tamara said in a low voice. Maybe the presence of her longtime friend would appease her anxiety and anger.

Dressed in a grey suit with a bright orange tie, Vassilli was soon on her doorstep. His massive body seemed to fill the entire entrance.

"Hello, Tamara," he said in his usual jovial tone. He hugged her and kissed her on the cheeks. "Last time we met you took off so suddenly that I really had no time to talk to you." He smiled, showing teeth that had seen too much coffee and tobacco. "Alone, I mean. Brad seemed to have a lot to say — he's a great talker."

"He surely is." Tamara preceded him into the living room, and gestured him to sit on the chesterfield. She wrapped her long skirt around her legs and sunk into the orange chair, her legs folded under her body. "Am I glad to see you, Vassilli. All the efforts I made to forget about the past and live a normal life seem to have been wiped out by what you folks have planned for me."

Vassilli patted her on her knees. "I'm sorry, Tamara. But let me explain." He crossed his legs, loosened his tie and undid the first button of his light beige shirt. "My government felt that the information we had gathered ought to be passed on to your government. At the moment they're bits and bites without a strong link — the use of the Modano Company for shipping being the only concrete element in the entire affair." He eyed the bottle that stood on the console.

Tamara rose and walked to the kitchen. She came back with two glasses, a bag of nachos and an ice bucket. She set everything on the low table in front of Vassilli, and got the solitary bottle of Smirnoff from the console.

"I don't have the same quality of vodka you're used to, so this'll have to do." She opened the bag and slid it close to her guest. "I wouldn't mind having a drink also."

Vassilli poured vodka for both. "I tried to convince Brad that involving you wasn't fair. You suffered enough because of political turmoil. Apparently his office was adamant. You were the right person. They wanted to approach you and get you on their side. You're working with the company suspected to be involved in the shipping —"

"Stop there!" Tamara said becoming very alert. "With all the talking I had to listen to, I still don't know what the real problem is. Who's doing the shipping, and what's being shipped?"

Vassilli wriggled in his seat, as if he felt uncomfortable. He took a long swig of his drink. "We don't really know much about the entire affair. Something dangerous — chemicals found in an old lab — could be on their way to this country. At least one person has been working in that lab in secret, and that person has disappeared. The only trace we have is that he or she had contacted the Modano Company in relation to a shipment. This was the first bit of information we had."

Tamara held the glass in her hand, but she didn't take any sips. "Come on, you must know more than that. How come your country is involved?"

"Because, unfortunately, the chemicals people have been working with have been found in a cave in the mountains of the Western Ukraine." Vassilli jiggled the ice cubes in his glass before finishing his drink.

"Why do both you and Brad think that the product involved in the shipping can pose a threat?" Vassilli remained silent, and Tamara pushed forward. "There was another piece of information, right? The one that made you folks act — and fast!"

Vassilli dropped two ice cubes into his tumbler and topped them with vodka. He took a handful of nachos and munched on them before replying.

"Yes," he said. "When an additional search was conducted in and around the old lab, the conclusion was that we could be facing an act of biological warfare. It was then that our governments entered into action."

Tamara sipped her drink, letting the liquor penetrate her body and the bad news sink into her mind. "Anything else?"

"No. The name Modano is the only link we have. CSIS thought that your position was ideal. They weren't going to pass on getting you involved. Brad assured me that they'll keep an eye on you. When I asked him how — how many people, and so on — he didn't answer me directly. CSIS has procedures for these cases, he said, and I couldn't get anything else out of him."

"Brad told me to report at least twice a week. If things become dangerous, they'll assign somebody to watch over me. He didn't go into details either."

"That's my point, and this is the main reason I'm here. I confronted Brad. If he didn't tell me explicitly how he planned to provide for your well-being, I'd withdraw my cooperation. He's in Toronto and I'm in Ottawa. What can *we* do for you? I requested that somebody should be available here, in London. Did he give you a name?"

"No, just a phone number that I can call if I need anything."

"Can I see it?"

"Surely." Tamara rose and went over to her purse. She pulled out the card Brad had given to her. "Here it is."

Vassilli took it and looked at it. "Do you mind if I make a call? I'd like to know a bit more about this contact Brad gave you." He rose, freed his cell from his belt and walked into the hallway.

Tamara could hear his voice, but couldn't grasp the words. She got out another bag of nachos, and placed it on the table together with a jar of hot salsa.

Finally Vassilli closed his phone and went back to sit on the chesterfield, satisfaction painted all over his face. He deposited the card on the coffee table.

"You got a name associated with that phone number, eh?"

"Yes. It belongs to Ron Brenner, an ex-officer of the RCMP. A man of trust, I've been told."

"Good to know," Tamara said with relief.

"I didn't get where his office is located, though. I'll work on it when I go back to the embassy." Vassilli remained pensive for a while, quietly munching nachos overloaded with salsa. "One issue is not addressed yet. What if you need a place to hide? Toronto and Ottawa are a long way from here."

"But at this very first stage I'm only collecting information on the people working at the Modano Company and the kinds of shipments the company deals with."

"Right for now. But if by any chance you bump into a key person in the criminal chain, which probably involves several people, then eliminating you could become an urgent, impellent necessity." Vassilli tapped on his lips, as he always did when his brain was in high gear.

Tamara remained silent, worried again.

"I got it. One of my friends lives around here — it's a person of absolute trust." From the table he lifted up the card with the phone number and scribbled on its back. "If you need anything or have to hide, you can go there, no questions asked." He slid the card toward her.

"I hope he's good looking," Tamara joked.

Vassilli wiggled his index finger at her. "I know your weakness, Tamara. She's a woman. A dear and old friend of mine."

"Girlfriend?"

"Ah, ah, I don't kiss and tell, Tamara, you should know."

Tamara picked up the card and read aloud, "Sophia Tadlova." She stopped. "She lives in St. Thomas? A bit far if I need a quick getaway."

"Twenty-five kilometres from here. She has a big farmhouse out of town. It's the best I can do for now."

"Better than nothing. Thank you, Vassilli."

"You're very dear to me, Tamara. I'll do everything I can to avoid you hardship." He looked at the grandfather clock that filled one corner of the living room. "Time for me to go. Take care."

Chapter 3

Almost equidistant from Lake Huron and Lake Erie, the city of London had been a rock fort of loyalists during the American Revolution. Faithful to their motherland not only in military action, the loyalists had named the river that meandered through the city, Thames, and the green area located in the heart of the city, Victoria Park. Over the years, London had grown to boast over 300,000 inhabitants and hosted several insurance and financial institutions, subsidiaries of large banks, the famous Labatt's brewery, a Bell Centre, and the second largest academic institution in the province, The University of Western Ontario, with its well-known Mustang football team. Large residential areas were filled with multi-million dollar dwellings — a testimonial to London's reputation of being the wealthiest town in Ontario.

When Tamara first settled in the city, she found it difficult to adjust to its rather formal, almost cold, atmosphere. Having spent her teen years in the southeast of France, Tamara often missed the warmth of the talkative French people, the closeness to the high peaks and the elaborate French cooking.

However, she had grown to appreciate the city, its theatres and concert halls, the fancy restaurants with traditional and international cuisine, and replaced downhill skiing with cross-country whenever a good snowfall filled the trails that coasted the Thames.

A few hundred metres from the art gallery was the Modano Company, housed in a medium-sized building with a shop at the front and offices at the back. The shop window paraded all sorts of objects: old pieces of furniture, vases, amphorae, statuettes and a myriad of pictures, both old and modern art. The company catered to a restricted clientele, collectors of antiques or people who wanted to ship valuables that required special packing and care. It had survived the fierce competition of powerful companies because of the personalized service it offered. In addition, once a month Charles Modano, the owner, ran an auction, which attracted customers from the far coasts of the country and across the border.

Tamara parked her Subaru in the spot reserved for the employees. As she covered the few steps that separated her from the entrance to the Modano building, she had a funny feeling, like being estranged from the place. A feeling opposite the one she'd had before the recent meeting with Brad Wilson. All the enthusiasm she had for her job had faded away. She had a double role now, and she didn't like either.

It was a Saturday morning. She would be alone until noon, when Charles Modano would join her to check on the list of objects to be presented at the auction.

Tamara entered her office. The carpet was a warm plum colour, similar in shade to the fabric of the upholstered chair. A metal desk and a file cabinet were the only other furniture. She plunked herself into the chair in front of her desk and logged on to an HP Media Centre. She opened the file with the list of the objects currently in the company inventory. In another window she displayed the names of the participants in the auction, together with a short profile of their interests and past acquisitions. It was always useful trying to match what was in stock with the interests of potential buyers. She made a list with the possible matches, printed it out and took it to Charles' office, which was contiguous to hers. Her boss's office was clogged with an incredible amount of boxes, paperwork, and folders, some sprawled on the floor. She zigzagged among the obstacles and deposited the list on Charles' desk, on top of a layer of papers. The way to Charles' office was through her own or through the office of his administrative assistant, Dianne Templeton.

The setup was ideal for snooping as she was in a position to hear when Charles was coming. The idea of spying — because that's what it was — still made her feel plenty uncomfortable.

She looked around to get an idea of how Charles separated the shipping business from the shop sales. Charles wasn't computer savvy, so he either depended entirely on his assistant, or he collected information — receipts, orders and customs clearance papers — in folders, sorted in alphabetic order. She started opening the metal file cabinet labelled 2006. The two top drawers were for shipments, the bottom, for sales. Tamara looked at the shipments and their invoices. Most carried the names of companies located in Europe, a few others from the States and Canada. The shop from which most of the shipments had been made was the parent company in Italy; so Tamara had no problems in memorizing all the others, a dozen in total. Later on she would go on the Internet and see what kind of business they were in. This would be the first step of her so-called covert mission. Brad Wilson could follow up and determine how legit each business was.

By the time she heard the main door buzz, Tamara knew about

all the clients who had been using the Modano Company for shipping — from January 2006 to the current time.

She retreated to her office, closed all the windows on her PC and put her HP on Stand By.

"Good morning, Tamara," Charles said cheerfully, and stopped in front of her desk.

Charles was 63, tall and skinny, with few white hairs. In his Ralph Lauren polo shirt and blue wool trousers Charles looked casually elegant, with the flare of an old country gentleman.

"How many customers?" he asked.

Tamara returned his greeting and said, "Twenty-three registered; a few more said they might come to the door. Things look good. I made up a list of the items that should interest today's crowd. I put it on your desk. If you approve of it, I can go to the storage, and take them to the auction room. The only item I might need help with is the boudoir. It isn't heavy, just old and delicate with those gold trims sticking out on the front of each drawer." She avoided looking at Charles, who hadn't moved.

"Something wrong?"

Tamara shook her head. "Nothing serious, just a headache that doesn't go away." She forced a smile and added, "I hope we can sell a bundle today."

"I'm sure we will. Since you joined the company, our sales have increased steadily. When you show an item, people are fascinated by the way you comment on it. You know what it was used for, the period in which it was made, at times even the past owners." He paused for a moment. "If things continue that way, I'll be forced to give you a raise."

"No need, Charles," Tamara replied. "I enjoy documenting what we have around. And I make sure the starting price is lower than in most of the other outlets."

"I know, I know. Well, what about lunch? Then we come back here and set up the show."

At that moment the door buzzed again, and a beautiful woman made a grand entrance. She was Dianne Templeton. Five foot seven in height with long curly hair that graciously grazed her shoulders, Dianne wore a two-piece red suit and high-heeled sandals. She threw her little purse onto Tamara's desk with disgust.

"Can you believe this?" she asked. "I waited two, I mean *two* hours down at the A-station for this three minute commercial about a new facial mask, and what happened? Nothing. The rep for the company never showed up."

Dianne had tried her luck in the movie industry, but had never made it except for a second-rate flick where she played the cashier in a bank robbery — shot the instant she had pressed the emergency button. At 35, Dianne still hoped for a break. She juggled her work at the Modano Company with any television contract she could get, no matter how small or brief her appearance would be.

"Sorry to hear that," Charles said sympathetically.

"Well, can I do overtime at the auction? Maybe Tamara would like to have time off."

Charles rescued Dianne's little purse from the desk and proffered it to her. "You can stay for the auction and help out, but Tamara has everything ready for the show." He took her arm and guided her out of the door. "Let's all go down to the Covent Garden Market."

"To Waldo's?" Dianne asked.

"Yes." Charles turned to Tamara who hadn't moved. "You coming?"

****

The Blackpox Threat

At Waldo's Bistro they lingered at the bar, waiting for a table. The big curved panels of the ceiling and the yellow-greenish artificial plant set in the middle conferred a bright look on the bistro. Tamara was tempted to join the others for a drink but opted for a juice. She reminded herself that she was on a mission. Better be alert and observe, and do it as inconspicuously as possible. She jiggled the ice cubes in her orange juice and tried to remember what she had learned about body language. Charles looked very much at ease, conversing with the barman about the weather. She shifted her attention to Dianne, whose enormous sunglasses covered half of her face. No chance to capture her expression. She sat on a stool, her shapely legs well exposed, one foot moving up and down. She had ordered a glass of mineral water and she was sipping it slowly, her head turned toward the entrance as if to monitor any newcomers.

They were ready to take a seat in a booth dimly lighted by a sconce, when Charles spotted two of his friends and invited them over. He introduced the man as Michael Devry, a knowledgeable merchant of paintings, and the woman as Stephanie Demoins, the owner of a shop in town. Michael was medium height with thinning, grey hair, brown eyes and metal-rimmed glasses. A chair was added to the side, and all five took a seat. Dianne had manoeuvred herself to be between Charles and Michael, leaving Tamara between Charles and Stephanie.

A server glided to the table, apologized for the wait and took the orders.

"I heard that you're the new person in charge of the auctions at the Modano Company," Stephanie said.

"Just started," Tamara replied.

"I'm thinking of remodelling my shop, and I'm looking for a piece to brighten up the entrance. A show-off piece. Maybe I'll drop by, sometime."

"I'm sure we have something for you. What kind of shop?"

"An atelier."

Tamara listed the décor items that could suit any shop, from the cheapest piece to the most expensive.

"Oh, you have fountains?" Stephanie said. "That's great. "I was thinking of making the entrance of my shop look like a miniature garden. That would do nicely. How big are they?"

"One is four by six metres. A dolphin in the middle squirts a jet of water every 15 seconds. It's a striking piece. We also have a matching bench, all in natural stone."

"There may not be enough space for all that."

"The one with three otters could do, then. It's about half the size."

"Sounds interesting."

Soon the entrées arrived and were set in the middle of the table, so everybody could share them.

Normally Tamara would savour every bite of her food. But today it was different. She should observe each of the guests carefully. The people around her were players in a big game; she had a job to do — so how should she do it? One forkful of linguine and one scrutinizing look, which, of course, should be as casual as possible? Is that how it was done? She should also give a tag to the relationships among the four people she shared the meal with. Casual, business-like or intimate? What she had learned at the seminars she had recently attended came back to her in spurts, and in a disconnected fashion. She had templates to refer to, but those, obviously, were at home. Well, Dianne Templeton was flirting away with both men. Charles reacted with bonhomie and courtesy, Michael kept at some distance, answering her questions in a rather curt way. That was all she could find out.

"Do you expect a big crowd at the auction?" It was Stephanie talking to her.

"Oh yes."

Stephanie wore a two-piece suit of raw silk, which combined softness with style. Bright green, it gave her eyes greenish reflections. Suddenly a recollection pierced Tamara's mind.

"Did I see you before?" She tried to flashback the recent places where she had been. "Weeks ago, at the Governor's reception?"

"I was there," Stephanie admitted. "Great party, but I don't remember seeing you."

"I left early."

"That's why I don't remember you. Normally I say hello to all the women at any party as they are my potential customers. My shop downtown is *The French Look*." Stephanie surveyed Tamara's sober outfit. "With your figure anything I have in my shop will look great on you. I can't think of even one item that wouldn't fit you."

Tamara laughed. "It might fit my figure, but not my wallet. I've heard of your place. Quite expensive."

"Well, if you drop by, we can come to terms." With the help of a spoon she rolled some spaghetti on a fork and graciously brought it to her mouth.

"I'll make a point to come in."

Tamara stretched her arm to pick up a stuffed jalapeno pepper, as the conversation began to set between each of the two couples. For the time being she should be content with making the acquaintance of some of Charles' friends. The name *Devry* had appeared as one of the companies that shipped items with the Modano Company; Dianne was Charles' assistant and Stephanie frequented the Modano auctions. As far as she could judge, everybody around the table had an interest in items shown, sold, or packaged and shipped via the Modano Company.

In principle, each of them was a suspect.

Chapter 4

With a crowd in a spending mood the auction had been very successful. Twice Tamara had to run to the storage room to add a few garden statues, which were in great demand. She was too busy presenting the items and later on wrapping them up for the customers to have much time to observe any of the participants in detail. She had the buyers' names though, and the list of objects they had purchased. Monday, at home, she would do some checking, maybe even find out their addresses using *411.ca*, as she had most of the customers' phone numbers. Nothing suspicious had surfaced at the auction.

Today it was time for her to attend a new type of seminar and learn how to become an efficient spy. Spy? Efficient too? Tamara inwardly laughed at the idea. She would do her best — and that was that. She climbed into her Subaru and in 20 minutes she arrived at her destination.

From the outside, the building looked like any other farm located along Vanneck Road. The walls were painted red; the roof, with two vents stemming out at the top, was dark brown; the only existing windows, on the upper floor, had dark panes. As Tamara entered the premises, she stopped on the threshold and said, "Oh, I should have worn my sunglasses!" The inside was high-tech, with metal desks, a counter filled with computers and computerized equipment, and lamps that spread bright light all over.

Brad approached her and welcomed her.

"Let me make the introductions. Tamara Smith," he said. "And this young man is our surveillance and computer communications specialist, Duncan Brown."

"The teacher?" Tamara asked, as she shook the hand Duncan offered her.

"More of an advisor," Duncan said. "I was told to give you practical hints and some equipment that's easy to use."

Duncan was short, overweight, with a mane of curly reddish hair and a long bushy beard. He wore metal-rimmed glasses through which two vivid eyes revealed brain activity.

"I'm going to leave you two, now." Brad grabbed his coat from a nearby chair and waved goodbye. "I'll be away for a few days. Report on the Modano activities by the end of the week, Tamara." And Brad was gone.

Tamara shook off her scarf and took a seat beside Duncan, at the longest counter.

"Let me start with the essentials," Duncan said. "First I have to find out if you know of all the capabilities that a cellular phone offers today. It might be the best gadget available to you to call for help, take a picture quickly or save vital information."

"I know how to use a phone."

"Yes, yes, I understand. But this one, the one Brad wants you to use to communicate with him or in case of an emergency, has special features. I programmed some keys for you. For instance, a soon as you take a picture, that is sent over to Brad. Even if they catch you shooting, by the time they grab your phone, the image you took will be on the air, ready to be caught by our team."

"Stop there for a minute," Tamara said. "What team are we talking about? I see equipment, instruments, but no people. Where are they?"

"This is a covert operation, Miss Smith," Duncan said in a grave tone. "They send specialists to different places to work in secluded quarters. We don't give away anything, anything I say, that is not indispensable for you to know."

Tamara scowled but remained silent.

Duncan continued. "You need a recording device that isn't too conspicuous, so I suggest a watch." He opened a drawer underneath the counter and extracted a rather big watch, with a metal band.

"That's for men," Tamara said. "People will immediately notice that I wear a strange watch, especially with all the fancy models available for girls." She unfastened hers, a Lady J. Breitling. "Could you insert your recording device in mine?"

"No." Duncan petted his beard, pensive. "You're right. I never dressed up — that means equipped with — a woman for the job. The size is needed to contain the chip." He turned over the watch and then put it back in the drawer. "You come back in three days, right?"

"Yes. Brad thinks I need a few sessions to become comfortable with the use of these devices."

"Good. I may look for a different case, smaller with a fancy bracelet. It may be difficult to find it, though. Let's forget about the watch for now." From the same drawer he extracted a couple of pens. "These are recording devices. You can keep one in your purse and leave the other in somebody's office. They record up to eight hours of conversation." He opened a slit on the pen's side. "There is a tiny battery in here. I'll give you an instrument to measure the voltage. Be sure there is juice at all times."

"Juice?"

"Jargon. You have to be sure that the battery is operational." Duncan sighed as if he was forced to do a very painful job. "And be sure you turn them on."

"Oh," Tamara said, ignoring the air of sufficiency Duncan had assumed. "So let me recap. I'll have a phone that can take pictures and transmit them instantly and I'll have gadgets that can record conversation. If I want to take pictures of documents, would the camera incorporated into the cellular phone be adequate?"

"For text, maybe in poor lighting? Is that what you are asking?"

"Yes."

"The answer is no. You'd need a mini-camera with higher resolution. I'll get you one next time, digital, of course, so that the documents can be downloaded to a computer and analyzed immediately if necessary." Duncan gave her a scrutinizing look. "Other questions?"

"Yes, an important one. How can I be sure that there are no spying devices of any kind in my home, in my purse or in my car?"

"Oh. Brad didn't mention anything about that." Duncan was genuinely surprised.

"Well, if somebody suspects I'm snooping, he may want to find out what I know. Doesn't that make sense?" As Duncan remained quiet, she pursued her argument. "I'd like to get a Sweeper, the multifunctional bug detector that is good for audio and video, be these either wireless or hardwired."

"Where did you get that information?" Duncan's tone was suddenly suspicious, his eyes showing astonishment.

Tamara smiled. "Did you think Brad would get a bimbo to work on his team?"

The trill of Duncan's phone interrupted the conversation. "I'll be right there," he said into the phone. Turning toward Tamara he said, "An emergency. We have to leave. See you in three days."

Tamara watched Duncan lock up the facility and enter his Hyundai, spinning the wheels as he drove out of the courtyard. When she had arrived, she had no time to glance around because she was late. Now she did. Nothing would give that barn away as a high-tech place. The door on the main floor needed painting badly, and the ramp that led to the upper level was in extremely poor condition, paved with disconnected stones and half covered with grass. Outside, an old RV lay neglected in a corner.

The cover was perfect.

****

For two weeks Tamara endured Duncan's instructions that often sounded more like pedantic lessons and stoically supported the air of sufficiency the man displayed every time she asked for a clarification. Then Duncan and Brad came up with the idea that she practice with the new wonder on the weapons' market, the electroshock weapon called a Taser, after having had to listen for two full hours about the marvels of this stun gun. It could deliver 1200 volts to the body by means of two barbed darts. Shooting charges of opposite signs, one into the heart muscles and the other into the skeletal muscle, would create a circuit within the body, making the victim temporarily inoffensive.

Tamara had clearly shown her pessimism. If her life were in danger she would like to rely on something more traditional.

After the murder of her parents, Tamara had registered her father's handgun, a Smith & Wesson Model 60, in her name. The easiest way to legally own a handgun was to become a member of a target-shooting club, and practice there regularly. However, Tamara intended to keep that gun for self-defence and carried it hidden in a pouch she had made at the bottom of her everyday purse. She didn't see any reason why she should spend time becoming familiar with a toy weapon. The one she owned was real, functional, reloadable and, most important, deadly.

Between the work at the Modano Company and the hours spent snooping and profiling the people she met, Tamara had been left with little time for herself. When, for the third time, Brad had called asking her to join him in another briefing session on the Taser X26, she had flatly refused.

She intended to go to a party and needed time to get ready. No way would she let Brad and his gang ruin the fun weekend that was ahead of her.

Vassilli had invited her to a costume party. It was going to be held on an enormous houseboat, which, wind permitting, would coast Lake Huron between Kettle Point and Goderich.

Tamara fetched the duffle bag she had just packed with her clothing, and climbed into her Subaru, riveting in the pleasure of the fun time ahead.

She was on County Road No. 81, directed to Grand Bend, when her car swayed left and right. She had a flat. She steered the vehicle to the road shoulder and stopped. She put the car in park. She was getting the small tire out of the trunk, when a car slowed down and coasted the road shoulder. It was a sports car, low and silvery-looking; as it stopped behind her Subaru, the four circles of the Audi shimmered in the late afternoon sun. She exchanged the tire for the jack and waited to see who was getting out.

"Need any help?" a young voice asked. A man in shorts and polo shirt with a cap of the Toronto Raptors got out and approached Tamara. "I'm always ready to help a woman, especially one in need." The man was at least four inches shorter than Tamara, but his build was pretty husky. About a dozen cars had moved in both directions since Tamara had stopped.

For a moment Tamara weighed the pros and cons of continuing to change the tire versus returning to the car. Then her nature — trusting, daring and playful — prevailed.

"You surely can," she said and swung around the jack. "By staying where you are and see if I do it right."

She positioned the jack under the car and unscrewed the lug nuts. She turned the lever until the wheel was off the ground, an eye on the man who had frozen a couple of metres away from her. She rolled the tire with the flat to the trunk, tossed it in and took out the small tire. She did the inverse operation, closed the trunk but kept the jack in her hand. Trustful she was, but prudent, too. She opened the driver's door and climbed in, the jack still in her hands. She locked the door and lowered the window a notch.

"How did I do?" she called out.

The young man walked toward her car.

"Excellent," he said. "Never seen anybody change a tire so fast." He approached the open window. "Justin, Justin Devry. I'm going to my father's country home, on Highway 21. Only 40 kilometres from here."

Tamara dropped the jack onto the passenger seat. "Good bye," she said, and turned on the ignition.

"Wait, wait! What's your name?"

Tamara shook her head.

"Nothing personal," Justin said, and opened his lips to a charming smile. "Just in case I need road assistance. You changed the wheel in exactly 12 minutes. Impressive."

Tamara laughed. "I like to impress people. But thanks for stopping by."

"I think I saw you before. At some party."

Tamara shot him a teasing look. "I bet you go to a lot of those. You probably mistook me for a dozen blonds." She put the car in gear.

"No. Impossible. You are...special." He paused and searched his shorts pocket. "Look, I'll give you my card, in case you need *real* help." He managed to slip the card through the slit Tamara had left opened.

Graciously, Tamara took the card.

"Thanks," she said, and drove away.

Chapter 5

When she arrived at the Colonial Hotel in Grand Bend it was dark. She registered and entered the room she had booked two weeks ago. Room Number 12 was on the second floor, down a narrow carpeted corridor. The drapes were parted, and she could see the lights of the intersection between Highway 81 and Highway 21. There were no luxuries; just a low dresser with a TV set on top; in a corner two chairs and a floor lamp provided a cozy nook for the reader. A door opened onto the bathroom.

Tamara unzipped her duffle bag and spread its contents on the bed. It was the costume she had bought at *eBay.ca* for $99.99. A glance at her wristwatch made her rush to get a shower. In less than an hour Vassilli Petrovic would come to take her to a costume party. *A Night Among Pirates* was the theme.

She sprayed plenty of extra-hold mousse on her short hair, still wet, to make it nice and spiky. With brisk movements she got dressed. The square mirror above the dresser allowed only a partial view of her figure, so she bent and stretched to see a full reflection.

She was satisfied with the way she looked. The red corseted vest was one piece with the white, mock sleeves, and the black skirt, short, was rimmed with ruffles. She discarded the high-heel boots that came with the costume and opted for flat shoes; at six feet in height she was taller than most people — something that some men would resent.

Holding a black purse on which she had pasted a white skull, she left the room and walked to the hotel bar.

Vassilli was there, sipping a beer. He wore an impressive costume: brown trousers and jacket, white shirt, covered boots and a long sword attached to a belt via an enormous buckle.

He took off his pirate hat and greeted Tamara. "Ready to go?" he asked. "They're just waiting for us."

"Let them wait no longer," Tamara said cheerfully, and linked arms with him.

****

Both decks of the houseboat hosted a buffet with platters full of food and drinks. The lower deck played contemporary music, the upper deck, sheltered by a tarp, was more suited for older folks. Vassilli moved with self-assurance amidst the crowd, introducing Tamara to the many people he knew. He had made it clear that the invitation to the party had nothing to do with her mission or any of the issues they had discussed with Brad Wilson.

Deciding to have a good time, Tamara had agreed to accompany him.

Only a few minutes had gone by when the band struck a tune familiar to both of them. It was a kazachok dance, and Tamara lost no time. She took Vassilli to the floor and led him in its frantic rhythm. Halfway through Vassilli disengaged himself, clapped to step the time and let Tamara continue alone.

A young man, dressed as a pirate first mate tapped Vassilli on the shoulder. "You lost your sash, Vassilli," he said, and then, pointing to Tamara, he added, "That's a fast pace!"

"Too fast for me, I was getting dizzy. It's a Ukrainian dance where the woman leads the man. Tamara needs a much younger partner." He took the sash and put it in his pocket. "Thanks for rescuing my scarf." The music stopped and Vassilli waved at Tamara, who was catching her breath.

She crossed the floor and joined him. "That felt good," she said.

"Here, Justin, I want you to meet Tamara Smith. She's like a daughter to me."

Justin was soberly dressed with a white shirt, black vest and trousers and a skulled headscarf. He lifted his eye patch and shook Tamara's hand.

"Justin Devry. Small world, isn't it?" Turning to Vassilli, he said, "I'll talk to you later." He took Tamara by the waist and whirled her into a waltz. "How do you like the party?"

"Pretty fancy. Several nice costumes. I counted two Jack Sparrows, one Captain Hook, one Captain Blood and one Captain Morgan. The women's costumes are the most interesting, though. Some are very elaborate." She looked at Justin's outfit. "You're a simple sailor?"

"Oh yes, I am. The rule is that every pirate with a status, that is carrying some sort of knife, has to participate in a duel."

"Oh, oh! Good for me I didn't wear my dagger — with my cheap costume I got a knife with small skulls wrapped around the handle. It looked impressive but it was cheap. It bent like a snake." She pointed at the cutlass swords. "By the way, those swords, so curved and long, aren't they dangerous?"

"Nah. They're plastic. They checked them at boarding time."

The music stopped and the band members left the deck for a break.

Tamara and Justin walked away from the crowd and stood by the gunwale, enjoying the warm breeze.

****

For a while neither of them spoke, as they looked down at the dark water first and then at the light of an approaching vessel.

"What do you do for a living?" Tamara asked.

"Work here and there, mostly for my father. He's a collector of art objects, mainly paintings." He took off his headscarf.

"Oh. Michael Devry is your father?"

"Hmm, yes. Why?"

"I met him. Just before the auction at the Modano shop. So what do you do for him?" Tamara turned so that she could see Justin's face. On his crew-cut hair lay the blind patch.

"I'm a kind of technical consultant. I analyze paint and varnish. They tell a lot about the chemical components used, and their times. What about you? I just learned that you're a friend of Vassilli's. Tell me something about yourself."

Tamara liked him when she had met him on the road. The man was young, handsome, and outgoing; now she liked him even more. He was not conjecturing anything about her; he was just waiting for her to talk about herself.

"My mother was Ukrainian, my father, Russian," she said. "Vassilli was their closest friend. He is actually the only member left from the old days since my parents died." She stopped for a moment. It wasn't the right moment to tell him that her parents had been assassinated, presumably for political reasons. Better divert the subject. "I'm in charge of public relations at *Ship Me Safely*, the Modano Company."

"Interesting. We use that company for our shipments."

Yes, she knew. It was one of the names she had memorized.

An announcement resounded loud and clear. The duels were going to start and the contenders were ordered to line up in the middle of the deck. There were 10 couples in all.

"Interested in watching?" Justin asked.

"Not really. It's breezy here. Under the tarp it's a bit stuffy, isn't?"

"Yes, besides, I like to be here with you. I feel I have you all to myself."

"Possessive?"

"Absolutely. If I could, I'd take you with me so I could hear all about you, from when you were a little girl up to now."

The man was a charmer. Likely, he had practiced his lines many times over.

"How old are you?"

"Twenty — three."

Tamara snapped her fingers in disappointment. "Too bad. I can't afford to like you. Too young for me."

Voices from the duelling contestants increased on the decibel scale. The referee announced the elimination of three of the contenders, provoking cheers and boos.

"The combat didn't last long," Tamara said.

"In general it's short-lived."

"Have you been to this kind of party before?"

"Oh, yes. They're organized by the owners of the cottages along the coast — by those who had a cottage for some time. My father doesn't care to come, so often I'm here alone."

There were screams.

"There's action over there," Tamara commented.

Justin turned around. "Let's go see."

They both moved toward the centre of the deck, trying to find a spot that would provide a good view.

In the middle of the floor, his shirt and jacket spotted red, stood Vassilli. His opponent, a Captain Hook, waved his sword to claim victory.

Tamara lurched toward her friend, but Justin held her by the arm.

"It's a show," he murmured. "The blood is likely cheap ketchup."

"Oh." Tamara gave her old friend a second look. "Oh," she repeated, "That's why he's still standing and laughing." She turned toward Justin. "Any other surprises?"

"Probably." Justin hiked his shoulders. "Let's wait and see."

A huge cutter had silently approached the houseboat and a rope had been wound around one of the poles that supported the deck tarp.

"What now?" Tamara asked, suddenly alerted by the manoeuvre that had taken place close by.

"A sailboat is hooking up to us." Justin perched over the rail, bending sideways. "Can't see much. Oh, there's an older woman at the helm. She isn't wearing much of a costume."

All at once from the cutter's mast a pirate woman, illuminated by a powerful light, held onto the rope and descended to the houseboat. She wore a short red gartered dress with a laced ruched bustle, and black stockings with bows. She waved her buccaneer hat with one hand and brandished a sword with the other.

"You clear out, dead man," she screamed at Vassilli. "I'm going to take on this Captain Hook." And another fake duel started.

"What about going down to the lower deck?" Justin asked.

"They're still playing music."

Tamara looked at her wristwatch. "It's already three in the morning. Vassilli has to get off at the next stop in Grand Bend. He has to be in Ottawa by the afternoon."

"No problem. The houseboat is circling around. We still have a half-hour before docking." He took her arm and guided her to the stairs. In one swift motion he led her to the floor where they were playing a salsa.

Then an English waltz followed, and Tamara became totally oblivious of her troubles. This time they moved as one to the music. Justin's arms embraced her without the pretence of holding her. It was wonderful to be in his arms, Tamara thought, and closed her eyes, capturing the magic of the moment. As she reclined her head on Justin's shoulder she inadvertently brushed her cheek against his, feeling a new growth of beard. She enjoyed the closeness of his body and the unmistakable feeling that Justin was going to be taken by her.

A thud coming from starboard stopped Tamara's reverie. They were docking. She opened her eyes and smiled at her partner.

"It was wonderful," Justin said. "We should do this again, sometime."

She nodded, looked around and inched away from him.

A loudspeaker announced, "We're in Grand Bend; hurry up if you want to debark."

"I have to find Vassilli right away," Tamara said with urgency. "I should have already looked for him a while ago." She left the dance floor and asked a waiter if he had seen him.

She was soon directed to a stateroom at the end of the deck. Tamara quickened her steps, followed by Justin. She knocked on the door a few times, from soft to hard. Then she tugged at the handle. The door opened.

Vassilli was stretched out on a bed, a raucous noise coming out of his mouth, blood dripping from the bedspread to the floor, a dagger plunged in his chest up to the hilt.

"Oh my God! Call for an ambulance!" she screamed at Justin, but Justin was already out of the room calling for help.

Vassilli opened his eyes and gestured her to come close. "I found out…oh, it's terrible…"

"Don't talk. Help is on the way." She unbuttoned his shirt and freed him of his belt. Slowly she lifted one of his legs so that he could lie completely on the bed.

Vassilli closed his eyes; his breath became more laborious. "Sorry, Tamara. So sorry." He opened his eyes and made an effort to lift his head and get very close to Tamara. "Don't tr —"

"What shouldn't I do?"

Vassilli's mouth opened but no sound came out. His head collapsed onto the pillow, and he closed his eyes.

"Vassilli!" Tamara shouted. "No, no! Don't leave me!" She bent to feel the pulse around his neck. It was intermittent, but it was present.

She dropped to her knees, her chest shaken by a convulse weeping. She couldn't lose him. He was the only person on earth who was family to her.

Chapter 6

In the hospital Tamara felt uncomfortable in the female pirate costume, the ruffles of her short skirt tickling her upper legs.

Vassilli had been airlifted to the University Hospital in London and taken to surgery right away. He was in a recovery room, guarded outside by a policeman in plainclothes. He was in critical condition — and that information was the only bit of news Tamara had been able to extract from the tight-lipped hospital personnel.

Except for an hour spent at the OPP station in Grand Bend, Tamara had stayed in the hospital for 10 hours waiting for news, afraid that Vassilli was going to die, and wondering what was the thing so important that Vassilli meant to tell her before passing out.

Justin had been with her on and off, bringing her tea, a pop or a snack. The last time, before leaving, he had pressured her to go home. Feeling totally useless, Tamara was ready to take off when an older lady walked into the waiting room.

She was dressed with a denim skirt that brushed the floor and a dark green hoodie. She approached Tamara and extended her hand.

"Sophia Tadlova," she said curtly. "An old friend of Vassilli's."

Tamara looked at her blankly, taking stock of Sophia's massive figure. Then she remembered the name Vassilli had scribbled on the card Brad had given her.

"Pleased to meet you," she replied. "I'm Tamara Smith."

"I know. A terrible thing, this accident. Such a nice man, Vassilli." She sat close to Tamara. "I heard on the radio. I always thought those duels were dangerous."

With effort Tamara swallowed. Her throat was tight, too constrained to swallow her own saliva.

"It didn't happen when they were fighting. The show was well over when it occurred."

She looked at the woman with curiosity. In general Vassilli's female friends were glamorous women. Sophia was in her 60s with white hair gathered in a knot at the nape; she wore no makeup and her clothing was plain.

"How is he?"

Tamara shook her head. "I can only report what I overheard from a nurse when Vassilli came out of surgery. 'They patched him up, but he won't last long.' " Tamara sighed. "Did you know Vassilli a long time?"

"Thirty years. He helped me to clear out of Georgia." Her lips opened to a little smile. "Not the one in the States, if you know what I mean."

Tamara assented and then said, "I'm not the next of kin, so the doctors don't say anything to me. I'm still in the dark about Vassilli's prognosis." She rose. "Well, I should go home and change, maybe get some rest. I dozed off an hour here and there — it's been a long wait."

"Let me know if I can help," Sophia said, and in a rapid move she hugged Tamara. "Vassilli's friends are my friends."

"Thanks. I'll be back tomorrow and the day after tomorrow. Vassilli can't be moved. I want to be here as much as I can."

"We can take turns. I'll stay here to start with, and see if I can find out a bit more."

"It won't be easy. There's a guard outside his room. You can't get close." As Sophia seemed surprised, she added, "Don't forget that they're investigating an attempted murder."

"Oh, it wasn't an accident?"

"Not by a mile," Tamara said, and grabbed her purse. "Bye now."

****

At home Tamara disposed of her costume and took a long shower, enjoying the soothing feeling of warm spray over her body. She made herself a coffee, stretched out on the chesterfield, and called Brad.

"I expected your call, Tamara. How do you feel?"

"Rotten. I couldn't get much information about Vassilli's condition. They relegated me to a waiting room in the opposite wing and told me they'd let me know if there was any change."

"I can guess why. Only a member of the Ukrainian embassy was allowed in his room." He paused. "Difficult to say if what happened goes a long way back in Vassilli's political life or if it's linked to our new operation."

"I see. The police questioned me and Mr. Justin Devry — I was with him when we found Vassilli — for over an hour first, and then again in the hospital. I couldn't help them. I saw nothing suspicious for the entire evening."

"Nothing at all?"

"Zilch. The houseboat's guests form a restricted, selected

crowd; most of them have known each other for a long time."

"You were his date but you weren't with him?"

"No. Vassilli participated in a duel, as customary, then went around chatting and visiting with old friends. I was mostly with Justin Devry, who also knew Vassilli."

Minutes went by without either saying a word.

"How many stops did *The Floating Tortuga* make before docking in Grand Bend?"

Surprised by the fact that Brad knew the name of the houseboat Tamara took a long swig of coffee, trying to remember the number of stops. "Three or four, I believe. I didn't pay much attention."

"Tamara! You need to be alert at all times!"

"Brad! Don't be such a —" She stopped. "I was invited to a party to have fun."

Diplomatically, Brad didn't push the issue any further. "The police have the guest list, but it won't do us any good. Clearly somebody came aboard clandestinely and left before you two found Vassilli. In a hurry, probably. The plan was to eliminate him."

"That somebody made it, I'm afraid," Tamara murmured. "Vassilli is in real bad shape, I gathered. Talk to you later, Brad."

"Just a minute. Please use the cell Duncan gave you. Any call you make in connection with our operation should be made with that phone. My line is secured, so you can speak freely — provided nobody is close to you, of course. Use your other phones, the one at home and your regular cell for normal communications. And remember your role: to get acquainted with as many people as possible among those who come in contact with the company. At the same time, don't let these people become familiar with your habits or whereabouts."

Tamara wasn't in the mood to listen to Brad's lecturing, and she was definitely too tired to stay on the phone any longer.

"Got it," she mumbled, and put the phone back in its cradle.

She had gotten a refill of her coffee when the phone rang again. It was Sophia.

"Any news?" Tamara asked.

"No. Nothing transpired about Vassilli's condition. The reason I called is —" Sophia hesitated and then continued. "What if I pick you up and take you out for a good meal? You looked exhausted when I saw you today."

Tamara found her invitation an unnecessary intrusion. "Kind of you, Sophia, but I've made other arrangements."

"Some other time, then."

"Sure." Tamara put down the receiver. She didn't care for the woman, but she should juggle feelings versus opportunity. Her best friend was in Toronto, and she hadn't had much time to make new ones in London. Having a secure place to hide in case of an emergency could make the difference between life and death.

The phone rang again.

"It's Justin, I'm outside the gate of your complex and I wonder if I can come in. I have food with me, and a bottle of wine."

Tamara couldn't avoid smiling. Justin was a fast operator and she wondered how he had found out where she lived. Unessential at this point.

"Real good food?" she asked.

"I don't have any beluga, if that is what you mean."

"No beluga? Then I'm not sure I'll let you in."

"Wait, wait. I got Chinese, and a lemon meringue pie."

"All right. I'll tell the super to let you in."

"There is no superintendent around."

"Oh, well, punch in 4742. My condo is Number 19."

Tamara opened her door and stood on the threshold, in wait, until Justin stopped his silver Audi in front of the condo and hopped out of the car. He was dressed in jeans and a checkered polo shirt. With one hand he carried a big paper bag, with the other a bottle.

"Hello, Tamara." He brushed his lips against her cheeks and looked around. "What does my beautiful hostess prefer? Candlelight dinner or picnic camping style?"

Tamara laughed as she stood aside to let him go by. "Camping is more my style. Let's go to the kitchen."

"There's no table!" Justin deposited the bottle and the boxes onto the granite counter.

"Over there," Tamara said, and pointed to the oval table in front of the bay window.

"Oh, I see. Glasses?" Justin asked.

"I don't use any when I camp. I drink from the bottle." She extracted a corkscrew from a drawer.

"Oh, I see. Sharing wine and germs. A new experience."

Tamara lifted the bottle and read, "Chateauneuf du Pape, 2002." She smiled at Justin. "I think this wine *does* deserve glasses." She opened a cupboard and took out two sparkling crystals.

Together they deposited food and utensils on the table. Justin pulled back a chair and invited Tamara to sit on it.

"Ready?"

"Ready for what?" Tamara teased him.

"To enjoy a good meal, of course. You wouldn't think I had any other intention, eh?" He sat opposite her and stretched an arm to squeeze Tamara's hand. "I bet you didn't have a good meal in the last 24 hours."

"True, but I wasn't hungry. I'd have gone straight to bed had you not come."

Justin filled the glasses, careful not to touch their rims with the bottle. "I like when people make me feel useful."

Tamara sniffed the wine. "Wonderful bouquet." She took a sip. "Excellent. Thank you."

Justin opened one box after the other. "Beef with vegetables, mandarin-almond chicken, sweet-and-sour chicken balls, fried rice, shrimps with water chestnuts. Help yourself."

"What are you trying to do? Get to my heart through my stomach?"

Justin laughed, showing perfectly aligned teeth. "Nothing of the sort. At the moment I'd like to know you better. You're an exciting woman."

Suddenly Tamara felt uneasy. The man could become a dangerous breach in Operation Bullfrog. She should discourage him but before doing that, she should find out what he knew.

"What's so exciting about me? You hardly know me!"

"Oh, I know more than you think. Had plenty of time to find out. You came to London six months ago, when Charles Modano hired you to promote his business. Charles has two lines of work: shipping, and selling décor items. The shipping is irregular since it depends on people like my father, who, from time to time, want to import objects of a delicate nature. The shop needed to expand its clientele outside London and vicinity. That's the reason he hired you. I knew of you before I met you on the road."

Justin dug into the beef and vegetables, then into the shrimps. He drank some wine, closing his eyes in delight. Slowly Tamara helped herself to a few chicken balls. Justin was very much alive, not afraid to show his feelings, clearly not hesitant to do battle for what he wanted.

"What else?" she asked.

"After your parents died you stayed for a while with Vassilli, then you wandered away — where, I couldn't find out." He stopped and grinned. "Maybe you care to fill me in."

The Blackpox Threat

Tamara didn't want to say much about herself; on the other hand speaking about her past was a way to avoid talking about the present and having to clarify her current position.

"I travelled a bit — all by myself. One day I packed my Subaru with my tent, my sleeping bag and other essentials. I wanted to know this country and its people. I also wanted to find my soul; I wanted to find out what to do with the rest of my life. After a year of moving around my nomadic instinct was totally satisfied. I settled in Toronto and found a job in a health club. It was there that I met the Ferreiros. One brother owned the club, the other a chain of take-out eateries. There's also an outlet here, right downtown."

"I know of the shop. Father orders cakes and bread from that store when he has special guests. They deliver everything to his door."

"They're famous for the quality of their products and friendly service." Tamara paused. "I became friends with Catherine Ferreiro, the young sister of the two. She was about my age. We jogged together."

She missed Catherine, her impish jokes and her easy laughter. Catherine's marriage had been a wake-up call for her. It was then that she realized that Tamara, too, had to settle down. And now that she was ready, she got involved in a horrible covert operation. She sighed, attracting Justin's attention.

"Try these shrimps, they're delicious." Justin hooked three on his fork and brought them close to Tamara's mouth.

Tamara savoured them. "They're really good."

"And then, what made you come to London?" Justin asked.

"Well, I met Charles at a party. He wanted somebody who would be willing to scout around looking for antiques."

"He wanted a looker, too. Important for his business."

She had spoken about things that didn't give away her current mission. Now she should contain Justin's enthusiasm into digging further into her life. But how? She sipped her wine and concentrated on the food as a way to gain time.

Between one mouthful and the next, Justin said, "Your parents were assassinated and now Vassilli has been targeted for murder. It doesn't take a genius to figure out that you need help — and friends." Nonchalantly he finished the chicken.

"I need a coffee."

Tamara rose and set up the percolator. She lingered around the counter until the coffee was ready. She returned to the table with two mugs full of coffee, the creamer and the sugar.

"You cheated," Justin said. "No perked coffee on a campsite."

Tamara sipped on the coffee before talking. "Justin, you can't help me. If you care even only slightly for me, stay out of my life. That's the absolute best you can do." She looked sternly into his eyes.

"Can I at least enjoy looking at you? When you entered the hall at the Governor General's party people stopped chatting for a moment. In your draped white outfit you looked like a goddess out of a Greek mythology book. Right away I wanted to have an occasion to meet you." He poured himself another glass of wine, ignoring the coffee. "Try the pie," he said quietly.

To get his attention Tamara tapped the fork on her glass stem. "Justin, did you hear what I just said?"

"Yes." He lifted a wedge from the meringue pie and re-invited Tamara to do the same. From one bite and the next, he said, "I just want you to know that I have a friend at the police station in London — we went to school together — if that can be of any help."

"I'll keep that in mind," she said dryly.

"I'm also a nerd when it comes to gadgets and communication

devices. I can set up a spying station with hidden cameras and the like," he said, and rose. "I worked for a while with a company that installed security systems and helped them install the one in our house." He rounded the table and kissed Tamara on the neck. "Just in case you need something of this sort. Just in case, I said. You have my phone and address."

He swiftly moved toward the door. "I'm going. Out of your house, but not out of your life."

Chapter 7

The voicemail was blinking, and Tamara, though reluctantly, dialled her password to listen to the messages. There were three, all from Brad Wilson, asking whether she had discovered anything important. Tamara slammed down the receiver. Didn't the man have any feelings? Vassilli was still in critical condition! She had been going to the University Hospital every day and spent time in the waiting room, hoping to hear that her friend had moved or said a few words. Nothing had happened.

Still upset, she picked up her purse, climbed into her Subaru and drove to the Modano shop. After all, that was the place where she earned her living. As she entered the building she heard voices coming from the office contiguous to hers. She quietly settled in her office and eavesdropped.

"You promised!" Dianne Templeton was hollering. "Harry, do you know how important that commercial was for me?"

"I understand," a man's voice replied. "I recommended you for the ads. They told me they'd use you, but then they approached another TV station. Before I knew of the change, they had another woman for the show."

"But you're the boss of *Pamper Yourself*! Can you do anything for the next round?"

"Yes, Dianne. Come to my spa next Saturday, around five in the afternoon. I'll be giving a big party, and you'll have a chance to meet people in show business. I could even have a contract ready for you." The silence stretched and then the man lowered his voice. "You could stay overnight, if you like. I can give you the best beauty treatment my spa offers."

"I don't think I'll be in the mood," Dianne replied dryly.

Tamara wanted to get a look at the man Dianne had called Harry. She tiptoed out of her office and went back to sit in her car. As the man came out of the building she opened the door, exited the car and said a curt "Hi" to him. The man responded with a wave of his hand.

Without another look at him Tamara quickened her steps and re-entered her office. On purpose she made noise by tripping on a chair.

Dianne came to see what had happened. "I didn't expect to find you here, today."

"Oh, with all the time I spent at the hospital I find myself behind in my work. I have to get some ideas for a new, attractive arrangement for the shop window."

"I see. Can you believe that man? The one who just left? You must have seen him in the parking lot when you came in. He promised me a contract for a series of commercials; nobody showed up for the signing, and then... he expects me to spend a night with him! Men!"

Tamara shuffled some papers around, not wanting to show how much she was interested in knowing who the man was.

"Maybe he was just bragging about being in charge."

"Oh, no. It was his business that was being advertised. He's Harry Pearson. I can't believe he had no say in choosing the type of commercials or the actress." She sighed and slumped onto a chair.

"Harry Pearson? The owner of the spa?" Tamara used the information she had overheard moments before.

"Yes, have you been there?"

"No. But I heard they offer very relaxing treatments."

"Expensive too, but the balms and lotions they sell are really good. I don't care for the fragrances. Too strong for my taste."

"One day I should go there," Tamara said. "I like the outdoors and my skin dries up quickly when it's exposed to sun and wind. Maybe he has a product right for me."

"I'm sure he has."

"Can I do anything to cheer you up?"

"No, but thanks for the thought." Dianne strode back to her office.

Tamara spent a couple of hours reorganizing the main window and then left. It was time to do some snooping. She looked up the address of the spa Dianne had mentioned and drove there.

She stopped her car far away from the parking lot of *Pamper yourself, A Unique Centre for the Beautiful Body.* She walked under a circular portico and reached the main door, which was flanked, on the left side, by a statue of a woman summarily wrapped in a draped cloth and, on the right, by a naked muscular man posed in the gesture of inviting people inside.

The door opened as Tamara stepped on the threshold, and she found herself in a large hall. A waterfall on the back wall conveyed a sense of perpetuity; the murals with abstract art in pastel colours gave the place a sense of tranquility; in a corner was a dais with a male receptionist.

The Blackpox Threat

The man rose, introduced himself as *Armand* and welcomed her to the spa. "What can I do for you? Are you here for an appointment or just inquiring?"

"Inquiring," Tamara said, and shot him the best artificial smile she was capable of.

"I can show you around, if you like."

"That'd be nice." She gave him a coy glance. "Even if I probably won't be able to afford any treatment offered in this centre."

Armand waved off her remark. "Come with me."

He took Tamara through an archway and into a corridor. He opened a door to show her a small room which was simply furnished with a bed covered with lilac sheets, a stool and a counter full of all sorts of containers. Towels, also in lilac, lay folded on the bed.

"One of our massage rooms. We have six of them. Five are unoccupied. The red light on top of the door indicates when one is in use." He walked toward the end of the corridor and showed her into a room with tiles from floor to ceiling. "Here we have our whirlpool." Armand pointed opposite the entrance and said, "Over there are individual saunas and showers."

"Very impressive," Tamara said.

"It's the best there is," Armand commented with pride.

They retraced their steps and Armand moved into an exercise room. "Equipment of different kinds to keep the body in shape."

A bell resounded, forcing Armand and Tamara to go back to the entrance.

"A new guest…well, then let me give you some brochures. Maybe you'd like to see who our patrons are." He pointed to a lacquered counter where photographs alternated with bottles of perfumes and jars of creams.

Tamara graciously accepted the flyers and approached the counter. She lifted a few jars, read the scripts and deposited them where they were before.

Another customer entered the premises, and Armand got engaged in a new welcoming ceremony.

Unhurriedly Tamara slipped outside and circled the building, noting that the total footage of the centre largely exceeded that of the facilities she had just visited. She was puzzled. Were the spa and its owner important players? Hard to know, she thought as she climbed into her car.

When she arrived home, the phone was ringing. As she expected, it was Brad Wilson again.

"I've been calling and calling you," Brad said. "No answer!"

"I was busy. I have —"

Brad interrupted her. "Use the other phone. And leave it on all the time!"

Annoyed, Tamara got the cell out of her purse and dialled Brad's number.

"As I was saying, I have one new name for you but nothing related to the shipments. There haven't been any this last week. However, I have something very important to tell you." She paused. "First, let me remind you that so far your office didn't pay me a cent for the work I did, so don't get impatient. I have to earn my living. Second, you'd better come up with some way to pay for my expenses, and give me a few extra dollars if I have to contact wealthy people on their own turf. Charles' clients are loaded with money. I can't go around in jeans and T-shirts."

"We'll work out something."

"How much?"

"I can't tell you right now, I have to consult my boss and the administration."

"I need $100 a day — minimum, and I need some by the end of this week." As she didn't get any answer, Tamara added sternly, "Agreed?"

"Yes. The name?"

"Harry Pearson. He owns a fancy spa just outside London. He was around to visit Charles' assistant. He's a friend of hers. The relationship looks very personal. Dianne would like to do some commercials for his business. Up to now there was nothing shipped to Pearson."

"I see. I'll pass on that name and find out more about his activity and financial status. Anything else?"

"No, except that Vassilli cannot be moved. He's in bad shape, I've been told. No sign of recovery."

"Sorry to hear that, I know how hard it must be for you."

"Very hard. So please send the money and wait for my call. While Vassilli is in the hospital I'm busy visiting him, and don't ask me why. If I don't call you it means I have nothing new to report."

"But I want to be sure you're okay…"

Tamara clicked off. She had done plenty for the time being. After all she was only a spy apprentice.

Chapter 8

Bergamo, Northern Italy
June 2007

At the crack of dawn, Boris Youkenoff unloaded the first metal box from his pick-up truck. He wondered whether any of his valuable biochemical products had been damaged during the long journey. The transfer from what he considered *his private* research lab to a new operative base in northern Italy had been planned for months, but none of the packing had even been considered until three weeks ago. It had been a delicate and nerve-wracking journey, considering the sensitivity to light and temperature of the cultures and the fragility of the vials.

For years Boris had worked in a covert location in the Beskids, that part of the Carpathian Mountains located in Western Ukraine. In a natural cave 50 metres underground were the remains of an old research lab for the development of biological weapons. Secretly established in the '80s by the former Soviet Union, its location, together with what had been left of the lab, had gone unnoticed for years, leaving Boris free to operate as he pleased. And did he! He made a good living manufacturing beauty creams, emollient solutions and other skin products he sold on the ever-growing global market. Two years ago, however, he made an encounter that had radically changed his life.

He vividly remembered the evening he had met with Frank Milton in a café in San Marco Square, where, to his astonishment, a band filled the air with rock-and-roll music. He often met his clients in Venice. He loved the city, its multitude of small and tiny canals meandering among the buildings, the many art exhibitions and especially its elegant municipal casino. Often he spent a night at Ca' Noghera playing Black Jack or at Ca' Vendramin Calergi gambling at the Chemin de Fer table. Taking a trip to Venice was an escape, almost a must for his mental health, as his lifestyle didn't allow him to make friends or have a family. At times, in fact, after having spent days underground, he had a feeling of unbearable, oppressing seclusion.

Frank Milton, his new client, had responded to an advertisement he had made over the Internet, offering low-price quantities of octocylene and titanium dioxide, two ingredients often used in the making of sunscreen lotions.

After the first beer Boris had sold three kilograms of each, and after the seventh beer Boris had started to tell Frank Milton about his lab, about the raw chemicals that had been left behind and were now at his disposal, and the hundred possibilities he had to create new products, some for the cosmetic industry, others for different uses. Unlimited possibilities, he had bragged. It was then that Frank Milton had accompanied him to the *La Lanterna di Marco Polo,* the hotel where Boris was staying, and gave him an appointment for the next day at the Lido, the world-famous Venetian beach. For the following week they had met every day at the beach, where a bottle of vodka, compliments of Frank, had stood deeply in the sand, available for a quick sip at any hour of the day. At first, Frank Milton had gotten vague answers to his questions, but by the end of the week Frank had a pad full of sketches together with formulas Boris could recite by heart; they referred to chemical compounds and micro-organisms still present in the cave, in addition to those he had created, mostly targeted to a market of beauty products. After all he had been hired, months before the official dismantling of the lab, as the chief biochemist! Then other questions had surfaced: were those elements still active? What could they be used for? At first Boris had hesitated, since the primitive goal of the lab had been biological warfare, and some of these substances were still present and active, even if the lab had been declared officially closed in 1992. These substances were stored in boxes accessible only by following a narrow trail that branched off the main path and was well camouflaged by the presence of a cluster of stalagmites.

Boris' hesitation had vanished when Frank said, "I feel we've a great future together. We should unite our forces and start a new business."

Then Boris had answered all of Milton's questions exhaustively.

With Frank's expertise in biology and Boris' thorough knowledge of microbiology and organic chemistry they would design a product that would make them rich. Very rich.

Boris smiled inwardly as he unloaded the last box and carried it inside the house.

****

Hours later, after having savoured a tasty salami sandwich and drunk a glass of Bardolino wine, Boris surveyed his new accommodation in the outskirts of Bergamo, a city situated in the foothills of the Italian Alps. He would remain here for a few weeks, that is, until the last phase of the operation he had concocted with Frank was completed. He had rented an old two-storey house with a nearby shack where he could store his truck. The kitchen was spacious; in the middle, an ancient wood stove had been covered with a formica board to serve as a table; the sink and a modern gas range lined up along one wall; cupboards and a pantry stood on the opposite side. Cast-iron pots hung from the beams above the old stove.

As he had requested, the refrigerator and freezer had been plugged in. Boris checked the temperature of each and then stored his precious vials in the freezer, and his equally precious cultures in the fridge. He continued his inspection of the premises. The two bedrooms were small, with only the essentials: a full bed, a dresser with a mirror and two barrel chairs in each. The bathroom, at the end of the corridor, had a gas heater for hot water. Boris moved to the upper floor, his boots making the stairway squeak at each step. There was only one large room, clearly used for storage since old light fixtures, broken chairs and boxes took one third of it. In one corner an enormous number of magazines and newspapers were amassed in casual order. Once cleaned up properly, the place could be used for some of his work, in case the second bedroom didn't provide enough space for his experiments. For the time being his new accommodation was adequate, Boris thought, as he descended to the main floor.

It was time to have a good rest.

The following day Boris performed a meticulous cleaning of the premises. In the spare bedroom, he set up all the containers and equipment he had taken with him from his lab in the Carpathian

Mountains. When all the preliminaries were over, he checked on the status of the substances he had to work with. To his great satisfaction, everything was exactly as it was supposed to be.

Finally he decided to turn on his cell and listen to his messages. There were three, all from Frank Milton, pressuring him to go ahead with the preparation of their new product. His partner was an impatient man who couldn't grasp that his research needed time and accuracy — it couldn't be rushed.

Reluctantly, Boris dialled Frank's number.

"Finally you decided to answer!" were Frank's first words.

"It isn't trivial to set up a lab, even a small one, in a strange place. I had to make sure that the environment in which I'll operate is germ-free. I did the work myself, and disinfected all the tools and containers. My little lab is operational now."

"I thought most of the components were in their final stage when you left the Beskids."

"You said it right: most components, not all. The latest version of the virus I created needs a new culture to be effective. I left in such a rush that I had no time to prepare it. I told you all that, right?"

"Yes," Frank mumbled.

"That's the work I still have to do. It isn't simple, without my usual apparatus. I'll make it; I just need a few days. By the way, are you ready with the testing of the final product?"

"Don't worry about that. I got plenty of Guinea pigs. Send the samples and I'll test them right away. Can you make it this week?"

"Yes. There'll be three containers, each inside an old amphora, nicely packed with the fake label 'penta-oxide-polyvalent — doesn't attack old terracotta. Used for restoration.' You remember the temperature you have to keep them at?"

"Yes. When will the second batch be ready?"

"In two weeks. But I'll ship it only after you tell me that the testing has been successful."

"If not, what would you do?"

"Frank, we went through this already. I'll use a different culture, different nucleic acids, until I find one that makes the virus ready to multiply at will. Trust me, I know what I'm doing."

"And the vaccine?"

Boris hesitated. "As we agreed, after I receive the final payment for the product."

"What about a couple dosages for me and the boss?"

"No. Money first. Deposit it at the Clariden Bank in Lugano, as usual."

"I resent you don't trust me, Boris."

Boris didn't reply, and Frank finally said, "Well…once you're done, clear up everything and take a vacation."

"Sure thing, bye-bye."

Boris didn't need to be told to go on holiday. For the last six months he had worked hard; he surely could use a break. He already had a great plan. Move from casino to casino, playing Black Jack and trying his luck at the slot machines. Normally, the hotels that hosted green tables were very nice, the girls, friendly and the food, fabulous.

It was time to get acquainted with the topography of the city and find out where the subsidiary of the Modano Company was located. The presence of the Modano's Italian branch was the reason he had selected Bergamo for his temporary stay. A company specializing in the shipment of antiques and art objects would not raise any suspicion at customs and treat his items with the utmost care.

He looked at a tourist's manual and soon realized that there were two sections of the city. Bergamo Alta, the once fortified part of the city, rested on a hill, with a maze of narrow, cobbled streets often tightly skirting churches and buildings of composite styles. This was the historical part which attracted tourists and artists in equal numbers. The lower town, reminiscent of the city's long allegiance to the Republic of Venice, combined clusters of old buildings which exhibited outstanding architectonical motifs with suburban and industrial areas.

Finished his exploratory tour, Boris parked his pick-up at Porta Osio and proceeded on foot to via Broseta, looking for the Modano shop. He was surprised to see how small it was, with only one window that showcased antiques and statuettes in every inch of available space. As he pushed the door open, melodic chimes revealed his presence.

An older woman, severely dressed in a dark grey outfit with a pearl necklace, moved forward to greet him. Boris asked to speak with the manager and was right away ushered to the back of the shop. He entered a small office whose walls were covered with oil and watercolour paintings. An imposing mahogany desk stood in the middle.

"Boris Youkenoff. I called you a month ago about a shipment of a very delicate nature," he said in English, not trusting his Italian for such an important transaction.

Behind the desk was a man in his 50s with grey hair and thick-lensed eyeglasses. He rose and extended his hand to Boris. They shook hands.

"Mario Rossi. Oh yes. I remember well. Do you have with you the object in question?"

"Not with me," he said. "I just wanted to be sure I had the right address." He looked around, wondering how such a small shop could handle intercontinental shipments.

"You surely do." As if interpreting Boris' perplexity, Mario Rossi said, "We have our trucks and the courier plane in another part of the city. Shipment is once a week."

"The cargo will be kept above zero temperature, right?"

"Yes. It's part of our specialty. Temperature between 15 to 25 degrees centigrade, humidity around 30 per cent. Otherwise, some components used in old paintings could be damaged, some experts claim."

"Insurance?"

"Minimum is 5,000 euros, included in the price. We sent you a bunch of flyers. Did you not receive our mail?"

"Mail?" Boris looked at him blankly. He had not received any mail from them before leaving. Besides, how in the world did Mario Rossi get his old address? He had never given it to him.

"Yes, our little package about the services the Modano Company offers. It included the prices per weight and dimensions, and the insurance rates."

Boris was speechless.

Mario's eyes brimmed with satisfaction behind the think lenses. "About a month ago you called us from your hotel in Venice, remember? La Lanterna di Marco Polo, correct? I called them and got your address."

If he had a gun in his hand, Boris would have shot the man on the spot. That mail could leave a dangerous trail. His house had been sold and it was now in the hands of the new owner, a man he only vaguely knew.

He slowly recovered from the shock. "Yes, yes, I remember."

"You spoke of precious and fragile objects. Would you like to increase the insurance?"

Boris actually didn't care about any insurance. His material was very valuable, actually irreplaceable. He wanted it to arrive safely in Canada.

"Hmm, what is the probability of my parcel being lost or damaged?"

Mario Rossi gave him a very reassuring smile. "Only one in 50,000." He adjusted the heavy eyeglasses on the bridge of his nose. "See that painting?" He pointed to an oil hanging on the side wall. "It's an original Fattori, valued at a quarter million euros. Your vases will travel with it." He smiled with pride. "The Modano Company is expensive, but very reliable."

****

Boris walked to his car, still upset about the mail that the Modano Company had sent to his old home address. They had no business poking into his life! And then, shouldn't guests' records constitute confidential information? He had been at that hotel for years, long before he had become involved with Frank Milton, so no wonder the hotel staff knew him well.

If Frank ever got scent of the incident he would be furious. He'd better leave him in the dark.

It had all happened because of the highway that was going to cut through the mountains where his underground lab was located; it was very close to his property. He had sold his house at a reasonable price and cleared out in a hurry. He wondered what the new owner had done with the package the Modano Company had sent him. Probably nothing, as he had been very careful not to leave a forwarding address — he had not even mentioned where he was going. Maybe he should give him a call and tactfully inquire if there was any mail for him.

That night Boris couldn't fall asleep. He could handle hours and hours of work, do and redo tests, improve his products incessantly but he couldn't handle the threat that the mail sent to his old address posed. He had to speak with the owner of his old house, Peter Stalovic, and find out if he had received any mail addressed to him. If so, he would ask Peter to open it. If it consisted of the flyers sent by the Modano Company, he would dismiss them as advertising material and tell Peter to dispose of them.

Finally, at eight o'clock in the morning he climbed into his pick-up truck and drove to the bus station in downtown Bergamo. He stopped in front of a phone booth. With the phone card he had bought in a coffee shop in viale Vittorio Emanuele, he placed a call to Peter.

"You can't believe what happened," Peter said. "I'm almost a prisoner in my own house!"

"Oh — what's the problem?"

"You know that the highway was going to pass through this area, right? So they came with bulldozers, backhoes, cranes and an army of men. They started digging all around when suddenly the soil caved in. There were caves, a lot of them. And they found — oh, I can't believe it! — they found that somebody had been working down there for years, using the stuff left in the lab. It was dangerous stuff, the police told me, and they wanted to talk to you. I'm happy you called. Where are you?"

"As I told you I was taking a trip." Boris had to think fast. "At the moment I'm in the Maldives."

"Mal — what?"

"They're islands, in the Pacific Ocean."

"You should come back, they have questions for you. They say you're the only person who can help them find out what was going on in those caves."

"Well, I don't know anything about that. I lived in the house I sold you, with my three sheep and four cows — the ones I left with you. That's all."

"Yes, yes, but you have to come back soon. To explain about all the fruit bats that were in the caves, some dead, some still alive. Somebody had been feeding them. Old peelings and fruit pits all over. What a mess! You have to talk to the police." Boris could hear Peter's laborious breathing. "I can't move around; they took away all my stuff: magazines, books, tapes — oh, it's terrible! They're treating me as a criminal."

Boris was overwhelmed with the desire to cut off the conversation, but he wanted to know what happened to the flyers that the Modano subsidiary had sent to his old address.

"Calm down, calm down! My vacation will end in three days, Peter. I'll be there to explain that you and I have nothing to do with any cave, bat, or chemical."

"Three days?"

"Yes. My return flight is set. I can't change it. By the way, did you get any mail for me while I was away?"

"Yes, I did. But I don't have it. They took everything with them, even the card that my daughter sent me for my birthday and..."

Boris had heard more than he wanted to know. He clicked off, more worried than before he had made the call.

The conversation with Peter, however, rang a bell, tolling nostalgia and pride as he remembered the exciting work he had carried out in the Carpathian caves for more than a decade. It was a sudden plunge into past glory. He couldn't avoid reliving the feelings he experienced when he had been hired to work at the secret laboratory. He had been so proud, then, and so eager to get new findings!

The Soviet Union, at that time strongly involved in biological warfare, had initiated a project on the genetic alteration of smallpox. Researchers had discovered that several areas of the smallpox genome, the DNA, were open to the introduction of new genes while leaving intact the smallpox's high contagiousness. The ebola virus soon proved to be a viable candidate for supplying the wanted genes.

The new genetically engineered virus that Boris had worked on, named *Karjak*, inherited the short incubation of ebola but also its lack of airborne transmission and its inability to be transferred by skin contact.

Boris' mandate had been to improve on Karjak. To this end, he extracted new genes from the ebola's RNA that would render Karjak absorbable by soft tissues, making it easier to propagate, and therefore, more dangerous. His colony of fruit bats had been very useful in testing the different viruses of his making — the new one always more deadly than its predecessor. He had pursued that goal even after the official closing of the laboratory — only to satisfy his scientific creativity. *"Only to satisfy my scientific creativity"*, Boris claimed aloud.

Until he had met Frank Milton.

Chapter 9

East of London, Ontario
June 2007

Dianne arrived at the spa past ten o'clock, when the party was in full swing. Her black chiffon gown, trimmed with sequins, left her arms and shoulders completely bare. It was three-quarter length and clung to her feminine body like a second skin. Her auburn hair was combed in tiny braids and two long heart-shaped earrings adorned her neck. A companion chain circled one of her ankles, tingling rhythmically as she walked.

The party at The Pamper Yourself Spa was a promotional event. For the occasion, the entrance hall had been decorated with balloons and banners spelling the spa's name in capital letters. Patrons' support was acknowledged with a donation of beauty products; potential customers were offered a coupon for a free treatment.

Harry Pearson rushed to Dianne and kissed her on the cheeks.

"You look fabulous," he said. "I was afraid you weren't coming."

"Well, I'm still upset with you, Harry, but, what the hell...a party is always good exposure."

"Come with me. I'll introduce you to some important people." He took Dianne by the arm and circuited her around.

Harry was medium-height, with grey hair that descended to the neck, and quick brown eyes. His velour brown trousers and vest were brightened up by an orange long-sleeve shirt and a matching silk scarf, giving him the look of an artist.

The band alternated modern dances with old tunes, but the preponderance of women limited the number of couples who could be on the floor. Dianne chatted with people here and there and danced every time somebody asked her, but she kept thinking how depressing the party was. It was almost midnight when she approached Harry.

"What about my commercials?" she asked. "Is the rep here?"

"Yes, yes. He said he was coming a bit late."

Dianne didn't move an inch. "Harry!"

"Don't worry! He'll bring the contract."

"When?" Dianne said, her eyebrows arched in disbelief.

Harry looked at his wristwatch. "Oh, it's midnight. Let's go to my office, at the mezzanine." He gave her an ingratiating smile. "You see, my spa needs a...what should I call it? A financial injection, so to speak, and this friend of mine, a nice man, has promised me a loan, if —" He hesitated and took Dianne up the staircase. "If I do him a favour."

"What do I have to do with this favour?" Dianne stopped at the fifth step and frowned.

"Nothing big. Come, come upstairs."

Reluctantly Dianne followed him.

The office smelled of recent cigarette smoking, and Dianne's first reaction was to vent out the strong smell; instead she took the ashtray and asked where the washroom was located. She dropped the cigarette butts into the toilet, flushed it and came back to the office.

"Oh, he came and left already," Harry said, and looked at the papers lying on his desk. He gestured Dianne to one of the chairs, but Dianne stood and waited. "Here it is! Your contract!"

"So, what's the deal?" Dianne asked dryly. Still standing she extended her arm to get the papers, but Harry rolled them up, kept them in one hand and banged them slightly against the other.

"This important friend of mine is expecting a shipment from a client who used the Modano Company. Three little vases, and he'd like you to personally clear them at customs."

"Oh, oh, count me out if we're talking drugs."

"Nothing of the sort."

"Oh, illegal export, then?" Dianne asked.

"Not really, even if he isn't sure of the objects' provenance. He told me that at customs sometimes they're very particular. My friend thought that since you're known there, you could smooth the problem, if a problem arises."

Dianne asked, "Hmm...antiques?"

"Yes. Precious."

"And they were not declared as such?"

"I'm afraid not."

"Hmm...our country favours the import of art objects. However there may be a duty to be paid."

"No problem with any duty or fee; my friend just wants those vases in his hands as soon as possible. The package should be arriving the day after tomorrow."

Finally Dianne sat. "I'll see what I can do. The contract? Can I

The Blackpox Threat

see it?"

Harry handed her the two sheets of legal format. He smiled. "It's all here. Two sessions, a thousand each. Your line of ad: moisturizing soap and shower gel." He attempted an ingratiating smile. "You'll look great in either."

Perplexed, Dianne took the papers and read them slowly. Who was Harry's mysterious friend? What did he have to do with her contract? On purpose she took plenty of time reading.

"Maybe you wonder what I have to do with the vases," Harry said timidly. "Nothing at all. It's just a favour to a friend."

Dianne folded the papers. "I'll go fetch the package as soon as it arrives and bring it over right away. The name?"

"It's addressed to me."

Dianne rose. "I'd like to be paid in advance for the sessions I'll be doing."

"But I can't do that. I'm not the one who signed the contract."

"Never mind."

Harry remained speechless as Dianne neared the desk. "Sign the cheque," she ordered.

"But I can't!"

"No money, I don't bother picking up the parcel."

"What about half?" Beads of perspiration covered Harry's forehead. "I told you, I, myself need money. Badly. And what guarantee do I have that you'll do the commercials?"

"I will; don't worry. It's very important that my face appears on TV. One job brings another."

"Half. I'll give you half."

Dianne shook her head vigorously, a couple of her little tresses getting loose in the process.

"All two thousand, Harry. Get them from your friend. And remember, before clearing the customs for your precious vases, I'll go to the bank. If your cheque bounces, I won't bother with your friend's antiques." She looked sternly at him, "As for you, you won't have to bother calling me again."

Harry didn't move so Dianne motioned to leave.

"Wait, wait!" he shouted. He dashed to the desk and opened a drawer. "You're a hard woman to deal with." He wrote a cheque and handed it to Dianne.

"Cheat me and you'll learn how hard I can really be."

****

For 20 years Frank Milton had worked in the cosmetic industry, experimenting with new products designed to address the needs of people with a variety of skin problems. He was in charge of the Orlane's Laboratory in Toronto, when he was suddenly fired. They didn't use that word, of course; they just told him that his position had become redundant. Frank knew better, however. His illicit business of using the company's formulas to produce his own products and sell them under cost had somehow been discovered and, in lieu of trying to prove his illegal doing and spending a fortune in lawyers, the company had cut its losses by terminating his contract. It would have been difficult to prove that his rejuvenating and cleansing creams were the same as the company's because he had systematically added a few extra ingredients, such as colour and fragrance.

The problem remained, however, that at 45, Frank Milton had found himself unemployed and unemployable in the industry. Clearly the Orlane Laboratory had passed the information about the real cause of his lay-off to other companies, competitors included. His little business had allowed him to accumulate a good half a million dollars, which he had used to set up his own company, the

The Blackpox Threat

Iridient. The most profitable outlet for his products was the Pamper Yourself Spa, owned by his friend Harry Pearson.

Once more Frank carefully checked on the contents of the three Petri dishes that lay on the counter. Everything was ready for the chemicals Boris Youkenoff would soon ship over. He jumped when he heard a knock on the door.

"Who is it?" he said.

"Who can it be but me, at this time of night?" Harry said.

Frank approached the door and opened it. "What's the problem?" he asked. "You know I don't like to be interrupted when I work at night." He gave Harry a penetrating look. "You're shaking."

"You bet I am." He removed the scarf that wound around his neck and used it to dry his perspiration. "I have a big problem. I asked my friend, Dianne, to go fetch your package at customs, as you asked, but the woman won't do it for free." Harry moved in and slumped on a stool, making it sway left and right.

"What?"

"You know the contract — the one for advertising the products we use at the spa?"

"Yes, it's done. They'll call her up next week."

Harry looked at Frank sheepishly. "She wanted to be paid in advance. The whole amount or she wouldn't go get your stuff."

Frank stood right before Harry. "So — " he said, scowling.

"I signed a cheque Frank, but...but it isn't covered." Harry glanced around. The place was spooky; the fluorescent lights cast dark shadows of jars, bottles and tools over the walls. Finally he mumbled, "I need the two thousand. By tomorrow morning, that is, in six hours."

"You mean to tell me that you don't even have two grand and you threw that big party that is still going on?"

Music resounded in the lab, even if the sauna, the massage rooms and the indoor pool were located in between.

"It's a promotion — I'm sure I'll get a lot of customers thanks to the party. It always pays off."

"That's what you said last time, and here you are again, broke as usual." Frank took off his white coat and threw it on the counter. "Let's go to the office. You'd better make sure that my vases arrive intact to my door."

Chapter 10

Fascinated by the activities that kept her little friends in permanent motion, Tamara stood in front of the aquarium where fine grey gravel, white rocks and seaweeds recreated the ocean's bottom. Five monos insistently crossed the path of a royal grandmother; three dominos swam close to the surface; several clowns appeared and disappeared behind the rocks. Tamara checked the bulb of the bluish light that was flickering and fastened it in its socket. Watching the fish kept her vision busy while her mind relaxed.

The grandfather clock tolled ten, reminding her that it was time to go to the hospital and find out whether there was any change in Vassilli's condition. Phoning had proved to be totally useless.

She grabbed her purse and climbed into her Subaru.

When she arrived at UH she soon discovered that Vassilli wasn't there anymore. Inquiries at the nurse's station on the fourth floor, where the man had been confined until yesterday, did not produce any results. Upset, Tamara descended to the main floor and went to the information desk. The volunteer in charge knew absolutely nothing about a patient named Vassilli Petrovic.

The wall of privacy that had surrounded the stay of her Ukrainian friend at the hospital was still impenetrable. Tamara used the cell that Brad had given her and called him.

"Vassilli has vanished," she said, skipping the greetings. "What do you know about it?"

"You mean to tell me that he isn't there anymore?"

"Apparently not. Nobody seems to know a thing about the man. Can you find out what happened and call me back?"

"Right away," Brad said, and clicked off.

Tamara helped herself to a muffin and a cappuccino and sat in one of the easy chairs located in the spacious entrance hall. She feared the worst.

Nothing happened for more than a half-hour, when finally Brad called.

"Sad news, Tamara. Vassilli died. It happened last night."

"Dead? Oh, no!" What she had feared for days and anguished her to no end had indeed happened. "Are they going to perform an autopsy?"

"It's already been done, and his body transported to Ottawa."

"The result of the post-mortem?"

"I'm not at liberty to say, Tamara."

Tamara switched off the phone. Was she part of the operation — actually the main player so far, as she had been made to believe — or was she only a peripheral participant?

The phone rang again.

"Tamara?" Brad said. "Don't get upset, I have to follow rules, you know."

"Upset? I'm furious, Brad, and if you want me to continue to work on this project, Bull — Bull — whatever, you'd better inform me of the essentials. There's been a homicide. Details are important; they may be crucial in keeping poor little me alive. So I want to know the results, and what kind of killer the police are looking for."

Only a few seconds passed, and Brad complied.

"It seemed that Vassilli had put up a struggle; he ripped off some of his assailant's clothing, as there was fabric in one of his hands. The knife, a double-edged blade, barely reached his heart, but the man wasn't in the best health condition. He was a diabetic, and massively overweight. He died of kidney failure." He paused as if he needed to catch his breath.

"What about the killer?" Tamara asked.

"I'm getting to it; I'm getting to it. There are fingerprints on the handle. The authorities made a search in their database, but unfortunately no match came up. It appeared that the killer exited by the door opposite the one you and Justin entered from, probably when he heard you two approaching the stateroom. Vassilli never said a word after he was taken to the hospital." Brad paused, but Tamara remained silent. "His murder is still being investigated, no suspect yet, and no assumption on the motive. What kind of killer? Nobody knows."

"Is that all?"

"All that they told me, I swear."

"I see. Vassilli never recovered, I guess." She sighed. "Funeral arrangements? I'd like to be there."

"I don't know yet. I can't go, and I suggest you don't go either, Tamara. We don't know whether his murder is linked to our operation. Your presence could blow your cover."

"What cover? It's public knowledge that I was a good friend of Vassilli's. I stayed with him after my parents died. Why should anybody link my presence to anything else?"

After a moment of hesitation, Brad said, "It'd be wiser if you stay put, Tamara."

"Just let me know when the service is and the place. I want to go and that's final."

****

It had started raining just east of Toronto and never stopped until Tamara arrived at the all-faiths chapel. Rain had pounded her windshield without mercy, the wipers seemingly unable to keep up with the clearing. Fortunately her GPS had guided her to her destination, Ottawa, without a hitch. She parked the car as close to the chapel as she could.

The building was a striking example of modern architecture. It had a round shape and a roof that sloped down gradually to form an arch on top of the entrance. The steps, semicircles, decreased in size from bottom to top, as they led to the entrance.

Holding tightly onto her umbrella, Tamara neared the chapel and ascended the few steps in front of the entrance. To her surprise, Justin and Michael Devry were standing near the imposing portal. They each wore a dark grey trench coat draped loosely on top of a black suit. She acknowledged their presence with a nod, closed her umbrella and entered the chapel.

The Devrys followed her, entering the same pew where she sat.

"Sorry about Vassilli," Justin murmured.

"Thanks," she replied.

Soon bouquets of flowers were brought in; some were set around the podium in the middle of the nave, others on the left side close to the organ. As the chanting started, six pallbearers carried the coffin and deposited it in front of the podium. When Tamara saw the blue and yellow flag on top of the casket she closed her eyes, made fists with her hands and tried to dismiss the sight. The image of another coffin, also draped in the Ukrainian flag, appeared in her mind. She tried to chase it away, but was unable to. That casket was her mother's, set beside her father's. Finally she surrendered to the inevitable. She exhaled deeply and let tears flow freely on her face, her shoulders shaken by tremors. As she rummaged in her purse to get a package of tissues she felt Justin's arm around her shoulders in a caring, brotherly embrace. Instinctively she leaned against him and stayed in that position until the ceremony began.

Overwhelmed by sorrow, Tamara hardly followed the eulogy and the speeches. To her they were sound without a meaning. Then her mind shifted to the presence of the Devrys. Why were they at the funeral? Who informed them of the time and place of the service? Were they a link to Vassilli's participation in Operation Bullfrog? Or were they present because they knew him much more intimately than Justin had implied? Or were they there for her?

The service over, Tamara didn't follow the crowd trundling out of the chapel. She genuflected and mentally said the prayers she had so many times recited when she was at the French boarding school.

"Ms. Smith?" a man in black clothing with a chauffeur hat in his hand called out.

"Yes?" Tamara turned, and rose.

"I'm a member of the Ukrainian Embassy. I'd like to let you know that we'll contact you. Soon."

Tamara put her hand on the man's arm. "What for, may I ask?"

"Mr. Vassilli Petrovic left an envelope for you." He gave her a sympathetic look. "Oh, I forgot. My deepest sympathy for your loss."

Tamara looked at the man, trying to memorize his facial

features. "Thank you. And you are — ?"

"Kikk, I drove Mr. Petrovic when he was in town." He bowed slightly and quickened his steps toward the exit.

Tamara didn't lose any time. She grabbed her purse and umbrella and followed him out of the chapel. She saw him reach a black limousine with *Corps Diplomatique* status and drive off. Slowly she walked to her car. Justin and his father were standing near her Subaru Impreza, clearly waiting for her. "We'd like to take you out for a bite to eat," Justin said. "There are no refreshments after the service."

"Thank you for the offer," Tamara said politely but firmly. "I have to go back to London right away. I have to catch up on a lot of work." She opened the door of her car and climbed into it.

The rain had stopped, giving way to a cold wind that swept dead leaves and broken branches across the road. She turned off Highway 31 and stopped at a Tim Hortons.

She was just sitting down at a table with a ham croissant sandwich when her cellular rang.

It was Brad. "Everything well?" he asked.

"Yes. I meant to call you, by the way. The Devrys were both there. Any connection with Vassilli that you know about?" Tamara nibbled her sandwich.

"Not really. They have a house on the shores of Lake Huron, not far from Vassilli's cottage. Why do you ask?"

"Just curiosity. I thought very few people knew of the funeral service."

"That was my understanding. Anybody approach you?"

"I have my mouth full," she said, and waited a second or two. Did Brad send somebody to monitor the crowd attending the funeral service? Probably. "Yes, a member of the Ukrainian Embassy approached me."

"And? What did he want?"

To gain time, she made munching sounds, quickly pondering whether she should tell him of Vassilli's envelope. It was probably something private, so she decided not to disclose its existence. "He offered his condolences."

"Of course, that was a must. So you're on your way back to London?"

"Yes."

"Good. Call me as soon as you discover anything new. Bye for now."

Tamara finished her sandwich and went to the counter to get a coffee. She had a long drive ahead of her.

****

In Justin's Audi, Michael Devry complained about being hungry. They were parked away from the Tim Hortons' entrance, their lights off.

"Be reasonable," Justin said. "We can't go in without being noticed. The place is almost deserted."

"But then she may take off for London, and that's another eight hours' drive. We brought me along to justify your presence. You were sure she'd accept your invitation." He paused. "Too presumptuous, that's what you are."

"We came here to offer moral support or help her in case she needed any. You agreed on the mission, because you wanted to give her another closer look. I never said that it'd be a fun trip."

"It surely wasn't." Michael pouted. "I didn't see too much of her either. She had a long raincoat, black; high boots, black, and a hat. Black too. Couldn't see her hair, without mentioning her eyes. She had an enormous pair of sunglasses — and it was raining!"

"She was dressed for a funeral, not a party."

"Hmm...I understand, but she looked old, more suitable for a man my age than for you."

"Sure, you belong to the generation according to which a woman had to be much younger than the man — 20 years or so. But women nowadays don't fall into that trap anymore. You may not have realized it, but there has been a women's lib. They choose their man."

"Oh, it could be, but then you are not the chosen!" Michael pointed to Tamara who was taking off, the taillights of her car disappearing in the dark. "She's gone. Let step in and have something to eat."

Justin put his Audi in gear. "Nah. We tag along until the first food outlet on the 401."

"And what would be the reason?"

"Father, try to understand. I care for her, and her past speaks tragedy. Her dear friend Vassilli has just been murdered. Her parents too, years back. She may be in danger. I want to see if she's followed."

Chapter 11

Tamara was back in London late at night. In painful moments like these, she really appreciated having a place she could call home. She stripped off her black coat and boots and flounced about on the sofa. She closed her eyes. She had lost a dear friend, the only person who had been around her for most of her life.

Vassilli's large frame appeared in her memory, together with his quick smile and loud laughter. The first time he had come to see her at the private school in Grenoble, he was dressed as Santa Claus, carrying a big bag. It contained the gifts that her parents, still in protective custody on the other side of the Atlantic, had wrapped up for her. Since that time — she was six years old then — they had exchanged gifts every Christmas. And the season's celebration wouldn't end there. They would go to a show together and have a midnight meal afterward. That nice, simple tradition was now gone as well. She sighed and opened her eyes.

A light flickered on the control box of the aquarium, dismissing her memories. She rose and gathered food for the fish. She filled the automatic dispenser that provided the correct amount of nutrients her little friends needed every day. Then she made a cup of tea and after finishing it, she walked into the bedroom. She would snatch as much sleep as possible. Tomorrow she should go back to work.

****

Just before nine o'clock Tamara entered her office at the Modano Company. She decided to put aside her sorrow, at least for the day. She had just draped her coat on her chair when Charles walked in and silently hugged her.

"I didn't expect you to be here today," he said. "I was going to call you and let you know how sorry I am for what happened to your friend, Vassilli."

"Thank you, Charles. I thought coming to work would distract me from my thoughts. So, a lot of customers for the upcoming auction?"

"I called it off. I didn't figure you'd be back in time. Next one in two weeks."

"Any new items I should catalogue?"

"Seven. The four we picked up together at that Toronto brocanteur who was going out of business, plus three I ordered when you were away."

"Anything that has to go through customs?" Those were the items Tamara should keep an eye on.

"Only two. Dianne offered to clear them. She already had to go fetch a parcel of a personal nature shipped by our company overseas."

"Oh, the Modano Company has a subsidiary?"

"Yes. In Italy. That's where the family business started. The ideal place for customers who shop for art objects."

Tamara's ears pricked with attention. She needed to find out the sender's name and the *real* recipient of that personal item. Then she would also discover where the Modano subsidiary was located — important information she could pass onto Brad Wilson, assuming he didn't already know of its existence. The shipment order should be in Dianne's office — but would she be able to see it?

"Where are these shipments normally cleared?" she asked nonchalantly.

"At the Canadian Border Security Agency, London Airport." Charles walked into his office and when he came back he gave Tamara a set of sheets. "These are the purchase slips of the objects that arrived. We can go down to the storage room, look at them and see what price we should tag them with for the auction. The starting price, I mean."

"Great. I'll do a bit of research, find out whether there are similar items on sale on *eBay.ca* and adjust the price, if necessary."

Charles looked at her. "You look in need of care, and food. Did you have breakfast?"

"Not yet."

Charles took her coat and handed it to her. "Me neither. Let's first get something to eat. Then we'll come back to work. Oh, by the way, we have to slip downtown to see Stephanie. She wants some advice on how to set up her new fountain. The plumber is coming today. She's very happy about that piece. She gives you a lot of credit for showing it to her."

****

When they arrived at The French Look, Stephanie was busy with a customer. The plumbing for the fountain hadn't been done yet; a few pipes of different lengths lay on the floor together with a tool box.

Stephanie showed up and said, "You're just in time. The plumber has stepped out for lunch." Her eyes sparkled with excitement. "I have an important guest in my office." She gestured to a man sitting on the other side of the glass partition, his shoulders towards Charles and Tamara. She turned to Tamara. "You were at the party of the Governor General, right? Do you remember a striking gentleman in a tuxedo?"

Tamara looked at her puzzled. "Most men wore a tuxedo. I don't remember anybody in particular."

"Well, he's here. I can't let him wait. He's interested in my atelier or..." She giggled. "Or in me. I should be going. Place the fountain where it should be. I rely on your judgement."

And she was gone.

"No problem." Charles called after her. "We'll be done in a minute and be out of the way."

A little basin collected the water trickling from the sides. Fastened to the flat rim were three happy seals, their dark colour contrasting the light grey of the natural stone. Charles and Tamara moved around the little fountain to expose it to the best lighting available in the vestibule. They'd positioned the décor item in its final position when the plumber walked in.

Charles and Tamara pointed to the place where he should set the fountain and left.

Once outside, Charles said, "I wonder who the man was that Stephanie was so excited about. You don't remember seeing a striking gentleman in a tuxedo?" Charles said, imitating Stephanie's high-pitch intonation.

"Not really." Tamara couldn't tell him that at the party she had been almost sequestered by Brad Wilson as soon as she had set foot

The Blackpox Threat

in the reception hall. "So many people at the party; the place was packed full."

"It makes sense. Well, I'll be leaving you. I'll stay at a cottage on Lake Simcoe with some friends of mine. See you in three or four days." He waved Tamara goodbye.

Tamara reciprocated and walked toward her Subaru.

Back at the Modano Company Tamara knocked on the door of Dianne's office. There was no answer so she entered and extracted one of Duncan Brown's recording pens from her purse. She dropped it into the pen holder on Dianne's desk. Clearly Dianne had left early, probably directed to the customs office.

Tamara startled when the phone in her own office rang. She quickened her steps to grab the receiver. It was Stephanie.

"Oh, Tamara, you don't know the troubles I'm having with the fountain. The plumber hooked up the pump but the pipes are set higher than the top of the fountain. They're completely exposed. That ensemble looks nothing but horrible."

"I see," Tamara said, her tone uncommitted.

"Can I exchange it for something else? Something big so that the pipes would be hidden. Half a foot taller. You see…oh, the troubles…the plumber turned the water off but he refused to clear out the pipes. He can come back only the day after tomorrow, he said. Oh, what a disaster!"

"I'm sure Charles won't mind replacing the fountain with something else when he comes back. He's going to be away for a few days."

"Oh, but I can't leave things as they are now. I have a show tomorrow morning. An important event."

Tamara hesitated. Dianne was away and she didn't feel comfortable exchanging the fountain with another object. She didn't know what the policy was for something like this.

The Blackpox Threat

"I'm alone at the office, Stephanie. Try to understand. I can't make any decision. I'm rather new around here."

"Oh, I understand, but you surely have something you can bring over. Anything tall enough that can hide those horrible tubes! Please, Tamara, I'm having a show right here, at the French Look, tomorrow morning. From 9 a.m. to noon. Please!"

Tamara had seen an ensemble of about the same price in the storage room. There was no fountain, but the group sat on a stand. It would do for height, probably.

"Tell you what, Stephanie: temporarily, I mean temporarily, I can bring over another piece, big enough to cover the pipes. It's a mother bear with three cubs."

"God bless you! When are you coming?"

"As soon as I can pack it and load it in my car."

Chapter 12

Finally a day of freedom and relaxation. Tamara sat on the leather chesterfield, stretched her legs on top of the low table in front of her and picked up the remote for the TV. Time to see what was happening in the world. The phone rang, forcing Tamara to reach for the table where the phone was located. From the caller ID she recognized Dianne's number. She immediately pressed the *Talk* key.

"Tamara? The maintenance man told me that you sold the ensemble with the mother bear. That piece was reserved for Mr. Thomas Sarcin."

"Oh, I didn't sell it. It was just that…" Tamara explained what had happened with the plumbing of the fountain and Stephanie's predicament about having a show scheduled in the morning.

"I don't care what Stephanie's problem was or is. That piece has to be delivered to Mr. Sarcin *today*. He's one of our most important customers." She sneezed. Dianne suffered with allergies, especially in the spring. "The truck is here. I'll dispatch it to the

French Look to pick up that sculpture."

"Wait, wait. When does this Mr. Sarcin expect to get it?"

"Today."

"Oh, can you have it picked early in the afternoon? The show will be over by then."

"No good. The trucker has his rounds all scheduled. Mr. Sarcin's country home is in Barkway, more than 300 kilometres from here. I'll call Stephanie myself and tell her she can't hang on to that piece."

"Wait, Dianne. If the truck driver can't modify his route, I'll take that statue to Mr. Sarcin myself. I can be there before dusk."

There was silence on the other side of the phone line. Then Dianne said, "But it's a big piece; it must weigh about 50 kilograms. And you'd have to pack it in its original box."

"No problem. I delivered it myself yesterday. I'd need a bit of help to load it into my Subaru. No doubt somebody at the French Look will be happy to give me a hand."

"Are you sure?" Dianne asked.

"Positive. Just relax and leave things in my hands."

****

Guided by her new GPS, the Maestro, Tamara arrived at the Sarcin country residence within the predictable five hours. She had called ahead, introduced herself and explained that the statue was on its way. Around six o'clock she pressed the bottom of the intercom on the entrance column of the gate, and spelled out her name. The gate, two solid pieces of steel, painted green, opened quietly. She followed the driveway, which was flanked on each side by statues representing wildlife or hunting scenes. Clearly the bear with her cubs would fit nicely among them.

Tamara stopped in front of the house, one-floor with a portico at the front. She stepped out of her car and opened the hatchback.

Immediately two men came to help her and quickly unloaded the big box; one of them opened it, discarded the packaging material, and lifted it out.

"Wonderful!" one of the men said. "Mr. Sarcin will be pleased."

They placed the ensemble on one side of the entrance, opposite a group representing a doe with a fawn.

"I'm Samuel, the gardener," "the other man said. "And he is Jacob. The statue that was here before got smashed and Mr. Sarcin was very upset about the empty spot."

Tamara could very well see the urgency of such delivery. Clearly Mr. Sarcin was loaded — with money and arrogance. She got the invoice out and asked Samuel to sign it. He did.

Tamara was ready to leave when a voice called out, "Miss?"

Tamara turned and saw a tall man approaching her.

"Tamara Smith," she said as she shook the man's extended hand.

"Please to meet you. I'm Thomas Sarcin. Did you come here all alone?"

"Yes. Dianne Templeton, Charles' secretary, said the delivery was of vital importance." She tried to keep sarcasm out of her voice.

"Oh. I see. Much obliged for the fast service. It must have been a long drive. Would you like to have a drink? I was ready to sit at the table for a quick supper."

Tamara was anxious to clear out, but, first, she was really thirsty; second, she didn't want to look impolite, and third, she could gather information on one of Charles Modano's most important customers.

"Sure, thanks."

She grabbed her purse from the passenger seat. She wouldn't go into a strange place without her precious Smith & Wesson. Thomas Sarcin gestured her to the door and led her into a small solarium. A maid quickly added another place setting to the table. In a jiffy a huge glass of lemonade appeared in front of Tamara, followed by a chalice overflowing with shrimps.

Thomas smiled. "I don't know how Charles does it. He's always surrounded by beautiful women."

Tamara emptied half of her glass in one big gulp and dabbed her lips with the white napkin. She felt uneasy. The place was secluded, five kilometres away from the closest hamlet; the walls surrounding the property and the heavy gate meant that the man had something or somebody to be afraid of or something to hide. Maybe it had been a mistake to accept the invitation of even entering the house.

"You should ask him," Tamara said.

"I will," Thomas said at length. "And what do you do when you don't deliver parcels?"

"I'm in charge of PR at the Modano Company. Unfortunately your statue had been misplaced and the truck driver in charge of deliveries couldn't come." She squeezed a slice of lemon on top of her shrimps. "I offered to replace him."

"Nice of you." Thomas sipped on the white wine the French maid had silently poured in his glass. "Do you also help with the auctions?" he asked.

"Yes, I do." Tamara dipped a shrimp into the Tabasco sauce, trying to hide that she was mentally building his profile. She ate the shrimp, and then another one. "Nice sauce," she said. The man was in his 40s with regular facial features, hazel eyes and greying hair. He could be attractive if it wasn't for the look in his eyes. When he had smiled, a while before, his expression had been confined to his mouth; it had never reached his eyes.

The maid cleared out the cups that held the shrimps and replaced them with two plates, each with a quiche, artily surrounded by baby carrots and green beans. She deposited a basket with small buns in the centre of the table.

Tamara looked at her watch. "I should be going," she said, and finished her lemonade.

"Nonsense. You have a long drive ahead." He smiled again. "Just a few more bites — and maybe a coffee?"

Tamara reciprocated the smile. "Okay. Coffee will keep me awake while I drive."

Jacob entered the room, approached Thomas and murmured something in his ear.

Thomas jumped to his feet. "An urgent matter just popped up," he said. "It'll take a minute. I have to step into my office. Please go ahead with your meal."

Tamara wasn't too happy about the situation, but she didn't want to be rude. She savoured the vegetable quiche and the steamed greens. Behind a frosted glass wall she could see the silhouettes of Thomas and Jacob. They gestured nervously. No noise reverberated into the solarium, which made Tamara believe that the glass wall was soundproof. Spooky, she thought. She finished what was on her plate, suddenly discovering how famished she had been.

She was ready to rise, when Thomas returned.

"Just enough time for you to drink your coffee and I'll be back," he said. "Please, don't disappear. I have a message I'd like you to take to Charles. It's important. Be right back."

Jacob had already fetched a car. The motor was running.

As if by a silent command, the maid appeared carrying a tray with a silver coffee pot and a china cup with saucer. Cream and sugar were held in containers with the same floral pattern as the cup.

The maid retreated and Tamara poured herself a full cup. The coffee was very hot, so she took small sips at a time. The message for Charles could be an excuse, she thought. On the other hand, spending a bit of time here could be invaluable for Operation Bullfrog.

Suddenly Thomas re-entered the house and made a beeline inside his office, leaving the door ajar.

Tamara got a little mirror and a comb out of her purse and ran her fingers through her spiky hair. She angled the mirror so that she could have a view into the office. She saw Thomas open a laptop and type a few keys. He then frantically clicked on a few icons. In no time he was out of the office again. He disappeared outside and into the car, followed by Samuel.

Tamara finished her coffee, waiting for the noise of the car engine to fade. She presumed that only the maid was in the house. Where was she? Tamara took a few tentative steps around, to see if the maid would appear. She didn't.

From her purse she extracted her flash drive and her handgun. She quietly entered Thomas' office and sat in front of the computer, the Smith & Wesson in her lap. Thomas had not logged off. She hit the keyboard space bar. A list of directories appeared. She inserted the flash drive in one of the UBS connectors and downloaded all the files.

Thirty minutes later Tamara climbed into her Subaru, clutching at her purse. With her she had a full gigabyte of secrets. She aimed at the entrance gate. She banked on the fact that most remotely — controlled gates opened automatically to exiting vehicles.

She was right.

Chapter 13

"No, no!" In her sleep Tamara screamed so loud that she woke up. Drenched in perspiration, she was hot and at the same time she was shaking. That dreadful nightmare was back. After her parents' murder she often dreamed of being ambushed, a killer assaulting her from behind. He would try to slash her throat. That horrifying sensation persecuted her for years, and had disappeared only when she was in her late 20s. Now she had to deal with it again. She sighed deeply.

Her little bravado in Sarcin's house had probably been the triggering factor. She had been scared, afraid to be followed and searched by Thomas' men. She had driven at maximum speed on the gravel road from outside the gate up to Barkway, where she had quickly turned into a side road. Here she had stopped and programmed her GPS with destination London. She didn't intend to follow the most direct route indicated by her GPS, though. If Sarcin's men were following her, they would catch up with her in no time. Instead she would use the satellite guidance system to re-route her toward her destination every time she wandered away.

So as soon as she reached a highway, she skirted away from it by taking the next accessible secondary road. Strangely enough, the more she drove, the sensation of being followed increased. Any car behind her posed a threat. She was frightened. Clearly dangerous situations were not her cup of tea. The whole affair proved once again what she already knew. She didn't have the makeup of an undercover agent.

With that zigzagged travelling it had taken her seven hours to return home.

Tamara looked at her watch. It was one o'clock in the afternoon. She rose and showered. Still in her satin robe she sat in front of her Lenovo PC and jotted down the impression she had had of Thomas Sarcin, avoiding the fact that she had downloaded his files. She had done something illegal, and didn't want Brad to know. She would use the information contained in the files with discretion. She typed away until she had created Sarcin's profile. She added to it the first names of the two men living with him, and mentioned the presence of an unnamed maid who had not said a single word during her entire visit. She made sure to comment on the security around the premises. When she was done she emailed the file to Brad Wilson. That should keep the man happy for a while, she thought. As soon as the transfer was completed, she deleted the file from the directory and also from the Recycling Bin. She kept her computer sanitized of any compromising material.

She moseyed on into the kitchen and decided on her lunch: noodles with pesto sauce. She put a pot of water on the stove, went to the fridge and took out the sauce she had prepared two days ago. She impatiently waited for the water to boil, shook in some salt and then dumped in the noodles. Three minutes later she added an ounce of cold water to prevent overcooking. She poured the noodles into a strainer and then onto her plate. She covered them with the pesto sauce revelling in the smell of basil, olive oil, pine nuts and garlic. She was mentally savouring her meal, when Brad Wilson called.

"Got your email, Tamara. We're aware of this Thomas Sarcin and his activities. He's a mysterious character, that's true, but nothing ever emerged against him. Some of your information was new and important though, since we didn't know he had a second residence."

"What would he do up there?"

"That's what we're going to find out."

"Good. What struck me the most was the urgency with which he took off. And the insistence in making me stay longer than I wanted."

"Perhaps he wanted to enjoy your company. I wouldn't blame him for that."

Tamara sprinkled the noodles with Parmesan cheese. "It could be so," she said, even if she wasn't convinced. She fretted to eat her pasta. It smelled delicious.

"Nevertheless, I'll make some inquiries, maybe find an excuse to contact him. Talk to you later."

"Bye, Brad."

Tamara took her wall phone off the hook, silenced her two cellulars and sat at the table to enjoy her meal.

****

In the afternoon the mail arrived and with it, two little packages, one from Duncan Brown, the other from Justin. She opened the latter first. It contained a fancy medallion, the shape of a daisy, hanging on a short chain. There was a handwritten note with it, which read: "There is a one-way transmitter underneath the daisy. It will put you in direct contact with me. Use it for emergency or...to send me a love message (preferable). Your friend Justin."

Tamara couldn't avoid smiling. Justin was such a sweet guy — too bad she had to keep him at a distance. She opened the second package. Inside was the new watch Duncan Brown, the specialist in surveillance, had designed for her. She looked at it with a critical eye. The wristwatch was still big and the bracelet, ugly. It surely would attract attention, raise questions and even suspicion. She tossed it in a drawer. No money from Brad, Tamara realized with disappointment. She needed new clothes and a new purse. The bottom of hers, of suede material, had taken the shape of her handgun. It was time to go to the French Look; later on she would swing over to the Modano Company and recover the recording pen she had left on Dianne's desk.

Stephanie welcomed her with open arms.

"I tried to call you but there was no answer, yesterday," she said.

"I was out all afternoon." She didn't tell her the marathon she had to run to deliver the statue to Mr. Sarcin.

"Well, I have to tell you — big news! The show, yesterday, was for atelier shops — the big chains that will produce my designs with the fabric and in the sizes they think would sell best." She paused, her eyes sparkling. "I sold three! It was a great day. Now I'd like to thank you properly for coming to my rescue with that nice sculpture. I have two outfits the shops didn't buy that would look great on you. Come, come to the dressing room."

Tamara hesitated, so Stephanie took by her arm. "No charge. It's a gift."

"Actually I'd like to buy a new purse with a sturdy bottom and big enough to carry all my stuff. Shoulder strap, even if it isn't fashionable anymore."

"Well, I sure have a few of them. Tan or black? Your choice."

****

Two hours later Tamara was the proud owner of a raw silk pantsuit, pale blue, and a chiffon cocktail dress, green, together with an elegant tan bag with sparkling studs at the front. She drove to the Modano Company whistling the tune of *La Marseillaise*, as she often did when she felt like celebrating.

When she arrived at the office it was past five o'clock and everybody had left for the day. It was a golden opportunity to search for the invoice that Dianne had received from overseas. She entered Dianne's office and went through her input tray. There were only three invoices, all from Canadian customers. She tried to open the two file cabinets, but they were locked. She opened the drawer in the middle of the desk, to find only stationary, scotch tape, a stapler and a container full of colourful clips. Disappointed, Tamara retrieved the recording pen she had previously dropped into the pen holder and replaced it with a new one, then left.

She had work to do, namely listening to what had been going on in Dianne's office and looking at the information she had extracted from Thomas Sarcin's laptop.

Chapter 14

The country residence of Michael and Justin Devry stood on concrete pillars at the front, to level, at the back, with the top on an incline. Designed by an architect known for his daring structures, it presented two special features: a huge round terrace that jutted five metres out over the shores of Lake Huron, and a parallel round hall at the back that served as a showroom for contemporary and old art pieces.

Justin had spent a great deal of his life here, where business, art and family life mixed without conflict. His great-grandfather, a carpenter from Holland, had collected art works for fun. His grandfather had enriched the family collection focusing on portraits, and made a business out of it. Justin's father, Michael Devry, had made it his life. Justin knew that his father expected him to follow the family tradition. He had disappointed him when he refused to attend college. For some reason, Michael, who held a BA in Visual Arts from the University of Toronto, thought that his son would outdo him. But Justin had been intolerant of anything that even vaguely resembled formal education. However, from the University of Toronto he had taken a course on the technologies needed to examine the chemicals used in old paints — an effective tool to assess the approximate age of a painting. He could now estimate the value of an old oil every time his father considered an acquisition.

Father and son were sitting on the terrace, stretched out in two lounge chairs.

"How do you feel about helping a friend of mine?" Michael asked.

Justin looked at his father, waiting for him to continue.

"Tony Esposito asked me if you could set up a small lab for in-house testing. At the moment he depends on consultants, who charge him a bundle."

"Hmm...that's something I could sure help him with. Where is he?"

"Vancouver."

"Vancouver! Are you trying to get rid of me?"

"Get rid of you? No! I have lost all hopes for that. You were 18 when I wanted you to go to college, and you didn't go; when you took that course for testing the authenticity of paintings you drove up and down Toronto; you refused to take a job with several museums..." He paused and shook his head. "I can't even hope for you to get married, since your relationships are short-lived. In our business a feminine presence would attract clients."

Justin gave him a lopsided look. "Why don't *you* get married? Barbara's been around a long time."

"Barbara? She's an academic and an artist on top of that. Blue jeans with holes; hair that never sees a hairdresser — sometimes a comb, once a year the scissors. Our clients would scatter away."

"The reviews she writes are of substance. Clear too. She gives the historical background of a painting, the techniques used at that time to obtain certain effects and shades, and then she gives her artistic evaluation."

"I give you that. She's good, and a dear friend — but that's all she is."

Silence followed as father and son admired the sun coming up high over the lake.

"How is the business with the new portraits?" Justin asked.

"Booming. Barbara sent me two of her students, eager to paint anything, just to be able to pay for their tuitions."

"I can't understand why wealthy people want to fake important ancestors. Besides, in this country only people of strict British or French descent ever had a portrait painted by a famous artist."

Michael shrugged. "I told my customers the truth; I told them that a simple test — X-ray diffraction, for instance — would reveal that the oils were painted recently. They say it isn't important; the paintings would look impressive at the end of a hall or in their dens. They didn't even want me to introduce any craquelure. Can you believe that? A bit of artificial aging would give a nice old flare." Michael shook his head and gave out a soft laughter. "They're in a real rush to hang the paintings in their multi-million dollar homes."

Again, father and son sat in companionable silence in their patio chairs.

Then Michael said, "By the way, I don't know if I'm going to use the Modano Company anymore. I don't want to deprive Charles of our business, but the last time the paintings had a very funny smell, and I tell you, that smell had nothing to do with paints or varnish, or special chemicals used for restoration."

"Drugs?"

Michael shrugged. "Can't say, and, frankly, I don't want to know. When we have something extremely valuable to ship, you can go there, supervise the packing, and take it with you." He looked at his wristwatch. "Let's wait for the next shipment, and then decide. Time for lunch. By the way, we have a guest: Karl McKenzie. He has just finished building a huge mansion 20 kilometres from here. He wants some advice on how to decorate some of his rooms." He tossed *ARTnews,* the magazine he had in his lap, onto the corrugated iron table and rose from his chair.

Justin's eyes followed Michael as he moved inside the house. His father was 55 and took good care of himself. He was a businessman who had earned the respect of his clients. And he was a wonderful father. Justin had never known his mother, who had died giving birth to him. He grew up in a happy home. He liked to stick around. He didn't mind taking trips for business or pleasure, but after a couple of weeks he always longed to return home. If he accepted his father's proposal he would be gone two to three months — the minimum time necessary to set up the small lab Tony needed. He should think about it — the last thing he wanted to do was disappoint his father again.

He sniffed once and then once again. A delightful aroma of roasted peppers fanned out of the house. Lunch would be ready soon.

****

Justin savoured in silence the dish his father had just taken out of the oven. Pork ribs curved upright to form a small crown. In the middle was a mixture of green vegetables; on the outside were French potatoes, sprinkled with herbs.

From time to time Justin observed his father's guest — clearly an important client. Mr. McKenzie was dressed casual, with a Blue Jays T-shirt, jeans and gym shoes. He was slim, about six feet tall, with regular facial features. His grey hair stuck up high, almost as if he was wearing a poorly fitting wig. He wore turtle-rimmed glasses that gave him an intellectual aspect. He talked slowly, almost weighing each word. He had an accent, but Justin couldn't place it.

Michael carried most of the conversation as they ate their entrées suitably accompanied by red wine. He spoke of his love for the arts, the resources he had available for finding new, interesting works of art, and the attachment he had for the place where he lived. Last but not least, he mentioned the increasing cost of transportation and insurance, and praised Justin for having installed the newest security gadgets on the market for the protection of his conspicuous artistic investments.

Justin admired his father once more. He had presented himself as a lover of the arts, but had subtly sent a message that his services would not be cheap. After all, his father was a successful businessman. He rose to refill the glasses with this year's Beaujolais wine while Michael cleared out the main dishes and carried them into the kitchen.

"So you're planning to establish your main residence around here?" Justin asked.

"Oh, yes. This part of the country is beautiful." As if responding to a silent question, he added, "I inherited from my Aussie uncle. He had no children and I was his only nephew — " He paused. "Not the only one, really, but the only nephew who spent time at his ranch. He left his fortune to me."

That would account for his accent, at least partially. "You carry a name with a rich heritage in Canada. Any connections?"

McKenzie shook his head no, and Justin waited expectantly.

"My ancestors came from England and settled on the eastern coast of the States."

Michael was back, carrying three bowls filled with blueberries topped with whip cream. He placed one in front of each person. He sat and addressed Mr. McKenzie.

"So when do you want me to come to see your new home?" He turned to Justin. "Mr. McKenzie wants some advice on how to decorate his hallway. It's 10-metres long with a skylight."

"Tomorrow will be fine; I'll be home all day."

"I'll come around 2:00 p.m. then," Michael said. "Coffee anybody?"

"I prefer not." McKenzie looked at his wristwatch. "In half an hour I have to be home." He hurried to say goodbye, and Michael saw his guest to the door.

Justin grabbed a coffee from the kitchen and went to sit outside. Fifteen minutes later Michael joined him and sat close to him.

"Got a new customer. We already have a deal for the hallway. He also wants me to look all through the house. He's envisioning paintings to fit the furniture, both in age and colour. I don't have a clear idea of what he wants, but I'm sure I can sell him plenty."

"Are you sure the man has money?"

Michael opened his arms wide in a gesture of 'who-cares?' "I always get paid half in advance, and I want a cheque right after the final delivery."

"Good for you. McKenzie's behaviour puzzles me. He's very reserved, almost as if he's afraid of something."

"All millionaires are a bit peculiar. He is no different from the others I know. He said he was in a rush and yet he stood at the door for a while, talking about his plans for his new home." Michael stretched his legs on the low table in front of him. "What a beautiful place we have, son. Look at the birds getting their catches."

A flock of seagulls, seemingly having spotted a school of fish, began a systematic dive, one gull after the other. Once the catch was secured or just swallowed, a seagull would line up for another dive. The scene seemed synchronized by an invisible sentinel.

"Beautiful indeed," Justin said. "Nature is full of wondrous ways.*"*

Chapter 15

London, Ontario
Beginning of July 2007

Frank Milton checked the temperature and the humidity of his lab — the two critical components for experimenting with the blackpox of Boris Youkenoff's trademark. On its way from Bergamo to Canada two of the vials had suffered a slight crack; he already knew of the incident before seeing the vials, as he had noticed an unusual smell. He wondered whether their contents had been contaminated. Wearing a mask and protective gloves Milton spread the liquid contained in the three vials over the three Guinea pigs' backs, mouths and ears. He would have to wait and see if the desired effect took place. He had already blown his top with Boris for the way he had packed the vials inside the art vases shipped via the Modano Company. The vases were intact, not a scratch on them, so clearly Boris had left the vials free to jiggle inside their containers. He had ordered him to immediately send another small batch for testing.

Frank opened a red folder where he kept records of his experiments; on the enclosed calendar he circled the current date and wrote *started experiment #1*. He was thinking of contacting Harry at the spa when his phone chirped.

The voice on the other side didn't leave room for pleasantries.

"The experiment?"

Keeping his voice natural and cool, Frank said, "In the making. In 10 days we'll know the result."

"Not before? You told me you could see some effects already after a week."

Frank wanted to gain time in case he had to run the test with a second batch. "True, but unfortunately some of the Guinea pigs got sick before I started the experiment. I had to buy new ones. We need 10 days, maybe more." He had to say something to appease the man. He was as neurotic as they come. "We want to be certain of the outcome before we go all the way with our little operation, right?"

A silence first, and then, "Hmm. How come I feel you don't tell me all the truth?"

"Oh, oh…we're in this together, remember? You for the power, me for the money. That's why I want to carry out the necessary testing." After all, he was the scientist; his boss was just a megalomaniac in search of more power, or glory — or God only knew what. "Trust the expert," he said jovially.

The answer was just a click.

Frank sighed and dialled Harry Pearson's number.

"I need you to pick up another parcel for me," he said without preambles. "It should arrive the day after tomorrow."

"What? Another one? I can't…that was a special case…Dianne wouldn't do it without…without compensation."

The Blackpox Threat

"She was paid $2,000, remember?"

"Frank, try to understand. That was for her appearance on a TV commercial. Did you see it? It was pretty good and —"

"Cut it off, Harry. I need that parcel."

"Why can't you go yourself?"

"Because I can't. It's been sent to Harry Pearson."

"I didn't give you permission to use my name again! I did you a favour once. I thought it was a one-time deal."

"Harry I can shut off your spa tomorrow, if I decide to do so."

"No, no. For heaven's sake, don't! It's going so well now. Between the party and the TV commercials people don't have enough of my spa. The body lotions and showering gels disappear as soon as I put them on the counter. The new rejuvenating night cream you made last month is such a success! It sells like hot cakes; you have to prepare more of it, much more. And that's not all. Plenty of people have booked for a massage — I'll have to hire an assistant if things keep going this way."

"Good," said Frank, keeping his voice as icy as he could. "Glad to hear you're back in business. Just get that package, as soon as it arrives. It should come the day after tomorrow."

****

It was the story of his life, Harry thought. When one thing seemed to go well for him, another problem appeared on the horizon. He had just re-established a friendly atmosphere with Dianne and now he would spoil it by asking her to go fetch a new package. Harry sighed. His friend was a powerful man who seemed to have connections in high places. He had helped him to set up the spa in less than six months; he had gotten Dianne a contract within a few days, and, most surprising of all, he had managed to have the commercial aired in record time. Yes, Frank was a powerful man, who obtained what he wanted. Few people would refuse him a favour — he least of all.

He sighed again. The new package had to be picked up.

Dianne had been reluctant to do it the first time, and now he had no incentive to convince her to do it again. Immediately after her TV appearance, advertising the spa's activities and products, a cosmetic company had offered her a contract for a commercial on a new foaming bath. That, Harry knew, would keep her busy for a while, so she would have a good excuse not to fetch the new package. He couldn't even lure her with the promise of another commercial. Frank wouldn't go along with it as the spa was now swamped with clients.

Harry drummed his fingers on the desk of his office, uncertain what to do. Finally, he picked up the receiver and dialled Dianne's number at the Modano Company. It was worth a try.

"I saw your commercial," he said. "You were fantastic."

"You liked it? I got a couple of fans calling me all the time, and I signed a mini-contract with another company. But you knew that."

"Yes, you did. Listen, Dianne, I need another little favour —"

"Oh, oh, what would that be?"

Harry whispered. "To pick up another package for me."

"Oh no. Why do you insist on using the Modano Company if you don't want them to take care of the delivery? Besides, *you* could go to pick up these stupid parcels. I'm very, very busy."

"Just once more, the day after tomorrow?"

"Absolutely not. We shoot a new commercial that day."

"But they shoot after office hours, you told me."

"Right, but I can't go just the same. I'm busy at the office and after hours I have to rush and get a new hair colouring. No way. Bye, Harry."

Chapter 16

It had been a very busy week. With plenty of customers at the shop, a lengthy preparation for the auction, with over fifty collector's items to be tagged, and then the auction itself, Tamara was happy that it was all over. Justin had come to the show and bought a three-hour glass clock — a huge item that had been in the storage room since the day she joined the company. It was something that would have gone unsold otherwise. Justin was such a sweet guy, genuinely interested in her. Too bad she was involved in a mission that didn't allow her to make friends. He had quietly helped to clear out the hall where the auction had been held, and then he left with just a wave of his hand.

Tamara slipped on the jacket of the pale blue pantsuit and was ready to leave, when Charles entered her office.

"Lunch Monday? he asked. "One o'clock at the Idlewyld Inn. I have a customer I'd like you to meet."

"Sure. Bye for now, Charles." Her spying mission had gone dry of candidates, recently. Maybe the luncheon would be an occasion to add one to the list.

She waited for Charles to take off and then went to Dianne's office to retrieve the second recording pen Duncan Brown had given her. She hoped it would reveal something interesting about Dianne's activities outside the company as the first hadn't provided any insights.

She then climbed into her car and drove home.

Once inside her condo, Tamara got rid of her dressy shoes, took an orange juice out of the fridge and lay down on the couch. From her purse she extracted the recording pen. She opened the slit carved on one side and flipped over the little switch. She listened to all the phones calls and conversations that had occurred in Dianne's office days ago. After a sequence of business calls and chats, there was a message from Harry asking Dianne to go to customs to fetch a parcel. Bingo! That established a link among Harry Pearson, the Modano Company and one of the overseas shipments. She immediately called Brad Wilson and left a message, briefing him on what she had just discovered.

She would get her supper and then devise a plan to enter the spa and find out what was going on inside that building. Too bad tomorrow was Sunday and the spa was closed. She would have to wait until Monday to go snooping. She had already remarked that the square footage of the property well exceeded that of the facilities of the spa itself.

****

At the Idlewyld Inn, located in the southern part of London, the table was set for three with the reservation held in place by a miniature silver teapot. Charles was seated at the table, sipping a margarita.

"I see your guest isn't here yet. I was afraid I was late." Tamara shook off her white shawl, revealing a sleeveless cotton dress of vivid coral. She had combed her hair straight instead of in the spike fashion she usually adopted. The mother-of-pearl medallion Justin had given her adorned her bare neck, reflecting light in all directions. It was fairly flat, considering that it hid a radio-transmitter, with one ear protruding on each side. Once squeezed together, they would activate a broadcast.

"You look great," Charles said, and smiled. "But, of course, you always do."

"Thanks," Tamara answered, and turned to look at the person Charles was waving to.

It was Thomas Sarcin.

"Thomas," Charles called. "Over here."

Thomas joined them, shook hands with Charles and stopped him from making the presentations.

"I already know Ms. Smith." He flashed Tamara a long smile and sat close to her. "Nice to see you again."

Tamara recovered from the surprise quickly. She addressed Charles. "It was when you were away, those few days you spent on Lake Simcoe. I offered to deliver a statue to Mr. Sarcin."

"I hope it wasn't in that desolated place he has up north, 300 kilometres plus from here!"

"Right, that one." And Tamara explained what had happened with the fountain that she had delivered to Stephanie, and the need for replacing it.

"She's an amazing woman," Charles said to Thomas. "A great addition to my company."

"I'm sure she is," Thomas said. "Unfortunately that day I couldn't enjoy her company the way I wanted, since I had an urgent call and had to leave."

"Your maid was very kind to me. I'm sorry I didn't wait for you, but it was getting very late." Lying wasn't in her nature and she resented, once more, the need for it. That Brad Wilson! It was all his fault!

"I understand perfectly," Thomas said. He turned to Charles. "So you can ship my merchandise from overseas?"

"No problem. What kind?"

"Manuscripts. Ancient and precious manuscripts. Kept in a special container from which the air has been sucked out."

"Oh? Why is that?" Charles asked.

"To preserve them. No air movement and no dust."

"How old are these manuscripts?"

"A few hundred years. They belonged to a friend of my father's who passed away recently. Apparently they're very valuable."

A waitress approached the table, presented each of them with a menu and asked if they wanted a drink.

Tamara declined the offer and glanced at the menu. She was puzzled. Thomas didn't fit the personality profile she had mentally built when she had first met him in his secluded refuge near Barkway. She couldn't believe the man had any intellectual interest. Or maybe it was a smokescreen?

For a while, Charles and Thomas sat in silence, sipping on their margaritas and studying the menus. Tamara alternated a glance at the menu with one at Thomas. Dressed in casual clothes, the man looked at ease, and somewhat different from the person she had met up north.

The waitress took their orders, chicken parmesan for Charles, a tenderloin steak for Thomas and a caesar salad for Tamara.

Charles removed his reading glasses. "So what is your interest in these precious manuscripts?" he asked.

Thomas laughed. "Absolutely none. But I'm interested to see if the container I built for them stood up to my expectation." He paused and finished his drink. He then addressed Tamara. "My business was building safes, but this container was far from my usual expertise. It was one of a kind. I incorporated a mechanism that would let air sift through slowly when the owner wanted to open it. There is a gadget that measures the pressure inside the inner layer." He paused. "But let me start from the beginning. Two layers protect the object. The external, thick layer is insulating material. The other is a chamber where air is pumped in or out: in, if one wants to open the container, out, if one wants to store the contents for a long time."

"I see," said Charles who had already savoured half of his chicken. "If I understood correctly what you told me on the phone, you want to be sure somebody travels with it, so nobody attempts to open it without precautions."

"Pre-cise-ly."

"Well, you're in good hands. I have a couple of people who can take care of your precious cargo."

Tamara had followed the conversation with interest.

"Who would be interested in those manuscripts?" she asked.

"Oh, several scholars would be very happy to study them." Thomas pushed his dish, only half-empty, toward the middle of the table. "But let's talk about you. Charles told me you work only two days a week for him, plus the time at the auctions." He looked into Tamara's eyes. "Interested to work a few days for me?"

Chapter 17

When she arrived home a little later, Tamara was still puzzled by Thomas' offer. She had dismissed, more than refused, his offer of work, saying that at the moment she was still busy decorating her new home.

It had been a long lunch as Charles and Thomas seemed to enjoy each other's company. It was now past four o'clock in the afternoon. What's more urgent? Tamara asked herself as she exchanged her fancy outfit for a pair of jeans and a T-shirt. Digging into Thomas' life by looking at his files or going to the spa? Thomas' presence was intriguing, but the information on the special shipment that Dianne had cleared at customs days ago and the new one that Harry Pearson wanted her to get the day after tomorrow could be crucial. It was the first time that the spying pen had provided a useful insight in the mysterious deliveries. She left a message for Brad Wilson, telling him she was going to take a peek at the spa. With her new purse and the faithful Smith & Wesson well concealed inside it, she drove to the Pamper Yourself Spa.

With big sunglasses and a bandana that covered most of her hair, she figured it wouldn't be easy to recognize her.

The parking lot was full of vehicles — a big difference from when she had been there the first time. Great, she thought. It is easier to pass unnoticed when there is commotion. She went through the fancy entrance and lingered unattended since Armand was very busy at his dais. She approached the counter where all sorts of beauty products were on display. She stood sideways, one eye on a jar's label, the other monitoring Armand's movements. Even though the fountain wasn't functioning she couldn't capture any of Armand's words — too much noise. In fact, seven people stood in line before the dais, talking to each other as they waited.

Armand consulted his planner and directed the first customer, a plump woman, toward the side of the hall where a big sign on top of an arch said *Massage Centre*. The second customer, a young man, needed to book an appointment, Tamara figured out, as Armand wrote something in his planner, and the man left shortly after. Tamara held a jar in her hand, turned it around, deposited it back and then picked up a suntan lotion. The third customer held a piece of paper in her hands, and Armand first consulted his planner and then shook his head. Both Armand and the female customer bent over the desk.

Tamara lost no time. She slid the suntan lotion back onto the counter and smoothly aimed toward the staircase. In a jiffy she was on the mezzanine, ambling along a corridor. The door with a plaque reading *Harry Pearson and Frank Milton* attracted her attention. First, she had another name to add to the list of suspects; second, she might find out what Harry was up to. The door was unlocked. She entered the room and looked around. The office was big, with several file cabinets, two desks facing each other, and a small table surrounded by three chairs. No computers. An enormous ficus plant, situated in a corner of the window, was the only décor piece. There was no way to see which desk belonged to whom. Tamara approached the one closest to her and opened the main drawer. From underneath loose sheets she lifted a red folder and leafed through it. Dates filled the first column of a page, names the second and third, and numbers the fourth. She flipped over a divider to find a page labelled *Calendar of Events*. Here there were dates and some of these belonged to the next two months. Somebody is planning ahead, Tamara thought, and these aren't appointments for massages or beauty treatments. She was just about to look at the pages after the next divider, labelled *Bills*, when she heard noise in the corridor coming from the direction opposite the one she had entered. Tamara slapped the folder closed, took it with her and darted to the door.

She hastened her steps as she heard, "Hey, you! Stop right there!" She descended the stairs two by two, barely skirted three people near the main entrance, exited and dove into her Subaru.

Tires squealing as she took off, she glanced in the rear mirror. On the spa's threshold stood Armand and another man talking into a cell. He looked like Harry Pearson.

Was the folder she had stolen worth the trouble? Tamara called Brad Wilson. She could surely use some advice. His phone mail came on, asking her to leave a message. That Brad! Where was he when she needed him? She had to think about her next move. But first, she would drive around and see if she was followed.

Chapter 18

Her heart pounding, Tamara passed through the gate of her condominium complex. She parked the Subaru in the area reserved for the handicapped and locked it. She put the documents she had extracted from Harry Pearson's spa in the trunk. As a precaution, she would check that no stranger was in her house before taking the folder with her. Breaking into the Pamper Yourself Spa had been an enterprise she hoped she would never have to repeat. She definitely needed a rest. She was looking forward to stretching on her couch, and, in total comfort, reading the files. Maybe she would find out something about the activities that were going on inside the spa in addition to massages and beauty treatments. She walked to Number 19 and entered her house. She listened attentively. There was no noise. She unlocked the box inside the entrance closet and turned on the video that had registered, for the last 10 hours, the movements around the main door, the kitchen entrance from the garage and around the windows. Nothing had been going on. She reset the video to zero, walked into the kitchen and dropped her purse onto a chair. She poured herself a pomegranate juice and got a slice of cheese with a few crackers. She walked into the living room and slouched into one of the big easy chairs. She would eat her snack and then go recover the Subaru.

She had just bitten into the first cracker when she heard voices coming from the outside. A man and woman were near her door. Tamara rose, hopped over the newspaper basket and neared the bay window. Through a corner of the sheers she saw that the woman had a gun in her hands. In no time somebody was fiddling with the lock. Tamara turned around to make a beeline for her gun. She tripped over the newspapers basket, spreading its content over the floor. By the time she was up again, the intruders were walking in the hallway, talking to each other. The only thing she could do was hide. She swiftly bent between the couch and the easy chair.

"Oh my god!" Tamara thought, "They've followed me!"

She suddenly remembered that she was still wearing the medallion Justin had given her. She waited until the intruders moved to the opposite side of the house. She simultaneously squeezed the medallion's opposite sides and whispered, "Justin, Justin! It's me, Tamara. I need help. Please get the documents that are in my car at the entrance of the condo and give them to the police. Hurry! Somebody broke into my house. I'm scared."

She waited, hopeful.

One person had turned on the light in the living room; the other had opened the door leading to the garage.

"She isn't home," a man with a raspy voice whispered.

"I saw her turning into the street of this condominium," the woman replied in a hardly audible voice. "Where else could she be going?"

"Maybe to visit a neighbour; anyway we can't go around and ask if anybody has seen her. So, let's search."

The Blackpox Threat

Tamara heard the fridge door open. The man was probably snatching a beer. Then she heard heavy steps pounding on the carpet of one of the bedrooms.

A few minutes elapsed and then the woman whispered, louder this time, "Let's search for the files and clear out."

"I already looked. I saw no files anywhere. They were in a binder, red, you said. It should be easy to spot."

"Hmm. I'll go search in the basement; you look under the beds, and the couch. She's an agent — don't forget. She's trained to deceive."

Tamara's knees were hurting, crouched as she was. She didn't dare to move or even breathe heavily. She heard her cell ring five times. It could be Justin, she thought. Then she heard her wall phone chirp.

Justin's voice came up from the loudspeaker she had left on.

"Got your message. No reason to worry. A friend of mine is taking care of your car so I can come to see you."

Justin was smart. He had captured the essence of her predicament and its priority. He had mentioned the car first. Now she could only hope that Justin's friend would spot it, since it was in the big parking lot at the entrance of the complex. If they killed her, at least part of her mission would be accomplished.

A good half-hour went by. Tamara's knees and legs were crumpled in a very small space. They ached, but she didn't make the smallest sound or move. Then two shoes, size 11 or higher, appeared in her view.

"You, get up!" the man said. "I found her," he screamed to get the attention of his companion in the basement.

Tamara rose to face the man. He was corpulent, his head shaved bald, his eyes closer to his nose than normal, his forehead small. He wore a sweat suit, black with white vertical stripes. The top stretched to the maximum over his chest and resembled an extended accordion. He deposited a beer bottle on the coffee table and pushed Tamara to the centre of the living room.

"What do you want from me?" Tamara asked. "This is my home; you have no right to be here. You broke into my house!" She heard hurried steps from the basement.

In front of her stood Sophia Tadlova, her cheeks red, her eyes flashing anger.

Tamara was stunned. "You?" Tamara said, after she recovered from the shock. She frowned. "You, a friend of Vassilli's, a criminal?"

"And a consummate one, you can well say." She emitted a short, bittersweet laugh. "Don't you even think of pulling a fast one! Where are the papers you stole from the spa?"

"I don't know what you're talking about."

Tadlova slapped her on the cheek.

Tamara was ready to retaliate, but the man grabbed her arms and held them behind her back.

"Once more, the papers!" The pitch of Tadlova's voice was high.

"I don't have any papers. Search, if you want."

As the noise of an approaching car became louder and louder, the man with the raspy voice said, "We have to clear out. The papers aren't here. We have to walk to the back of the compound. It's a bit of a walk and then we have to jump over the fence. Let's go. Now!"

Tamara began screaming with all the wind she had in her lungs as the man dragged her out of the house.

"Gag her, Stan," Tadlova said with an icy tone.

And a piece of duct tape sealed Tamara's mouth.

Chapter 19

Justin had stopped his Audi two houses before Tamara's and tried to assess the situation. A monster of a man was carrying Tamara. She was kicking him in his stomach and pounding on his shoulders with all her might. The older woman didn't look dangerous, but she was probably armed. He watched them cross the lawn and disappear behind a copse of trees. Clearly they had parked their vehicle outside the compound at the far end, and vaulted over the fence.

He decided to turn around, look for them and follow them, hopefully without being noticed.

His friend at the London Police Service had already taken custody of Tamara's car.

At the beginning, Justin had no problem following the Chevrolet Optra driven by the assailants. As they both passed Lambeth and took the overpass across the 402, the traffic became scarce. Justin turned off the car lights and kept behind the Chevy at the maximum distance that allowed him to see it. His eyes were strained; he was finally relieved when the car slowed down and drove into a gravel road leading to a farm. On the far left stood a big barn and a silo; on the right was a one-storey house. Justin noticed a light in the barn. As the Chevy skirted the farmhouse and headed toward the barn a sudden barking filled the air.

Justin stopped the car on the road shoulder and observed the scene.

The woman climbed out of the car, walked to the barn's sliding door and opened it. Only then did the man follow her inside, carrying Tamara.

Justin opened his cell, glanced at his GPS and gave the coordinates of the farm to his friend, Bill Hartwart, who worked at the London Police Service. It was not London's jurisdiction any more, Bill told him, and it would take time to alert the OPP.

Disappointed, Justin got out of his Audi and tiptoed to the barn — a Swiss army knife and a penlight in his pocket. The only point of entry seemed to be the main door and that was not a good idea. He rounded the barn and noticed a small door at the base of the silo, and that the silo was one piece with the barn. Light filtered from the back section of the ceiling toward the silo's door, left ajar. Circumspectly, he pushed on the door. It opened into a small room shaped like an atrium, with three doors. Strange, Justin thought. He expected the silo to be full of grain or other feed for the livestock. He opened the door to his left and circled his penlight. He spotted a wagon, a baler and a small tractor. He repeated the operation with the second door, which contained hay, packed in small cubes, one bale on top of the other. Then he opened the third door. This led to a corridor with a stairway winding upwards. Justin hesitated a few minutes, and then went up the stairs. At the top was a balustrade from which he could look down into the barn.

Tamara was bound, her arms tied around a chair's back. Behind her was the huge man he had spotted before; in front stood the older woman, who was swinging her gun up and down.

"Talk," she said to Tamara. "Those files have to come back; one way or the other I'll get them. Where are they?"

Tamara shook her head. "I don't know what you're blathering about. I never took, saw or touched any files." Her voice was calm, her posture erect.

With the barrel of her revolver, Sophia signalled the big man to leave the room. "Let her spend the night here," she said. "Seal her mouth. Get the dogs and leave them outside."

Both the man and the woman strode out.

Justin retraced his steps and stood outside until Tamara's abductors entered the farmhouse. He then returned to the silo, climbed upstairs and leaned out of the balustrade. He whistled the tune of the last pizzica he and Tamara had danced together on the houseboat.

Tamara turned her head up but her position didn't allow her to see him.

"My friend, Bill Hartwart, got your car," Justin said. "The papers are safe with him. With a bit of luck I'll get you out. Besides, the police should be here any moment. They've been alerted." He looked around. "Don't move," he joked. "I'll look for a rope and slip down." He paused and listened. "They're getting the dogs. I can hear them."

Justin kept quiet until he heard the steps of the man fade, that noise soon superseded by the barking of the dogs and their scratching the barn door. Good. The noise would cover Tamara's escape. Using his penlight, he searched for a rope but couldn't find any. He returned to the balustrade.

"No rope," he said. "I'm going to drop a few bales of hay and come down that way." In no time six bales dropped close to

Tamara, submerging her with strands of hay. "Sorry," murmured Justin as he jumped on top of them and then rolled onto the floor. "They weren't pressed very tightly."

The dogs outside intensified their barking.

Swiftly Justin extracted his knife and cut Tamara's ropes.

"I'll let you take off the duct tape. It may be painful."

Tamara nodded and freed her mouth. "That hurt!" She wetted her lips. "What's next?" she whispered.

"Let's go back the way I came down," he said. "I parked my car not too far away."

They had just reached Justin's Audi when they saw a man approaching the barn's entrance. They stood in silence, holding their breath. The man deposited food for the dogs, which quieted instantly.

When the house door closed behind the man, Tamara climbed into Justin's Audi and sat in the passenger's seat.

"I was scared," she said. "I'm glad it's all over."

"I'd like to know what kind of troubles you're in. I know they're serious. Start by explaining how those two people managed to break into your home."

"They were fast operators. I had just entered the condo and hadn't yet inserted the alarm that rings directly at the security company. I was planning to go back to get my car. They had no problems in forcing the lock open."

Justin had put the car in gear. Still without any light he made a U-turn and then began driving normally toward London.

"I was lucky you remembered the code that opens the gate at the entrance of the condominium's compound. Thank God I gave it to you a few weeks ago." She brushed off the strands of hay from her top and slacks. "Thank you. You probably saved my life."

Justin extended his hand and caressed her cheek. "Welcome.

Want to stop and have something to drink or eat?"

"I'd prefer to go home. I must make a call with the special cell I keep in my purse. What about the police? Shouldn't they be on their way to the farm? We didn't meet them on the road."

"Right. That's strange. Let me call my friend." Justin tried a few times. "He doesn't answer. How crucial is it that the documents be in safe hands?"

"Very. They may help prevent a catastrophe."

For a moment Justin drove in silence. "I understand you may want to wait to tell me what this is all about in detail, but can you give me a hint?"

"It appears that dangerous substances are being smuggled into this country. They constitute biological warfare. What kind and in which timeframe this is going to happen we don't know. Sophia and her acolytes are the first people with a name and an address that have been finally identified. Before we had only intermediate persons who might not even have been aware of the role they had been playing. It's essential that Sophia and that goon, Stan, be arrested and made to talk. Even if they're not aware of the entire operation they surely know who else is involved."

"You work for CSIS?"

"Yes, I'm an informer, even if nobody dares to call me that."

Justin didn't speak until they reached Tamara's condo. "You can go ahead and make your calls and whatever else you have to do. I'll check the alarm, and call the station to find out what happened to Bill and your car. I'll make us a bite to eat. I'd like to sleep at your place, in case there are new…new…how should I call them? New developments."

"Fine."

Justin parked his Audi in Tamara's garage. Briskly, Tamara got out and entered the house through the kitchen. As she stopped in front of the small mirror that hung near the window she glanced at her reflection.

"It looks like I'm wearing a wig. The hay is almost the same colour as my hair."

"Quite becoming," said Justin. As he walked by her he kissed her on her neck. He reached for the fridge and set two cans of cola on the table.

Tamara neared the chair where she had deposited her purse before being abducted. She rummaged in it and got her cell. "I'm going to make a call," she said, grabbed a cola and marched into the living room. She shut the sliding glass door behind her.

****

Tamara drank half of her cola while dialling Brad's number.

The answer was immediate. "Tamara, where have you been?"

"At Sophia Tadlova's farm." She gave him the approximate whereabouts. "She and her goon, named Stan, abducted me and kept me in the barn, threatening me. They wanted the papers I'd managed to steal from Harry Pearson's spa."

"Who has them now?"

"Don't know. They were in my car — I had it parked away from my condo and a policeman from the London Police Service was supposed to bring them to safety."

"Did you have a chance to look at them?"

"Just a quick glance. I saw invoices, bills and a schedule of events. Also a spreadsheet with payments and dates, but no names." Tamara finished her drink.

"The name of this policeman?"

"Bill Hartwart. I know only that he's a friend of Justin Devry." Tamara paused, for the first time stunned at Brad's lack of concern for what had happened to her. "Are you going to do something about these people who kidnapped me?"

"I have to consult my superiors, first."

"Good. Consult your superiors, and then meet with me. Tomorrow at 11:00 in the morning. My house. If I don't see anybody I march to the closest police station and report my kidnapping. I have a witness. You can forget about secrecy. It's my life we're talking about. You don't seem to care about it, but I do."

"Tam —"

Tamara had already snapped the cell closed. She sat in an armchair, pondering the situation. She had to rely on Justin, even if his father was on the list of people who participated in the shipments. But how much should she trust him? She had the uneasy feeling that Operation Bullfrog was fighting a multi-cell criminal ring, where each cell had only partial knowledge of the whole. What did Brad Wilson know that he wasn't telling her? She wanted answers, and tomorrow she would get them, and they better be convincing, or she would take the first flight away from London. Any destination would do.

Now, she should find out what happened to her car.

Tamara opened the door that separated the living room from the kitchen. Justin had set food on the table, together with two plates and two bottles of Dasani.

"News about my car?" She rubbed her wrists, where the rope had left red marks.

Justin shook his head "no" as he made himself a sandwich of ham, lettuce and mayo.

"I can't understand what happened. Nobody has seen my friend, Bill Hartwart. Not at the station and not at home. Nobody has spotted your car either." He ate his sandwich in big bites. "I think we should go to the police right away. They can send a message to all cruisers."

"I talked with my contact," Tamara said at length. "He'll come down tomorrow morning at 11:00. We wait and see what his advice is." She looked at Justin. "I'd like you to meet him. Whether CSIS likes it or not, you're now involved." She got an apple and bit into it. "Let's see how much they want to tell you and if they think you should be part of the operation." She finished her apple, took a bottle of water and said, "Good night, Justin. I'm exhausted. Thank you again."

Chapter 20

It was early morning when Frank Milton glanced at the clock. The time was up; by now the toxin should have reached its maximum effect. He looked with satisfaction at the cages on the rack. The three Guinea pigs bled from their noses and mouths and their eyes were red. They hardly moved. Their physical characteristics were now terrifying. Frank focused his camera onto them and shot a video as the little pigs took on different positions. These pictures would scare anybody because people would immediately assume that the disease could be transmitted to humans.

He rubbed his hands together. His time had finally come.

He looked for the bottle of Rémy Martin he kept underneath the counter and filled a brandy glass with it. A celebration was in order.

The phone rang, interrupting his moment of jubilation.

"Sophia, here."

There was a pause and Frank already knew it was bad news.

"Is it Frank?"

"Yes."

"We didn't get the folder."

"What happened?"

"Tamara didn't have it with her, and we couldn't find her car. We searched and searched."

"So, keep looking. Harry Pearson was fairly sure Tamara was the woman who stole them."

"Fairly sure or sure?"

"Well…he'd seen her once at the Modano Company. He said he recognized her by her height."

There was silence, then Sophia said, "Stan and I are in trouble; we have to clear out, and fast."

"Would you mind explaining why?"

"It's a long story…"

"You already got $20,000. They're worth a few words."

Sophia hesitated, then continued. "When we couldn't find the papers we took Tamara to the farm and tied her down in the barn. We thought that would soften her up."

"You kidnapped her?" He had asked Sophia to steal the papers back, never told her to use force! "Don't tell me she escaped!" He couldn't believe his own words as he spelled them out.

"That's exactly what happened. Somebody must have followed us and got her free. I don't know who or how. We had left the dogs outside, to guard."

"You can't leave, not now." He couldn't replace them at the last minute. "We need you for broadcasting the big message and the distribution. It will happen in two, maybe three weeks." Christ almighty, the woman was as stupid as they could get. "Can you not operate from another place?" Silence greeted him. "Just take the CD with the email addresses and get a new computer. Stay put until I tell you to broadcast my message and the pictures! And all that

Stan will have to do is deliver a couple dozen items!"

There was heavy breathing on the other side. "Stan is already gone. I'm leaving, Frank. Tamara knows me."

"People don't cross me, Sophia." He paused for effect. "Don't fail me either. I'll reach you wherever you go."

A click was all that he heard next.

****

Sophia…he had been an idiot to engage her. The woman only wanted revenge against Vassilli and Tamara.

The best subjects for his experiments with blackpox would have been fruit bats, like Boris used, but he didn't know anybody who raised them. He'd opted for Guinea pigs. He was familiar with those because he ran tests on live animals for his work on beauty products.

One day he had approached the Tadlova's farm to get a few new ones, carefully concealing the fact that they would be used for illegal purposes. Raising those little animals was what Sophia, 67, did to round out the meagre income of her farm. In the course of his first visit, he had noticed a large framed picture, the only one in the house, standing on her desk. He had asked her if it was her husband, and he had gotten to know that the picture belonged to Vassilli Petrovic, the man of her dreams. Vassilli had married a Canadian woman who had left him a bit of money and a nice cottage on the shores of Lake Huron. Then Sophia had started to talk about him, how he had helped her escape from the Soviet Union via Hungary, and gave her a bit of money to start the farm. Ten years ago he had become an important diplomat, Sophia had added. For the last few years, he had held the position of commercial attaché at the Ukrainian Embassy. After the death of his wife, Sophia had hoped for a relationship, but Vassilli had become more distant than when his wife was alive. He was often in the company of attractive women.

When Sophia had mentioned the word "Ukraine," Frank had become all ears. Would this Vassilli still come to visit her? Sometimes, she answered. Recently? Yes. He wouldn't make a special trip for her, but when he went to the cottage he would make a detour to go see Tamara, the daughter of an old friend of his, and then drop by her farm for a drink. Was Tamara his girlfriend? No, but she surely was close to his heart. He cared very much about the young woman's well-being.

It was then that Frank thought he could use Sophia to do some checking. He told her that he was very much interested in visiting the Ukraine and especially the mountain regions. Did her friend Vassilli know anything about the Carpathian Mountains?

After having bought a few more pigs, Sophia informed him that that particular mountain region was going to be extensively developed and a new highway constructed. This information, which agreed with what Boris had told him weeks before, had prompted the relocation of Boris's lab.

Unfortunately, Sophia had grown bitter, unsatisfied with her life at the farm, which cost money without producing an adequate revenue, and angry with Vassilli who ignored her more and more.

Frank needed people to work for him. Sophia could easily dispose of his discarded products. If she wanted to take revenge for Vassilli's neglect, fine, he would not interfere with her doing that. At the time, it seemed such a good idea...

Frank drank his brandy and poured himself another. After Harry Pearson had seen Tamara hurry away with the folder where he recorded his lab experiments and payments, he had asked Sophia to recover it. He never thought she would go to the extent of kidnapping Tamara! She had endangered the entire operation, now that it was so close to its final phase. And that other idiot, Harry! With all his preaching about security, he had left the door of their office unlocked to go to the john! He was surrounded by incompetents — that was his problem!

He was still trying to figure out why this Tamara Smith could be interested in his activities — Harry Pearson had just seen her working at the Modano Company. She wasn't even a full-time employee. Harry had found out from her friend Dianne Templeton that Tamara had been hired to help with public relations to beef up the sales, but, especially, to organize the auctions, which often dragged until late on Saturdays. So what was the connection? Or maybe she was just looking for something to steal? Had she maybe removed the folder out of the drawer in search of something better and just got caught with it in her hands?

And now, the big dilemma: should he inform the man who financed his operation of what had happened? Fortunately, all the important correspondence he had with Boris Youkenoff was encrypted and safely stored in the computer he kept in his lab. That was locked at all times, day or night.

Chapter 21

When Tamara woke in the morning, Justin wasn't there. On the kitchen table lay a note.

Last night my friend, Bill, had an accident. He was taken to Emergency. Only minor injuries. They'll discharge him today. I know where your Subaru has been taken. I'll go get the papers.

Oh, oh. She didn't like that Justin would get at the papers. And she'd be without a car for a while. What an annoyance! Tamara sighed. Well, compared with what she had gone through yesterday, these problems were only minor inconveniences. She put coffee in the percolator, bread in the toaster and opened the fridge. She was hungry like a bear out of hibernation. She fried two eggs with five slices of bacon and took her plate to the living room. She turned on the television and walked back to the kitchen to fill a mug with fresh coffee.

A commercial had just finished, when the bell rang. Justin? Brad maybe? Too early for Brad. Still in her satin robe, she looked through the pinhole.

The Blackpox Threat

It was a policeman.

Tamara retreated to the kitchen, grabbed the intercom and called the superintendent. Keeping her voice to a murmur, she asked whether he had okayed the entrance of a police officer. When she received a negative answer, she asked whether there was a police car in the parking lot. No, was the answer. Tamara called Brad and reported the fact.

"Things are getting worse by the minute," she said. "Where are you?"

"My partner and I are just an hour from your condo. Don't open the door and get ready to use your gun."

The bell rang again. Tamara fetched her purse. She turned the television off and screamed, "Just a minute. I need to get dressed." She stood in the hallway, the safety off her weapon. She waited.

Ten minutes had elapsed when she heard a car stopping outside. Justin, she thought, hopeful. She looked through the pinhole. It was indeed Justin. To be sure he didn't have company, she tiptoed into the living room and looked through the sheers. Justin was alone.

Tamara opened the door and Justin entered, waving a red folder in one hand and a box in the other.

"Got the papers out of your car," he said triumphantly. "Took your car to a garage. It needs a new door, passenger side." He paused. "How is this for service?"

"Super," Tamara said, and grabbed the folder.

"That's all you have to say, *super*?" Justin closed his eyes. "Don't I deserve a kiss?"

The warmth Justin managed to spread was always uplifting and his cheerfulness was contagious. She felt like kissing and hugging him to no end. She should resist, though. Justin was now involved, it was true, but she should him keep at a distance. Things had already gone nasty, and the visit of the fake policeman she had received moments ago confirmed it. Whoever was involved was not going to stop hunting her down. She posed a danger to Justin.

She caressed his face and gave him a kiss on the tip of his nose. She sniffed. "What do you have in the box? Donuts, by any chance?"

"Yes. I didn't bring any coffee — I knew that, if you were up, it would be brewing already."

He moved into the breakfast nook, followed by Tamara. He deposited the box on the table and opened it.

"Get one," he said to Tamara as he moved to the counter to pour himself a cup.

"I will," she said. "But I'd like to give a look at the folder before CSIS comes and takes it away. I want to discover what was in it that was worth kidnapping me for."

With the folder under her arm, she walked into living room.

There were four sections, each separated by a divider. The first one was a spreadsheet listing date of acquisition, company, item and price. Neither item nor company raised any suspicions in Tamara's mind. The second section was only a couple of sheets thick, with handwritten notes on purchases to be made, and a check mark on most on them. The third section was a calendar, with ample space for each day of the year. For the months of April, May and June the annotations were frequent. She perused the annotations, neglecting, for the time being, the dates. A few caught her attention immediately. They read:

contacted S.; B. leaves today; B. arrived; contacted H.; got 3 new Guinea pigs; shipment ordered; shipment arrived; experiment #1 started; shipment reordered; contacted H. She proceeded to the next section, which contained only bills.

Tamara was puzzled. Sure, that material could be relevant to Operation Bullfrog, but it could also be simply a record of activities linked to the spa. They would not incriminate anybody. So why kidnap her?

The bell rang. Brad Wilson, accompanied by a woman, was at the door.

Chapter 22

Frank Milton exchanged the police officer's hat with his helmet and started his Harley-Davidson. On foot, he had cleared out from Tamara's house as soon as he heard the noise of a car. He was now circling the condominium complex and was ready to go back to his lab, when he changed his mind. He parked his vehicle underneath the trees at the back of the complex, as he had done before. He got his binoculars out and moved to the extreme corner of the woods so that he could have a view, even if partial, of the movements taking place around Tamara's house. There was an Audi parked in front of it and another car was approaching.

A man and a woman descended from a blue sedan; both were dressed casually. The man wore a fishing hat with a lure pinned on one side and the woman, in a sweat suit and wearing huge sunglasses, carried a large bag.

So, Frank reasoned, there are at least four people in the house. What could the occasion be? Maybe he should wait and see what happened. His cell rang. He looked at the number. Oh, no, it was

Harry again!

"Dianne refused to get your parcel," Harry said.

"So, you go."

"What if they ask questions? What have you shipped this time?" Harry's voice was querulous.

"The same thing as last time. Three vases, antique. Delicate, that's why I used the Modano Company."

"Yes, but —"

Frank wanted to focus his attention on Tamara's house and its surroundings. Harry was a desperate case of logorrhoea. He would have dropped him a long time ago, but, unfortunately, he needed the spa as a smoke screen for his activities. So Frank responded to Harry's complaints and questions with vague comments and sympathetic noises.

Then Harry said, "There may be duties…"

"So, pay them!" Frank replied, at the limit of his patience. He shut his cell off.

There was movement around Tamara's house. The man and the woman he had seen before came out of the main door followed by a young man carrying a big cooler. A tall woman dressed in jeans and a yellow top exited last and checked that the house door was locked. Tamara Smith, probably. The foursome seemed heading for leisure times, gesturing and chatting cheerfully as they climbed into the sedan.

Frank was puzzled. Was Tamara the woman Harry had seen fleeing with his documents? Was it possible Harry was mistaken? After all, Sophia and Stan had not found any red folder in the house. Should he follow the foursome and find out what they were up to? It would be a good idea, even if he was pressured for time. He wanted to go back to his lab and observe closely the status of his Guinea pigs.

Finally, he decided to follow the blue sedan. He would see where they were heading and then rush back to the lab.

After three-quarters of an hour, spent driving, plus a coffee break at Tim Hortons, the sedan stopped at the entrance of Fanshawe Park, in the northeast part of London. Clearly they were on a leisure excursion. Nothing to worry about, Frank thought.

He turned around. He should forget about the folder. It contained information that only a person aware of his activities could interpret and use. It was the one he carried along when he had a meeting with the man who financed him. He reminded himself again that his planner and the day-by-day documentation of his experiments were encrypted and stored in his computer, which was duly protected by a password.

He should go back to the lab, check on the little pigs and get everything ready for the big, final act.

****

Brad Wilson had introduced his partner as Major Heather Motta and urged Tamara, still in her satin robe, to get dressed, so that they could take off and go talk in a safe place. He had suggested they play as if they were going on a picnic and asked Justin to find a cooler. When Tamara had rejoined the group, dressed in white Capri slacks and a bright yellow top, Brad was ordering Justin to leave.

"Justin comes with me," Tamara had said with a firm voice, coming into the room from behind Brad's shoulders. "He's involved now, and I expect you folks to treat him with respect."

"Tamara, you have to understand that this operation is going out of its perimeter if we allow him to stay," Brad had said with a sharp tone.

The Blackpox Threat

Tamara had not replied. She had taken her purse, reset the surveillance system and opened the door. "Let's go," she had said with authority, and gestured the threesome outside.

They were now seated at a picnic table sheltered by the foliage of a majestic maple; the blue cooler containing the folder was underneath the table; the box with Justin's donuts lay on top of it. Justin sat beside Tamara, opposite Brad and Heather, and opened the box of donuts.

"Dig in," he said, and helped himself to one.

Tamara extracted a small notebook from her purse, and said, "I'd like to know something about your jobs, what you do, and where your offices are located."

"This is a covert operation," Heather Motta said, "We can't give you that information. It would endanger us all."

Tamara closed the notebook. "Fine, then give me a CSIS office where I can meet the person in charge of Operation Bullfrog. Every time I ask Brad for something, he tells me that he has to check with his superiors. It's time I meet them, on their turf. I don't want a meeting in a park. It looks as if we were playing a game, and I would dismiss it as a stupid game, if it wasn't for the fact that I have been held at gun point." As she received no reply, she asked, "And the money, Brad, did you bring it?"

"Oh yes, I forgot about it." He slid an envelope toward Tamara.

Tamara counted $3,000. "It will do for the time being," she said dryly. "Now, I'd like to go home."

"Wait, wait, Tamara. We came to talk, so let's talk." He gave Tamara a suave look. "I do have some authority, you know. Power too. And we're in this operation together. First of all, Tamara, tell us what you've seen at the spa, so we can take appropriate actions."

Tamara sighed. "The spa looks legit, except that there's much space that isn't accounted for in relation to the facilities open to the public. It can still be perfectly legit, however. I have no way to know." She paused and closed her eyes as she concentrated on her recollection. "Yesterday I went to the spa. I managed to go up the stairs and found a corridor with several doors. On one, the brass tag read *Harry Pearson and Frank Milton*. Pearson is the spa's owner. I entered that office and looked around. No computers; no typewriters; just two desks and a small table with chairs. I opened the drawer of one of the desks and found a folder, the red folder we hid in the cooler before coming here. You can have it." She opened her eyes and kicked on the cooler hard enough to hit Brad's feet.

"Ouch!" Brad said. "No need to get violent." He smoothed his words with a smile. "And what about the people who kidnapped you?"

"One was Sophia Tadlova, as I told you earlier; the other was Stan: a big man, bald, with dark eyes; muscular, about forty; somebody must have broken his nose at some time, so maybe he's an ex-boxer."

"Anything else?" Heather asked.

Tamara quickly reported on the parcel Harry Pearson was supposed to free from duties at London Airport.

"Oh, good," Brad said. "That can be a real breakthrough! We finally have a lead on the shipments." He turned to Justin. "By the way, who is the officer who took care of Tamara's car?"

"A friend of mine, Bill Harwart. He knows that there were important documents hidden in the trunk of Tamara's Subaru. He isn't aware of their contents, though. I got hold of them once I found out that he had a car accident."

"What else does he know?"

"Not much, but by now he may be curious enough to ask questions."

"Anybody else involved?"

"The police, obviously. I called for help when I saw they were abducting Tamara and then again when she was detained in the silo."

Heather and Brad said at the same time, "So both The London Police and the OPP know of the kidnapping?"

"Of course," Justin replied.

Brad extracted a card from his pocket and offered it to Justin. "If your friend or anybody else asks about the incident — the kidnapping, I mean — tell him to give me a call. Don't say anything." As Justin didn't reply, Brad bore his eyes into Justin's. "Understood?"

Unperturbed, Justin turned to Tamara. "Tamara, do you agree?"

Tamara assented. "We'll keep everything under wraps for a couple of days. To give Brad time to go after Tadlova and her accomplice." She paused. "But in that frame of time I'll have to be reassured that this operation has a coherent plan of action. If not, I'll march to the police and report every single detail of what happened." She looked at Heather and then at Brad. "Clear?"

"Yes, Tamara. I want you to know that we have already requested to have you shadowed." Brad looked at Heather. They exchanged a knowing look. "Meanwhile we'd like to ask you folks to do one more thing."

"And what would that be?" Tamara asked.

Brad stretched his arms on the picnic table and crossed his hands. "Find out who is the sender of the package that Frank Milton is so anxious to receive," Brad said.

"Unfortunately I can't go. Harry Pearson may be there."

"That's right." Brad addressed Justin. "Can you go, Mr. Devry? Tamara would wait for you in the car in case you need a fast getaway."

"I'll go if Tamara asks me," Justin replied.

Tamara put up a hand. "Just a moment. Do I interpret correctly what you're saying — that nobody would be assigned to shadow me by tomorrow?" Tamara asked, unable to disguise her frustration.

Nobody spoke for a long moment. Silence was only interrupted by the soft munching of Justin, who was savouring the last of the donuts.

"Unfortunately, that's correct," Brad finally said. "You see, Tamara, we're working around the clock and have to brief an officer on all aspects of this operation. It isn't easy to select the right person, who has to be competent and totally trustworthy."

"But you can get an order to confiscate the package — find an excuse. It shouldn't be difficult."

"That's what Heather and I are going to work on as soon as we're back," Brad said.

"Then why don't one of you stick around and go to customs tomorrow morning?"

"Not possible," Heather said with a firm tone. "We're both working on a problem that we have to solve as soon as possible."

"Problem?" Silence greeted her, so she reiterated the question, "What problem? I want to know!"

Heather took off her sunglasses and glanced at Tamara and Justin in turn. "Operation Bullfrog started with eight people, which included you and Vassilli Petrovic. After Vassilli died, a new member of the Ukrainian government took his place. We don't know him well and we have no way to find out how accurate his information is." Brad put a hand on Heather's arm in an attempt to refrain her from continuing but Heather didn't budge. "In short, this new member claims that there's a leak in our group." Heather fiddled with her sunglasses.

"Heather —" Brad called in a sharp voice.

"Brad, let me continue. Tamara has the right to know. She has just risked her life for us. We're holding an internal investigation, which can't be delayed. The life of millions of people may be at stake."

"So there're four more active members participating in the operation. What are they doing?" Tamara asked.

"They're hunting down scientists who may be familiar with biological weapons and reviewing all the reports of the labs which, at one time or another, were involved in these kinds of experiments. One member is in Geneva to gather more information at the World Health Organization, where they keep samples of all known viruses and microbes."

Tamara sighed. "So there are only two spies — the new Ukrainian attaché and myself?"

"Actually you're the only active one. With the death of Vassilli, that source has contributed little in terms of new information."

Tamara reached for the box of donuts. With disappointment she noted that it was empty.

"Tomorrow morning Justin and I will go to the customs office at the airport," she said. "We'll try to find out all what we can about the package addressed to Harry Pearson." She rose. "Let's go. I need to collect my thoughts."

Chapter 23

Justin had taken Tamara out for supper and then home. Still standing outside the door, he asked, "Do you know that we were followed on our way to the park?"

"I noticed that a motorcycle drove behind us all the way on Fanshawe Road. I thought it was going to pass us but we were going at the speed limit. I thought that was the reason he didn't."

"I wouldn't have suspected anything, except that he turned around as soon as we entered the park. So why come all the way? The driver wore a dark outfit, and the motorcycle was a Harley-Davidson. Black with big yellow stripes." Justin paused. "Be careful if it shows up again."

"You'd think Brad would've noticed," Tamara said, pensive.

"He was driving, if that's an excuse for a super-agent as he prides himself to be. I don't have much respect for your CSIS guys. Probably less than you do, which says a lot. In any case I got the license plate; I stored it in my Motorola i580 and I'll pass it on to my friend Bill; he can find out to whom it's registered." He pulled on Tamara's sleeve. "I feel we should take some actions." They were still standing outside the condo. "Do you know what I think?"

"Yes. That we should have a look at Sophia Tadlova's farmhouse."

"Right on the dot. My guess is that by now she's cleared out. Brad didn't mention searching her house."

"But he could have the police doing it."

"Maybe or maybe not." Justin looked at his wristwatch. "Let's go."

"Fine. I'll go change into a dark sweat suit, get my digital camera and a new flash drive. A few small plastic bags. I intend to collect samples of everything of interest we find in Sophia's house."

Within a few minutes they climbed into Justin's Audi and began driving.

There were no lights outside or around Tadlova's house, and no light in the barn. Justin stopped the car on the shoulder and together they proceeded on foot, listening intently for any noise.

They approached the garage first. Using a penlight they looked into it through a broken glass crescent, one of the many that decorated the top of the garage door. There was no car.

"Sophia is gone," Tamara said. "What about the dogs? Where do you think they are?"

"Maybe inside."

They rounded the house and tugged at the backdoor. It wasn't locked. They tiptoed inside.

"Nobody's home," Justin said. "Let's turn on the light, here, in the kitchen. What should we look at first?"

"Find where she keeps her books, her mail, anything on paper. I see a desk in the living room." Tamara moved toward the centre of the house. "A coffee mug too; good for fingerprints." She quickly dropped the mug into a plastic bag and into her purse.

"There's a computer — something I didn't expect from an older woman," Justin said.

"Great. I'll look for papers; see if you can find any interesting files on her computer."

For a while they worked in silence, then Tamara said, "Got something! There is a copy of a cheque for $20,000 signed by Frank Milton, who shares an office with the spa's owner. I wonder what that was for."

"Nothing important in this old Gateway. Just a list of addresses under Christmas-2006 and some emails. No password whatsoever."

Tamara rummaged in her purse and gave Justin a flash drive. "Copy all that is stored. The list of addresses may provide useful links to people she knows." She continued her search, at times taking pictures of documents. "More cheques signed by Frank Milton, and some records of sales. Sophia and Frank had some kind of business together."

There was noise outside, soon followed by a soft whining at the main door.

"The dogs!" Tamara whispered.

Justin retrieved the portable drive and walked to the door.

"Yes, the dogs are outside," he said. "Tadlova might have let them free before leaving. We should clear out. They may attract attention."

"And how? They'll jump on us right away!"

"Hmm. Let me think."

Tamara dropped her camera into her bag and moved close to Justin. "We're trapped inside, I'm afraid."

"Not really. Go out the back door and run toward the car. Drive to the back of the house. Meanwhile I'll open the main door, so they can see I'm an intruder. They'll get ready to attack, only temporarily refrained by the storm door. In the little time it'll take them to jump through it I'll run to the back and hide in the kitchen, until you show up."

Justin waited until Tamara reached for the back door and then opened the front one wide, making a lot of noise. Soon after he ran to the kitchen and shut the door behind him. The dogs were inside the house in a jiffy — their barking furious and menacing.

Finally the lights of the Audi appeared and Justin walked outside, without realizing that one of the dogs had turned around, leaped outside and was now chasing the approaching car. While he was opening the passenger door, the Doberman got hold of his jeans, and ripped off a big portion of them.

"You okay?" Tamara asked as soon as Justin dashed inside. She immediately started driving toward the road.

"Yes and no. The beast managed to nip at me." He massaged his injured spot. "And half of my pants are gone."

Tamara turned on the interior lights and laughed. "I can see your shorts, white with a little red maple leaf. Very patriotic." She switched the lights off. "Sexy too."

"Laugh, laugh, after I saved you from being bitten."

"Well, the operation was a success. We have some material that may reveal the depth of Tadlova's involvement."

"Yeah. A costly success. My jeans were designer's jeans."

"Designer jeans? Oh my, oh my. You'll have to be happy with a pair of less distinction. Wal*Mart is probably the only store open at this time of night."

****

The morning came too early for Tamara. Her sleep had been intermittent, punctuated with sudden awakenings due to a fast heart beating. The recurrent nightmare about her parents' horrible death had surfaced with violence, leaving her soaked in perspiration. Toward the morning, when she had finally managed to fall asleep again, the alarm clock called her to duty.

Tamara showered slowly, hoping that the water would refresh her spirit and not only her body. She combed her hair flat and put on a pleated skirt and a sleeveless top. She slipped on Justin's medallion and set it underneath her shirt and then checked the batteries of her two cells, her own and the special one that Duncan had given her, well aware that her life might depend on them. She felt uneasy, out of her league, called to fulfil a role that was too big for her and, worst of all, poorly defined. She thought of Justin, of how dependable, yet unpretentious and sweet he had been. For the first time in her life she felt the need for a steady relationship, the need to have a family, the need to build a home for herself and her companion, the need to be needed. These feelings had been lurking for some time, she realized, but Justin's presence had prompted their awareness. Now that she could satisfy her needs, she found herself involved in an operation that endangered Justin's life and her own.

She should take some actions to get out of Operation Bullfrog — but how? She had no friends she could count on, nobody she could resort to for advice.

The noise in the guest bedroom's shower stopped her musing. Justin was up and would be around in minutes. She moved into the kitchen and set up the coffee maker.

In no time Justin appeared, his short hair still wet.

"Good morning, my Mata Hari," he said. As Tamara responded with an empty look, he said, "Father and I are movie buffs, old ones in particular. There is an oldie starring Greta Garbo as Mata Hari, a German spy."

"Don't know much about old movies or movie stars," she said, and gestured Justin to a cup of coffee she had deposited opposite her. "Good morning." She took a sip of her own and asked, "Plan of action?"

"Just go to customs and see what we can find out. My father uses the Modano Company too, so I know the place and I can inquire about a phantom parcel supposedly addressed to my father."

"Resourceful, eh? I like the idea."

"One more thing I'd suggest we do."

Tamara waited for him to talk and then said, "So, what is it?"

"Something Brad wouldn't like. Take Sophia's coffee mug to my friend at the police station and ask him to check for fingerprints. He'll do it without asking questions."

"Sure?"

"Well, almost sure. Then we'll courier it to CSIS."

"Agreed," Tamara said. "Let's have breakfast and then move on."

****

Remodelled about a decade ago, London Airport sported a round, stylish glass façade. It housed the local customs at the end of the northern wing.

Tamara parked the Audi as close as she could near the building. "Ready?" she asked.

"Almost. Can you give me a rough description of Harry Pearson?"

"Medium height and weight, well, maybe a bit shorter than average. About 40 years old. He looks like an artist: fairly long hair, grey. I saw him wearing a loose top and a scarf around his neck, bright colour."

"Thanks." He blew a kiss to Tamara and got out of the Audi.

Tamara stayed in the car. She didn't want to be recognized by Harry Pearson or anybody who might accompany him. Her thoughts went back to her predicament and the uneasiness she felt about the entire operation. There was a lack of cohesion; the information that the two governments had gathered on the biological threat was fragmentary; the involvement of the Modano Company in the conspiracy, as far as she could judge, was marginal. The Ukrainian Government had revealed that new viruses had recently been produced in an old lab and that the person suspected to be in charge had left the country leaving only a feeble trace: the possible use of the Modano Company for shipping.

Was Operation Bullfrog one step further in the investigation than at the beginning? Tamara doubted it. There were a number of issues CSIS should clarify. Did they know who worked in the secret lab, and more important than anything else, had he taken any of the potentially dangerous material with him? She suspected that CSIS had an affirmative answer to both questions. That's why it was vital to keep an eye on all the recipients of parcels shipped through the Modano Company.

Half an hour had passed when she spotted Justin coming toward the car, whistling.

"Don't turn your head and don't move yet," he said as he climbed into the car.

"Why?"

"You may not have seen Harry Pearson entering the building. He came in from the far side while I was there. He's now walking in this direction." He turned toward Tamara, hugged her and kissed her. He whispered, "Our mission was very fruitful. Got the name of the sender and the declared content of the package Harry Pearson has just picked up."

Chapter 24

Bergamo, Northern Italy
First week of July 2007

After a week of intense work, Boris Youkenoff needed a break — a break from Petri dishes and vials, a break from the nagging calls he kept receiving from Frank Milton and a break from the confining space in which he was forced to operate. Sightseeing would relax him and get him ready to manufacture the next batch of blackpox.

Satisfied with his decision, Boris drove to Bergamo Alta and parked his pick-up in one of the rare spots available. With a brisk walk he reached Piazza Vecchia where he admired the many buildings surrounding the square and the beautiful fountain with lions and tritons that attracted the curiosity of so many tourists. He proceeded to visit the nearby church of Santa Maria Maggiore, marvelling at how well the statues and other pieces of art from the distant 1400s had been preserved. Following a vociferous group of schoolboys and girls, he ascended to La Rocca to admire the view of the old city and the imposing far-away mountains.

Around noon he felt like taking a break from walking. He took the funicular to San Vigilio and entered the Bar Pizzeria Ristorante for a midday meal. Seated close to the large windows that took an entire side of the restaurant, he absorbed the peace that the view exuded. Hills alternated with short plains where mansions and clusters of dwellings seemed to find their natural place. Green was everywhere, in the woods, the lawns around the buildings, and the vineyards built up like stairs to fit the irregular terrain.

The fondue of local production was excellent and the little warm biscuits that came with it were exquisite. Boris Youkenoff enjoyed every bite of his meal, confident that many more were in store for him once the business with Frank was over. He savoured the last drop of Lacrima Christi that was in his glass and extracted a map of the region. Red dots marked the cities where a casino was located. He retrieved a pen from his coat pocket and measured the distance between Bergamo and each of the red dots. Venice, San Remo and Saint Vincent were far away, but Campione d'Italia, which hosted Europe's larger casino, was reachable within a couple hours of easy driving.

He dropped 40 euros onto the table and headed home.

Boris changed into formal attire, got 500 euros out of his piggybank and adjusted his red bowtie in front of the mirror located at the entrance. Sightseeing had relaxed him, but a bit of gambling would fire him up.

Just then, his phone rang. Sighing, he turned it on. As he suspected, it was Frank Milton.

"Need to speed up production," Frank said.

"I'm on time; I'm following the schedule we agreed on," Boris retorted.

The Blackpox Threat

"I know, but something came up that may endanger our operation. Manufacture the last batch of virus as quickly as you can."

"I want to know what the urgency is all about," Boris said, hoping to gain time.

"There's been a breach of security. Somebody got hold of some documents, and one person dropped out of sight."

"Oh, I see. By the way, how did the experiments with the Guinea pigs turn out? Did the new virus work as well as the old on the fruit bats?"

"Yes, yes. It did well. Got some frightful pictures, I can tell you. Boris, listen. Work as fast as you can."

"Wait, not so fast. One, what kind of documents? And two, what was the role of the person who cleared out?"

"Somebody stole a file where I kept a coded list of the experiments; nothing a stranger can understand. The person who took off — well, she was an absolute idiot. She was in charge of disposing of the dead Guinea pigs and broadcasting the blackmail messages once everything was ready. Only after that should she have cleared out. She panicked."

"Who is going to replace her?"

"I don't have anybody at the moment. Don't lose time talking, Boris. Get busy." He paused. "The vaccine, is it ready?"

"Of course."

"Send a small quantity that I can try on the pigs."

Boris hesitated. He wanted the full payment for the blackpox before shipping the vaccine. On the other hand, it might not be a bad idea to test it on the pigs.

"Okay," he said finally, and clicked off.

Boris threw his phone onto the upholstered settee that stood underneath the mirror. He undid his bowtie and dropped it over the phone. Work, work, work. If it wasn't for the anticipation of a life of luxury and pleasure he would tell Frank to go to hell.

He dragged his feet upstairs, where his temporary lab was located. His mood had radically changed and had taken a turn for the worse. Having missed a trip to a place of fun and pleasure was one reason, but there was another problem that had troubled him for quite some time.

The vaccine for the blackpox was not foolproof. When he had tested it on five fruit bats only two had recovered. He had never mentioned this fact to Frank. In the back of his mind was the nagging worry that they could be starting an epidemic that could not be controlled. Could they be among the victims?

Chapter 25

London, Ontario
Mid-July 2007

I should have expected it, Tamara murmured, disappointed. She had inserted the flash drive with Thomas Sarcin's directories into one of the Lenovo's USB ports and started to examine its contents. The first few directories were password-protected. She bit her lips as she often did when she was disappointed or scared. All the troubles she'd gone through to download his files had been a waste of time. She shivered at the memory of how scared she was when she had snuck into Thomas' office, and how shaky she was when she had taken off at high speed through his gate, then zigzagged through secondary roads to reach London, always afraid of being stopped by Thomas' men. She should have thought of the protection and avoided a lot of suffering. To add to her frustration, she had to admit that Thomas didn't look all that dangerous when she had lunch with him and Charles.

The Blackpox Threat

Tamara continued to click on one directory after another. As she scrolled down the list, she came across a file folder named *Down-Under*, which was not password-protected. It contained only two files. She opened the first one, *Hannibal*. It was a sequel of long paragraphs, interspaced by a blank line, in the same fashion that school assignments are formatted. It read:

Why do you have to be so judgmental? I accept you the way you are. It does not matter what you do, where you go, which friends you have. There is no right or wrong — these are definitions introduced by society to justify what the powerful want to do and what they don't want others to do. It is that simple.

Moral principles? A big laugh! Slavery was a way of life for centuries. Slaves were a commodity. Robbery? In ancient times, governments imposed tax even on people who would have to starve their families in order to pay them. The strong had the right of death or life over the weak...

And killing? Still today people genuflect in church reciting a creed of compassion and love — and then what do they do? They sit on a bench and sentence a person to death. They call that kind of homicide "making justice," because it fits their goals. Everybody likes to play God. So why shouldn't I?

Look at people — look how they rush to pray when they are in trouble. Even non-believers half-mumble prayers they hardly remember from when they were children. This act is nothing more than a helpless attempt to control God. Everybody wants power. There is nothing in life worth pursuing except the achievement of power — a lot of it. There is enormous satisfaction in controlling people, making them do what you want, seeing them afraid of defying you. And I will soon have so much power.

Tamara stopped reading and tried to recall if anything in that file could be connected with the protagonist of the movie *Hannibal*.

She didn't think so. She also excluded the Hannibal she knew from the readings on ancient civilizations. That Hannibal was a man of action, crossing waters and high mountains with an army and in the company of elephants; he was not a cheap philosopher. Probably the file had been so named for its extravagant contents. Without another thought, she closed it and opened the second file, *Old-Addresses*.

There were only 25 locations mentioned, and one referred to her parents' house.

Tamara jumped off her seat as if a monster had popped up out of her computer. She bit her lips so hard that she tasted blood.

Still mesmerized, she rose and looked for a tissue to clean up her lips. Slowly, she closed the file and put her Lenovo on Stand By.

****

"I won't come," Stan said firmly to Sophia. He walked around the Chevy Optra and stood near the trunk. He banged on it. "Open up, I'd like to get my bag."

Sophia popped her head out the window. "Stan, listen to me. We just have to go to the farm and back. It'll take only a couple of hours."

"But it isn't safe to be on the road. The police may be looking for us."

"And why? There was no news of Tamara's kidnapping." Stan had not moved, and Sophia gestured him to climb into her car. "Come on, Stan. I told you Frank promised me another $40,000. Forty-thousand! You can have half of it. Think. A full $20,000!" Sophia opened the passenger's door. "When Frank called me on my cell last night, he convinced me that there was no real danger. All we have to do is to get my CD where I stored the list of people I have to contact when the operation starts, and bury the Guinea pigs Frank had deposited in the barn yesterday. That's all. Frank thinks our operation can start as early as next week. Next week!"

His huge shoulders slumped and his head down, Stan moved to the front and entered the car.

"What about the red binder?" he asked. "Frank was going to search Tamara's house; did he manage to get it back?"

"No, but he said not to worry. The information he collected in that binder wasn't critical; it'd be almost impossible for anybody to deduct anything useful about our little scam." Sophia put the gear in drive. "For safety, I'm going to approach my property from the far end through the trails that cross the fields. It's already dark now. There will be nobody around when we arrive."

They drove in silence. The car swayed left and right as they tried to stay on the uneven trails that divided Tadlova's farm from the neighbours' properties. They parked in the little enclave between the silo and the barn.

"Can you handle the pigs?" Sophia asked.

"Yes. I know the ground. The light inside the barn is just enough to let me do the digging." He got out of the Chevy and then said to Sophia, "Hurry up with your chores. I don't feel at ease hanging around here, no matter what your dear friend Frank says."

Sophia walked to the house and entered from the back door, which she usually left unlocked. She turned on the light in the kitchen and left its door open to give her enough visibility to move around safely. She approached the desk where the computer was located and opened the first drawer. Here she kept that important CD that held a copy of the addresses she had gathered for Frank. She put it in her pocket and, following the contour of the wall, she reached the staircase. She climbed upstairs and walked into her bedroom. She couldn't see much, but she had no problems opening her closet. She palmed the clothes, trying to recognize what they were. She needed a few more slacks, a couple of tops, and a coat. She bent to feel around until she came across two pairs of sneakers. She gathered everything in her arms — she might need them in case she had to stay away more than the week Frank had anticipated. Cautiously she descended the staircase and turned off the light in the kitchen. For a change, she locked the back door and joined Stan.

"Still digging?" she asked.

"Well, hmm…yes."

"How come?" Stan didn't utter a word. "What happened?" Sophia demanded.

"I dug out a few of the old ones while I was burying the new ones." He shoved a couple scoops of soil into a hole.

"So?"

"So, so! Why do you ask stupid questions? I had to bury the old ones again!"

"Oh. Did you dig deep enough for the new batch? One time you didn't and the dogs pulled them out."

"Stop complaining or do the job yourself!"

"Okay, okay. By the way, where do you think my dogs are?"

"At the neighbour's for sure. She feeds them scraps from the table. They like them better than dog food."

"Hmm. I miss them," Sophia said in an undertone, and walked to the Chevy. "I'll wait for you in the car."

****

When Justin arrived home at night, he tried to sneak out of the common area. His father was having guests and he didn't feel comfortable making an entrance in his crumpled clothes. He hadn't crossed half the hallway, when he heard Michael Devry's voice.

"Justin, in here!"

Justin stopped in the doorway of the dining room. Professor Barbara Fattori and Mr. Karl McKenzie were savouring a dessert and sipping bubbling wine from crystal flutes.

"I didn't see you for almost a week," Michael said. "I started to worry."

Michael was casually dressed in a green and blue chequered shirt; Barbara was wearing a shapeless grey top made more sombre by a double set of black beads. McKenzie looked classy in a long-sleeved shirt of raw silk in a musky green colour.

"I'm not presentable." Justin tried to excuse himself.

"Come on, join us!" Barbara said cordially. "You look great to me." She gave him a friendly smile.

"This dessert is fabulous," McKenzie said. He moved the chair closest to him from underneath the table and gestured Justin to sit. He pointed to the tray in the middle of the table. "Try the pastry."

Justin willingly complied.

"We were through talking business if that is what you were worried about," Michael said, and rose. "I'm going to make some coffee."

"Your father tells me that you're a communications nerd — all self-taught," McKenzie said.

Justin hiked his shoulders. "I like to play with gadgets, that's all." He savoured a mini puff and then turned to Barbara. "Before I forget I'd like to tell you that your latest piece, published in the *University Gazette*, was very interesting and easy to read. It made the reader understand the static beauty of Pier de la Francesca's paintings." He turned to McKenzie. "I don't have my father's aesthetic talent, so I appreciate when an expert takes the trouble of explaining the artistic significance of a painter in lay terms."

Barbara looked pleased. "Thanks. Sometimes I write two versions on the same topic, one for a scholarly magazine, the other for the public."

Michael came back with the glass container of the coffee maker and set it on a metal holder. "Coffee everybody?"

"A small cup, please," Barbara said.

"No, thank you." McKenzie said. He looked at his wristwatch. "Time for me to go." He deposited the white napkin on the table and rose. "Thank you for the wonderful supper, Michael. I'll see you when you get that Delft pottery we talked about."

"Sure enough. They should be available in a week or so. Since you're in a hurry, one of us will go and get them. I'll call you, then."

McKenzie shook hands with Barbara and Justin, and waved Michael away from seeing him to the door.

Justin took the coffee cup Michael handed him and stretched his arm to reach an éclair.

"So what have you been doing?" Barbara asked Justin.

"Helping a friend of mine." Justin said. "She had some problems."

Michael laughed. "He has a new girl."

"Oh, that's the age," Barbara said. She drank her coffee in silence. "I should be going, too. I still have to put my lecture in PowerPoint format. Sometimes it takes me more time to set up the slides than preparing the content of my presentation." She sighed. "I envy the new generation. They grow up surrounded by technology and master all those computer utilities with ease. Not to mention the jargon!"

"Very true." Michael rose. "I'll see you out."

Justin said goodbye to Barbara and then walked to the kitchen to return with a plate full of what he guessed was Beef Stroganoff.

The Blackpox Threat

He sat at the dinner table and ate one forkful after the other, realizing that he was famished.

He had almost cleared his entire plate when Michael returned.

"A long goodbye," said Justin, giving his father a teasing look.

"Don't start that music again. Barbara and I have business together."

"I know. I know. You don't have to explain or justify. Besides, I like her."

Michael rolled his eyes. "Stop that nonsense. Oh, by the way, your friend at the police station called twice. It was urgent, he said. You better call him back."

"Thanks, dad." Justin rose and hurried to his bedroom. He placed a call to Bill Hartwart.

"The troubles you're causing me — oh man!" were Bill's first words. "They asked me a ton of questions about that mug and its fingerprints."

"And?"

"I said what you told me — and I hope it was the truth — that the mug's owner had asked you for a lift after the costume party aboard the floating house. That she left it in your car and you didn't think anything of it until, later on, you realized that it could be important evidence."

"Did it work?"

"After I repeated it for the third time, they *almost* believed me. But there're two problems." Bill paused and cleared his throat. "First, they want to talk to you and — listen to this one — the object in question has been sequestered by the RCMP. They warned me to stay away from anything connected to that mug. I am not even supposed to know that *there was* such a thing."

"I see. Thank you, Bill."

"Yeah. But don't come up with anything else. First those

mysterious documents I had to rescue from the trunk of a Subaru, then this mug business. Leave me out of your troubles. You tread dangerously, my friend."

Chapter 26

There was no solace in anything Tamara tried to do. When the memory of her parents' murder surfaced there was nothing that could put her mind at rest. She experienced a mixture of physical and emotional reactions, over which, she knew from experience, she had little control. It was pure and simple torture.

What was the reason Thomas Sarcin had the address of their old house? The property had been sold a year after the murder. It's true that the file Thomas had on his computer was listed under the directory *Old-Addresses*, but still, what was the reason for it being there?

She paced back and forth in the living room, only once in a while glancing at her fish. There was no way she would leave that issue unresolved. She placed a call to Brad.

"Anything new?" Brad asked anxiously.

"Yes and no. I told you of Thomas Sarcin, right? You said you're going to do some checking. Did you?"

"I have a file on him. Let me get it." He let her wait on the line for more than five minutes. "Not much in it, Tamara. His family owned a firm that built safes; Thomas sold it out after a bitter litigation with a client that claimed foul play."

"Was he at fault?"

"We don't know. It was settled out of court. The family had money; Thomas managed the company after his father died. There's nothing that points to any connection with our present problems, Tamara."

"I see. Anything else on the man?"

"Not really. He travelled a lot. Why are you interested?"

"Nothing in particular." She couldn't tell him what she had found in Thomas' files because she had never mentioned that she had downloaded them. "I met him again. He's a good friend of Charles Modano." She paused. "I thought it'd be good to know more about him. Bye, Brad." She clicked off. Clearly Brad was not aware of any link between Sarcin and her parents' death. But then, why was that address in Thomas' computer?

A glance at the grandfather clock made her realize that she was running late. She mentally made a point about the situation. So far there wasn't anything suspicious about the behaviours of Charles Modano, Michael Devry or Dianne Templeton; likewise for Stephanie Demoins. She had some suspicions about Thomas Sarcin — only faint shadows so far. Harry Pearson and Frank Milton were definitely involved in illegal activities and, of course, Sophia Tadlova and her goon, Stan, had committed a crime. Not much progress for weeks of work, Tamara concluded.

The bell rang. It was Justin, coming to pick her up for the meeting with the CSIS officials in Toronto.

****

The Blackpox Threat

They were early, so Tamara and Justin took a leisurely walk along Front St. West. They stopped by the CBC building, appreciating the originality of honouring Glen Gould with a statue set in front of the entrance. They crossed the street to head toward a tower of hexagonal shape.

Coming from behind, Brad Wilson tapped on their shoulders. "Come with me," he said, and led them inside the building and up to the fourth floor. Once on the landing, an agent asked Justin to follow him while Brad ushered Tamara into a conference room.

Tamara blinked and blinked until she adjusted to the bright light of the room. On one counter was a coffee maker, on another lay computer equipment. Standing close to the oval table was a man in his 30s, who quickly moved to greet her.

"Dale Romano," he said, and gave her hand a firm shake. He wore a dark grey suit and a polka-dot grey and black tie. "Please sit down."

Tamara complied, telling herself not to be intimidated by the formal atmosphere.

"You know Brad Wilson, right? Together we're going to give you a brief overview of our operation."

"Another briefing?" Tamara asked.

"Yes. It's important, Tamara. This is a delicate operation; an amateur can blow it easily, without even knowing it."

Reluctantly, Tamara accepted the explanation.

Dale Romano began talking in a melodic tone, pronouncing each word clearly. With each sentence being the logical follow-up of the previous one, he reviewed Operation Bullfrog. When he was finished, he invited Brad Wilson to continue. Brad gave the usual pep talk on the important role Tamara Smith had in the operation.

Tamara listened patiently. After a moment of absolute silence Romano said, "So we're all done, right?" He rose and added, "Glad to have met you, Ms. Smith. Now I have to go back to work."

Tamara didn't lose any time. "Please sit down, Chief. We need to discuss a few issues, and I want answers." She paused for effect. "And I want answers from you, Mr. Romano, since you're the one in charge."

"What?" Romano gave a quizzical look to Brad, who opened his arms in a clear sign of resignation.

"First, I need CSIS to cover my expenses. Regularly." She took a void cheque from her purse and slid it across the table. "Please deposit $2,000 every month in my bank account. Gas is expensive; I had to pay for a new car door in the course of this operation. I use my own car and computer. They cost money. Then there's hydro and other incidentals; also, I'd like to buy a Bowflex since I have little time to go to the gym." She paused and wiggled in her chair to sit comfortably. "Second, I want the file CSIS has on my parents' murder, with all the details collected over the years."

"Tamara," Brad interrupted with an indulgent tone. "You shouldn't be distracted from Operation Bullfrog. Once the danger is over we can focus on the old stuff."

Tamara dismissed the issue. "Not negotiable. Third, I want answers — satisfactory answers, I mean, to my questions. I have several, but there are four that can't wait. Question one: why don't you charge and arrest Sophia Tadlova? Number two: why don't you question Harry Pearson about the shipment he picked up at customs? Number three: why don't you search the spa and the adjacent building? Number four: how many people are involved in this operation?" There was an embarrassing silence, so Tamara pushed ahead. "Mr. Romano, I'm asking *you*."

Romano sat down, his demeanour spreading a sense of calm around the table.

"As you probably know," he said, "we received, some time

ago, fragmented information from what was an isolated part of the Ukrainian Mountains. Somebody had been experimenting with smallpox and ebola. We suspect they were trying to revive an old warfare project aimed at creating a combined virus more dangerous than each of the two separately. Even today we don't know if that is true. As Brad told you, the only clue we had pointed to the Modano Company. It was connected with one or more shipments that may have originated from the secret lab located in the mountains. We're in contact with the World Health Organization and other laboratories, which are familiar with the apparatus needed to create this deadly virus, commonly referred to as *blackpox*. There are reasons to believe that the varieties that can be created are very infectious but have short life spans." He stopped and asked, "Can you follow me?"

"Yes. Brad already briefed me on the subject."

"So you know that we're very worried. The situation is serious."

"I know that too, but that doesn't answer my questions."

Romano pushed his eyeglasses up his nose. "Brad, who until recently has been the brain behind this operation, suggested that it was better not to alarm our suspects. They could take off and put somebody else in charge. In other words, Harry Pearson could be an intermediary, easily replaced once he's caught." For a split second Romano seemed tired. He tagged at his tie knot and then continued, "That answers two of your questions. No official action at the moment. We have a court order to search the spa and the adjacent building, but we wouldn't do anything of the sort at the moment. We prefer to wait for their next move. Now I come to question number one. We're actively looking for Sophia Tadlova, hoping that she can lead us to the place where this new blackpox is manufactured, or simply handled. We're doing so as surreptitiously as possible." He paused again and then continued. "We've alerted the Italian Government and told them that we suspect that illegal substances are being shipped to our country via the Modano Company. We didn't want to say anything more. Finally, there are three dozen members from CSIS, RCMP, Public Safety and CSE, all working together, even if in different places. They form a tactical task unit under my command." Romano rose and poured himself a cup of coffee from the thermos that lay on the counter.

"CSE?" Tamara asked. "What does it do?"

"The Communication Security Establishment keeps an eye on telephone, cable and satellite communications to detect if the messages being transmitted deal with warfare." He sipped on his coffee. "Harry Pearson's phones, at home and at the spa, are tapped. The same for Sophia Tadlova's phone. Her email messages are relayed directly to us, even if I seriously doubt that she'd use any of these communication devices. After all, she's on the run. At this very same moment we're conducting a search of her premises." He finished his coffee. "Oh, I forgot. One member from the CBRNE, the Chemical, Biological, Radiological & Nuclear Explosives Resource, will join our tactical task unit tomorrow." He looked at Tamara and asked, "Coffee?"

"Yes, with a bit of cream, please."

For a moment the only noise in the room was the trickling of liquid. Romano handed the mug to Tamara and sat beside her.

"Brad, did you tell her about the newly formed detachment in London?" Romano asked.

"Well, no. I didn't have the time." Brad quickly extracted from his pocket a container of aspirin and ingested four caplets.

Romano seemed surprised. "It was decided yesterday. Four people of the task unit, under Brad Wilson's supervision, will be operating from a house on Vanneck Road, just outside the city limits of London. It's an old house, a bit far away from the road, with a row of tall poplars at the front, and a big barn at the back." He sipped his coffee. "You're familiar with the place, right? It's where Duncan Brown holds his pep talks and demonstrations on surveillance techniques." He paused. "So what was I saying? Oh, yes…the detachment…it has two main tasks: the stakeout of the spa and the adjacent buildings, and the selection of a hospital or part of it; this would be sealed off temporarily and equipped to handle special infectious diseases, in a style similar to that adopted for SARS a few years ago." Romano addressed Tamara, "Satisfied so far?"

"Yes." Tamara breathed with relief and smiled at Romano. "But I still have one quick question."

"And what would that be?"

"Did you get anything out of the red folder I sequestered from the spa?"

"The purchases listed in that folder deal with containers and chemicals often used in the cosmetic industry. Nothing suspicious about that. Then there are meetings and shipments taking place. No clues from where or to where or with whom. The only suspicious item is the mentioning of Guinea pigs. Associated with that kind of lab, this means illegal experimentation on animals. That too, in itself, wouldn't mean much, but in the context of our operation it takes great significance."

"Great significance?"

"Yes. If they're involved in producing blackpox of some variety it means one of two things; they're experimenting on the toxicity of their invention, or they're experimenting on a vaccine. Of course, we hope the first would be the case, which will give us time to stop them before they go public and blackmail the world."

"I see." Tamara drank her coffee in big gulps. "I have a

confession to make." She rummaged in her purse and put a flash drive on the table. "Justin and I went to Sophia's house. Before Sophia's two Dobermans chased us out, we managed to copy the only file we could find on her computer. It's a list of addresses, some of which refer to well-known people." She slid the flash drive on the table.

"You didn't tell me." Brad scowled.

Tamara looked defiantly at him. "It was kind of personal, Brad. After all, the woman kidnapped me and kept me at gunpoint. I hoped to find out why."

"No more of that!" Brad said. "I have to know everything you do, and where you go."

"You have to understand my position. I've been kept pretty much in the dark. And often, when I need advice, I get your voicemail." She paused for a moment. "Here is some evidence that Milton and Tadlova had some kind of business together."

Brad jumped up and quickly grabbed what Tamara had thrown onto the table. They were the copies of the cheques issued to Sophia Tadlova and signed by Frank Milton. "I had my digital camera with me and took pictures of the cheques' carbon copies."

"Now! Is that cooperation?" Brad shot a dirty look at Tamara.

Romano put up his hands in the silent yet effective order of stopping the bickering. "The last couple of weeks I've worked my people pretty hard. I'm sorry we failed you, Tamara. I'll schedule a weekly meeting in the new office in London. Be there. Satisfied?" Tamara assented. "We've been very active, Tamara, and most of the leads we're following at present are thanks to you." He put a hand on her shoulder. "Of all the people involved you're the key person; the one in the position to point us to the mastermind of this dangerous plot."

Chapter 27

The night was clear and the road deserted. Justin was asleep, his head reclined on one side. Tamara, at the wheel, pondered on the recommendations of CSIS. They didn't want Justin involved any further as his father was one of the people who used the Modano Company for shipping. Tamara sighed. It would be difficult to continue seeing Justin and keep secrets from him.

However, things were definitely moving forward; Brad would soon send her a copy of the file with the results of the investigation into her parents' murder. Overall the meeting had cleared out much uncertainty. The only thing that still puzzled Tamara was the absence of Heather Motta. At the gathering held in Fanshawe Park, Motta had mentioned an internal inquiry. Had she been demoted or excluded from Operation Bullfrog? And, if so, why?

A cruiser, all lights and sirens, appeared on the left lane, brusquely interrupting Tamara musings and Justin's placid sleep. Justin turned his head and looked in the side-view mirror. A second police car was rushing in.

"An accident, probably," he said.

"I hope not. It'd delay us considerably, and I'm anxious to dive into my bed."

"Want me to drive?"

"Well, let's see what's ahead. If we have to stop within a few miles, you take the wheel." Tamara turned toward Justin. "So, what did you do while I was in the meeting?"

"Me? Nothing. I just followed the agent you saw on the landing. He took me to a room with a lot of magazines and newspapers from all over the world and let me wait; then another agent — he didn't introduce himself either — came in and asked me a lot of questions about the work I do for my father and the circumstances in which I met you. Finally he made me an offer."

"An interesting offer?"

"No! They'd like me to follow a course on civil protection. To start with, I'm not interested. Second, I'd have to stay in Ottawa for five weeks, and I don't like to be away from home more than a week or two." The traffic came to a crawl and soon progressed in spurts. "It looks like they wanted me out of the way."

Tamara suspected that that could be indeed the purpose. If Justin decided to go to Ottawa she would miss him; on the other hand she wouldn't have to keep him distant. She had no doubts Justin was on the level; she thought the same of his father. Michael Devry had not shipped anything for the last two months. Of all the so-called suspects, he was the only one who used the Modano Company for what he needed, that is, the careful packing and shipment of art objects. When she had pointed out that fact at the CSIS meeting, the answer had been that the most unsuspected persons are often cleverly manipulated by criminals and used as smoke screens. Michael Devry could be one. That argument had silenced Tamara. Either way she was going to lose a person in whom she could confide and who had the talent of cheering her up. She emitted a long sigh.

"Something wrong?" Justin asked.

"Not really. What bothered me at the meeting was the fact that there was no proper introduction of the members. Just the name, no title, no mention of expertise. The same had been before when I made a search about Brad Wilson." She paused. "Once I tried to find out what degree Brad Wilson had, since he was very secretive about his rank. When I Googled, I got nowhere. Now what's the expertise of Dale Romano and our old friend Major Heather Motta?"

"In my interview they referred to Romano as *Doctor* Romano," Justin said. "For Heather Motta, I can find out what her training was through my friend Bill."

Silence followed as the traffic stopped; in front of them a myriad of red backlights punctuated both lanes.

"Romano is a doctor, you said? He's quite young — early 30s I'd say." Tamara reflected for a few moments. "Could he have a doctorate in criminology?"

"It'd make sense."

"When I snooped around to find Brad Wilson's qualifications, I discovered that you can't get hold of a list of graduates through university records on their Web sites. I came across the names of graduates in emergency medicine and high-energy-particles physics from the University of Toronto because they were posted directly by those two groups. Otherwise, zilch."

"Let me think," Justin said. "If Romano has a doctorate in criminology, he probably got his degree in the States or at the University of Toronto."

"Good thinking," Tamara said. "But that takes me nowhere."

"Not true. My father is a U of T graduate; he can query the

alumni's database. Actually, I'm the one who takes care of all his computer interactions. I'll check it sometime tomorrow."

"Great," Tamara said, and yawned. "I'm going to let you drive." Tamara and Justin exchanged places. "I'll take a nap," said Tamara.

"You better rest well, since tomorrow morning we're due for the big match."

"Match?" Tamara asked as she reclined the seat and stretched out in it.

"Don't tell me you forgot about the tennis match. Charles and Stephanie against the two of us. We play for a dinner at the Armouries, remember?"

"Oh, that!"

"Are you any good? Charles is, you know, and Stephanie plays twice a week. It's her way to keep in shape, she says."

"I told you I am. I haven't played for a while, though."

"When was the last time you played?"

Tamara hesitated and then said, "Last year of high school." She pulled her sweater up to her neck and fell asleep.

****

After a three-hour match, all tired and dowsed in perspiration, Tamara, Justin, Stephanie and Charles grouped under the veranda of Charles' home to have a drink. Colourful lawn furniture and flowerpots added a cheerful look to the backyard, in contrast with the severe look of Charles' Tudor-style house.

Tamara had banked on her excellent physical condition and past expertise to rake in a win. However, Charles and Stephanie had played often together and compensated in strategy what they lacked in strength. At the beginning her serve had been weak and, therefore, an easy target for a fast return on the baseline. Justin was a good player and definitely a gentle soul. He never said a word about any of her bad shots. Fortunately, as the game progressed her serve became stronger and, with that, her confidence increased. Never give up, she told herself. Finally when the score of the first set was 17-16, it was her turn to serve. With the game at 30-love, she read expectation on Justin's face. She didn't deceive him. With two aces she sealed the set in victory.

Relaxed in a lounge chair Justin shook his head. "When we started, I thought my partner was a beginner," he said. "For a while, my only concerns were losing with dignity and not hurting her feelings." He raised his beer in Tamara's direction and said, "What a tiger! I will never pick a fight with you."

Tamara laughed softly. "I was the school champion for five years. I forgot a few things, however, that even a new racket can be a handicap. And that one has to get to know her partner before engaging in a match that serious!"

"I enjoyed it. I don't remember having had so much fun in years," said Stephanie. "Nobody slacked off; everybody fought as if it was a question of life or death. Never played such a long set! We should do it regularly, folks."

Charles appeared with a tray of sandwiches.

"We can set it up right here: every other Saturday morning, except when I have an auction," he said. "All in favour?"

"I'm game," Tamara said, followed by the others. "It's been a long time since I felt so good."

Her cell rang, breaking the relaxed atmosphere that had reigned until then. She quickly moved away from the crowd.

It was the superintendent of her condominium.

"A special courier just came in and left an envelope for you, Ms. Smith," he said. "It's Saturday, so it isn't one of the usual deliveries. I thought it could be important."

"Thank you," Tamara said. "I'll be right over."

She rejoined the others and, making sure her body language wouldn't betray her anxiety, she turned toward Charles and said, "An old friend of mine just came to town. I should be leaving."

****

Once inside her condo Tamara dropped her sports bag on the bearskin that covered the entrance floor and rushed into the living room. She sat on the armchair closest to her and ripped open the envelope she had just received. It was from the Ukrainian Embassy and contained only one letter. It was hand-written. It read:

Dear Tamara,

If you receive this letter it means that the recent threat made to my life (stop passing information to the Canadian Government or else...) was for real. It also means that you are in double danger; first, because you belong to the company that is involved in the suspicious shipments of the dangerous biochemical, and, second, because somebody at CSIS may be playing a double game.

I spent an evening with Major Heather Motta — a delightful person, by the way. She was puzzled by the enormous time that occurred between the day I passed on the information about the findings in the Carpathian Mountains and the day those findings were given serious consideration. After she had pointed out that incomprehensible delay at a CSIS meeting, there was a reshuffling of duties and people, and a new boss, a one Dale Romano, was put in charge. The first thing Romano did was to order an internal inquest, which obviously will take some time to conclude.

I am still a crucial player, since I regularly channel the information coming from my government to the Canadian

The Blackpox Threat

Government as soon as it becomes available. A team of experts is at work in the now-famous cave to examine even the most miniscule remnant of what is estimated to have been an active lab until a few months ago. From the corpses of the animals used for testing to the residuals left in vials and containers or discarded items, the experts hope to determine the stage at which the dangerous biological component being created was before the person or persons who worked on it took off.

If I am no more, look over your shoulders.

You are my heir, Tamara, as you were the daughter I wished to have and had not. In due time, the embassy will notify you of my will. There is not much, but I know you will enjoy my cottage on the shores of Lake Huron.

Take care and be very careful.

Love,

Vassilli Petrovic.

Her hands shaking, Tamara put the letter back in its envelope. Then the words Vassilli had pronounced in the berth of the Tortuga came to her. *Sorry, Tamara. So sorry.* And then the warning he had never finished, which started with, *Don't tr* —. He had probably recognized his killer and tried to warn her.

Her heart was pounding as her anxiety mounted. What should she do? Vassilli had been eliminated; was she next? If they could find Vassilli's assassin, there would be a chance to know where the danger came from. The threat of spreading the blackpox virus was part of a conspiracy that involved several individuals. Was it possible that a CSIS member was sabotaging Operation Bullfrog? Clearly the stakes were high. People would pay millions to avoid being infected and, once the disease spread, they would pay even more for a vaccine — if there was one.

Chapter 28

Bergamo, Northern Italy—
Mid-July 2007

Sciopero was a word Boris Youkenoff had to look up in his pocket dictionary. It was written in capital letters on the glass door of the Modano shop. It meant strike and, in fact, the shop was closed. Disappointed, he wandered about town, thinking what to do next. He was anxious to ship the batches of blackpox that Frank Milton badly wanted. He calculated that the virus would be active from two to three weeks; the culture he had used could deteriorate after that, even if he had no time to make exhaustive tests on the matter.

Not knowing what to do, Boris entered a coffee shop and ordered a latte with a croissant.

The customer seated at the table next to him was hunched over a phone book with yellow pages. He seemed to have found what he was looking for, because he transcribed something on a piece of paper and left.

Boris rose and picked up the phone book. He leafed through it and stopped at a page that carried the word *spedizioni*. There was a UPS listing. He didn't wait for his order of latte. He gathered his five packages containing "antique vases with floral arrangements" and strode out. He hailed a cab and ordered the driver to go to Orio al Serio, Aereporto Road.

The driver hesitated. "It's UPS, right? Not open. The unions — we have many — have declared general strike. Not everybody agrees, but most companies remain closed."

Boris made a sign to proceed. It was worth trying.

When he arrived at the shipment centre there was a picket in front of it, with a dozen people talking and gesturing agitatedly. He entered the building and lined up at the only open counter. Half an hour later he was given a sheaf of papers to fill in. With relief he noticed that they were similar to the ones he had completed at the Modano Company. Finally he managed to unload his packages, even if at the cost of 725 euros. They would travel in a temperature-controlled compartment.

As soon as he was back to his living quarters, he placed a call to Frank Milton. There was no answer. Glad to have shipped his precious cargo and having avoided speaking with Frank, Boris felt like celebrating. He changed into a formal suit, got 500 euros from his piggybank and climbed into his pickup. In an hour and half he would be in Campione d'Italia, the four-kilometre-square enclave carved out of Swiss territory.

****

Boris approached the Nuovo Casinò di Campione slowly, observing with curiosity the massive construction that extended upwards in bulky vertical blocks. He parked his truck in the underground garage and took the elevator, thus reaching the casino's entrance. As he neared the counter, a woman in dark uniform asked him for his ID. Boris looked around, uncertain. He wasn't fond of showing his passport to anybody. The rows of slot machines that lay behind the glass wall, however, were too tempting to make him overly concerned with bureaucracy. He showed his ID and let the woman take his picture. He then proceeded toward the semi-dark room where only a handful of people were gambling. He chose a place where he could play for only two cents at a time and introduced a 10-euro bill. An hour later, tired of losing, he took the escalator up and went to the refreshments counter. He got a vodka, and attempted to engage the barman in conversation. Boris wanted to know why the third floor, which housed the French Games, was closed. Chemin de Fer was the game that excited him the most.

"Not enough patrons," was the laconic answer.

He received the same answer when he inquired why the restaurant wasn't open. Boris looked at his watch. Obviously, midday was not the time professional gamblers preferred. He moved to a table with Caribbean Poker and began playing. The game was not his favourite, but he was good at it. A few hours later, he had 85 more euros in his pocket than he'd had when he arrived.

His first contact with the casino had definitely been positive. Once the operation with Frank was over, he wouldn't mind spending a few enjoyable hours here.

It was night when he decided to return home. He then remembered he should call Frank. He freed his cell from the leather belt and opened it. There were no bars. He went to the casino's main desk and scribbled Frank's number on a post-it. Without saying a word, he deposited a five-euro bill on the desk. The employee assented, pocketed the money and dialled the number for him. There was no answer. Not to worry, Boris thought. UPS assured him that they would deliver the merchandise directly to the spa.

Chapter 29

Two hours after she had opened Vassilli's letter with his farewell message, Tamara was still shaking. She felt trapped, isolated, with no place to go, nobody to talk to. Her parents had been killed 13 years ago, and the last proven friend she had on earth, Vassilli, had succumbed to a deadly conspiracy. She was involved in an operation that could hide a traitor, a person working on both sides and ready to become a mass murderer for the ancient evils of control and greed. She had compiled, in her mind, a list of people, each now more suspicious than before. What about Justin? Was he involved, too? Maybe his father was one of the main players and had carefully manoeuvred around Justin so that his son could get close to her. Maybe the kidnapping had been a show orchestrated by Michael Devry to make Justin a hero in her eyes. Father and son were unusually close. Maybe there was a reason for that, and it wasn't love.

The internal inquest that Heather Motta and Vassilli had both mentioned, even if in different circumstances, took a menacing consistency. She sighed.

Carrying her cup, Tamara walked into the kitchen and poured the cold coffee into the sink. Slowly, she opened the fridge and looked inside. Except for milk, orange juice, a head of lettuce and bread, there was nothing. She needed to keep up her strength if she wanted to defeat her adversaries. She should increase her physical activity. She should start with devising little traps to test the sincerity of the people around her. She should dig into their turf.

Information is power.

She would check her email and then go out for a good meal. She sat in front of her Lenovo. There was a message from Justin; its subject was: "Bingo!"

It read,

Hi Tamara: I got lucky with the search. Dale Romano has a Bachelor of Science in Biology and a Ph. D. in criminology, as you conjectured. He graduated under the supervision of Prof. Anthony N. Dobb (University of Toronto) with a thesis entitled How to Fight Bioterrorism. Heather Motta is an OPP officer, a Sergeant Major, but he didn't want to dig any further. I suspect Bill is mad at me. He had some problems with the story of the mug we took from Sophia's house.

Love, Justin.

So Dale Romano was the right man in the right position. He knew about biochemicals and how to counteract their use for criminal purposes. Was it possible he knew too much? Tamara pondered the idea for a moment, but then dismissed the suspect. Romano was too much in the spotlight, she thought. If there was a double-crosser, that person had to be somebody high enough in the ranks to have clearance, and therefore capable of grasping what was going on, but low enough that his actions would not be rigidly scrutinized or monitored.

The Blackpox Threat

Tamara deleted the message, grabbed her purse and left the house.

The first stop was at the Bertoldi Trattoria on Richmond Street. It was 5:30 in the afternoon and the place was almost deserted. Right away she was served a basket of fresh bread, bread sticks and an aromatic dip based in olive oil. She savoured two slices of bread as she looked at the menu. The pasta with a sauce of shrimps and octopus made her drool in anticipation. She ordered it and declined the offer of any of the drinks the waitress observantly listed. As she waited, she tried to define a plan of action. She was curious to find out if the spa was already under surveillance, but even getting close to that building could be dangerous. It would also be interesting to discover a bit more about Sophia Tadlova. A talk with her neighbours could be harmless, yet deeply enlightening.

Her entrée arrived and she enjoyed every forkful of it. She accepted a second cup of coffee but declined the offer of a dessert. A feeling of some urgency was dribbling inside her. She quickly asked for the bill, paid cash and left.

She drove by the Tadlova farm, located on Meadows Road, taking in the environment. When she had been there the two times before, it had been dark and she had not noticed that two farms surrounded Tadlova's, one at a distance of about two-hundred metres, the other by at least half a kilometre. Tamara made a U-turn and stopped at the farmhouse closest to Sophia's. This was a two-storey building, with vinyl siding on the upper part and yellow bricks on the lower part. The garage was detached from the house, and the roof was in urgent need of repairs.

Tamara rang the bell and waited.

An older woman appeared, a shawl on her shoulders even though the air was pleasantly warm.

"Yes?" she asked.

"I was told that the farm close to yours is for sale," Tamara said, pointing to Tadlova's.

"Oh, I don't know about it, but it'd be a grace of God if that awful lady clears out. Her dogs run free all the time. She doesn't feed them well, so they're always around, looking for food. They go into the garbage. A mess, I tell you."

"Oh, I see." Tamara gained some time, thinking about the next question. "Did you see her recently?

"No. I think she's away."

"Do you know who takes care of the place?"

"Nobody."

Tamara had exhausted the set of questions she could ask without raising suspicion. "Thanks, Mrs.?"

"Bev Roland. You can try the Rossiters, down the road. They may know more."

Tamara thanked her again and went back to her car.

The farmland around the Rossiters' house was cultivated in neat rows of corn for a number of acres. Voices came from the back of the house, and Tamara hesitated to ring the bell. Finally she decided to go ahead with it. After all she had come to collect information.

"Come in; it's open," a male voice said.

Tamara took a few steps into a large room that was partially kitchen and partially living room.

A man in his 50s came to meet her. He wore a pair of green coveralls and working boots. He had a worried look painted on his face.

"Sorry to call you on a Saturday evening, but my wife and I didn't know what to do with the dogs," he said. "They behaved strange all day, and now they look sick. Come, come and see."

Tamara didn't move.

"What's the problem?" the man asked.

"I'm not here for the dogs," Tamara said. "I was just inquiring about the farm next to you. They told me it was for sale."

"Oh, you are not from the Humane Society?"

"No. Sorry." Tamara was ready to leave when a woman joined them.

Much younger than the man, she was dressed in a long cotton outfit held in place by two shoulder straps. Her short curly hair, golden brown, framed her oval face.

"Hi, come in," she said in a soft voice.

"She is not from the Humane Society," the man said to her. "I'll go call the Health Department." He walked out of the room.

Tamara addressed the woman. "I see that you and your husband are very busy. I'm interested in buying a farm in this area, if one becomes available. That's why I dropped by." She gave the woman a big smile. "I won't trouble you any longer." She said goodbye and quickened her steps toward her Subaru.

Once at home, Tamara called it a day. She hid Vassilli's letter under her mattress and went to bed.

Chapter 30

The following day Tamara would have liked to doze off in bed until noon, but the doorbell rang inexorably at 9:30. As she expected, it was Duncan Brown, the surveillance specialist who had coached her on surveillance techniques. He was supposed to install a security system in her house. Yesterday she had given him the code to enter the compound.

Duncan kicked in a heavy metal suitcase, fighting with the bearskin that covered the floor. He went back to his Hyundai and returned with a number of small boxes, loose gadgets and wires. A few fell onto the floor and he rapidly picked them up. Finally he closed the door behind him and greeted Tamara, still in her robe.

"Good morning, Ms. Smith," he said, looking at her through his metal-rimmed glasses. "I understand you went up in rank. I was told to secure your house with the latest system available. Immediately. So here I am, working on Sunday." He looked at her figure with appreciation. "I was ordered by the man himself."

"The man himself?"

"Doctor Dale Romano."

"Oh, good." Tamara ignored his ironic tone and the implication of his words. "Then you have an excellent reason to do a perfect job."

Without another exchange of words she grabbed the *Time Magazine* from the basket in the hallway and retired to her bedroom.

She showered and slipped on a pair of old jeans and a sleeveless top. She doubled up the pillows and stretched on the bed. She had just finished reading the main article when the house phone rang. It was Catherine Ferreiro. After she had moved to London, Tamara had not seen her anymore; they had just communicated by phone or email.

"Nice to hear from you," Tamara said.

"You'll soon see me, if you come to the gate and let me in!"

"Are you here?"

"In person. I came down to deliver some hors d'oeuvres for a party. It was a late order and my brother worked all night to meet the deadline. I already dropped it off and thought I'd stop to see how you're doing."

"Great. I'll come to the gate right away." In the small stretch Tamara had to walk to reach the entrance of the compound she tried to figure out how to explain the presence of a person working in her house on a Sunday morning. Catherine was a good soul, but curious as a groundhog.

The hugging and kissing and the exchange of the latest news regarding Catherine's family took a good half-hour, during which Duncan kept out of sight, working quietly on a sensory device for the door that opened onto the kitchen from the garage.

Comfortably seated on the leather couch, Tamara and Catherine sipped an herbal tea. Tamara hadn't been able to think of a credible fib to explain the situation as Catherine, who was expecting, kept describing the preparations for the baby's arrival.

Then Duncan appeared on the threshold of the glass partition.

"I need to wire the windows," he said, ignoring Catherine. He dropped some equipment on the floor and began working.

"Who is he?" Catherine asked, keeping her voice low.

"Oh, just a man from the security company," Tamara said with nonchalance.

"Security? In a gated place?"

"Well, there was a break-in. Sometimes I receive clients of the Modano Company and Charles suggested I show off some pieces of his collection." She pointed to the Louis XV console opposite them. "That's the one I have here now, together with those two winter scenes above it. They're one of the reasons I'm installing a security system."

"But it must cost a fortune," Catherine said.

Tamara laughed inwardly. She had an occasion to get even with Duncan. "My employer pays for it," she said aloud. She ignored the dirty look Duncan shot her.

"Oh, I see." The grandfather clock tolled 11. "Maybe I should be going," Catherine rose. "Make a point to come to Toronto soon. I miss you." She kissed Tamara and headed for the door.

Tamara saw her leaving and then shouted to Duncan, "When will you be finished?"

"In a couple of hours."

"Great. I'm going jogging inside the compound. Be back by then to test the system."

****

Tamara had planned to spend a relaxing afternoon with a good book in her hands when the bell rang. She looked at the closed-circuit TV that gave her ample view of the road in front of her door. Impatiently shifting his weight left and right was Justin. He wore a pair of khaki shorts, a black shirt with the insignia of the Raptors and a matching cap.

She opened the door feeling ambivalent about Justin, as usual. He was a nice alternative to any book, no matter how interesting the reading was; on the other hand Justin could severely endanger Operation Bullfrog. She opted for danger. She greeted him and invited him inside.

"I need a drink," Justin said.

"It's only three o'clock!"

Justin walked into the living room and slumped onto the chesterfield. "And a snack," he added.

Tamara stood in front of him, perplexed. "What happened? Your father kicked you out?"

Justin shook his head. "Four hours at the police station."

"Oh — the mug!" Tamara said, remembering that the London Police Service wanted to talk to him about that object.

"Yeah, that fucking mug!"

Tamara laughed. "You deserve a drink. Vodka or beer?"

"Don't you have anything better?"

"No." Tamara left and headed to the kitchen. She returned soon after with a sandwich of smoked salmon on rye bread and a Labatts lager. She handed both to Justin. "They go well together. That's what I had for lunch."

Justin ate the sandwich in big bites and took long swallows of the beer.

"Good," he said. "Can you double up?"

Tamara was back with a second sandwich, which Justin ate with equal enthusiasm. "I feel better."

Tamara sat in a corner of the sofa and watched him savour his second beer.

"Let me guess," she said. "They didn't believe the story that you gave a ride to Sophia Tadlova at Grand Bend."

"Maybe not, but I kept saying that I was in a state of confusion. They believed that. No, the problem was another. They hinted that I knew who killed your friend Vassilli. They even hinted, at one point, that I was an accomplice." Justin finished his beer. "They insisted that I knew where the mug is now; can you imagine that? The RCMP took it from them! How in the world would I know where it is?" Justin took his cap off and raked his hair. "It was a crazy situation — I tell you."

"Did you tell them you knew that the mug had been confiscated by the RCMP?"

"Of course not. I got the impression that they wanted to find out whether I knew more about it than they did. But I don't." He gave Tamara a quizzical look. "Maybe you do."

"Not in the least."

"Well, let's forget about my troubles. They're over. Let's think about this afternoon." He gave her a smile. "I'd like to take you with me. Show you my house; maybe have a swim together and let my father have a chance to know you better."

Tamara was surprised. Things sounded pretty formal. On the other hand, this was an occasion to get to know Michael Devry and ask him a few questions about his shipments.

****

Justin's Audi offered a smooth ride and Tamara truly enjoyed the trip from London to the shores of Lake Huron. Justin kept talking about his father's gallery and his unconditional love for the arts. Just after Bayfield they took a side road and in no time they stopped in front of a very distinctive building.

"Is this your father's house?"

"Yes. It's three-in-one. It's a family house, a shop at the lower level — my shop — and a showroom at the front. See the glass facade? That's the showroom."

"Impressive. No wonder you want to live here."

"We got it right." Justin parked the car and asked, "Feel like going for a dip?"

As Tamara agreed he guided her to the side of the house where a pressure-treated deck extended toward the shores to end up with a stairway leading to the beach.

"There are two cabins where we can change. Go to the Ladies. It's the yellow."

Tamara slipped on a pale blue bikini that left very little to anybody's imagination. She wanted to impress Justin. From Justin's look when she came out of the cabin, she knew she had been successful.

The water was unusually warm and together they swam for more than an hour, often stopping to do small talk. When the sun dipped down Justin suggested they get ready for supper. His father was the cook.

"He's preparing a *blanquette de veaux* — I told him you're fond of French cuisine." Justin talked from the blue cabin, as Tamara, in the other, slipped on a sleeveless gold blouse on top of a tan leather miniskirt. She knew that the flimsy blouse accented her small waist and round breasts.

Hand in hand they walked into the dining room.

Wearing a colourful apron on top of casual clothing, Michael Devry moved toward Tamara, took her hand and kept it between his. "I heard so much about you, that I feel you're already part of the family. We met a couple of times but we only exchanged a few words."

"Heard a lot about me? I hope it's nothing bad."

Michael released her hand. "Nothing but the best," he said. "Justin was right. He said you'd make any artist anxious to immortalize your effigy on canvas."

Tamara blushed. "Thanks," she whispered.

From the bar located in a corner, Justin called, "Tamara: white or red wine?"

"A glass of white would be fine."

"I made some vol-au-vents as an appetizer," Michael Devry said, pointing to a tray on the table. "Help yourselves. Dinner will be ready in about ten minutes." He walked out of the room.

In the background, Pavarotti sang an aria from Puccini's *Tosca*. Tamara glanced around, admiring the elegance of the oval table and the Queen Anne chairs. She neared the many pictures that almost covered an entire wall.

"It's like being in an art gallery," Tamara said. "National artists or foreigners?"

"These?" Justin looked at them closely. "Mostly post-Van Gogh Dutch impressionists. The artists aren't very well known, but good, nevertheless."

"Does he travel a lot to acquire new paintings?"

"Some, but he has connections in the field, friends who inform him when an auction is up, or of people in financial troubles who have to sell their collections."

Tamara sipped on the wine. "Always shipping through the Modano Company?"

"So far, yes."

"It must be very expensive."

Justin laughed. "He's reluctant to take the risk of commercial carriers. Besides, his clients are loaded." He extended his hand over the wall. "Most of these are already spoken for."

With a terrine held by its handles Michael made his entry. He deposited it on the table and gestured Tamara and Justin to sit. He poured himself a glass of white wine and said, "Bon appétit." He approached Tamara and scooped a portion of the blanquette onto her dish.

"Don't be cheap," Justin said. "The lady has no weight problems. I saw her wolfing her food last time we were out together."

Michael scooped another portion onto Tamara's dish and then served Justin.

"Busy these days?" Michael asked Tamara.

"So-so. Dianne, Charles' assistant, has asked for a few days off — she has to do a couple more shootings — so some of her work finds its way to my desk."

Tamara complimented the cook noting how tender and tasty the veal was. She was wondering how to inquire about Michael's future shipments when Michael surprised her.

"I heard that Vassilli Petrovic's cottage has been left to a Ms. Tamara Smith," Michael said. "That's you, isn't it?"

Tamara was flabbergasted. She had just received Vassilli's letter. How did Michael Devry get to know about her inheritance? Hastily, she took a sip of her Sauvignon.

"Vassilli mentioned once that he might remember me in his will. He was a long-term friend of my family and helped me out when my parents died." She paused. Michael Devry already knew too much about her; there was no need to add or confirm information he already had. "I haven't seen any will, however, and haven't been notified of its existence by an attorney." She took another long swallow. She had come to pump the Devrys and here she was, being pumped. Nonchalantly, she said, "I'm surprised with what you told me. How did you get that information?"

"From the bartender of the lodge along the road. Probably Vassilli told him. He used to have a drink at the lodge now and then."

Tamara turned toward Justin and said, "Perhaps we'll become neighbours. We just have to wait and see."

Michael rose and cleared out the dishes, replacing them with smaller ones. He moved to the kitchen and returned with a black-forest cake, which he served to his guests.

Tamara savoured a bite of her cake and then steered the conversation to the Dutch impressionists. When the evening was over, she could have written a five-page report on the subject.

On the way back to London she dozed off, blaming the wine for her drowsiness. Her mind, however, was alert, still puzzled by how tightly bound the ring of suspects seemed to be.

Chapter 31

In general, Charles wasn't in on Mondays. Dianne was still away, so Tamara searched their offices to check on incoming mail and old and new records. Nothing unusual or suspicious surfaced. She retrieved the recording pen she had left in Dianne's office and replaced it with another. Unfortunately, it seemed that Dianne was currently out of the business of fetching packages, which left spying on her useless.

Not much Tamara could do. Operation Bullfrog was temporarily on hold; she'd better think about the next auction. She went to the storage room, examined the items that had recently arrived and assigned them a starting price. Tomorrow she would consult Charles to see if he wanted to make any price changes.

Her desk cleared of clutter and old papers, Tamara was ready to head home when she received a call from Brad Wilson, asking if she could help set up the new quarters on Vanneck Road.

Even if surprised by the unusual request, Tamara agreed and drove there.

The two-storey house was situated close to the barn where she had gone to "spying device school", and was at least 100 feet away from the road. With grey vinyl siding and a steep dark roof, the building looked like a million other houses. Two men were unloading furniture from a U-haul truck and carrying it piece by piece through the garage to the interior. Tamara parked at the back and looked around.

Tamara noticed Duncan Brown, on top of a scaffold, busy installing a satellite dish. She waved at him, but got no reaction. As she entered the premises she met Ron Brenner. Ron was the contact person that Brad had told her to call in case of an emergency, when he first made her part of Operation Bullfrog.

"Glad you came," Ron said. The man was around sixty, tall and skinny, with wavy silver hair and dark eyebrows. His short-sleeved shirt was drenched in perspiration. "I can use some help. Of the five members that should form the nucleus of this operative basis, only Duncan and Mark Farin showed up this morning. Mark is on duty at the spa, so I called Brad and asked for reinforcement. He said you'd come to help."

"And here I am," Tamara said. "However, I don't know what I should be doing."

"We have to set up an office on the main floor and make the rooms upstairs into sleeping quarters for eight people. Mr. Romano wants a permanent contingent here, since it appears that London is the centre of trouble."

"Fine," Tamara said.

For the next hour she helped Ron unpack the desks and chairs and assemble the bunk beds for the upstairs. It was becoming increasing difficult to read the instructions in the twilight.

"Hydro will be installed tomorrow; Duncan will come back to set up the receiver for the dish and test the system." Ron looked

The Blackpox Threat

exhausted. "It's dark now and there's nothing else that we can do." He picked up his coat, checked that all windows were closed and descended to the main floor, followed by Tamara. He locked the front and back doors.

He walked Tamara to her car. "Lamps will come tomorrow morning, but we still need bed sheets and linen," Ron said. "Would you mind going and buying them?"

"Just tell me how many."

Ron extracted a sheet from his pocket. "Here is the list."

Tamara took the list and pocketed it. She waved goodbye and climbed into her Subaru.

"Thank you, Tamara," Ron shouted after her.

For the next four days Tamara helped make the new base functional. In spite of her efforts during that time to glean any insights into Ron, she hardly came to know him, as the man talked little about himself. An ex-RCMP officer, he had served in several isolated stations of the Northwest Territories.

On Friday evening as Tamara was preparing to leave, a message was broadcast over the newly installed loudspeaker.

"Mark Farin here. Just reporting about the surveillance of the spa and adjacent building. I photographed every vehicle that entered either building. Nothing unusual to report, I'd say. There was one delivery by UPS. That's all. I'll go back to Toronto and let them analyse the photos. I don't see any point in setting camp in London. It's Friday; tomorrow my colleague will relieve me and I plan to spend some quality time with my family. Bye-bye."

"Wait, wait!" Tamara screamed, but the caller had already clicked off.

"What's the matter?" Ron asked.

"That delivery could be important."

"And why so?"

"It could consist of the dangerous biochemicals shipped from Europe. We should find out who the sender is! Call him back!"

As Ron didn't move, she dialled Brad's number. To her great disappointment, Brad didn't answer. She left a message urging him to do something about the recent shipment.

"You worry too much," was Ron's dry comment. "Mark Farin is a qualified officer, not an amateur. He's been briefed about this operation and its dangers. If he felt that there was any cause for alarm, he'd have informed Brad Wilson himself."

"Qualified officer? He was supposed to be here! And what does he do? He hightails it home!" She gave Ron a look of disdain. "And where are the other two members? Where is Brad Wilson? This is an outfit of incompetent people!"

She grabbed her purse and left.

Still upset, she tried Brad's number again as soon as she entered her condo. There was no answer. More worried than ever she walked to the kitchen and took a beer from the fridge.

She kicked her shoes off and sat on one of the orange armchairs, the local newspaper under her arm. She unfolded *The London Free Press* and leafed through it, barely even noticing any of the headlines. Then she came across an article that alarmed her. Two dogs in the St. Thomas area had died of a suspicious disease. As a precaution, livestock owners were advised to check on their animals daily. Further news would be issued as soon as the cause of death of the two Dobermans could be ascertained.

The word Dobermans made Tamara jump to her feet. It was almost midnight, but it was imperative she talk with somebody who cared about Operation Bullfrog.

Chapter 32

London, Ontario
Beginning of August 2007

The last call from his boss left Frank Milton shattered. Physically, because of the length of the call, a full hour, and emotionally, for the restraint he had to continually exercise. Frank was only 10 days past the scheduled time and the man kept complaining and throwing doubts on his ability. Frank was sure his boss was a sick egomaniac who didn't have a clue about the difficulties that a scientific enterprise entailed and who perceived the entire world as if it revolved around his persona. If it weren't for the $50 million that Boris's blackpox was going to earn him, he would tell him to go fly a kite. Frank had not mentioned that the first shipment had been contaminated and had justified the delay by saying that his Guinea pigs had become sick the day before the experiment started. He also didn't say a word about the last shipment. Contrary to all agreements, Boris hadn't used the

Modano Company — a fact on which his boss had specifically insisted.

Better forget about Boris and the boss, Frank thought. After all, things were proceeding well. A glance at the pigs confirmed his opinion. The biologically-engineered virus was definitely effective. His pigs were bleeding from their noses and ears, and the open buboes they exhibited all over their stomachs were revolting. They would be dead within minutes. According to the experiments Boris had carried out in the lab situated in the Carpathian Mountains, the contagiousness of the virus would last from two to three weeks, but those weeks would be enough to terrorize the entire world, and get their leaders eager to pay a handsome ransom.

He looked at the pigs one more time. They were stone dead. He turned off the digital camera, which had captured the effect of the virus right up to the Guinea pigs' end. He would send a copy of the video to his boss, hoping that the pictures would satisfy him and keep him happy for a couple of days.

Wearing the usual mask and protective gloves, Frank dumped his victims into plastic boxes and firmly closed their lids. He loaded them onto his Ford truck. As before, he would dump them on Sophia's farmland.

He had managed to convince Sophia Tadlova to continue in her role of messenger. When the time came, she would broadcast the terms of the blackmail and then clear out, but he had not succeeded in keeping Stan in his employment. Stan had refused to take care of the remaining dead pigs or to have any involvement in the delivery of the blackpox vials. Frank had told him that the vials contained free samples of a new anti-aging cream, and begged him not to quit. Stan, however, had been too scared to even listen to his plea.

Only a minor problem, Frank told himself. They were so close to the conclusion of their operation that he didn't have to worry about burying the carcasses of the Guinea pigs. No need to hide them anymore. He would deposit them directly in Sophia's deserted silo, away from indiscreet eyes. Satisfied with his resolution, he began driving.

Half a kilometre from Sophia Tadlova's farm he glanced ahead. Normally at night the place exuded peace with the relaxing sounds of the countryside: chattering crickets and a few isolated barks. Not so now. As he drew near, he noticed unusual activity along the road. A pickup truck from the Ontario Ministry of Health and a police car were stationed at one of Tadlova's neighbours. Another truck, powerful headlights on, was spraying a substance on the ground. Frank drove past Sophia's farm. After a couple of kilometres he stopped on the road shoulder, the hood of his truck pinned up as if he were experiencing car problems. He didn't know what to make of the presence of the authorities. The police car didn't worry him, but the other vehicles got his vibes up. He debated whether he should stop and make some inquiries. He was curious to find out what was happening so close to Sophia's farm. He pondered the issue for a while, then concluded he had better clear out.

He made a U-turn and drove past the trouble spot.

He knew of a little marina where he could ditch both pigs and truck.

Chapter 33

Frustration mounting by the minute, Tamara tried and tried to contact Brad Wilson and Ron Brenner. Neither answered her messages. Out of other options, she faxed a memo to CSIS, attention Dale Romano, saying she had information worthy of evaluation. She kept the message purposely vague because several people not involved in Operation Bullfrog would read it. She banked primarily on her name to provoke a response. Nothing happened.

She sat in front of the aquarium. Normally observing the fish's activities, diverse according to their schools, had the power of relaxing her mind. Not this time, unfortunately. For more than an hour she was seized by worry and fear, unable to think or move. Finally at two o'clock in the morning, she rose, took a shot of the old vodka and went to bed.

As soon as she got up Saturday morning she perused the local newspaper that was delivered to her doorsteps, and then, eager for more news, drove to a variety store to buy *The Globe and Mail* and the *Toronto Star*. Frantically she leafed through each page, hoping to find out more about the two dogs that had died on what she guessed was the Rossiters' farm. There was nothing. Disappointed, she returned home. She should put aside her worries — maybe even dismiss her involvement in Operation Bullfrog. The truth was, that even if CSIS claimed that she was the central player, she had no relevant part in the operation. She should accept that and think about the weekend ahead.

She began working out on her newly assembled Bowflex. She should be in shape for the upcoming tennis match. She was glad to have something to look forward to, something that did not present any political implications.

When the phone rang Tamara jumped up, for a few seconds thinking it was CSIS, then realizing that was not possible, since the chirping came from her house phone.

It was Charles. "We have a problem," he said. "My partner, Stephanie, called it off." Tamara could hear him giggling, imitating Stephanie. "She got an impromptu call from that gentleman she met at the Governor General's Party — you remember him, right? — and she can't make it to the game. Before I call Justin, I'd like to know what you prefer: call it off, play Australian or let the two of you play single?"

The last thing Tamara wanted was to be alone with Justin; the second last thing was to be left alone with her thoughts.

"Australian will be fine," she replied.

"Great. See you at 11. The Clublink in Lambeth."

They were only half an hour into the game when drizzle changed into rain. In a few minutes it poured so hard that they had to find shelter in the clubhouse. Soon after most of the golf players joined the crowd already inside.

Charles rushed to get a table.

"It won't stop raining any time soon," he said. "We'll have to give up our game for today." He asked Tamara, "Time to spare this afternoon?"

"Sure. What do you have in mind?"

"To go see a couple of old mansions along the shores of Lake Erie. There may be antiques worth buying." He turned to Justin. "You can come along; maybe you can find some paintings for your father's collection."

Justin laughed. "I doubt it, and in any case I wouldn't dare to buy anything. He's very meticulous in his choices, and I try to stay away from his work. One artist in the family is enough." He looked at Tamara. "I'd like to come, but at the moment we have only my car, and Father needs it, since he has to attend a vernissage. I have to go home."

"Too bad," Charles said. "Let's have a bite to eat and Tamara and I will be on our way."

The salad bar displayed a variety of meat platters, sandwiches, pasta and green salads and fresh bread. They helped themselves, ordered coffee and ate in silence. Then Charles turned to Tamara.

"Do you mind if we use your car? Just in case we find some big items to take with us."

"Be my guest," Tamara replied.

Soon after they waved goodbye to Justin, and they both climbed into the Subaru.

"I'm happy to have some time alone with you," Charles said as he secured his seatbelt. "I wonder whether you'd like to work fulltime." He waited for her answer, but Tamara didn't react, even if she was surprised. Recently there was hardly enough work for Dianne and her.

Charles continued. "Thomas — you remember Thomas Sarcin, right? — is interested in joining the company and expanding it. On this side of the Atlantic we chiefly operate on the selling of art goods, much more than on the shipping. He thinks he can beef up our activity as land courier. He'd bring in several clients, he assured me."

"Does he have experience in this field?" Tamara tried to gain time, as Charles, now, became a serious suspect in her eyes.

"No. The family business was in building safes. He told us that, remember?"

"Yes. He got out because of a bitter dispute and problems within the family, he said."

"Right. He inherited it from his father. When his father passed away, Thomas, who was in charge of the estate, stopped the long-lasting litigation by settling out of court. In the meantime, he and his brother inherited more money, from an uncle this time, and Thomas found himself quite well off."

They were on Highway 3 and the traffic proceeded slowly.

"Thomas' father was a very bright man, but difficult, argumentative — he was hard on his two sons, who grew up without a mother. Their mother left before the boys even started school."

"So what did Thomas do with all that money?"

"He travelled and collected art pieces. That's how I met him."

"He must be well into his 40s," Tamara said as she put her car in park. She noticed that the traffic had stopped completely. "Why does he want to start a new venture at this time of his life?"

"Boredom, I assume. I didn't ask, however. The proposition he made included a substantial injection of capital into my company. That definitely interests me. He'd like you to become his personal assistant. We'd share you in that capacity, that is."

Tamara was taken by surprise. Were both Charles and Thomas involved in the illegal shipments and trying to find a reason to keep her under close surveillance? Tamara turned her head to look at Charles. Was it possible that a man with such a flare of old-style-gentleman was also a callous criminal?

The sound of a horn blown behind her car made her realize that the traffic had resumed. She put the car in gear.

"I have to think about it, Charles. What you propose is quite interesting."

"Great. Next week our lawyers will meet. I'll know then if this expansion of the Modano Company is feasible."

The afternoon drive continued without any further conversation until they reached Leamington. Charles had the address of a house nearby where he wanted to buy two oil lamps for which he already had a customer. The owner wasn't in, so they proceeded to the next dwelling where Charles bargained on the price of a small credenza. He managed to get it for very little money. The visit to another old mansion produced two handmade rugs with Indian drawings.

When the search for antiques was over it was dark.

The ride back to London was spent discussing the starting price for the new acquisitions in view of the upcoming auction. Tamara was grateful for the conversation which helped ease her anxiety and temporarily deflect her thoughts from the potential threat the country was facing.

Once at home, Tamara checked her three phones for messages. There were none. Clearly, in spite of what she had been made to believe, Operation Bullfrog was not a priority on the CSIS agenda.

Frustrated but tired, Tamara went to bed.

As usual, the morning paper came very early. The Sunday edition of *The London Free Press*, of smaller size than the weekly version, was assembled in a book format with loose pages. She didn't hope to find much in it, as Sunday's edition was, in general, a rehash of previous news and an avalanche of ads. But on page 14, under *Comment* there was a title that intrigued her. She quickly focused on it. "Was the man careless?" A farmer in south-western Ontario had not waited for the Health Department to inspect the dead animals; he had burned them. Interviewed, the farmer had so justified his actions: "I asked for help that didn't come, so tired of waiting, I did what I thought was appropriate." Readers were asked to express their opinion on the farmer's behaviour. There was a Web site available for collecting the responses.

Those few lines reminded Tamara of the "suspected disease" and the "two Dobermans" mentioned in the Friday paper. The word "farmer" connected the dots: they were talking about the incident that occurred at the Rossiters — Sophia Tadlova's neighbours.

She was debating whether she should call the Rossiters, when Dale Romano was on the phone.

"You may wonder why nobody contacted you in spite of your messages, Tamara," he said with a tight voice. "Our group had pursued an important lead." Romano paused. "The fingerprints on Sophia Tadlova's mug were the same as those found on the dagger that killed Vassilli Petrovic."

"What? The two were friends. Their relationship dated decades! Vassilli helped her escape from the Soviet Union!"

"It may be so, but that was in the past. The truth is that Tadlova killed the man. We figured out she must have been aboard the cutter that approached the Tortuga — the floating house where the costume party was taking place — during the fake duels. That's how she slipped aboard, avoiding security." Romano paused again. "You were lucky to escape when she abducted you. Clearly she had a motive to eliminate you."

Tamara was speechless, and Romano continued. "So we were busy checking on the several tracks the woman left behind."

"Did you get her?"

The Blackpox Threat

"No, but we know where she spent a night two days ago. In a motel in Woodstock. We think she's heading back to her farm. That's where we're going, now."

"And Stan? Any trace of her goon?"

"No, nothing. I have to go, Tamara. Oh, what was the reason you called?"

"I think the disease — what you guys call blackpox — has already spread. The first two victims have been Sophia's dogs. In her absence they usually roam free. They may have come across some infected animals, probably on Sophia's farm. Saturday night they ended up, very sick, on the land of the Rossiters, Sophia Tadlova's neighbours."

"How do you know all this?"

"I was there. Mr. Rossiter called for the Humane Society first and, when he got no answer, he called the Health Department. They asked questions but didn't go to see what the problem was. He finally decided to burn the carcasses, making impossible any investigation on the cause of death."

There was silence on the other side of the phone line. Then Romano said, in a quiet voice, "The situation may be worse than we thought. I'll call for the direct intervention of CBRNE, the Centre for Chemical, Biological, Radiological & Nuclear Explosives Research, in case there's danger of an epidemic. They're the specialists." He paused. "Good work, Tamara. Let's keep in touch."

Tamara wanted to ask if anybody had found out who the sender of the shipment delivered by UPS to Harry Pearson's spa was. Probably not, she concluded. They were busy chasing after Sophia Tadlova.

Chapter 34

An OPP car, Romano's unmarked Buick and the special CBRNE unit, which was a van equipped to handle highly infectious diseases, had been in tactical position since dusk. Romano had tried to limit the number of people involved in this particular operation to avoid media attention and alerting the criminals. He had positioned a road sign with *Men at Work* and another one with *Broken Pipes* on Meadows Road, one kilometre from each side of Sophia's farm. The OPP car was on guard at that site. The CBRNE van was stationed five kilometres away, hidden behind an abandoned gas station. Romano's Buick moved along a perimeter that enclosed Sophia's land; Romano and Brad Wilson alternated in scrutinizing every movement in the area.

"Why are you so sure she would come back here?" Brad asked.

"You're never sure of anything in this kind of game. However...her Chevy Optra was found in a parking lot in Woodstock. Nothing in it, not even the car registration. So I assumed Tadlova and her man wanted to abandon the car and clear out. We showed her picture in a few motels close by, and one manager recognized her. She and her accomplice had stayed one night at his motel." Romano turned off the fan that had been going full blast until then. "We flashed out our badges at car rentals, always with her picture in our hands. No luck. We stretched our search to the dealers of used cars. We hit the jackpot. Sophia had bought an old motorcycle. The dealer had tried to sell her a car, but she had refused. She didn't have to go very far, she'd said; a motorcycle would do." Romano adjusted the fan once more. "My deduction is that she's heading home — for what reason we still don't know."

"I see," Brad said. He reclined the car seat and stretched out in it. "I'll take a nap, in case we have to spend the entire night here."

It was close to midnight, and the major events of the watch had been the coming and going to Mr. Subway for a couple of submarines and the refilling of mugs with fresh coffee.

Then a spotlight appeared in the distant cultivated fields, soon followed by the distinctive noise of a two-cylinder engine.

"Brad, wake up, it could be her," said Romano.

Brad raised his seat and focussed on the movement of the vehicle.

"It's either Tadlova or some boy practising his motocross skill," he said. "It bounces up and down and left and right."

"She's coming in from the back, so we can move toward the house and hide in front of it."

A few minutes passed and the noise became more pronounced. Finally the motorcycle stopped in the little enclave between the silo and the barn.

"Ask the police car and the van to come over. No siren, no lights. I think there's only one person, but we don't know if that person is armed." Romano stepped out of the car and cautiously moved to the corner of the house where he could see what was going on. He opened his cell. "It's a woman," he communicated to Brad. "She's opened the barn door and put the motorcycle inside. Give the order to move in."

In no time the OPP officer, Brad and Romano surrounded the woman.

"Ms. Tadlova, we want to speak to you," said Romano in an authoritative voice.

Sophia first tried to run away, then she kicked the officer who was restraining her.

"We only want to talk to you," Romano said.

In response, Sophia tried to shake away the policeman by throwing her body against his. Of course, she was no challenge for the man.

Within five minutes Sophia Tadlova was dragged inside her house. The sleeves of her coat had been ripped off; only pieces of her scarf remained wound around her neck. She was breathing heavily; her chest moved up and down in big heaves. She let her massive body slump into one of the kitchen chairs.

"Where are my dogs?" she asked, looking around.

"Not here," Romano said, and sat opposite her. "We're not here to talk about dogs."

"My dogs…they're all I have." Her eyes seemed made of water; they were so clear and moist. She wiped her nose with her sleeve and snorted. "They can drink from the creek, but they need food. Snapper and Blaze are their names." She pointed to a corner of the kitchen. "There's food in there." She motioned to rise but she fell back into her chair.

"They don't need food anymore," Brad murmured.

"Dead?" she asked, her voice a mere whisper. "Oh. My poor Snapper, and Blaze, so…so sweet."

Romano shot a severe look at Brad and then said, "Ms. Tadlova, we know you have accomplices. We want to know their names."

Tears raked Sophia's face; she first coughed and then snorted again.

Romano spotted a box of Kleenex on top of the refrigerator and put it in front of the woman.

"Can I have a glass of water?" Sophia asked.

"Sure." Romano locked his eyes into hers. "As soon as you answer my questions."

Sophia stared into the distance.

"Who is your boss?"

"I don't know."

"How do you receive orders?" There was no answer. "Why did you kill Vassilli Petrovic?" Silence greeted him. "I want names." He leaned toward her, almost breathing onto her face. "Names!"

Sophia moved her head away from him. She took the strands of grey hair that hung in front of her face and thrust them back together with the others.

"Can I have some water?" she asked with a feeble voice.

Romano signalled to Brad, who neared the cupboard in search of a glass.

"Who is Stan? He must have a last name. I want that name!"

Sophia shook her head no.

Romano sighed in frustration. He was going nowhere with her, and she was the only lead they had. He had to make her talk. It was possible that experiments involving blackpox had taken place in this area and the infectious virus could be in circulation within days if it was not already too late.

Brad filled a glass with tap water and put it in front of the woman.

"Here it is," he said.

For a moment Sophia looked blankly at the glass and then bent over the table, her face almost touching its surface. Then, in one abrupt movement, she tilted sidewise and collapsed onto the floor.

"Bring in the paramedics," Romano ordered. "If she dies, we're totally lost. No!" he shouted to the policeman who had bent to give Sophia mouth-to-mouth resuscitation. "No mouth-to-mouth. It isn't safe. Wait for CBRNE to take care of her."

****

On Monday morning Tamara drove to the Modano Company with the credenza and the rugs still in her car. The maintenance man wasn't on duty, so Tamara took the rugs to the storage room, tagged them with the price she and Charles had agreed upon, and left the credenza in her car. She would wait for someone to help her unload it.

Tamara could see that Dianne was in. The door between the two offices was wide open and Dianne was busy working at the computer. Tamara sat at her desk and began to prepare the list of items to be offered at the upcoming auction.

Within minutes Diane appeared in her office. As usual, Dianne was dressed in style: a trendy blue suit with short sleeves, yellow blouse and blue sandals with yellow stripes.

"Can I bother you for a moment?" she asked.

"Sure. I came in early because I had some new items to put on the list for Saturday," she said. "Charles and I went hunting for collectibles yesterday."

"Found the oil lamps he was so anxious to get?"

"No. The owner wasn't at home. But we did get a fantastic credenza, with inlays of fine woods and ivory. I still have it in my car, if you want to see it."

"Later, maybe. Now I'd like to talk to you."

Dianne hesitated, so Tamara encouraged her. "What is it?" she asked, and relaxed her back against the chair.

"You know Harry Pearson, right?"

Oh my God, Tamara thought. He had told her about the red binder she had taken from his office! Tamara tried to muster a calm demeanour even though her nerves were on edge. When she had gone to the spa on her spying mission, she had done her best to disguise herself. She had worn a pair of old Capri slacks, a discoloured top with sparkling beads and a bandana that covered most of her forehead and hair. She topped it off with big sunglasses. In spite of all that, though, she knew Harry Pearson had recognized her — her height had probably given her away. But did he say anything to Dianne? The odds were against it, considering he was in some way involved with her kidnapping.

"Yes, I've seen him around here. He's a friend of yours, right?"

Dianne's face showed annoyance. "He's a good masseur, I can testify to that. The special creams he gets from his friend the chemist? They're a miracle! My wrinkles disappear instantly. I look 10 years younger. And the massage? I tell you, after an hour at the spa I feel as if I've grown wings. That's how light my body feels afterwards." Dianne paused. "However, he wants to be my boyfriend — if I gave him the tiniest encouragement he would even want to marry me!" Dianne sat in the chair in front of Tamara's desk. "He's very much —"

"In love?" Tamara suggested.

"Maybe. But he's, he's…well, so sticky, weird too."

"Sticky? Weird?"

"He doesn't let go, he can't understand that I don't want to get tied down!"

"That's the problem?"

"That among other things." Dianne stopped and leaned toward Tamara. "You see, while I was on vacation I met an interesting guy, Gordon who I've been seeing regularly. I would like to keep Harry as a friend and my aesthetician, but nothing more." She emitted a suffering sigh. "He has this fancy that I should go get his friend's parcels, personally, instead of having them delivered through our carrier."

"You're right, that's strange. It doesn't make much sense. Do you know the reason?" Tamara's tone was subdued.

"Not really. Those parcels aren't for the spa; they're for a friend of his, Frank Milton. He supplies the creams and fragrances to the spa. Anyway, the parcels are some vases he has shipped via the Modano Italian branch."

"Vases? His friend is a collector, too? Maybe we should invite him to our auctions."

"No, please don't; he may come with Harry, and Harry would think it was my doing..." Dianne sighed again. "You see, between the work here, the commercials, which I tremendously enjoy doing and my new boyfriend, I don't have the time to do these favors." She paused. "Sometimes I stand in line for hours; one time it took me half a day to handle the duties and the brokerage. It's becoming a real pain."

"I understand," Tamara said, and tried to assess the situation. "Maybe I could go to customs for you." As she didn't want to sound too obvious, she rushed to add, "Maybe you can get me a cream or two. My skin is always very dry."

"Would you go? Oh, that would be great. That was the favour I was going to ask you."

"No problem, just don't tell him about the switch and I'll bring the parcel to you."

The Blackpox Threat

Dianne blew her a kiss. "Oh, great. You go get the next shipment when it comes. I'll give you a couple of hydration masks." Dianne, clearly relieved, motioned to leave. "Oh, one more thing. Harry said it's imperative I go to pick it up the day it arrives."

"So —"

"Answer my phone if I'm not in."

"Sure."

Dianne clapped her hands, satisfaction painted on her face. "That's settled. What a relief! Now, let's go see the credenza. Maybe I'll buy it myself."

They walked to the area where Tamara's Subaru was parked, the hatch pointing to the entrance of the storage room.

"Six hundred is the starting price?" Dianne asked, after they had lugged the old piece inside. "I'd have to make a few more commercials before I can afford something like that!" Dianne fingered the inlays of alternating light and dark wood that embellished the top, the front and the sides. "I can't even imagine the time it took to do such fancy work!"

"Surely out of my league," Tamara said. "It's incredible how the pattern repeats so precisely over and over."

"It'll bring in a lot of money, I can tell."

"I hope so." Tamara was ready to follow Dianne back to the office, when her cell rang.

It was Dale Romano. "Meeting at 12 o'clock sharp. Be there."

Chapter 35

It was a plenary session — all the members of Operation Bullfrog were in attendance. Romano asked them to introduce themselves together with their affiliations. Tamara, a legal pad in front of her her, managed to scribble down each name to the best of her phonetic ability. Most of the attendees brought laptops, crouching down under the long oval table to plug their computers into a common outlet. Everyone wore a suit, the majority of them dark.

Tamara, dressed in a plain beige pantsuit, had come to the house in Vanneck Road directly from her office; she had not expected the atmosphere to be so formal.

"Meeting to order," Romano said in his clear voice. He wore a blue suit, with a white shirt and a blue tie. "The agenda has only two main items. First, I'll brief you about what happened, second we'll decide what to do next. Duncan Brown, you're in charge of the minutes."

"Why me? Ask Tamara, she has nothing to do!"

Romano shot him a fierce look. "Mr. Brown, I issued an order. You take the minutes and make them available to us, in print, before we leave." Duncan wiggled in his seat, but Romano didn't bother giving him a second look. He stood and continued. "Yesterday we arrested Sophia Tadlova, whose fingerprints matched those found on the weapon that killed Vassilli Petrovic. As I am sure you are aware, he was the man who first informed us of the danger that a new form of blackpox was on the way to this country." He paused and adjusted his glasses up the bridge of his nose. "Tadlova was also guilty of kidnapping the here — present Ms. Tamara Smith. Tadlova died early this morning, without saying one single word about the motive of the murder or about her accomplices. She was apprehended when she came back to her farm to feed her dogs. The only items she had with her were a bag containing a laptop and two compact discs and some treats for her dogs. One of the compact discs was empty, while the other contained a list of email addresses."

"Any chemicals with her?" Ron Brenner asked.

"No, nothing. Preliminary testing seems to exclude that she was infected with any kind of contagious diseases. CBRNE will perform more accurate analyses, however."

"Nothing in her car either?" Mark Farin asked.

"She arrived at her farm riding a 1973 Yamaha. The old motorbike has been sequestered. CBRNE is analysing it, together with her possessions and the premises. On my request they've disguised themselves by wearing working clothes when they're in the fields and use their protective outfits only when they come in contact with objects that may be contaminated. The official version for their presence is an inspection ordered by Agriculture Canada."

Absolute silence reigned in the room, and Romano continued. "We have two extra men on watch at the spa owned by Harry

Pearson and the building adjacent to the spa. I made arrangements to have available the shipping records regarding the UPS delivery that took place at the spa last Friday. We'll soon know the name of the sender, what the declared content of the parcel was, and to whom it was addressed." He turned toward Duncan. "Did you get all that I said?"

Duncan assented. "Word-by-word, Dr. Romano. My voice recorder is hooked up to my computer. I'll be able to print out the copies right away."

Tamara was puzzled. What did this Duncan fellow have against her? He had all the means available to record the minutes of the meeting with a couple of clicks, but he would have liked to dump the job onto her, knowing full well she only had a pad and a pen. He's a woman-hater, she concluded.

"Two members of CBRNE will contact the neighbours on either side of Tadlova's farm and ask permission to run tests on their farmlands." Romano said. "We have court orders to do it, but we hope it won't be necessary to use them. The smoother we operate, the less publicity we get." He sat. "Tamara, Ms. Smith I mean, can you tell us the names of the people you think could be involved, even without their own knowledge, in smuggling dangerous substances into this country?"

"Charles Modano, Michael Devry and Thomas Sarcin could be involved, even if I couldn't gather one single element of wrong-doing. I'd be inclined to exclude the two women who gravitate around these men, that is, Dianne Templeton and Stephanie Demoins."

"We'll get court orders to inspect the premises of all five," Romano said. "Now it's time for questions."

"We were not aware that Ms. Smith was abducted," Ron Brenner said. "When did this happen?" Romano briefly explained the circumstances.

"But we have only her word for what happened," Brenner said.

"No, there was a witness, the man who helped her escape. We asked both, and the police unit involved, not to divulge the fact."

I have to add Brenner to women-haters, Tamara thought.

"Any other questions?" Romano asked.

"I have one," Tamara said, knowing well that each and every member present would hate her for asking. "What happened to Major Heather Motta and the inquest into the alleged leak occurring inside Operation Bullfrog?"

Romano bit his lips and said, "That's an internal matter, Tamara."

"Ahah. Not so anymore." Tamara glanced at each member, including Duncan who, instead of being hunched on his pet gadgets as usual, was glaring at her. "Weeks ago I received, from the Ukrainian Embassy, a posthumous letter written by Vassilli Petrovic. It was to be delivered to me in case he fell victim to an assassination."

Brad Wilson jumped up. "You didn't tell me that!"

"I didn't have to. It was personal. Very personal." Tamara looked around, as she had done before. "Vassilli suspected the presence of a traitor among the members of Operation Bullfrog; he had confided his suspicions to Major Heather Motta and in his letter he hinted that his murder would be the proof."

Tamara looked around again, and all she saw now were faces frozen by stupor and fear.

Finally Romano talked. "I'd like to see Vassilli's letter, Tamara, in order to ascertain its authenticity. I'll personally contact Motta. Meeting adjourned." He strode out.

Brad lost no time. He rushed to Tamara's side and sat at the table beside her.

"We have to talk," he said. "A long talk."

Tamara took the copy of the minutes that Duncan had printed out on his portable system, folded it in four and put it in her purse. "I have nothing to say," she said coolly, "and nothing to listen to." Before Brad had time to react, a muffled buzz emanated from Tamara's purse. "Excuse me," she said, and reached for her personal cell.

It was Justin. She took a few steps away from Brad.

"Yes, I hear you." She listened without a single interruption. Then she said, "It sounds exciting, but I'd need a bit of time to think about it and organize my things." She listened to what else Justin had to say. "In any case, thanks for the offer."

Tamara turned to Brad. "You can add another name to the suspects list: Justin Devry. He just asked me to accompany him to Holland to bring home three precious plates for one of his father's clients. Blue Delft from the 1700s. So valuable and so fragile that not even the Modano Company, specializing in the shipment of art objects, can be trusted."

Tamara turned off her phone, consternation and sadness washing over her. Justin, so attentive and lovable, could be a cold-hearted criminal.

Brad stood in front of her in silence, an enigmatic expression on his face.

Tamara wanted to get out of there and nurse her wounds in solitude.

"Good bye," she said curtly, and marched out of the room.

Chapter 36

Frank Milton waited until all the day campers near the marina left for the day. The small park along Lake Erie was now deserted. His original intention was to dump the boxes with the infected Guinea pigs together with the truck into the lake. However, the longest dock was only a hundred feet long. At that point the waters were just not deep enough to conceal his vehicle in a fairly permanent way. The last thing he wanted was to report his truck as stolen and have somebody discover it right away.

Disgruntled but firm in his new resolution, Frank carried the two boxes to the end of the dock, and dumped them into the dark waters.

Mission partially accomplished, he told himself. To complete it, he still needed to get rid of his truck. He would stop at a used car dealership and trade it in for a newer, better vehicle.

On the way back to his lab he contemplated how long it would take him to put together the two blackpox formulations. One was in liquid media, and would be contained in minuscule sterile vials.

The second would be boxed in small jars, to be mixed with a binding agent. While this version would be less effective, it could more easily pass as a cosmetic product.

With these thoughts running through his brain, Frank had just entered his lab, when Boris Youkenoff called.

"I have no time to listen," Frank barked into the phone before Boris had time to utter a single sound. "Have you shipped the vaccine?"

"Only one sample. For testing."

"Not the full amount?"

"No. I haven't, and I won't if I don't receive the payment — the full five million euros."

"The money should be there."

"I went to the bank. You said the money would be transferred to the Clariden Bank in Lugano, right?"

"Yes, yes. It's been done."

"They checked my account. Zilch."

"Boris, we're running out of time. The boss is getting hysterical and one of our members has disappeared. I need your cooperation."

"You had it. You tested the virus and confirmed my findings; that it is effective for at least two weeks. I've done what we agreed upon for the five million. Get me the money and I'll ship the vaccine."

"I need it now! We can't put the virus on the market without being vaccinated first."

"Sorry. Money first, vaccine second. Besides, there are other complications here as well. The labour strikes are causing additional setbacks. When the Modano Company opened for business yesterday their shop window was smashed. Now they're closed. We have to find some alternative for the shipping."

"Easy. You bring the vaccine personally, then. It's just one hop over the Atlantic."

The line went dead. Enraged, Frank dialled Boris' number. "Don't hang up on me, ever!"

In response he got another click.

****

To hell with Frank, Boris told himself. He had to get at the money. Boris was tired of living in the decrepit house he had rented in Bergamo, surrounded only by the bare necessities. It was okay when he had to check that all his substances hadn't suffered from being shaken during the tortuous trip through mountains and hills; it was fine when he had to add a culture to the virus to make it reproduce very quickly; but now he wanted to move. The virus has been perfected and the vaccine was ready. Of course, the final proof of the effectiveness of both the virus and the vaccine would require human trials and testing, something that was clearly impossible.

As far as he was concerned, his part was over. Single-handedly, he had achieved what many laboratories in the world would have done only by employing dozens and dozens of scientists. Too bad he couldn't publish a seminal paper, and be recognized for what he was, a shear genius.

What was his reward? Only the five million, and he was determined to get all of it, not one penny less, and the sooner, the better.

Seated on a park bench in the Parco Civico in Lugano, Boris relaxed as he watched the ducks gliding on the smooth waters of the lake. He wanted to settle down. Of course, not in Lugano — way too expensive. But in its vicinity, in a little place where he could afford to buy a house. He could be happy there. He would enjoy the orderly way of the Swiss life. And he could get a boat, so that he could just cross the lake every time he wanted to reach the casino in Campione...

The sun was getting down; the pedal-boats were rushing ashore, and the park would soon be closed. He should return home. For the time being he had to economise; he shouldn't go gambling and he shouldn't spend the night in one of the beautiful hotels along the lakeshore, no matter how inviting they were.

Frank had always paid him well and on time. When the dismantling of his lab in the Carpathian cave had begun Frank had given him 40,000 euros. It was more than he needed to set up his microlab in Bergamo; unfortunately he had lost 10,000 on the green tables.

For the time being he could only dream of a house.

When he arrived home, a red Fiat Punto was parked beside the farmhouse. Boris ignored it, entered the house and was ready to go to bed, when he heard a knock at the door. He glanced at his watch: it was two in the morning.

"Who is it?" he asked, and looked through the pinhole. It was a woman, medium height, dressed in a black smock.

"The landlord," she said.

Boris opened the door. Finally he recognized her. "Yes?"

"Can I come in?"

Boris stood aside and let the woman enter. "You rented my house for 15 weeks. Do you intend to stay any longer?"

Boris had forgotten about the contract and its expiration date. He had to gain time. "Maybe a week or two?"

"Then you have to pay. It will be 300 euros."

"Can you give me a little time? A friend of mine was supposed to come. I'm waiting for him. Together we're going to take a trip down south, to Rome. I don't know what happened to him."

The woman wasn't in the mood to show any interest or

empathy. "Two days," she said, and waived two fingers in front him. She made an about-face and strode out.

Boris cursed inwardly. He was planning on having a good night's sleep and now he had to face this complication. He didn't want to borrow money through his credit card. Until then he had taken precautions not to leave any tracks of his stay in Bergamo.

Problems, problems! He moved to the kitchen and poured himself a large glass of Bardolino wine.

Chapter 37

London, at the spa
Mid-August 2007

The following morning Frank began filling 50 vials with the deadly blackpox, careful not to spill a drop. He set them in a white plastic container with tiny compartments built in. The vials would sit tight in the insulating box, preventing any breakage due to sudden movements. He mixed a binding agent with the remaining virus and dispensed it in small jars. Those he packaged in a separate grey box. Unfortunately, two of the jars didn't fit in the box. He set them aside on the counter — an unfortunate waste, he thought.

He looked with satisfaction at the culmination of his efforts. All he had to do was to clean his lab and dispose of all other chemicals that were not related to the preparation of cosmetics.

It was four in the afternoon when he was finished. Now he would move to his cottage in the country. This was the place where he would hide after the blackmailing message was broadcasted and the vials deposited in selected places, which included emergency departments of hospitals, daycare centres and libraries — just to support the threat with facts. The little movie with the dying Guinea pigs, displayed on YouTube, would add an extra scare. He congratulated himself; everything was in order.

He grabbed his thick briefcase and his laptop. He had all he needed.

He called Armand, the receptionist at the spa, and asked him to bring his car, a newly purchased Chrysler 300 Touring, to the front of the building. Together they loaded the two boxes, the white and the grey. Frank waved him goodbye and began driving.

He still felt exhilaration, as always when he had accomplished what he had proposed to do. A nagging feeling, however, was settling in the back of his mind. Sophia Tadlova had the most updated copy of the addresses to send the threatening message. Where was she? She had promised him to complete her job before fading into obscurity.

On the side of a gas station he spotted one of the few still-existing phone booths. He stopped and dialled Sophia's phone number. A female voice answered at the first ring, but it wasn't Sophia's. He immediately hung up and resumed driving.

He couldn't count on Sophia anymore. He would have to do with the email addresses she had given him last month. It was too bad, but he could dig out a few more while in seclusion at his cottage.

Now he had to think of how to solve the problem created by the lack of vaccine.

****

Harry Pearson had just finished giving his last massage for the day at the spa. His shoulders were sore and his throat was dry. He'd had five clients to attend to, one right after the other and each more anxious than the next to make conversation. Exhausted, he called Armand in and asked him to go get a vegetable pizza at the take-out restaurant that was only a mile away.

"Maybe you should ask Frank if he wants anything. He's been working hard. He never left his lab all day."

"Mr. Milton left just a few minutes ago."

"Oh, is that so? I asked him to make me some of that antioxidant cream. I'm completely out of it and it sells like crazy." Armand's face was expressionless. Armand's role was to welcome clients and potential customers. He was good at it, but that was all he was good at. "Well, I'll talk to Frank when he comes back." He looked at Armand. "Move, Armand. I'm hungry."

Harry strode to his office and sat in one of the chairs arranged around the coffee table. The business was booming. He had many customers and the cosmetics the spa offered were very popular. Now that things were going well, Dianne didn't show up anymore. He shouldn't have asked her to go to the customs to get the shipment Frank was expecting. She had agreed to do it, but he knew she didn't like to. This was the last time Frank was going to boss him around. Soon he would be financially independent and wouldn't need him anymore. It would be an immense relief.

Armand was back with the pizza. He set the carton in the middle of the table.

"If you don't need anything else, I'll be going," he said.

"Fine, Armand, thank you."

Harry rose and got a bottle of wine and a glass from the cabinet. He started savouring the pizza and sipping his Chianti.

He had to do something to gain back Dianne's affection. The woman was beautiful. Not only did she have the power to turn him on, but she was a great asset to his company. She spoke highly of the spa's treatments and products — she represented an indirect and genuine advertisement for his business. Now that she was in showbiz, several of her co-workers had flocked to book an appointment, months ahead.

Tomorrow he would send her a fantastic bouquet of flowers and a basket with an assortment of soaps, fragrances and other beauty products.

****

First thing in the morning Frank Milton inspected the place where he would wait for the results of the blackpox threat to take its course. It was a cottage near Wasaga Beach that he had remodeled and equipped with modern technology, satellite Internet included.

Frank was puzzled. Until now his boss and Boris had played straight, but now, clearly, one of them was lying about the money. The simplest way to find out would be to call his boss, but he had to risk an explosion of anger that would ruin his day. Instead, he called the Clariden Bank in Lugano, and asked whether or not there had been a transfer of money from Canada to the Swiss account of Mr. Youkenoff.

He was put on hold, and after more than fifteen minutes he was told that the bank would not provide that information to strangers. And that was that.

Calling his boss remained the only solution.

"I hope the reason for waking me up is a good one," his boss said.

"An excellent reason. Boris affirms that he hasn't received any money. So he doesn't want to ship the vaccine. You assured me that the transfer would take place last week. What happened, Zaccaria?"

"Don't call me with my name, I told you a hundred times!"

"Okay, no need to shout."

"At the bank they asked too many questions, which I didn't want to answer." Zaccaria's voice was unusually calm, which hinted that he was in the wrong.

Frank pressed. "That money must reach Boris, or we won't get the vaccine. It was agreed upon."

"I understand. I had to use a different route."

"And?"

"A courier went to Switzerland with the money. He should arrive tomorrow."

"Is it safe?"

Zaccaria roared with laughter. "In our business nothing is safe; you should know that. If he betrays me he'll pay with his life, that's all."

"That doesn't solve our problem."

"Check with Boris tomorrow. The money should be there." Zaccaria hung up.

Frank walked to the den and hooked up his laptop to the wall to recharge its battery. He was preparing to surf the Internet and find a few more email addresses of important people to send his threatening message, when his cell rang. His glanced at the caller ID, hoping it was Boris. He was out of luck, it was his boss.

With reluctance he opened the communication line.

"Have you seen the newspapers?"

"No, I'm at the cottage; there is no delivery of newspapers here."

"Sophia Tadlova's farm is off limits for health reasons and so are two farms near hers. One paper hints at foul play. Do you know anything about it?"

"Me? And why should I know?" Frank hoped they wouldn't

check Tadlova's soil for some time. He knew Stan Glover, Sophia's goon, had buried the pigs near the silo.

"You told me you had a safe place to discard your Guinea pigs. Was it Tadlova's land?"

"No. Yes, that's what I told you but then I thought it was safer to dump the carcasses into the lake." Zaccaria had no way to check. "Very deep into Lake Erie."

"Hmm. Have you spoken with Sophia recently?"

This time he couldn't lie. "No, I couldn't reach her."

"Can you find out what happened to her?"

"Why don't you try? You have far better connections than I have."

"I would, but my main contact has disappeared."

"Oh. Who was he?" Frank had been curious all along to know who protected his boss from inspections and, who, often, provided him with important information.

"No need for you to know. As soon as you receive the vaccine, be sure you ship a dose here, and remember: I'm the one who pays you!" Zaccaria clicked off.

Frank kicked the desk close to him until his foot ached. This time his boss had managed to make him angry as hell. Why in the world did he go into business with such a mad megalomaniac?

He drove to town and bought all the newspapers he could find. He wondered what had really happened to Sophia Tadlova. Had she been arrested? Of one thing he was sure. No one would make Sophia spill the beans. She had undergone more cruel interrogations than any member of CSIS could ever inflict on her.

Chapter 38

London, Ontario
End of August 2007

Tamara had just settled in her office when she got a call from Justin, asking whether she had decided to accompany him on his trip to Holland.

"Only five days, but we'll have so much fun that you'll want to do it again," Justin said, his voice impregnated with optimism and cheerfulness. "We'd stay at the Grand Hotel Amsterdam, a place rich in charm and history. But I need an answer. My father wants me to leave today."

"What's the rush if you plan to stay that long?"

"There are some papers to be filed, and the certification of authenticity, which we asked for, will take place after the sale. The owner insisted that it should be done at our expense. That takes a day or so. Not much for us to do; we could go sightseeing."

She'd have liked to discuss Justin's offer with Romano but she hadn't been successful in contacting him. "I can't give you an answer right now. I didn't manage to talk it over with the boss."

"Yeah, I thought things were too rushed, but I gave it a try. I'll see you when I come back. Take care, Tamara."

For a moment Tamara stared into the distance, still puzzled by Justin's request. Who was the mysterious client his father was so obsequious to? Clearly someone filthy rich, if the story of the Delft pottery was true, but also a key player in the criminal ring if the acquisition of those art objects concealed the changing hands of dangerous biochemicals. Maybe a CSIS agent could shadow Justin on his upcoming trip.

A knock at the door interrupted her musing.

"Come in," she said.

A young man carrying a vase wrapped in cellophane stood on the threshold, balancing the vase and an enormous basket in his hands.

"I have a delivery for Ms. Templeton," he said.

"This isn't her office," Tamara said. "Come with me."

Tamara opened the door to Dianne's office and gestured the young man to deposit the flowers on the desk and the basket on a chair. There was no room for both on the desk. As she pulled open the cellophane to let the flowers breathe, she gave a furtive glance at the card. It said, "With undivided love, Harry." Clearly, Harry Pearson was still hoping to make up with Dianne.

She invited the young man back to her office and gave him a five-dollar tip, and received the man's profuse thanks.

It was time to call Brad and report her decline of Justin's offer. The line was busy. She made herself an instant coffee and then tried again. No answer this time, and the phone mail didn't come on. Strange, she thought. She'd better call Ron Brenner.

"Can I help you?" Ron asked as soon as he acknowledged that

he was speaking with her. He didn't sound at ease, though.

"Well, I don't know if Brad told anybody that Justin Devry invited me to go to Holland for what he said was the acquisition of Delft pottery."

"Ah, I don't know anything about it. Is there a problem?"

"No, Brad told me to let him know what I was going to do. I declined the invitation."

"I see."

Tamara was puzzled. "Meeting today?"

"I think so, but I'm not sure."

Tamara closed her cell, more confused than before. She looked at her watch: ten in the morning. She had time to do some work before going to the meeting. She sat in front of her HP and opened the file with the list of the objects currently in the company inventory. On a post-it she jotted down the items that had no price tag yet. There were only five. In Charles' absence it was her job to assign a starting value.

She went to the storage room to look at each item. Two were coffee tables; one was a Tiffany lamp, and two were the oil lamps Charles had been chasing for some time. He finally got them, Tamara thought, and probably he already has a customer in mind. She would leave a blank for the oil lamps. She tagged both tables with a 20-dollar sign and carefully examined the Tiffany lamp. It was old and small but there wasn't a single fault in it, and the colours of the glass inlays were very vivid. She pasted a hundred-dollar tag on it.

Once back in her office Tamara printed out the list of the auction's items and the list of the people who had already communicated their presence. She took both printouts to Charles' office and deposited them on his desk.

She went to the restroom and checked on her appearance. This time she would be in line with all the other members of Operation Bullfrog. Over her pale blue dress she wore a short white jacket bordered with the same fabric of the dress; her hair was styled behind her ears on one side with strands falling down on the other; her blue shoes had two-inch heels. A usual, she didn't wear any makeup, just a day cream to keep her skin moist.

She closed the office and climbed into her Subaru.

Three-quarters of an hour later she arrived at the house on Vanneck Road, now the official headquarters of Operation Bullfrog. Two cars were parked in the backyard and she lined hers up close to them. She entered the conference room.

Ron Brenner was pacing back and forth; Duncan Brown sat in one of the chairs, his legs stretched out over another in front of him. He was clicking on his laptop with alacrity. He looked at her from above his glasses and greeted her; Ron stopped before her.

"Hi, Tamara," he said. "Nice outfit you're wearing."

"Thanks," Tamara said. "I'm early, but not by much. Is everybody coming?"

Duncan put his laptop on the table. "We don't know. We can't reach anybody at CSIS except for a secretary, who keeps repeating that there's been an emergency. Most members are in session."

"Oh. That's in Toronto or Ottawa or where?"

Ron opened his arms in dismay. "We don't know."

Tamara glanced around. On the counter, which extended along one of the walls, the coffee machine was gurgling; several platters with food were covered with saran wrap; a big bowl showed a variety of fruits.

"The meeting may not be on, but the lunch surely is," she said.

Duncan approached her. "We're hoping you have some news." He looked up at her, expectantly.

"Me? I'm always the last one to know anything."

"Nothing at all? You don't know anything that may have triggered the emergency they're talking about?" Duncan's demeanour was strangely humble.

"I can hardly think of anything. I can tell you what involves our suspects. For one, Justin Devry is going to Holland to get some precious Delft platters. He invited me to go with him, but I refused. Brad's aware of this circumstance. I thought maybe a member of Operation Bullfrog would follow him, incognito. Justin could be a link to the import of dangerous bio-products. So this issue is in the air. Two, Dianne Templeton is away for a commercial; she'll come back later today; she's received a magnificent bouquet of flowers and a huge basket of smelly stuff from Harry Pearson, the owner of the Pamper Yourself Spa." She stopped and neared the counter to pour a cup of coffee. "As you can see, I don't know anything exciting. That's all, I'm afraid. What do you guys know?" she asked, and sat at the table.

"Only that the packages delivered by UPS to the spa were from a guy named Giorgio Tortorella of Bergamo, Italy, and that the declared merchandise consisted of flower arrangements in porcelain vases."

"Flowers arrangements for the spa?" Tamara asked. "That's curious."

"Not for a guy like Harry Pearson," Duncan said. "We checked him out. He's a fellow of strange taste and behaviour; he dresses in an extravagant way; when he was young he supported himself by painting on the streets and playing in a rock band."

"Gay?" Ron asked.

"I don't think so," Tamara interjected. "He has great taste and interest in women. Well, at least in the one I know of."

"Oh, right, I forgot. Dianne is his girl?" Ron asked.

"Was; now I believe he's trying to gain back her affection."

Tamara finished her coffee. "I'm starving. I think we can start with lunch." With sure strides she approached the counter, got a paper dish and scooped a helping from each platter.

The two men followed her example.

When lunch was over, Duncan looked at Ron and said, "What do we do now?"

"Wait. We wait for orders to come."

Chapter 39

Near London, Ontario
September 2007

"No! No, and no-ooh again," Thomas Sarcin said into the phone. "I don't want to hear anything of the sort, Zarathustra!"

"Don't call me that!"

"Hannibal, then. That's what they called you in school, when they found out you enjoyed eating live toads and frogs!"

"That story was made up. Stop right away, and remember that my name is Zac, short for Zaccaria, the saint."

"Okay, Zac. I don't want any part of your business. You're crazy!"

"Crazy because I want to make money?"

"You have plenty of it," said Thomas.

"Not as much as you do!"

"You don't know how much I have!"

"You still sell your safes to friends, oh, not commercially, of course, just as a favour — and they repay you handsomely in one form or another!"

"That's business; legitimate too, not like yours. You step out of the law anytime you please, with one excuse or another."

"A supreme goal justifies any means employed to achieve it."

"That what you said last time when you were a firm believer in the communist panacea." Thomas paused. "I wouldn't be surprised if you killed for them."

There was a laugh on the other side of the line. "Of course I did. But only once. I eliminated two enemies of the Great Cause. That was a must. It's in the past. This time politics has nothing to do with my action and what I propose to you."

"Then you're talking nonsense. My answer is no." Thomas slammed the desk phone down into its cradle.

His phone rang again and instinctively he lifted up the receiver.

"Thomas Sarcin," he said.

It was the same voice.

"I bought a nice piece of land in Fiji and I'm building a beautiful mansion up in the hills, away from the modern world. I know you liked that place. You stayed in those islands for months, and more than once."

"I was escaping then. I was escaping a difficult situation — and you know very well what it was: trying to please a father, who couldn't be pleased no matter what." Thomas paused, the many unbearable situations parading in his memory: the shouting, the reprimand, the belittling, the being sent to bed with no explanation or reason. "I'm not escaping anymore. And here's news for you. I'm going to sell the old place up north. I don't like it; actually I hate it. There's nothing there, and that nothing is surrounded by high walls and a reinforced gate. Father built it to protect himself from his demons." He paused. "He never realized, not even once, that the demons were inside him, devouring his mind and heart." The person on the other line didn't say a word, so Thomas pushed ahead to make his final point. "And don't bother emailing me all that rubbish that you call 'philosophical insight to the world,' Zarathustra!"

He slammed the phone down and pulled the cord out of the jack.

****

At the Operation Bullfrog headquarters in London, Tamara Smith, Duncan Brown and Ron Brenner had consumed all the coffee available. Ron Brenner had gone outside busying himself with pulling the many weeds that surrounded the house on Vanneck Road; Duncan was one piece with his laptop and the Internet; Tamara had gone to her car and retrieved the book she had just started, *Blood Work* by Michael Connelly.

Finally, at five in the afternoon, they reconvened in the conference room. It was then that Romano called. He wanted to talk to Tamara, but asked her to switch the phone to speaker, so that Duncan and Ron could listen in.

"Evidence points to Brad Wilson as being our leak." Tamara perceived pain in his voice. "If he contacts you, let me know immediately. Be on guard. He may be armed."

Tamara wanted to ask questions, but refrained herself from doing so to give Romano all the space he needed.

"We caught him as he was boarding a plane to Geneva. He had with him two and half million euros — a sum he couldn't justify in any way or shape. Brad was also the suspect Heather Motta pointed to in one of her reports to CSIS." He paused again, and Tamara already knew what was coming next. "He evaded our surveillance and he's on the loose."

"Sorry. I didn't suspect Brad," Tamara said. "He tried to keep me out of the loop, but I thought it was one of those things men do to women when they feel outplayed." She was flabbergasted. "I didn't picture him as a traitor to his country and humanity."

Romano continued. "Brad is aware of our plans. He may disappear from sight all together or he may alert his accomplices before doing so. A quarter of the police force in the country is out looking for him. We raided his house in Toronto. We didn't find any compromising material, not at first glance, at least, but we have some of his phone records. Brad was one of the most experienced and smartest agents. My guess is that he'll try to leave the country without contacting anybody. This way he'll be safe from a reprisal by his boss — whoever she or he is — and, at least temporarily, safe from us, since CSE has tapped all the phones of people he'd called for the last month." Romano stopped, clearly exhausted.

Tamara looked around; the eyes of Ron and Duncan, fixed on her, expressed a feeling between stupor and horror. Brad was one of them. The betrayal of a fellow officer was hard to take.

Romano continued. "We're running out of time. If the money Brad was carrying was a payoff, the virus is already in this country. The only clue we have is the spa and the adjoining building. We'll search it tomorrow morning. A team from CBRNE will be with us, and they'll assist us in analysing every square inch of it, testing on the spot for any kind of viruses, micro organisms, poisons and the like." Romano's voice was now raucous and low, probably for the talking he had done all day. "Tamara: keep an eye on Dianne and Charles."

"Yes, sir. I'll..." Tamara hesitated to add more burden onto Romano's shoulders, but she had no choice. "Justin Devry is going to Holland to import some fancy Delft pottery. He'd invited me to go with him, but I've declined."

"When was he leaving?"

"Tonight, with KLM."

"Too late to follow him. Know where he's staying?"

"The Grand Hotel Amsterdam."

"Good enough. I'll ask one of my Dutch colleagues to do some checking. Now, let me talk to Ron Brenner."

****

Frank looked with suspicion at the phone's little screen: unknown caller. It could be dangerous, he thought and didn't answer. Half an hour later he received the same call. He mentally reviewed the people who had his recent cell number; they were Zac and Boris. Then he remembered that he'd given that number to Sophia as well. It could be her. He would keep the call short. He clicked on *Talk*.

"Who is it?"

"It's Stan Glover, Mr. Milton, Sophia's friend."

"Are you alone?" Frank asked.

"Yes, yes."

"What's the problem?"

"Sophia is dead."

"Dead? Are you sure?"

"Yes, yes. They took her away in a big van."

"An ambulance?"

"No. Just a big van, almost as big as an RV."

"Then how do you know that she is dead?"

"Because..." Stan's voice faltered.

"Start at the beginning. Where were you when you saw the big van?"

"Don't be mad at me, Mr. Milton."

"I wouldn't. But you have to explain, give me some details. It's important." Stan was very loyal to Sophia, but he wasn't the smartest man on earth. "So —"

"After that girl escaped — you know of that girl, Tamara, right? — Sophia and I picked up a few things and left. We thought the police would come after us."

"I know that. She told me."

"We were in Kitchener when she thought about her dogs, Snapper and Blaze. She wanted to go back to get them." Stan paused, clearly embarrassed. "I didn't want to go, so I split."

The man wasn't as stupid as he thought, at least smarter than Sophia.

"Then I felt guilty. I went back to the farm. It was late and dark. I hid in a ditch along the road, and I saw two men dragging Sophia into the house. This big van drove in and stopped at the back door. I followed it and hid close to it. They were interrogating Sophia."

"Did she say anything about our operation?"

"I couldn't hear, Mr. Milton. I was outside. But she couldn't have had time to say a lot. She fell onto the floor."

"So you don't know if she was dead."

"There was a lot of commotion, then two men dressed in funny suits, like hazard suits, entered the house. They came out with Sophia on the stretcher and one said to the driver, 'They want us to take her to the hospital, even though she's dead.' Sophia was already in a bag."

Frank was silent. Somehow the authorities knew far more than he suspected. Time was getting critical; he had to act.

"Mr. Milton, are you there?"

"Yes, Stan, I am. We can't do much for Sophia, anymore. Just hide some place until I call you. You'll have to pick up a package for me at the spa." He paused. "The operation will be over very shortly."

"I don't know, Mr. Milton, if I want to do that for you. I'm kind of scared."

"Two thousand dollars, Stan, just for bringing a single package over here."

"I see. When would it be?"

"In a few days. I'll call you. Be ready. After that you'll be free as a bird. Agreed?"

"Okay. Two thousand you said?"

"Yes. Not one penny less."

"Fine," Stan said.

Frank shut his cell. He had to hurry up and call Boris.

It was night in Bergamo and Boris answered only at the tenth ring.

"Do you know that it's three o'clock in the morning?"

"Yes. I know," Frank said. "I can count the six-hour difference, Boris. Did you get the money?"

Silence.

"Boris, I asked you if you got the money."

"No. Not a cent — and you better explain why."

"It's a rather long story. That amount could not be transferred through a bank without answering critical questions, so the boss sent two envoys, each with half of the money. You'll get your money, don't worry, so ship the vaccine."

"I'd prefer to wait," Boris said.

"There's no time. One of my people is dead and the authorities have involved CBRNE, the centre specializing in dealing with epidemics. How they know is a mystery. We have to hurry up."

"Yes but —" Boris paused.

"Have I ever cheated you? Trust me. Ship 12 dosages of

vaccine to the spa. And use the Modano Company!"

"Okay," Boris replied.

"Don't use your name; do what you've done with the UPS shipment."

"That was that. I can't do it with the Modano Company. They know me. They traced my identity when I asked for information months ago."

"How was that possible?"

"The manager of my hotel in Venice spilled the beans."

"I see. You didn't send the vaccine for testing. Why?"

Silence again.

"Why Boris?"

"I need the money, Frank. I want to be sure I get it. You got all of the virus, and I haven't receive a cent yet!"

He didn't want to fight with Boris. He still needed him.

"Well, send over the vaccine as soon as you receive the payment, then, disappear."

"Will Switzerland be a good place to hide?"

"Hmm. Better farther away. Go back to the Ukraine if you have no other place to go." Frank stopped, exhausted. "But don't leave a single trace of chemicals and the like. Understood?"

"Yes. By the way, I better junk my old cell. I'll call you when I get a new one."

****

The temptation of going back to sleep was enormous, but Boris Youkenoff knew better. Five million euros was nothing to sneeze at. He should protect his capital. He stretched his limbs, jumped out of bed and took a shower.

He loaded the bit of equipment that was still in the house onto his truck. He packed what he had to ship and his personal stuff in two cartons and placed them near the entrance. He took the garden hose and carried it inside. He rinsed off every corner of the two-storey house. When he was finished, he opened the windows to let everything dry up.

He had made good time; it was only six in the morning. He went to the collective dump outside town and disposed of all the paraphernalia he had used for the experiments. When he returned, he hosed off each corner of the barn, which had served him as a garage, and then began washing his truck.

The red Fiat Punto of the landlady suddenly appeared behind his truck.

"Taking off?" she asked before she was out of the car. "You owe me money."

The last thing he needed was to have that greedy woman go to the police. Boris made sure to show how much he was annoyed as he pulled out his wallet.

"Here are 150 euros, one-week's rent for the extra three days I stayed." He threw the bills onto the hood of her car. "My friend called me. He had an accident and I have to meet him in Milan. I don't have to wait for him anymore. Please make up a receipt."

He began drying his car with a shammy, keeping an eye on the woman as she scribbled on a piece of paper.

"Here is the receipt," she said.

He stretched out a hand and took it, still wiping his car with the other hand. He didn't stop rubbing it until he heard the noise of the car fade away.

Chapter 40

The spa's parking lot was deserted, except for the CSIS surveillance van that was parked at the very end of the building.

"Ready?" Romano asked his crew.

All members silently assented.

They entered the spa and were welcomed by Armand's disarming smile.

"You're very early, gentlemen," he said. "Mr. Pearson isn't in yet."

"And you are — ?" Romano asked.

"Armand Belfleur, the receptionist." He stood, clearly puzzled.

"Mr. Belfleur, I'm Agent Romano and I have a court order to search this building." He showed him the paper. As Armand didn't take it, he put it on the dais. "Let's do it," he said to his crew.

Three CBRNE agents brought in a lab on wheels and began the testing. Followed by Ron Brenner and Duncan Brown, Romano stepped up on the stairs and forced open the door of Pearson's and Milton's office. He glanced inside and then proceeded further along the corridor that abruptly ended with a massive door. It was locked.

"Ask Armand to give us the key," he said.

Duncan descended the steps two by two and was back soon after. "He doesn't have it. He said Mr. Pearson told him not to let anybody enter the lab."

"I bet he did," Romano said, and called for the door to be torn down.

A big room faced them. As Romano looked at the long counter, he ordered the lab on wheels to be brought upstairs.

"This is the area that needs to be tested first." He inhaled a few times. "I can't smell anything. It's been cleaned recently."

He looked at one wall containing cabinets with glass doors. He neared them and opened them. Transparent pots with flower petals and seeds were neatly arranged in rows and labelled accordingly. He made a quick count. About a hundred containers. Was he in the wrong spot? Clearly this lab had been used for producing fragrances.

"Got something," a CBRNE agent said. "A few hairs. My guess is Guinea pig's hair."

So someone in the lab had been carrying out experiments on animals and whoever did it cleaned the place carefully afterwards. Outside the law, but nothing of what Romano expected to find. He sighed loudly.

"Anything wrong?" Duncan asked.

"*Nothing* is wrong; that's the problem." He gestured to Ron and Duncan to follow him. "The testing of all these premises will take hours. Let's hope they find something substantial. Meanwhile let's go down and look at the recording video the surveillance squad has made."

Once downstairs, a shaking Armand ran after him.

"Sir, there're clients scheduled to come; a few would want to

The Blackpox Threat

use the pool, others the exercise room." He looked at Romano, expectantly.

"The spa is closed," Romano said curtly.

"But we have to give a reason; we can't just brutally shut the door in our customers' faces."

Romano was on his way out. He looked at Armand and at the big waterfall at the end of the hall. "Tell you what, Mr. Belfleur. You make up a big sign with 'We regret to inform our clientele that the spa is temporarily closed because of a plumbing problem. We are addressing the situation and anticipate the reopening of the spa very soon.' Paste it on the door, Armand; everything will be fine."

Inside the van, Romano, Ron and Duncan reviewed the tapes that the surveillance team had recently made. There was nothing relevant in the first two tapes. As they started viewing the third tape, a zealous Armand drifted in sight onscreen. He drove a dark green Chrysler to the front of the spa's main entrance and helped a man load two plastic boxes. They zeroed onto the man first and the car's licence plate second.

"Anybody know who this man is?" Romano asked.

They all shook their heads, "no."

"Call Armand," Romano ordered Ron. He looked around at the interior of the van. It had been a camping site for day and night. Empty potato chip bags and nuts were scattered on the floor. "Duncan, clean a bit around here. I need to make Armand feel at ease. And then get some fresh coffee and tea."

When Ron did not return, Romano walked back to the spa, whose front door now exhibited the message he had dictated to Armand.

"Well, where is Armand?" Romano asked Ron.

"We can't find him," Ron said.

For the next half hour everybody searched the spa and the

adjacent building. No luck.

Armand Belfleur had disappeared.

****

When Tamara stepped into her office at the Modano Company, she found a bouquet of flowers towering her desk. Beside, was Dianne's post-it: "It's yours. I won't be in until Charles returns and I don't want to take it home. My new boyfriend may get jealous."

There was also a long note from Charles.

Thomas Sarcin invited me to spend a couple of days on his new boat. A bit of fun, a bit of discussion about our business together. I may not be back for the auction. You can cancel it or run it all by yourself. Your choice!

Charles.

Great, Tamara thought, upset by the notes. She was supposed to keep an eye on these two people, and what do they do? They take off.

The mail consisted of only one invoice for which she wrote a cheque right away. She turned on her HP and checked how many participants had already registered for the auction. Fifteen. With all that was going on in Operation Bullfrog, it would be expedient to cancel the event, but 15 people, in these kinds of auctions, meant at least 15 items sold. She wouldn't cancel it. She walked into Dianne's office to retrieve her recording pen, and replaced it with another, ready to be used. She had regularly utilized these snooping devices, even if they had provided her with only one clue. She listened carefully to what had been going on in Dianne's office the last few days. As expected, there were a few office calls and a couple of mushy conversations with Gordon, her new boyfriend. Nothing substantial.

The Blackpox Threat

Tamara looked around. There wasn't much else to do. She carried the flowers in both arms to her car and headed home.

Parked in front of her house was Justin's Audi. Justin immediately got out and waived at her. He helped her carry the floral arrangement into the house.

"I thought you had gone to Holland," Tamara said, recovering from the surprise.

Justin winked at her. "A bit of meddling, at times, gives excellent results." He deposited the bouquet on the living room floor. "I knew that my father's friend, Barbara was dying to go to Holland. So I suggested that it'd be nice to have our own expert examine the antiques that we were going to buy. Perhaps Barbara would like to take a look at the many other items that this Dutch collector has at his home; that probably she could take pictures and get a publication out of it." Justin gave Tamara a brotherly kiss on her cheek before continuing. "Barbara fired up and chimed right in. I said I'd gladly renounce the trip if the two of them wanted to go. At that point Father was trapped." He grinned. "So here I am, at your service." He slumped onto the couch and took off his baseball cap. "It's nice to look at you. You're my ideal woman. You have the perfect proportions above and below the waist, great legs and a cute face. You don't even wear makeup and you're gorgeous or else you've found one that's invisible."

For a moment Tamara didn't know what to do or say. She picked up the flowers, set them on the Louis XV console, and freed them of the cellophane.

"I understand you like me, Justin. That's great." She sat close to him.

"It's more than that. I'd..."

Tamara tapped a finger on his lips. "It isn't the right time, Justin."

"I see," Justin said, and kissed her finger. He pointed at the flowers. "Am I in competition with a florist?"

Tamara laughed. "No, flowers and florist have nothing to do with it. It's because of the position I'm in. I can't get involved."

"Not even for a brief romantic interlude? It'd be good for the spirit and the body."

Tamara shook her head no and reinforced her previous statement. "I can't get involved."

Justin pulled her close. "But you would later?"

Tamara tapped him on the nose. "You want to know too much."

Suddenly, Justin hugged her and kissed her on the neck. "I think of you in the day and I dream of you at night. You cast a spell on me."

His torso pressed against her breasts; his hair tickled her face; his arms around her unmistakably spelled strong desire. For weeks she had dreamed of Justin making love to her. Tamara closed her eyes, hoping that her body wouldn't betray her feelings. It was wonderful to be wanted. She had longed for that sensation, and Justin was now delivering it, forcefully and unconditionally. It was a magic moment and she wanted to capture it in her memory forever.

Slowly she disengaged herself from his embrace. She caressed his hair tenderly and said, "Let's get out of here. Would you like to take me out for lunch?"

Justin faintly assented.

****

From time to time Tamara gave Justin a furtive look from the top of her menu. Justin was busy reading his. She thought of what had happened while they were in her condo, how passionate and tender he had been.

Who was Justin? She asked herself. He was a person at ease as only honest people can be. At peace with the world. She couldn't picture him as being part of a conspiracy.

"I'll take the shish kebab," Justin said, breaking her musings.

"I was thinking of the same." Tamara closed the menu and returned it to the table. She had not given a look at it, too busy observing her companion. "Nice place," Tamara said, and complimented the cozy atmosphere.

It was past noon and Moxie's Classic Grill was getting busy.

"While you order, I'll go to the Ladies room," Tamara said, and rose.

"Anything to drink?

"Just water for me."

Her inseparable bag hanging from her shoulder, Tamara went to the Ladies' restroom. Fortunately, it was deserted. She placed a call to Romano and quickly updated him about the morning's events. She listened while Romano recounted the raid at the spa and the little they had found so far, and of the mysterious disappearance of Armand Belfleur.

"Anything you want me to do?" Tamara asked.

"Yes. Come to the spa at 1:30. Alone. You may be able to help us."

When she returned to the table the meal was already served.

"Fast service," she said.

"No," Justin said, and laughed. "Long call."

"How do you know that I was placing a call?"

"Intuition." Justin began removing a piece of meat and a cut of red pepper from the skewer. "I'm out of the loop, but I still can put two and two together."

Tamara indulged in savouring a piece of meat before asking,

"Why do you think you're out of the loop?"

Justin buttered a roll, bit into it and then continued. "First, there was this course CSIS wanted me to attend; then, I got some information at the police station. You remember Bill Hartwart? He was told to keep quiet about your kidnapping, and he did. But then he had to fill in a report about the car accident. They asked him what was he doing in your car and he had to tell the truth. CSIS had asked not to say anything about the kidnapping — but meanwhile several people knew." Justin finished his roll and then got another piece of grilled meat. "Rumours spread outside the London station and one of CSIS's top men came down to lecture to them. I was having a beer with Bill and his friends when they told me of Brad Wilson's visit."

"Brad Wilson came to the police station?"

"Yes, to tell them to keep quiet, but also to inform them that I was a suspect."

"The bastard!"

"Nobody believed him. Why would I save you from Sophia Tadlova and her goon if I was in with the bad guys?" Justin lowered the skewer Tamara had in the air, close to her face. "Watch your eyes. That stick is very pointed."

"Oh my God," Tamara said, and set the stick on her plate. "Beware of Brad Wilson. He crossed the line. He's dangerous. There's an order for his arrest. He was caught as he was trying to board a plane for Switzerland, with more than two million euros in his briefcase. Unfortunately, he managed to escape." Tamara paused. "You remember Heather Motta, the OPP member who was present at that meeting Brad insisted we disguise as a picnic at Fanshawe Park?"

Justin nodded. "She mentioned there was an internal investigation."

"Right. Brad had managed to have her removed from his group. She had evidence, not strong, unfortunately, that Brad was on the take."

"You mean to tell me that a senior CSIS was involved in biological warfare?"

"Yes. Brad is a double-crosser, and the worst part of it is that he knows all the moves Operation Bullfrog intends to make." She finished her meal and pushed away her dish. "Romano, who directs the operation, hopes that he'll not contact his accomplices for fear of retaliation."

"Oh my God," said Justin. "And you're in the middle of all that?"

"More or less." Tamara looked at her wristwatch. They had come with both cars, since Tamara presumed she had to join Romano's crew. "I've got to go, Justin. Thank you for the wonderful lunch, and the company."

Chapter 41

"Do you recognize this man?" was the first question Romano asked Tamara. Romano had shown her the frames in which Armand Belfleur appeared driving a Chrysler to the curb of the spa's entrance and then helping a man load two boxes. "The building's owner is Harry Pearson and it so happens that he's not available."

Tamara looked closely at the screen. "I've never seen him, but I believe he could be the man interested in the shipments that Dianne Templeton has to fetch personally. His name is Frank Milton."

"Oh, finally somebody who can give us some useful information." He called Duncan Brown. "Duncan, go after this Frank Milton."

"Know anything more about him?" Duncan asked.

"Yes, he's the person who supplies the ointments for the massages."

"He could be a chemist," Duncan ventured.

"Yes. He could be," Romano said. "Duncan, find his address,"

Duncan retreated to the back of the van and began clicking on his inseparable laptop.

"Did you find anything in the building that points to dangerous biochemicals?" Tamara asked.

"Not a thing. It's very frustrating and it'll be embarrassing when we'll have to justify our raid." Romano turned off the tape. "Anything else you can tell us about Frank Milton?"

"Not really, he's a friend of Harry Pearson, but you must have figured that out."

Romano nodded and said, "We can't find Armand Belfleur. Do you know anything about him?"

"Only that he's the receptionist and he does a superb job in making the spa's customers feel welcome."

"Armand escaped under our eyes. Do you know how he could have done it?"

"Not a clue."

"Let's go to the spa. You must have studied the layout when you seized the famous red folder," Romano said.

"Only enough to move fast and elude Armand when I went upstairs."

Romano opened the van's door and gestured Tamara to get out and follow him.

The spa was teeming with people, some wearing protective outfits.

"Can you think of any place where Armand could hide, or any passages through which he could have escaped?"

Tamara looked at the fountain. The water trickled from the top of the back wall in a soothing and continuous motion; it made noise only when it tumbled into the collector at the bottom.

"When I came here for the second time the fountain wasn't working. I noticed a door in the wall."

She neared an abstract painting hanging on the side of the

fountain. She set it aside and a casing appeared. She opened it and depressed a red lever. The water stopped. Carved in the wall was a door, painted beige, the same colour of the wall.

Romano approached it and opened it to reveal a long corridor.

"Follow the tunnel," Romano said to an officer close to him. "And see if there is any trace of our receptionist."

Romano gestured Ron Brenner and Tamara to come close. "We have Harry Pearson's address. Let's go there and see what we can find." He turned to Tamara and grinned. "I'm sure you don't want to face him — he may be able to recognize you — but I'd like you to stay in the van in case I have questions."

"No problem," Tamara replied.

Just off Fanshawe Park Road there was an old house with a frontage of at least half an acre. Unconcerned about the dust that they would create, the drivers of the van and the Buick rocketed on the parched driveway and stopped in front of the brick house, both vehicles shrouded in yellow dust.

Romano rang the bell and Harry Pearson, in a purple velvet robe and purple slippers, opened the door.

"What is this?" he asked. "It that the way to drive on somebody's property?"

"Dale Romano, special CSIS task unit," he said. "Sorry about the dust, but this is an emergency."

"Somebody died?" Harry inquired, and stepped aside to let the team enter.

"No." Romano said. "But many people could." He took a sheet of paper out of his pocket and said, "We're authorized to search your house."

"Search my house? And what for? I don't do drugs."

A faint smile appeared on Romano's face. "We're looking for something more dangerous than drugs. Can we sit down some place? I'd like to ask you a few questions."

Harry moved into a room with an enormous wall TV, a desk, a bookcase, a low table, a recliner and two upholstered chairs. He sat in one and gestured Romano to the other.

Without asking permission, Romano turned on a small voice recorder. "Do you know where Mr. Frank Milton is?" he asked.

"Away on business, I believe."

"Where?"

"Oh, oh, Frank never tells me when he takes off or when he comes back or where he goes." Harry's eyes followed the two agents who were examining his collection of books.

"You're the owner of the spa and the adjoining building. There is a lab in that building. What is its purpose?"

"Oh, Frank mixes oils with fragrances; I use them when I do the massages or I sell them directly to my clients. He creates new unguents and emulsions all the time."

"What kind of oils?"

Harry shrugged. "I don't know exactly. Coconut, almond, olive, something like that. Frank worked with a big cosmetic lab before he came to the spa. He's very good at what he does."

"So Mr. Milton works for you?"

"Oh no!"

"You aren't his boss?"

"Absolutely not."

"But you're the owner of the spa and the lab attached to it."

Harry wiggled in his chair, clearly uneasy. "You see, Frank gave me the money for my business in exchange…" He stopped. "The agreement was that I'd let him be free to experiment in making new cosmetic products. He thought that, with time, he could enter the market with his own company and make good money."

The Blackpox Threat

"But he didn't?"

"Well...too early to tell about the money. He got a license for the Iridient, that's the name of his company, only a few months ago. But I can tell you that my customers like and buy the products he makes."

"Do you have any of these products here, in your house?"

"Sure, in the bathroom."

"We'll take them," Romano said.

"Why? You didn't say what you're looking for."

Romano hesitated, then said, "We've reason to believe that a virus has been developed at the lab. We need to collect all products that have been recently created by Mr. Milton."

"A virus? You must be crazy. There's no way. You can't go around making claims like that, my spa will never recover from such bad publicity!"

Romano ignored him. "We need the addresses of Mr. Armand Belfleur and Frank Milton."

Without saying a word Harry went to the desk and opened the front drawer. He extracted a black notebook and dictated an address to Romano. "Frank has just moved out of his apartment. He didn't give me his new address." He consulted the notebook again. "The old one is 1005 Richmond Street, Apt.101."

"Thank you for your cooperation." Romano turned off the recorder and rose. "Mr. Pearson, the spa is closed until further notice."

Romano climbed into the van and slumped onto the rear seat.

"It seems Frank Milton is our key player. Unfortunately he's ahead of us."

"I got his address," Duncan said triumphantly. "It is — "

"1005 Richmond Street, Apt.101," interjected Romano. "He moved from there."

"Oh," Duncan said. "Too bad."

Tamara, who had not joined the team in Harry's house, said, "I called the Chrysler dealers in London and found who sold the car to a Frank Milton. They didn't want to tell me whether or not he paid with a credit card, but they'll release that information to police."

The crew had finished searching Harry's house and joined the others in the van. "Nothing, Mr. Romano. We couldn't find anything suspicious."

Romano covered his face with his hands. "What's next?" he whispered.

"The passport office!" exclaimed Tamara. "If this man is involved in biological warfare he must plan to leave the country."

Romano sighed. "Ron, give it a try first thing tomorrow morning. See if he has one. However, if he's our man, the odds are that he has a false passport, perfectly compiled and computer-readable."

"What about Armand?" Tamara asked.

"We have his address and we can pay him a visit. But I believe Frank Milton kept his activity — the criminal part of it — well concealed from his friend Harry and anybody else working at the spa." Romano pointed to two agents. "Go to interview Armand Belfleur; Ron, go to the Chrysler dealer, tonight. Everybody else, back to headquarters. Meeting at 21:00 sharp. We need to review our options."

A call came in. Romano listened carefully for about a minute.

"It was CBRNE. They didn't find any trace of smallpox or ebola in the soil of Sophia Tadlova's farm or her neighbours'. Nothing in Sophia's house either. No exposure whatsoever." He paused, looking exhausted. "The dogs were likely the only evidence we could have had — and their carcasses have been reduced to ashes."

The Blackpox Threat

In the van nobody moved or made any noise. Finally Romano broke the impasse.

"Tamara, when is the new shipment due to arrive?"

"Tomorrow."

"Call us as soon as you know something definite. We'll be there. Any ideas anybody?"

"What about Sophia? Will there be a funeral?" Tamara asked. "Maybe somebody would show up, maybe Stan — Sophia's goon — would attend."

"It's a possibility," Romano said, his face showing signs of enormous fatigue. "I doubt it, however. No one even came to claim her body." He looked around. "Can someone take Tamara back to the spa, where she's left her car?" He rose and turned to her. "I'd give you a ride myself, but on my way to headquarters I have to brief the Prime Minister. It'll be a long and painful call."

Chapter 42

Zaccaria had pampered the woman in every way, shape and form and yet she still wouldn't agree to take a vacation with him. What was the matter with Stephanie Demoins? Every Saturday night he had taken her out to the best restaurants in town and, recently, to a reception offered by the Russian Embassy in Ottawa. She had shown appreciation for the attention, but she had kept him out of her business. When he had offered to finance the new shop she would like to open in the capital, she had flatly refused.

"I simply don't mix business with pleasure," she had said with a flirtatious smile. "If I can afford a new outlet, fine; if I can't, well, that's fine too. I have to wait until the end of the year to see which is which."

He had then changed tactics. He had spent hours in her shop on Dundas Street, pompously named The French Look, and showed interest in her work and looking at her in action. Often, pins in her mouth, she personally knelt in front of a prestigious customer to mark how a dress should be altered. Other times he arrived at the shop early and watched her while she sketched a new outfit, or cut into a soft fabric to create a prototype she hoped to sell to the big ateliers.

At first Stephanie had been enthusiastic about being with him; with pride she introduced him to the people she knew. But the relationship had not gone much further.

Zaccaria wondered why. Stephanie, a former model of Versace, was a splendid creature. Her oval face was framed by curly hair that often rebounded on her forehead in a capricious way. Her green eyes sparkled with cheer, and her body moved with grace and vigour at the same time. At the Governor General's party she had been the focus of more than one man's attention. It was then that he had decided that she was the perfect centrepiece for his project.

Soon he would receive the virus that would horrify the world. He needed a subject of Stephanie's calibre to carry the maximum impact.

He toyed with the Fuji digital camera he always carried with him. He needed to do whatever was necessary to convince Stephanie to take a vacation out of the country. Only then would he put his plan in motion. He would photograph her beautiful body first, and then as the devastating virus ravaged her body he would again takes pictures after every feature of her face, every square inch of her skin had been devoured.

Yes, tonight was the night.

****

He sat at a table, wondering why Stephanie was so late. Normally she was punctual, give or take a few minutes. He ordered another martini, impatient to recite the speech he had prepared. The tables around him were served with dishes that oozed delicious aromas. The restaurant of the Delta London Armouries was well known for its superb cuisine. He was getting famished.

Finally Stephanie appeared in the doorway. She looked around and waved at him. Wearing a red outfit that didn't leave any guessing about her perfect anatomy, she attracted the attention of most people in the hall. Zaccaria rose as a waiter glided near Stephanie and moved out a chair for her.

"Sorry I'm a bit late. I got a late customer."

"Important, I guess." He tried to keep the frustration out of his voice.

"Quite, yes." She took the menu that lay on the table and said, "I'll skip the drink. Let's order." She opened the menu and consulted it for a good five minutes. "This Raclette sounds interesting; melted cheese, potatoes, ham and dried beef. I always like to try something new." She deposited the menu on the table.

The waiter was standing, waiting.

"Steak for me, medium rare, baked potato with sour cream and green beans," Zaccaria said quickly.

"Wine?" the waiter asked.

"Beaujolais?" Stephanie asked Zaccaria.

"Oh, yes. A bottle," he said to the waiter.

Stephanie gave him a big smile. "You said you had something important to tell me. You got me curious. What is it?"

He forced himself to recite the part of a lover consumed by passion. Out of his pocket, he took a little package wrapped in silver paper and said with a warm, tender voice, "As you probably have guessed, Stephanie. I'm madly in love with you."

Stephanie unwrapped the package and opened the box. Lying on blue velvet was a diamond of the marquis cut. "Oh, that's beautiful! Look how it sparkles!"

"I'm asking you to marry me, Stephanie." He couldn't resist

adding, "Soon."

Stephanie kept looking at it, clearly surprised.

She's very pleased, Zaccaria thought. She must think she has made it in life!

Slowly, Stephanie closed the little box and said, "I'm sorry, but I can't accept this."

"What?"

She reached for his hand and tapped on it. "Don't be upset, Zaccaria. When I met you, I fell for you. Love at first sight. Your masculine yet elegant presence, your flair — all of you impressed me." She paused and sipped the ice water the waiter had silently put in front of her. "I still like you, of course."

"So, what's wrong?"

"Our relationship is at a standstill. I don't know anything more about you than I knew the first night I met you, at the Governor General's party. You seem to be impenetrable. When I come close, you seem to avoid me...I told myself that maybe I was wrong, that the intimacy would come, given time. But it didn't..."

The waiter reappeared and gracefully put a dish in front of each of them. "Bon appétit," he said, and left.

Zaccaria stared at Stephanie, who had started to savour her Raclette. The nerve this woman had! Refusing not only to spend a vacation with him, but even his proposal of marriage! She will pay — oh, will she pay! Wait until he had all the power that the blackpox would confer him! She would be on her knees, begging for her life!

His heart pounded hard and he could feel the vessels in his temples throbbing. He closed his eyes, trying to gain control of his rage. He finally managed to reopen his eyes.

"Let's take things as they are, then," he said. "For the time being, at least."

Chapter 43

Tamara's sleep, troubled by her recurrent nightmare, had been intermittent and short. At eight in the morning she got up and jumped onto her Bowflex. The exercise reinforced her muscles, but didn't calm her nerves. The anxiety she had developed at the meeting of the previous night was taking its toll. There had been bad news as Romano commented on a report of the World Health Organization; they had established that the remains of the fruit bats found in the cave of the Carpathian Mountains did indeed contain traces of smallpox. The only positive result of the investigation was that the virus was no longer active. The centre was working on a press release that would be informative without raising unnecessary alarm.

Tamara showered, toweled dry and got dressed, a sense of urgency permeating her body and mind.

She drove to her office.

The auction was on and as she would have to run it all by herself, she had better get busy. She assembled all the items she could carry in the hall and lined up the chairs for the participants. Her mind, however, never ceased to think of the danger that was around the corner and of the little progress that they had made in the recent weeks.

It was two in the afternoon and the call that would announce the arrival of a package for Harry Pearson had not yet come. She grew impatient and worried, looking for things to do. Then the phone rang. For a split second the sound raised her hopes; until she realized it was her phone, not Dianne's, that was ringing.

Justin's cheerful voice lifted up her spirits. "I'm in town. Can I come to your office or is it off limits?"

"Oh, hi, Justin. Any chance you have something to eat with you?"

"Of course. That's my passport. Hawaiian pizza and apple crisp."

"Hmm. Sounds good, and would you also be available to do some work?"

"Anything for you. Open the main door, I'm just outside."

With Justin around she would never go hungry, Tamara thought as she unlocked the main door.

"Are you here alone?" Justin asked.

Tamara nodded. "The maintenance man doesn't come in on Friday and Dianne is away. Charles may still drop by, but he wasn't sure he could make it."

"What work needs to be done?" Justin asked as he set down the food on Tamara's desk.

"There is an auction tomorrow and a few pieces have to be taken from the storage to the hall. They aren't too heavy. The two of us can easily make it."

Justin extracted two orange juices from his jacket pocket and offered one to Tamara. He then sat in a chair and opened the carton from Papa John's.

"I can help you. Tomorrow too?"

"If you could it'd be great. The number of registrants had risen from the initial 15 to 35. It's going to be a big crowd. It's nice if there is someone to help carry the items to the clients' cars. I'll be at the podium and I can't leave until the auction closes. Some customers, however, prefer to take off early. Your presence will come in handy."

Justin nodded, pulled a slice of pizza free and began eating.

Tamara's cell rang. It was Romano. "I assume you didn't get any call, am I right?"

"Yes. Dianne's phone didn't ring even once."

"We're going to customs. If there's a package for Harry Pearson, we'll get it. We got the necessary authorization."

"Dale," said Tamara, rushing to speak before Romano would cut off the communication, "Do you know what to do with the package?"

"Yes. We talked to Armand. Upset about our incursion at the spa he had indeed escaped through the tunnel, where he kept his bicycle. He's a fitness fanatic, he doesn't own a car. This morning he was calm and cooperated fully. He told us that there's a kind of procedure in place. Dianne would inform Harry of the arrival, bring the parcel to the spa and give it to Armand. Armand would deposit it, unopened, outside the door of Frank's lab, at the end of the corridor." Romano paused. "And that's exactly what we're going to do — if the parcel is there. Anything else?"

"Yes, if the package doesn't arrive today do you want me to wait for the call on Monday and go get it?"

"Yes. If at all possible, we'd like to avoid any move that may alert Dianne Templeton, in case she's part of the conspiracy. The only reason we go to customs now is that we don't want to lose two days just because some lazy guy didn't call Dianne, and the package is sitting there waiting to be picked up."

****

The auction had required all her attention, taking Tamara's mind off the impending danger the nation was facing. Justin's assistance and his good nature had also helped restore her positive predisposition to life.

"You're a precious companion," Tamara said as Justin was busy massaging her feet. She had been wearing high heels at the auction, standing for four hours straight. Now she was home, stretched out on her leather couch, with her head propped on one arm of the sofa. Justin was sitting at the other end.

"Feeling better?" Justin asked.

"Yes. Thank you for everything. I'm happy I didn't cancel the sale. Did you see how people went crazy for the credenza? That little old lady defeated the competition and finally got it for $4,500! We raised a total of $31,000 and made a lot of customers happy. I feel I earned my position as PR person."

"You surely did. I heard a lot of comments about you, all positive." Justin stood up and unhooked the medallion Tamara was wearing around her neck. "I'll change the battery." He took a little metal disk out of his pocket and inserted it into the back of the medallion. "Done," he said, and refastened the necklace around Tamara's neck. "You all right?"

Tamara nodded. "I'm going to bed soon. While I was running the auction Duncan Brown came here to change the alarm system, in case Brad Wilson shows up at my door." She lifted the medallion and kissed it. "Together with this, I feel very protected."

"Good. If you need anything, call. I'm going to have a beer

with Bill, my friend at the station, and then I'll be heading home." He bent to kiss Tamara. "Bye, Tamara."

"Bye, Justin."

She hated to see him leave, but she needed to have a good rest, which, hopefully, would appease her anxiety. Things weren't progressing well. At customs they hadn't found any package for Harry Pearson and no one had spotted Milton's Chrysler on the road. The only positive result was the tracing of Milton's bank. Frank Milton had paid for his new car with a credit card issued by the Bank of Montreal. His related account contained only a few thousand dollars. They had also obtained Milton's picture from the provincial drivers licence office.

It was now a waiting game — a game nobody who belonged to Operation Bullfrog felt comfortable playing.

Chapter 44

After the dinner with Stephanie Demoins, Zaccaria fell sick. He had a severe headache; he felt dizzy; the world spun around him every time he tried to stand up. Of course, he wanted the world to revolve around him, but not in this way...his plan to take Stephanie away for a vacation had miserably failed. How was it possible that he had misjudged the situation by a mile? Stephanie was a flirting butterfly, a party woman, who giggled and laughed even at the stupidest joke! He found out that she thought of herself as a business person who knew what she wanted, and was capable of achieving it. She was crazy! Women were put on earth to please men; they had no other reason to exist.

He had to think quickly. Think of an alternative plan to scare the world.

Lying on the sofa with a pillow underneath his head and an icepack on his forehead, he mentally reviewed the females he had met recently and who could play the role he had invented for Stephanie.

The Blackpox Threat

At a recent promotional party for the launch of a brand new shower gel and ad campaign, the guests were invited to preview the new commercial and were introduced to the beautiful actress who had starred in the two-minute ad. Zaccaria recalled the scene of her lathering her body with the new soap and drying herself seductively in a soft pink bath towel. She had attracted the attention of more than one man. Zaccaria had gone to the party with Stephanie; the actress, he recalled, was escorted by a young man. He made an effort to remember her name but he couldn't. His headache was mounting. He decided to get some rest and postpone any more thoughts regarding his next victim.

A full eighteen hours later he woke up refreshed, his headache completely gone. He even remembered the name of the actress he had seen in the TV ads: Dianne Templeton. Satisfied with his recollection, he rose, showered and made himself a breakfast of bacon, eggs and toasted brown bread. Coffee was brewing in a corner of the kitchen counter. The sound of an approaching car at his gated entrance attracted his attention. Very few people were allowed on his property; only a handful of his men even knew his address.

Zaccaria quickly reached for the gun he kept in a kitchen drawer. His cell rang. It was one of his key men. "Yes," he said.

"Zac, I have a problem. Let me in."

Zaccaria clicked on the remote that would open the gate and then on the one that would unlock the house door.

"What are you doing here?" Zaccaria asked unceremoniously.

"You can't believe what happened." The man collapsed in a chair.

As his interlocutor didn't utter a sound, Zaccaria said, "Spit it out. We can't waste time."

"I was going through security at Toronto Airport when the

alarm went off. The woman in front of me triggered the alarm. She had dropped a knife onto the floor. She tried to flee and in so doing pushed me onto the ground. It was a chaotic situation. The area was cordoned off and everybody in the area was escorted to a room held by security where they were subjected to a thorough search." He paused. "They found my money and they began asking questions."

"Did they sequester the money?"

"Yes, all of it."

"Shit! Two and half million euros!"

"I managed to escape, but they're looking for me. The entire country is looking for CSIS agent Brad Wilson, armed and dangerous. I need a place to hide where they can't find me until the operation is over."

Zaccaria remained silent, quickly examining his options. The man appeared to be totally, irrevocably useless, now; worst than that, he had become a liability.

"I thought I could stay here, for the time being," Brad said. "I'll need a clean cellular, a gun and access to the Internet."

The trill of a phone intruded. It was Frank Milton.

"I'm ready with the new list of email recipients. I've got politicians, industrialists, news media contacts...I split the messages in groups of a dozen each, so they don't get flagged as spam. Are you ready?"

What was the matter with Frank? Was he trying to give orders, now?

"What about the vaccine?" Zaccaria asked.

"It's supposed to come in today. So are we ready to go? As I told you before, the virus is only active for two to three weeks."

Zaccaria was trying to evaluate the situation. Brad Wilson wasn't in the loop anymore so he could no longer monitor CSIS's moves and give him a chance to counteract them. Even worse, Brad couldn't slow down the actions CSIS was ready to take. Yes, they had to move, but another day or two wouldn't make that much difference and meanwhile he could get a woman for the big showdown.

"We wait a couple of days. I'll call you." He cut the communication off. He turned to Brad. "I have a job for you. Go out and get me a beautiful woman. Not a prostitute, though — a woman of substance. I want to infect her with the virus and take enough pictures of her to flood the Internet with."

Brad jumped up. "What? You always said you wanted to scare people bad enough that they'd pay; you never said that you wanted to create an epidemic!"

"And you believed me?" Zaccaria's dark eyes bored into Brad's. "You don't know what I am capable of!"

Chapter 45

"You're doing fine, Tamara," Romano said with his soothing voice. When she had climbed into her car she had exchanged Justin's medallion with a two-way transmitter that put her in direct communication with Romano. Romano wouldn't take any chances. He parked his unmarked Buick very close to the airport building and waited until Tamara had dispatched all formalities at customs and got the parcel addressed to Harry Pearson.

Tamara walked to her car, her stride as natural as she could muster, careful not to shake the package she was carrying. In the back of her Subaru two agents looked carefully at the box and created another one that, exteriorly, looked identical. So far so good, Tamara thought with relief. Dianne wasn't in her office so Tamara drove to the spa.

The big sign indicating the spa's closure had been temporarily removed and Ron Brenner had taken Armand's place.

Tamara gave the fake package to Ron, who took it upstairs and set it in front of the door that led to Frank's lab.

"What do I say to Dianne when I see her?" Tamara asked Romano over the transmitter. "She may get upset because of my initiative to take the package to the spa."

She heard a faint laugh. "You'll have to take the heat, *Agent Smith!*" He then added, "There's a Sunoco station on your way; stop there and let my two agents out. I'll pick them up. Hand them the special transmitter I gave you this morning. We may need it."

"Yes, sir."

Her duties discharged for the time being, Tamara headed to the Modano Company.

In the parking lot there was Charles' car flanked by another one she didn't recognize. Dianne's vehicle wasn't there. She quickly checked her hair in the rear-view mirror, combed it the best she could and changed her running shoes with a pair of dressy ones. Her pantsuit, soft green linen, was suitable for an employee in the PR business.

As soon as she passed through the main door, she heard loud voices, and then a "Come in, come in, Tamara," by Charles. "I'm happy you came. Come to share our improvised party!"

On Charles' desk was a tray with hors d'oeuvres and a bottle of champagne. Beside the desk stood Thomas Sarcin, looking great in a pair of jeans and a blue polo shirt.

"Hello Tamara," Thomas said. "Nice to see you again."

"Hello everybody," Tamara replied, and deposited her purse on a chair. "I see it's party time. Any special occasion?"

Charles waved two fingers in front of her. "One, because Thomas and I are going to be partners; two, because of the success of Saturday's auction." He stroked her on her shoulder. "I bet our storage room is empty!" He held up the glass he had in the other hand in a toast. "To the best PR this company ever had!"

Thomas had gotten an extra glass and filled it with champagne.

The Blackpox Threat

"Here, Tamara," he said.

"Thanks, folks. I see some wonderful canapés: salmon on rye is one of my preferred ones." She tasted one and then sipped her wine. "Dianne isn't in?" she asked Charles.

"She's has been sick the whole weekend and still is. She'll probably be in tomorrow."

Since she had entered the room Thomas had focused his eyes on her. She felt embarrassed and for a moment she didn't know how to divert his attention. Finally, it came to her.

"The last time I saw you, you were talking about manuscripts kept in a special container, one of the kind that you had designed and built for the occasion — air tight. Were they preserved as you expected?"

"Oh, you remember!" Thomas embraced her in a warm smile, clearly pleased. "Yes, the scholar to whom I donated the manuscripts complained about their status; he couldn't read some words, in some instances entire phrases, but I had made a photocopy of the documents before storing them. The comparison was almost perfect. Only the colour of the paper showed a bit of alteration; it was a bit more yellow, naturally." He refilled Tamara's glass even though it wasn't empty.

"Are you in business also along this line of expertise?" Tamara asked.

"Oh no. That was a special occasion. I don't build safes of any kind anymore."

"Attracted to the arts and antiques?" Tamara inquired. She couldn't figure out why Thomas had gone or was going into business with Charles.

"Not really. The Modano Company seems to be a good business in which to invest."

Charles stepped in. "I'm planning to decrease my involvement.

New blood is welcome and necessary."

Tamara didn't know what to make of the new partnership; why was Charles withdrawing? Did he owe money to Thomas he couldn't pay directly? Why would Thomas be involved in a business that required knowledge of antiques and a lot of scouting around for acquiring items at a low price? Or was Thomas acquiring a way to ship illegal items around the world? Finally she told herself that she shouldn't show her perplexities — after all, at the Modano Company she was a simple employee and the last comer.

Tamara lifted her glass and said, "To the success of your new venture!"

****

After a couple of stops to buy groceries and a bag of food for her fish Tamara went home. She felt relaxed, as things were finally moving in the right direction. There was no meeting scheduled for the evening or tomorrow; one group was busy analyzing the contents of the parcel just received; another was ready to follow the person who would pick up the fake package at the spa.

She looked forward to having a peaceful evening at home. She planned on doing a few of the domestic chores that had been sorely neglected of late. She started the cleaning cycle for the aquarium and later she would fill the automatic dispenser with food. Fortunately, fish didn't need company, or by now they would all be dead.

She closed the drapes and moved into the kitchen to bake some squares. She had not baked anything since the day she attended the Governor General's party. When she went to retrieve her recipe book from its regular location in the kitchen drawer, it was missing.

Assuming she misplaced it, she searched in all of the other drawers of the counter without success. Wondering where in the world she could have misplaced it, Tamara extended her search to the living room.

Entering the room, she heard a feeble, continuous rustling sound around the main door. As Tamara turned on the light, the noise stopped instantly. Her senses on high alert now, she went to the stereo and put a CD on, setting the volume down low. She closed the sliding door of the living room, made a bit of noise in the kitchen by moving around pots and pans, and then stepped into the hallway. Quietly she retrieved her purse. She took out the cell phone CSIS had given her and opened it. Waving lines filled the little screen. She got out her own and repeated the operation. Same result.

Suddenly the lights went off.

She reached for the wall phone, which, she knew, worked on an independent low-voltage power line. The line had been cut. Frantically she touched her neck, looking for Justin's medallion. Then she remembered. She had exchanged it for the CSIS receiver while driving to customs. It was still in her car.

With the cessation of the sound coming from the door, she knew that whoever was out there was ready to break in. The alarm system, along with all her other means of communication, had been cleverly bypassed, somehow neutralized by even more powerful devices.

She patted her purse; her faithful Smith & Wesson inside.

She hid in the entrance closet and left the door ajar, adjusting its opening to fit the gun's muzzle. She loaded the nine-round magazine and made sure the safety was off. To have more stability, she knelt down, pointing her weapon — the only protection she now had — slightly upwards.

As she waited in the dark, doubts began to surface. Would she be able to see the intruder? She had only practised at the shooting range, where the target was always well lighted and visible. The circumstances she was facing now were totally different. More troubling than all of those thoughts however, was her own self doubt. Would she actually be able to fire at a human being? Was she ready to shoot to kill?

Minutes, that felt like hours, ticked by uneventfully, her ears on full alert for even the feeblest of sounds.

Then it happened. The main door opened quietly and the silhouette of a man made one step into the hallway.

Tamara fired once, and then again and again.

****

Suddenly the shrieks of automobile brakes followed by approaching sirens filled the air. Next was the sound of approaching footsteps. The first to enter her house was Justin, who, a flashlight in his hand, stepped over the man lying on the floor and began searching for her and calling her name.

Tamara was still in the closet, shocked by what happened and nauseated by the smell of gunpowder.

"I'm here, Justin," she shouted with all the wind she had in her lungs.

"Thank God you're okay!" Justin bent toward her and helped her stand. "When I couldn't contact you in any way, I called Romano. They didn't put me through so I got my friend Bill to send a squad." Justin hugged Tamara tight.

"How is he?" Tamara asked, pointing to the man on the floor.

It was Brad Wilson.

"Bad shape."

Two policemen bent over Brad to give him first aid.

"We have to warn Romano. Give me your cell, Justin. Let's see if I can reach him even if the call comes from a number unknown to CSIS."

Chapter 46

On the shores of Lake Huron
The Devry residence
End of September 2007

A blade of rays cut into the bedroom, otherwise made dark by thick curtains. Tamara blinked, yawned, turned around and put her head under a pillow. Somewhere between asleep and awake, she felt totally relaxed, a sensation she wanted to last forever. A few minutes later she heard the whisper of her name.

She emerged from under the pillow and looked around. Where was she?

From the back of the room Justin walked toward her.

"Good morning, sleeping beauty." He sat on the bed, close to her. "How do you feel?"

"Fine." She rubbed her eyes. "Where am I?"

"In my house."

She remembered. "Oh God, I shot Brad Wilson! Is he dead?"

"No, but almost. He's being kept alive by machine."

Tamara sat upright, adjusted a pillow behind her back and leaned against the headboard.

"I can't figure out why Brad came to my place. I know less than any other members of Operation Bullfrog. Why me?"

Justin shrugged. "Let Romano figure that out. I'm just happy you were unharmed. Now you're here and I'd like to take care of you."

Tamara caressed Justin's cheek. "You're a precious friend."

"I know. Do you think CSIS has some other dangerous tasks planned for you?"

"Well...I have to keep an eye on a couple of people."

"I see. People under suspicion, I assume." Justin laughed. "Well, I'm a suspect in their book, so you should start with me. Hang around me all the time."

Tamara pushed him away. "I should get up and have a shower."

"Last night, before taking you here, I packed a bag with some of your clothes." He pointed to a chair. "It's over there."

"Great." She realized she was wearing only her underwear. "I'd like to have some privacy."

Justin rose. "Sure. I'll go upstairs and make some pancakes."

After a long shower Tamara felt physically rejuvenated, but also acutely aware of what had happened last night. She had shot another human being. She mentally prayed that he wouldn't die. She unconsciously recited the prayer of contrition she had learned at the French Catholic School where she had spent her early years. She had played God when she had chosen her life against that of her assailant. It was self-defence. He was a traitor, she told herself. But so were her parents, if judged by the standards of their country of origin. What was the difference? Well, for one Brad had everything a person could aspire to while her parents didn't have one of the most precious things a human being can have — freedom.

In spite of her philosophical reasoning, she felt guilty about having harmed Brad Wilson. She fervently hoped he would survive.

Justin was calling. "Tamara? Are you ready? Brunch is on the table."

Tamara quickly slipped on the first dress she found in her bag. She took a shawl with her and climbed the spiral staircase that led to the main floor.

On the small kitchen table there were pancakes, syrup, fruit, scrambled eggs and slices of fried bacon. Small croissants and biscuits hot from the oven, fanned out an inviting aroma.

"That's a feast," said Tamara as she sat in one of the chairs around the table. "What are you trying to do? Get me fat?"

"I've kept a close eye on you, Tamara. Since the day I met you on the road, you must have lost at least 10 pounds."

It was true. Tamara smiled. "Then I'll pig out."

****

After a tour of the Devry premises, Justin took Tamara to the terrace overlooking the shores of Lake Huron.

"It'll rain pretty soon," he said, scouting the sky with his sharp eyes.

The breeze had changed into wind; at the horizon, dark clouds blended with the grey waters of the lake and both seemingly headed ashore with urgency. The waves had gained strength and now broke forcefully against the protective stones of the little bay.

Perching on the terrace's rail, Tamara and Justin watched the storm make its entry. The sky had just begun rumbling with remote thunder when a bolt hit close to shore, followed by two others.

"Maybe it's time to go inside," Justin said.

"Agreed."

They stepped inside the elegant parlour of the Devry house. One set of chairs, upholstered in an arabesque fabric, clustered around an oval low table; another set, in Queen Anne style, stood on the opposite side, surrounding a long coffee table. The walls sported paintings and photographs framed in different styles. A lacquered black counter, full of bottles and glasses filled one of the corners.

"Nice room," Tamara said.

"Yeah. The upper floor is both a family and a public place. Father entertains his guests, that is, his potential customers, in here. Most of this floor is for public consumption, with the exception of Father's living quarters. The lower floor is my domain. Independent entrance and all the space I need for my gadgets."

"Not a bad arrangement," said Tamara.

"It's great." He moved closer to Tamara. "It's warm in here." Justin lifted the shawl from Tamara's shoulders and kissed her neck. He splayed one hand across her back while he gently pulled her close with the other. "I'm in love with you, Tamara. You're beautiful, and very much alive. And don't tell me that this isn't the right time. I know it is. And you're the right woman for me."

Tamara turned around. "Are you sure?"

"Yes. I knew it, the very moment we danced the English waltz, on that houseboat, the Tortuga. I felt your body leaning on me as if it was in need of support and tenderness."

"Pretty sure of yourself, eh?" Tamara scrambled to think how to resist him. The man's passion was piercing holes in the rational part of her thinking.

Justin didn't answer and brushed her lips with his. "I want to make love to you. I want to caress your body, all of it, and I want to make you mine."

She shouldn't get involved. She should not…but she was alive today and might be dead tomorrow. At least once, she wanted to feel Justin's body lie and move on top of her; she wanted Justin to enter her so that she could hold him tight inside her in the ultimate act of communion of soul and body.

With her hands she cupped his face and kissed him on the cheeks and the forehead, taking in the smell of his skin. "It's marvellous to be close to you." She closed her eyes and murmured, "It's the right time, Justin. Make love to me."

Chapter 47

When the bell resounded through the vast bedroom the next morning, Justin flew out of bed.

"Who is it?" Tamara asked.

"I don't know."

Tamara glanced at the clock on the nightstand. It was almost noon. She pulled the sheet up to cover her naked body and watched Justin walk to the end of the bedroom. The bell rang again.

"It's Romano."

"How do you know from here?"

"I have a sort of periscope pointed at the entrance. Very useful. That's how I escape the boring crowd that often drops in to see my father without notice." He fiddled with his viewing device again and said, "Your boss is pacing back and forth. He looks nervous."

Tamara got out of bed and grabbed her clothes. "Can you go up and tell him I'll be ready in a few minutes?"

"Sure." Justin slipped on a pair of jeans and a shirt and ran upstairs.

Romano, accompanied by Ron Brenner, greeted Justin and asked how Tamara was.

"Not bad, considering all the stress she's been through," Justin said. "She's resting. She'll come up shortly." He invited his guests to enter the spacious living room and asked if they would like a coffee.

"It'd be great," Ron said without hesitation. "We didn't have time to have anything to eat or drink this morning. Only go, go, go!"

"Come to the kitchen then. While you wait you can help yourself to some food. I'll get a pot of coffee ready."

In no time dishes and cutlery, cheese, crackers, cold cuts of meat, fruits and yesterday's pancakes were on display.

Ron eyed the cold pancakes, grabbed the syrup that was on the counter and dug into them; Romano nibbled at the cheese and grapes.

Her hair wet from her recent shower, Tamara soon joined them and greeted them.

"What's wrong?" she asked.

"There's been an incident with Dianne. Somebody got at her boyfriend and tried to abduct her. They were heading to the parking lot near the Grand Theatre when a man shoved her boyfriend to the ground. Dianne managed to click on the alarm button of her car's remote. The assailant took off but not before having thrown her onto the ground. She has a concussion."

"Oh, my God," Tamara murmured.

"It gets worse. Her boyfriend's head injury was more serious. He hit the sharp edge of a walking path when he hit the ground. He didn't make it." Romano paused. "Dianne has asked for you."

"Where is she?"

"She was taken to the University Hospital. Fifth floor."

Tamara hesitated and then asked, "May I ask why they called you?"

Romano smiled. "There's an executive order in the name of national security to call my office if anything happens to any of our suspects. Each branch of policing in the country is so instructed."

Justin had filled four mugs with coffee and passed them around.

"Oh, I see. Why didn't you call me?" Tamara asked.

"We tried. Apparently neither yours nor Justin's phones were on."

"I turned them all off," Justin said brusquely. "I thought Tamara needed at least a few hours rest."

Eagerly, Romano drank his coffee. "I figured that out. That's why I came. I can take you to the hospital, Tamara."

"No need, Mr. Romano. I can do that," Justin said.

"Okay with you?" Romano asked Tamara.

"Sure."

"Great then. There're a few administrative duties I have to attend to. You see — " he started and then stopped to take off his eyeglasses and rub his eyes. "The vaccine has been tested. Preliminary results show that what was delivered at the spa is the real McCoy. The CBRNE lab in Manitoba is gearing up to produce the vaccine."

"On large scale?" Tamara asked.

"Yes, we can't take any chances. But, of course, it might take a few months." Romano nervously adjusted his eyeglasses on the bridge of his nose. "You aren't aware of the latest development, Tamara. About Stan, Sophia Tadlova's goon."

"Oh, is he who picked up the fake package at the spa?"

"Yes, it was, and our van followed him. But then...at the crossing of Richmond Street and Highway 22 he went through a red light. A truck swerved trying to avoid him, but in so doing it hooked up onto Stan's car. The truck ran for a hundred metres with Stan's car hanging on the side until it toppled."

"On top of him?" Tamara asked.

"No, on the other side. Our agents were stuck at the crossing, of course. When they finally reached the scene of the accident, there was no sign of Stan. In the confusion created by the crash he'd disappeared."

There was silence in the room.

"Dale," Tamara said, her voice full of worry. "Is this ever going to end? Will we ever prevail in this battle of wits?"

Romano put his arms on Tamara's shoulders. "We're going to give it all that we have. We'll fight to the end." He paused. "But one thing is sure. If they overcome us they'll be in such bad shape that they won't even realize that they've won." He tapped on her shoulders. "For now, take care, Tamara." Turning to Justin he added, "Thank you for the refreshments. We'll make it up to you, Justin; soon, I hope."

****

When Tamara arrived at the hospital Dianne was asleep, a thick bandage around her head, her arms relaxed over the pale blue blanket. Tamara shrugged off the raincoat Justin had lent her and draped it on the back of the chair. She sat close to the bed.

Who wanted to hurt Dianne? Romano's immediate intervention suggested that he had linked the assault on Dianne with Operation Bullfrog. But why? This incident seemed more like a botched robbery.

Slowly Dianne opened her eyes. "Oh, Tamara, it's you! Thanks for coming." Tears began flowing out of her eyes, raking her cheeks. "Gordon, my boyfriend…is dead."

Tamara leaned toward her and took her hand. "I know," she whispered. "I'm so sorry." She offered Dianne a tissue from the box on the table.

"Just when things were going so well for me…" Her voice broke.

"You have to think how to get better." She clutched Dianne's hand in hers.

Dianne wiped her eyes. "I can't understand what happened." She turned slightly to face Tamara, still sobbing. "That man said, 'You'll come with me!' Who in the world would want to kidnap me? I have no money!"

Suddenly an idea hit Tamara. When Brad Wilson had broken into her house he didn't have a gun at the ready. Why was he there? Was he planning on abducting her? But then, why? She had no money either!

"Dianne, do you remember anything particular about this man?"

"I already told the police. He was tall. He assaulted us from behind. I just got a glimpse of him when I was lying on the ground. But that's all I can say about him. It was dark; it was pouring hard when it happened."

"I see. Is there anything I can do for you?"

"Would you bring me some clothes and my beauty case? My other coat too. The one I was wearing is full of mud and silt." She sighed. "They're going to take another CT tomorrow, so I'll be here at least one more day longer if there're complications and they want to take an MRI."

"No problems. I'll get your clothes from home and take the dirty ones to the cleaners."

Dianne closed her eyes, apparently exhausted.

"I'm leaving," Tamara whispered, but Dianne had fallen asleep.

Justin silently entered the room and neared Tamara. "Anything I can do?"

Tamara nodded. "Yes. More chauffeuring."

Chapter 48

Patience was not one of Frank's virtues; waiting, in particular, made him irascible. What in the world was Zac doing? Two days had passed and no news from him. Zac was his boss, he understood that, but after all they were in this endeavour together. Was he really still his boss? Zac had paid him 20 million and never even blinked an eye when he had asked for more money for his experiments; he had promised him another 30 million after the completion of their operation. But Zac wanted to be in charge at all times and have the final word on every important move. Hoping for a successful outcome, Frank had always complied with Zac's mood and behaviour.

Frank drummed his fingers on the side table, uneasy and uncertain whether he should call him. Zac had a temper, and a vicious one at that. However, time was running out. He dialled Zac's number.

"Yes?" was the scanty answer.

"Zac, we can't wait much longer. If you haven't found your

woman to show off with, that's too bad. We have to plan our final move."

For once, Zac didn't disagree. Instead, he said, "Did you get the vaccine?"

Frank hesitated. "Well no, actually. Stan had a car accident. He was lucky, he walked out of it with only a cut on his forehead. But the vaccine was left behind. But he's here now, ready to carry out your orders."

"It may be too dangerous to go ahead without the vaccine."

"Not where you're going. And not much where I plan to retire, either, I hope." Zac had in mind the Fiji Islands; Frank thought of his secluded cottage near Wasaga Beach. "Besides, Boris still has half of the vaccine. He says he'll give it to us when he receives the money."

"The bastard!"

"Yes, well, try to see his point of view. The money we're talking about is still for the virus. We didn't give him a cent, yet, for the vaccine itself!" Zac's prolonged silence worried him. "What does your mole at CSIS has to say, Zac?" He could sense that something wasn't right and wanted to know what it was.

Zac replied with a question. "Where is Boris?"

"I don't have his address, but he's in Lugano, waiting for the money. As a precaution, he was going to get a new cell and then call me. Don't worry about him — he's precise and reliable. He has already cleaned up after his temporary lab and closed his account at the Clariden Bank since we couldn't transfer the money legally. He's agreed to be in the Parco Civico, close to the stairs going into the lake, feeding the ducks from three to four o'clock every afternoon, waiting for our contact." Frank became impatient. "Just send a courier with the money and we'll be all set!"

"I don't have a courier handy. What about Stan, is he reliable?

Can we send him to Switzerland with five million euros?"

Frank hesitated because he really didn't know Stan well. But time was of the essence. The authorities were on their tracks; he could swear to it, even if he hadn't any concrete proof. He took a few steps into the living room and glanced at Stan. He was placidly watching *UFC Unleashed* on the Spike channel, his body taking up most of the sofa.

"I think we can trust him. You'll have to instruct him on exactly what to do when he's there."

"Send him over. Stan could take the money to Boris and come back with the vaccine."

"Yes, he could."

"Fine, then. Talk to you later."

For a few minutes Frank remained still, pondering the situation. Unfortunately, Stan's accident has been a big drawback, introducing a delay of at least a week. Sending Stan overseas was probably the best possible solution.

****

After the conversation with Frank Milton, Zaccaria felt uneasy — something that didn't happen too often. He would have liked to consult with Brad Wilson, but, unfortunately, he was nowhere to be found. The last he heard from him was that he was going to kidnap a beautiful woman and bring her to him. He had waited up all night in vain. No woman and no Brad.

So should he abandon his plan of stunning the world with the his photos of blackpox in a human being? Nothing seemed to be working like he planned. Even the attempt of abducting Dianne Templeton had miserably failed. Worst of all, the vaccine was not in his possession and he was paranoid about contracting the disease himself. Hell, he was paranoid about contracting any disease, but in particular one that compounded the deadly effects of smallpox with those of ebola. He wouldn't feel secure until he had inoculated himself with the vaccine.

Chapter 49

"Not a bad view," Justin said as he re-entered Dianne's apartment from the little balcony. "That's the advantage of being on the 11th floor. One can see for a long stretch ahead." He turned toward Tamara. "Did you find what you're looking for?"

"Yes. Underclothes, slippers, robe, two pairs of jeans and two tops. I should also get a pair of shoes since the boots she was wearing are basically ruined. One sole broke in the middle and the high heel of the other shoe must have been snipped off because it's missing." She packed everything in a big bag and handed it to Justin. "Can you get her red coat? It should be in the entrance closet."

Justin complied and Tamara moved into the bathroom, which was decorated in pale green with designer towels and a shower curtain of a matching shade. Dianne's beauty case was sitting on a stool. She picked it up and was ready to walk out of the bathroom when she noticed a big basket lying on the bottom of the bathtub. It was the one Frank had sent her a few days ago. Loose on the side were two small square boxes, empty. She picked up one and read its label: *Made for The Pamper Yourself Spa by Iridient Ltd.* She kneeled, deposited the beauty case on the floor and rummaged inside it, looking for the jars that were once inside the square boxes. She found both.

She lost no time and called Romano. There had been an order to gather all recent cosmetic products manufactured at the spa for an accurate analysis. "I found two of the spa creams," she said after Romano had identified himself. "In Dianne's apartment."

"Bring every cosmetic product you can find in her apartment to our quarters on Vanneck Road," Romano said. "I'll get Harry Pearson over and see if he can date when they were made."

"Roger," Tamara said.

Justin was standing on the bathroom's threshold. "That's a curious position for making a call," he said, offering her a hand and helping her rise.

"Do you mind taking me to my place? I'll need my car, since I have to stop at headquarters before going back to the hospital."

"Sure, no problem. I'll go home, then, since Father returns tonight."

****

What weeks before was a 60-acre uncultivated parcel of land with two rundown buildings was now the centre of a sophisticated and covert operation. The entire perimeter had been enclosed in six-foot-high vinyl privacy fencing, punctuated, about every thirty or forty metres, by the sign *'Environmental Research. DO NOT TRESPASS'*. One parcel of the land had been mowed to a minimum and three concentric circles marked with red paint to guide helicopters in their descents; a large lane had been excavated to lead directly to the back of the house and to the edifice which contained the reconnaissance equipment; a satellite, pointing upwards, had been mounted and connected to two receivers, one in each building. Four tall halogen lamps allowed day vision in any corner of the compound.

The word *emergency* wasn't written anywhere, but one could perceive it in the way things were structured and the urgency with which people and vehicles moved.

As Tamara passed the sentry, two agents unloaded the items she had been told to bring from Dianne's apartment.

Ron came outside and knocked on her window. Tamara lowered the glass.

"I'm on my way to the hospital to see Dianne," she said.

"No, don't. Harry is here and so is Romano." He opened the door for her. "They're waiting for you."

When Harry saw her, his face reddened and he pointed to her. "She is…" He stuttered and couldn't continue.

"Never mind who she is or is not," Romano said curtly. "Mr. Pearson, you're here for a precise purpose — to tell us when these jars were filled with constituents made by your friend Frank Milton."

"He isn't my friend — I mean he is my friend, but I didn't know — " He stopped and coughed.

Romano pushed the jars across the table, close to him. "You gave these creams to Ms. Dianne Templeton. The label reads *Iridient Ltd*. When were they manufactured?"

"I don't know." He got an orange hanky out of his pocket and dried the drops of perspiration from his forehead.

"When did Frank Milton give them to you?"

"He didn't. He left them on his counter before leaving. I took them, as usual."

"And that was when?"

"A week ago."

"And you put them in a package for Ms. Templeton?"

"Yes. It was a gift. She's my...no, well, she was my girlfriend but then — "

"Did you give her any other item produced by the spa in the last month?"

"No. Frank was too busy to make me the creams my customers like so much. The soaps and perfumes I put in the basket for her had been around a while."

"How long?"

Frank made some mental calculations. "The last time Frank made them was about three months ago."

Romano gestured an agent to come close. "The basket, the beauty case and those two containers have to go to the CBRNE lab. By helicopter." He turned toward Harry Pearson. "Mr. Pearson, we have accommodations in this house. We'd like you to stay here in case we have other questions."

"But why?"

Romano rose and said, "National security." He tapped Tamara on the shoulder. "Come with me. We have a meeting."

It was the first held without Brad Wilson. His empty seat meant more than a simple vacancy. It spoke betrayal, shame and sadness. Imperturbable, however, Romano, called the meeting to order.

"We had no time to make up an agenda," he said with his even voice, "but I requested a meeting to brief everybody on the newest events." He cleared his throat and continued. "First, no prognosis on Brad Wilson's condition. He doesn't talk or move. At the moment we don't see how we could get information out of him. The search in his house didn't bring to light anything substantial about his involvement in the act of terrorism we're trying to prevent. Second, we lost an important lead. The man who got hold of the fake package at the spa had a car accident. In the midst of the confusion created by the crash, he managed to flee. So we don't know who was supposed to receive the vaccine. The vaccine has been analysed, and estimated to be effective; however, only a test of the virus itself would confirm whether this is indeed the case."

Duncan Brown took advantage of Romano's temporary break and asked, "Are the two tied together?"

"Yes, they are. The virulence of a virus is a factor. A powerful virus requires a vaccine different than a less active one. So I come to point number three. None of the chemicals found in the spa contains any trace of virus, disease or poison. However, just today we came across two recent containers which *may*, I emphasize the word *may*, contain traces of blackpox. They're being analysed as I speak." Romano paused and asked for questions. There weren't any, so he continued. "Fourth, we got a name of the scientist who may have developed this new biological weapon. The Russian Government made a huge effort to help us by searching the archives regarding the dismantled lab in the caves of the Carpathian Mountains, at that time under Soviet control. The only member, still alive, that they could trace is one Boris Youkenoff, a biochemist and microbiologist of high scientific repute. His photo of 20 years ago is now in our hands."

Romano turned toward Duncan, the computer wizard, and asked, "Are you still working on it?"

"Yes, I'm applying a few aging algorithms. I'll end up with four or five versions of how Boris might look today."

"Good. We'll make them available as soon as they're ready, with priority to Europol, since we have reason to believe that Mr. Youkenoff is in Europe." He paused and asked, "Questions?" Romano drank from the bottle of mineral water in front of him. "No questions? Then I come to the fifth piece of information. We've requested the surveillance of one of our suspects, Michael Devry, as he took a trip to Holland to acquire some antique artefacts. The timing, and the fact that he's a regular client of the Modano Company, which we now know has been used to ship illegal substances, made us take such an action. According to the Dutch Government, the purpose of Mr. Devry's trip was totally legit." With one long swallow he finished the bottle of water.

"Now we come to the last and most critical item," Romano continued, his voice a tad firmer and louder. "Until yesterday there were rumours and suspects regarding a dangerous virus being shipped to this country. The seizing of the vaccine has put to rest all speculations. An act of bio-terrorism is in the making. The Prime Minister has decided to inform all other anti-terrorist agencies around the world of the impending danger. Requests from these agencies to our group will be collected and coordinated by Mr. Ron Brenner. A release will occur only upon my authorization."

"What about the press?" Duncan asked. "They'll be breathing down our neck."

"Only if there's a leak. If this happens — and I'll climb hard on who is responsible — we'll let them breathe as much as they want and ignore them. The Prime Minister will issue a televised communiqué only if necessary for the safety of the country and at the latest possible time."

"They'll be camping outside," Duncan said in a querulous voice.

"So far Operation Bullfrog-o-one has been a well-guarded secret. We're entering a second phase, namely Bullfrog-o-two and I hope I'll be able to say the same of the new one. It'll take time for even the sharpest of reporters to find where we are and what we're doing." He paused, as if he was extremely tired. He looked around.

"Any items from the floor?" He waited only 10 seconds and then announced, "Meeting is adjourned."

Chapter 50

Tamara had not been to many meetings, but certainly none so short and poignant. She wondered if Romano's show of confidence and determination was in part enacted for the benefit of his team. If so, it was effective, according to the comments she had heard as she was leaving the conference room.

She drove to a drugstore and bought some supplies for Dianne, including a new day and night cream to replace the ones that were confiscated. When she arrived at the hospital it was almost closing time. She scrambled to take an elevator on its way up and stopped at the fifth floor. She passed in front of the floor desk and briskly walked to Dianne's room. She wasn't there. She doubled back to the desk, and asked for Dianne Templeton.

The nurse had just started her shift and wasn't aware of any change.

Tamara deposited the bag with Dianne's belongings on the floor and waited for the nurse to strike a few keys on her computer.

"Here it is," she said. "Ms. Templeton has been transferred to a private room on the third floor."

"Oh, thanks." Tamara bent to recover the bag and was ready to walk away.

"I'm afraid you can't go there!" the nurse said. "Visiting hours are over."

Tamara stopped. "I have with me a robe and a few toiletries she asked me to bring over. I'll drop them off at the nurse's station. I won't disturb her."

"Be quick!"

"I will." She waved goodbye and strode toward the elevator.

At the third floor the nurse accepted the bag Tamara gave her. She didn't appear to be too busy and so Tamara engaged her in conversation.

"Do you know why Ms. Templeton was transferred?" Tamara asked, worried that Dianne's condition might have suddenly deteriorated.

"No particular reason. Somebody paid the supplement for a private room."

"Oh. Do you know who that was?"

"Yes, her boss. He also left a bouquet of flowers for her."

"Oh, I see. Well, I'll come back tomorrow. Oh and please be sure she gets her things, she almost begged me to get them for her."

"For sure. Good night."

Tamara thanked the nurse and left. She was tired, but happy to have accomplished all the chores she set out to do. She headed home. She would go straight to bed as she planned and get up early in the morning to be at the office before nine o'clock.

****

When she reached the Modano Company, the following day,

only the maintenance man was around. He was vacuuming the storage room, almost bereft of any piece of furniture or art object. There was always work to be done, thought Tamara. She should bring in the Louis XV console and the two pictures Charles had lent her some time ago. To start with, the console would make a great show piece in the entrance window and it surely would sell quickly at the next auction. She logged in on her HP and went to eBay to search for items that could interest the Modano's clientele. She scribbled down a reference to a grandfather clock.

There was noise at the door and soon Charles walked in.

"Hello, Tamara. I wasn't expecting you here today. Isn't Wednesday one of your days off?"

Tamara rose and greeted her boss. "Yes, it is. But our storage room is empty and we need to refurnish our inventory."

"We surely do after last week's big sale," Charles said, ready to move into his own office.

"It was nice of you to move Dianne to a private room," Tamara said, and started to punch a few commands on the keyboard.

Charles stopped on the spot. "What are you talking about? Private room? Where?"

"At the hospital."

Charles looked blankly at her. "Dianne is sick?"

"Weren't you there? Did you not bring her flowers?" Charles didn't make a sound. "Don't tell me that you weren't the person who passed for her boss at the hospital!"

"I don't know anything about Dianne or any hospital."

Tamara rose, and frantically looked for her purse.

Charles grabbed her arm. "Was Dianne in an automobile accident?" he asked.

"No. A man tried to abduct her. He threw her onto the ground, where she hit her head. She's in the hospital with a concussion."

Charles fell into a chair. "A serious blow?"

"Not on first examination. But her boyfriend, who was attacked from behind, hit his head on a concrete step and died on the spot." She pulled free from Charles' hold. With the bag hanging on her side she ran toward the washroom. "I'll be right back," she said to Charles.

Tamara placed a call to CSIS hoping to talk to Romano. She got Ron Brenner instead. She briefed him of the unauthorized change of Dianne's room and of her suspicion that someone might be trying to harm her. She asked him to convey her worries to Romano and clicked off to dial The University Hospital.

When she got through to the hospital, she was put on hold for several minutes and then the news she dreaded hearing came. Dianne Templeton had left the hospital without being properly released. Nobody had seen her since the night before.

Tamara closed her cell. She returned to her office, hoping to hear soon from Ron Brenner or Dale Romano.

Charles was pacing the room and looked at her expectantly.

"Oh, I am so sorry for poor Dianne…did you see her?"

"Yes, I did, yesterday. She asked me for some of her stuff and I brought her what she needed." She couldn't decide whether she should tell Charles that Dianne's life might be in danger. If he was part of the conspiracy, he knew that for a fact…

Charles slumped in the chair in front of Tamara's desk.

"Dianne has been very good for my company," he said. "I organize the shipments and Dianne takes care of the remaining administration. She puts in long hours when it's needed, and takes off when we have slack times." Charles' eyes were moist. "She's been with this company for eight years."

Tamara remained silent for a moment, surprised by Charles' emotional attachment to Dianne. "Do you need me to fill in while

The Blackpox Threat

Dianne is out? Is there anything I can do to help?"

"I suppose you could just go through the company mail and pay the bills for now. That would be a help. Be sure you record the extra hours you put in." Charles didn't move. "It appears that the deal with Thomas is going through. He'll take over the shipping, and I'll work on the antiques. We'll split the income 60-40 for the next three years. Then we'll re-evaluate." He paused. "Thomas would like you to work fulltime, you know, but it's up to you to choose."

Tamara fiddled with the piece of paper where she had jotted down the reference for the grandfather clock. Working for Thomas would give her a chance to discover if he was involved in illegal activities, but then she wouldn't be able to help the cause, now that Operation Bullfrog was at a critical phase. There would be no time for both.

"I find the agreement we have, Charles, to be the best. Fourteen hours a week, plus one Saturday a month for the auction is the absolute best for me."

"Fine with me."

Maybe she should add a bit of an explanation. "I have a friend, right now, and I enjoy being able to go to the opera in Toronto or to take a short trip. The arrangement we have is gold for me."

"I'll tell Thomas, then." Charles rose. "and I'll go see Dianne, today."

"You better call the hospital first, Charles, to check on the hours and if she can accept visitors." She didn't want Charles to make a totally useless trip.

"Good idea," Charles said, and walked to his office.

Chapter 51

Within one week the life of Dianne Templeton held no secrets for the members of Operation Bullfrog. Romano had linked her disappearance with the ongoing operation and had, therefore, mounted an aggressive search for her and the person who had taken her out of the hospital. In a desperate attempt to establish a link with her abductors, the special task force had interviewed the teachers of her elementary and high school, the staff of the School of Drama she had frequented, the members of the television companies she had worked for, and given Harry Pearson the third degree. Only after these inquiries failed did they contact her parents and brother. To avoid worrying them unnecessarily, they had dispatched an agent who played the part of a reporter eager to find a special angle in the life of Dianne the performer. Nothing of substance had surfaced. The search of her apartment had not provided one single clue. The idea that Dianne had taken off on her own had not been given any serious consideration. She left wearing only a robe, leaving behind all the other belongings that Tamara had taken to the hospital.

In the last meeting Romano hammered out the point of the situation. The contagious cells found in the two cream jars that Harry had put in the gift basket for Dianne had revealed traces of blackpox; it was the scientists' opinion, however, that they had probably been inactive by the time Dianne had used the cream.

The hunt for Frank Milton and his Chrysler Touring had turned up no results. No one at Europol or Interpol recognized Boris Youkenoff from the age progressed images Duncan Brown created and forwarded to them. After tactfully interviewing Sophia Tadlova's neighbours, the Rossiters, Romano was able to extract a fairly good description of Sophia's goon — though his last name was still unknown. So now both Stan and Frank were on the loose and left behind no obvious clues as to their whereabouts.

For the time being there was nothing to work on, Dale Romano concluded. There were only questions. Did the criminals involved give up on their plan? Or were they trying to fit Dianne into their scheme? How much of this blackpox did they actually have? Were they going to blackmail one government at a time or many at the same time?

At the moment they could only conjecture and wait. And the wait was unnerving.

****

Tamara's worries about Dianne continued to mount. The woman needed medical assistance and more than likely was not receiving any. Tamara believed Dianne was clearly part of the blackmailing package Frank Milton and associates had planned. Tamara wondered if she would ever see her alive. She had carefully hidden her feelings as she worked at the Modano Company.

Charles was very grateful that she was doing some of Dianne's work as it allowed him to put off the decision as to whether he needed to replace Dianne.

Meanwhile, Tamara had the occasion to observe Thomas Sarcin, who had redecorated the main office and brought in a new desk for himself.

By the tenth day following Dianne's kidnapping, Tamara had collected a substantial number of items for the next auction. Furthermore, she returned the items Charles had loaned her and was contemplating buying a piece of furniture herself, to replace the antique console.

Just as she was about to leave for the day, Thomas entered her office. He was soberly dressed in a pair of flannel blue trousers with a striped shirt and vest that matched the blue stripes of his shirt. He was the kind of man who exuded elegance from his lean, tall body and fluid movements.

"Can I buy you supper?" he asked her.

Tamara put on her coat. "Thanks Thomas, but I planned on going shopping."

"For a new collector's item?" Thomas asked.

"Actually, no. I'm looking for a piece of furniture to install in my own condo. I'd like something nice to display my good china and a few nice glasses. I still keep them in the kitchen cupboard."

"Want some company?"

Surprised, Tamara's first instinct was to refuse. But, on second thought, Thomas would soon be one of the bosses.

"Sure. But I warn you; it may take a couple of hours."

"Fine with me."

After a stop at Leon's and another at Sears they drove to the Ikea store which had just featured a promotional sale. There Tamara found a teak cabinet that matched the style of the coffee table she already had. It was long, and one end opened to a built-in-bar.

"It's big enough for my lonely bottle of Vodka," commented Tamara as she decided on the purchase. She had a chance to probe Thomas. "I used to keep a bottle of Vodka on hand for my old friend, Vassilli Petrovic. He would stop by now and then," she said as nonchalantly as possible, watching for Thomas' reaction.

"Was he the old gentleman who was injured on the boat?"

"Yes. Did you know him?"

They walked toward the service counter to arrange for the payment and delivery of the furniture.

"No, but I heard the news of his death from Charles. He told me he was family to you. I'm sorry for your loss."

As Tamara gave her credit card to the salesman, Thomas looked at his watch. "Do you have time for supper? I'd like to get to know you a little better and also tell you something about myself."

****

It was late that night when Tamara entered her condo. She had learned a lot about Thomas or at least a lot of what Thomas wanted her to know. His father had carried on the family business of building safes and vaults; his uncle, a free spirit, had spent most of his life flying hot-air balloons and, later in his life, learned to build them. After both his father and uncle passed away, Thomas and his older brother had inherited in the millions.

"My childhood and a great part of my life were spent in an atmosphere of emergency, when, really, there was no need for any. Money didn't compensate for the constant state of anxiety in which I grew up." He had paused and then continued. "Remember that evening when you delivered the décor ensemble to my place up north? My brother had broken a statue when he had come to visit me and had called the Modano Company ordering an instant replacement." Tamara had listened attentively, hoping he would also explain the urgency in which he had left. She wasn't deceived. "That was the last time I seriously listened to my brother. That night, while you were there, he called me with the excuse that he couldn't open one of his safes, and he badly needed to get at its contents. Made it sound like a case of life and death. When I arrived I found out that all he wanted to do was talk." Thomas had sipped his wine and added bitterly, "Talking about a lot of nonsense, as only he could do."

Tamara wondered whether there was any information about Thomas that needed to be passed on to Romano. She was still debating the idea, when her special cell rang.

It was Romano. "Come over at once. We got a blackmail request from a guy who calls himself Nekton. He has the virus and Dianne."

Chapter 52

Along the Maritime Coast
Beginning of October 2007

Alea jacta est, Zaccaria screamed into the wind, his arms high in the sky, his exhilaration incommensurable.

His boat was sailing toward open waters, or, as it seemed to him, toward the conquest of the world. Nothing would stop him now. His plan was perfect; he had worked out all the details with mathematical precision. Once the first phase of his operation was completed, people would be so frightened that they would pay whatever he asked for — any time he snapped his fingers.

He had gotten the vaccine from Frank Milton and managed to give him only 20 million with a promise to pay him the remaining sum after conclusion of their operation. For the time being he wouldn't have to deal with Frank — and what a great relief that was! Often Frank made him feel like an ignoramus, just because he, Frank, held a science degree.

The Blackpox Threat

Zaccaria had only four men with him, but none of them would ever question his actions and each was ready to die for him. Not as many as Julius Caesar might have counted in his army when he crossed the Rubicone River, he thought, but just as committed to their leader's cause.

He checked the fastenings of his boat's grey tarp that would, at first sight, appear as an awning set up to protect guests from the sun. He checked the control room and all its commands.

Satisfied that everything was in order, he descended to the lower deck where Dianne Templeton was. The woman didn't look sick at all; every time he entered the stateroom she imprecated against him with renovated vigour and an astounding richness of vocabulary. He had to tie her to the bed in order to restrain her. He needed her, and needed her badly. Her picture, broadcast over the Internet for the world to see, would show the increasing horrors that the blackpox threat posed to humanity, day after day, week after week. But first, he had to receive payment from the Canadian Government under the pretence that the ransom's request would be a one-time deal.

Zaccaria congratulated himself on his great plan as he savoured the pleasure of holding the world in the palm of his hand.

****

Lugano, Switzerland
Mid-October 2007

At the distance of about 24 metres, Stan Glover could hear the two men speak, but he couldn't understand their words. They were standing on the steps that led to the lake in Lugano's Parco Civico. One man was in uniform, the other was casually dressed; medium height and bold, he corresponded to the description that Frank had given him of his contact, Boris Youkenoff. Stan moved a few feet closer.

A third man, in plainclothes, joined them. He addressed Boris in English, explaining that it was forbidden to feed the pigeons.

"I was feeding the ducks; it isn't my fault the pigeons just took over!" Boris said with indignation. "They came begging for food, one climbed on my shoes to get it!"

"That's because there're people like you who feed them," the man in plainclothes said. "Besides, when you entered the park, you walked on the lawn. We've seen you." He pointed to a sign. "Look right there: it says it's forbidden. You have to pay a fine. Twenty franks."

"I don't have twenty franks!" Boris pointed across the lake. "That casino of yours cleaned up all my money — in less than three hours!"

"That casino doesn't belong to us," the uniform stated with a condescending tone. "It sits on Italian soil."

"Please come with us," the man in plainclothes said, and took Boris by the arm.

Stan followed the threesome at a distance as they walked to a car. He didn't know what to do — except that he shouldn't feed the birds and shouldn't walk on the lawn. He would find lodgings in one of the many hotels on the lungolago and try to meet Boris Youkenoff tomorrow at the same location. All he had to do was exchange his bag, which contained the money, with Boris' bag, which contained the vaccine.

****

Frank Milton held his briefcase tight in his hands. Twenty

million was a large amount. Together with what he managed to extort from Zac on the day-to-day operation of the lab, his financial situation amounted to over 22 million. It was the culmination of his efforts and the assurance that he could spend the rest of his life in luxury. For weeks he could feel the authorities breathing down his neck. It was a sensation, something that floated in the air, impalpable, yet real. That was the reason he pushed Zac to launch the blackmail message. Finally it was done. Of course, if Zac ever discovered that the vaccine he had sent him consisted of common antibiotics, he would never see the remaining 30 million. But he had no choice. The problem was that he had lost contact with both Boris and Stan. Boris had not answered any of his calls and Stan never appeared on his front step.

Better to forget about the other 30 than lose everything, or, worse, end up in jail.

****

The atmosphere at the headquarters of Operation Bullfrog on Vanneck Road was a complex mixture of relief that the waiting was over, expectation for the upcoming engagement, and anxiety for Dianne's precarious situation.

The terms of the ransom had come by fax two days ago. The modalities seemed to be simple. Within three days from receiving the fax the government had to provide raw diamonds to the equivalent of a quarter billion dollars to be delivered by helicopter to a place that would be communicated later; 24 hours after the consignment of the gems the locations of all the blackpox containers spread around the country would be disclosed and Dianne Templeton released. There would be no publicity on the deal, and no subsequent requests. It should be considered a once-in-a-lifetime transaction. A picture of Dianne's face and neck, showing red spots all over, took a full page.

Tamara had squeezed a seat between Duncan Brown and Ron Brenner and was listening to Romano's presentation as a number of people she had never seen before filled the room and stood in a row behind the seated members.

"If we knew that Ms. Templeton would be where we have to drop off the diamonds, we could attempt a raid," Romano said. "But we don't."

"Can we get so many diamonds in three days?" Ron Brenner asked.

"Yes, we can and we already have some, but the Prime Minister does not intend to pay any ransom."

"Is he more concerned with money than with the safety of people?" a member new to Tamara asked.

Romano's answer was swift and matter-of-fact. "We all know that what blackmailers promise to do after they get the ransom seldom happens. So our strategy is, first, to rescue Dianne and, second, to catch the criminals. We can use a small quantity of diamonds to engage them in communication and trading so that we can get an idea of how many people are involved and maybe a hint of their MO. We can justify the small quantity by saying that it will take us more than three days to get the full amount." Romano stopped and adjusted the eyeglasses on the bridge of his nose. "Remember, if they indeed have the virus or a method to fabricate it at will, they won't stop with us or with this occasion. They'll continue blackmailing until they're caught."

After a moment of silence, Ron asked, "Do we know from where the fax originated?"

"Downtown Toronto."

Duncan Brown, his red hair longer and bushier than usual,

raised his hand. "I have something interesting to show you." Everybody's eyes riveted toward him. "I had the forensics team analyse this photo of Ms. Templeton." On the large screen hanging from the far wall Dianne's face appeared. It was full of red spots and smudges. With his electronic stylus, Duncan marked all of them with a black circle, except one. "There is only one spot in this photo that may actually be interpreted as the effect of the disease in question. All of the others appear to be fabricated, probably painted on her skin with a lipstick or some other cosmetic device. In short, this picture doesn't show the real state of Templeton."

"What are the implications of this? She's still in the hands of a megalomaniac or criminals who won't hesitate killing her," Mark Farin said.

"True," Romano hastened to admit. "That's why her rescue is our main concern."

"When will our own vaccine be ready?" Ron Brenner asked.

"In three to four months."

"Do we have any leads as to the locations of where the containers with the blackpox may have been or will be deposited?"

"No, but we can assume it will be in locations directly accessible to the public. Remember, that from the little we've gathered about this kind of virus, we know there is only a two to three week time span before it is rendered inactive."

"To whom was the fax addressed?" another member asked.

"To the Prime Minister. All communications are automatically rerouted to this office and to my cell."

Then came the question everybody in the room wanted to ask, but hesitated to. "What about Brad Wilson? Can he talk?"

"No. He has received multiple blood transfusions, but his prognosis is still not good. In fact, his case is exhausting the hospital's supply of O-negative blood, which is his blood type."

The Blackpox Threat

Just then, the fax machine whirled and spit out a sheet of paper which Romano immediately grabbed.

"It's the location of where to make the drop — a boat off the coast of the Gaspé Peninsula." He gestured to one of the agents. "Get the chopper ready," he said to her. To another, "Inform your group at CSE to focus on this area and record all calls in and out. We've already discussed the type of surveillance we need. Get it started." As the agent didn't immediately move, he added, "On the double!"

Most of the agents present left. Clearly each had a pre-assigned role that he or she would have to play once the location became known.

Romano, Brenner and Brown remained in the room. Duncan furiously hit key after key and then turned around his laptop so that they could see where the boat was.

"International waters," he said with disappointment.

Romano couldn't refrain from chuckling. "It doesn't make any difference what kind of waters. We're going after them."

"How?" Tamara asked.

"A unit of the coastal defence, The Kingston 700, is moving into the area. Besides, in about half-an-hour we'll have a web of satellite channels zooming on that location, feeding us information continually." He paused. "That boat will have no secrets from us."

Chapter 53

With pleasure Zaccaria licked the salt that had been accumulating on his lips. Being at sea gave him a sense of immensity, enhanced by the excitement of the imminent action. With his BPC field binoculars he once more scrutinized the waters around him to detect whether any vessel was approaching. None. He looked up in the sky. No aircraft in sight. The field was clear. From his dealings with Brad Wilson he was well acquainted with what to expect from Doctor Romano, of Operation Bullfrog, and of the CSIS task force. He expected delays and uncertainties, and was prepared for them.

After the three days specified in the ultimatum had gone by, Zaccaria, using his new satellite phone, reinforced the blackpox threat by calling Romano directly.

The answer came quickly. They needed more time to gather the requested amount of gems, but they were ready to deliver a small percentage of them as a sign of good will if one of their agents could come aboard the boat and talk to Dianne Templeton.

Zaccaria paced the deck back and forth. How did they know that the woman was aboard? They were guessing, he concluded. He firmly denied that Dianne Templeton was on his boat and refused to let anybody come aboard without all of the gems. He would wait another 24 hours, he added, and then the full-scale dissemination of blackpox containers would start.

Pleased with his firm stand, Zaccaria mentally reviewed the many features that he had added to his boat so that it could face any contingency. The boat could face any sea, provided all comforts, and hid several getaways that only he knew about.

He looked forward to showing Romano and CSIS what he was capable of.

****

In the operational centre on Vanneck Road, half a dozen people, each equipped with a cell and a computer, were busy acquiring as much data as possible on the blackmailer's boat and its geographical location, together with weather conditions along the coast of Quebec. They had assembled an impressive amount of information that Romano was trying to process in view of a possible raid. From the first set of pictures the boat appeared to be an old freighter, maybe 60 by 45 metres. There was movement on the boat, but they couldn't spot more than three or four people at any given time. The Communication Security Establishment, CSE, which was monitoring any transmission coming from or directed to it, had not detected any calls, except the ones dealing with the task unit. The only breakthrough was the shop where Nekton's satellite phone had been purchased; the buyer's name would be soon known through his or her credit card.

Another set of pictures arrived, showing a huge grey awning

covering one third of the upper deck. The boat, pompously christened *The Master of Masters*, was circling around the area at slow speed, and it was impossible to guess which kind of engine was aboard.

A third set of satellite pictures reached the task unit. On deck a silhouette, partially concealed under the awning, seemed to struggle with a tall man. Duncan Brown asked to have the pictures sent to his laptop so he could apply image analysis.

Romano stood behind Duncan, impatient to see if the silhouette could be identified as Dianne's. Duncan applied one algorithm after another, making Romano more and more impatient.

"Please do sit down," Duncan said to his boss. "I can hear you breathing. I need to think, I can't rush what I'm doing."

Romano refilled his mug with coffee and sat, his eyes zeroed in on Duncan.

"I have something here, Dale," Duncan said half an hour later. "Look." He turned the monitor toward his boss. "Look at the clothing. It could be a long skirt, a woman's skirt. Look at the next three frames. The skirt whirls as a man's arm grabs the woman by the waist. I got only five good frames to work with. Can you get anything out of all this?"

Romano approached the monitor and examined the three frames that Duncan had lined up one next to the other, thus providing the perception of motion. "Maybe we can." He opened his cell. "Let's get Tamara here and see if she can identify the fabric as belonging to one of Dianne's outfits."

****

For the last few days Tamara had juggled her time between the task force's meetings and her work at the Modano Company, where she did her best to conceal her anxiety regarding Dianne's well-being.

Romano's call reached her on her way home, so she quickly changed route and drove to the headquarters of Operation Bullfrog. She immediately recognized the robe as the one she had taken from Dianne's house and delivered to the nurse at the hospital.

Romano lost no time. He compiled a message for Nekton, the blackmailer. They had evidence that Dianne Templeton was indeed aboard his boat, he said, and they were prepared to give him an advance of $250,000 in diamonds if they could land on his boat and talk to Dianne. There would be no deal until they were sure that Templeton was alive and well. Romano ordered the pilot of the chopper stationed at the back of the field to be ready for takeoff.

An hour passed uneventfully. Every participant of Operation Bullfrog-o-two needed a good rest, so they took turns sleeping in four-hour shifts.

The answer arrived at dawn. A chopper would be permitted to land on the boat in the next 24 hours, with one stipulation. Only two people were to be aboard, the pilot and Tamara Smith and only Tamara would be allowed to set foot on deck.

If a bell had rung throughout the building, it wouldn't have woken up everybody any faster. In a jiffy the eight members of Operation Bullfrog-o-two took a seat, commenting on the new proposal.

"Double danger," Mark Farin said. "First, Tamara isn't trained for this kind of operation; second, that maniac could end up with two hostages instead of one."

"I agree," Ron Brenner chimed in.

In a corner, Romano was talking into his cell. He made a gesture to keep the noise down. Duncan busied himself making a pot of fresh coffee.

"We're in," Romano announced with a steady voice, as he closed his cell.

"Too dangerous!" two members shouted at once.

Romano addressed Tamara. "Do you feel like helping us one more time?"

"Yes, I do."

Romano smiled at her. "I knew I could count on you." He cleared his throat and said, "The Prime Minister has okayed the tactical approach I lined up when you folks were asleep. Remember that the code for this phase of engagement is Bullfrog-o-two." He looked around to be sure he had everyone's attention. "This is what we're going to do."

****

Lugano, Switzerland
Mid-October 2007

For the third day in a row Stan Glover took a leisurely walk on the lungolago, admiring the mountains profiling against the clear sky, the blue waters of the lake and the enormous amount of flowers that brightened the shoreline. It looked like paradise to him, and he wondered how people could be so fortunate to live in such a beautiful place. He mentally compared that setting with Tadlova's property where he had spent the last 10 years, after having been badly injured in the ring. Of course, he was grateful to Sophia, who had taken him in as a helping hand, doing chores on the farm. With time his brain had recuperated some of the most important functions; however, at age 40, and without a trade, he hadn't been able to find a permanent job. Sophia Tadlova didn't pay much, but he had free lodging and enough money to go to a movie, spend a day on the beach in the summer or go ice fishing in the winter.

Sophia's financial situation had been deteriorating with the passing of years and the farm was poorly kept. Sophia planted corn but then didn't use any fertilizers, herbicides or insecticides or even practice crop rotation. She was left with a field of corn she couldn't unload. Even the Guinea pigs were a hard sell, as experimenting on animals was now strictly regulated. The 10-hectare farm provided only for Sophia's basic necessities.

Stan remembered the big change that occurred when Frank Milton had come into the picture. At first Frank had come to see Sophia to talk about her motherland, then he began to purchase her pigs on a regular basis. Before long, Frank had engaged Stan, directly, to dispose of the spa's chemical refuses first, and the dead pigs, later. Frank had given Sophia a computer and taught her the rudiments of computer technology. Stan had never questioned the kind of business Frank Milton was dealing with; he seemed to be successful in what he was doing and that had been enough for him. After Sophia's death he had wondered what he would do all by himself, and had been happy to be of service by becoming a courier for Frank Milton.

Stan Glover looked at his wristwatch. It was almost time for the rendezvous with Boris Youkenoff. He stopped to get a cone of fruit ice cream. Licking it slowly to make it last as long as possible, he strolled toward the Parco Civico. He hoped, yet doubted, that Boris would be there.

He sat on one of the benches. He waited and waited, absorbed in the thought of what his life would be from now on. Sophia was gone, Frank was an ocean away, and his contact was not showing up. He stroked the bag that contained the packets of euros, each packet neatly folded in a transparent plastic sachet.

Maybe it was time he thought about himself.

Chapter 54

Wearing a jogging outfit and companion shoes, Tamara sat in a corner of the conference room, waiting to play her role in the next phase of Operation Bullfrog. Her eyes were trained on Romano, who had been on the phone for the last half-hour. It was impossible to guess what the conversation was all about. Romano often answered with monosyllables, or short sentences like "I don't think so," "I repeat, it's dangerous," or "In this case I can't take responsibility for the operation." Finally he said, "I'll wait for your decision," and closed his cell.

"A delay," he announced with a steady voice. "The Minister of National Defence made a case to the Prime Minister that they should be in charge of operations." He took off his eyeglasses and slid them onto the table. "We have to wait."

Duncan almost exploded. "They can't come in at the last moment!" he said. "They don't know anything about what has been going on, not to mention all the preparations we've made!"

"Not completely true. Reports have been sent to them on a

regular basis. Unexpectedly, the delivery is going to take place in open waters, and we need the support of the navy. A unit of the Coastal Defence, the HMCS Kingston 700 has been moving into the area. It's now an internal fight for control within our ministries and agencies. Of course, our boss, the CSIS director, won't surrender easily."

"Who is going to decide?"

"The Prime Minister." Romano stretched out to grab his eyeglasses and slipped them on again. "They granted that I have experience in police raids and hostage rescues, and hold a cross-appointment with Public Safety Canada, but they pointed out that I never served in the armed forces — which is true. I may need their cooperation and advice, but I believe I'm the best man for the case." He paused, pensive. "And that is not all. Our neighbours from the south want to get involved too."

"What?" Duncan said. "It'd be a complete disaster! A *de facto* takeover!"

"That's only a minor concern of mine. Besides, I know several of their people. We can work it out, if that's the case. I might have to spend some time talking to them and keeping them posted." His phone rang and Romano assumed a deferential attitude as he listened for a few seconds. "Let me understand, sir. You don't want to spell out what happened but you also don't want to lie?" Romano listened to more. "It's going to be difficult, sir. My undergraduate degree is in biology, not psychology." Romano closed his eyes. "Yes, I'll try. Two paragraphs. I'll put something together for you." The call was clearly over and Romano closed his cell.

Romano looked at the other agents. "As you've probably guessed, that was the CSIS director himself. Brad Wilson died three hours ago. The press is already investigating and conjecturing, so some official statement needs to be made. London police managed to get out of the impasse by saying that Mr. Wilson was a CSIS officer involved in a special operation. So now the reporters want to know, not only what happened when he got injured, but also what the special operation was all about." He sighed audibly. "Duncan, come close. I'll dictate a short memo."

Duncan slid his laptop toward Romano and dragged his chair close to him.

"Ready," he said.

"CSIS is currently investigating the circumstances in which Mr. Brad Wilson, a senior officer with the Canadian Security Intelligence Service, suffered severe injuries as he broke in — no, cancel 'broke in.'" Romano pondered for a second or two. "If we say 'broke in' they come back to ask for the place where he broke in. Write: as he carried out an operation not authorized by his superiors." He drummed his fingers on the table. "In the course of his career with CSIS, the late Mr. Wilson served, both at home and abroad, in different capacities, mostly aimed at safeguarding the security of the country. More information will follow as it becomes available." Romano stood and said, "That's it. One paragraph more than was requested. Fax it to the CSIS press office. They're experts in these kinds of situations; they should be able to keep the media at bay." He moved away from the table. "I'm going to rest for a while. Be back when we get word from the Prime Minister."

Tamara neared the place where Duncan was and smirked. "That memo says nothing!"

Duncan, who was sending the fax directly from his computer, nodded vigorously. "It takes a lot of training to do that. At this precise moment we can't give away anything that isn't absolutely indispensable. We want the organizers of this horrible blackmail to wonder if Brad talked."

"Meaning what?"

"Meaning that they may accelerate their plans, go ahead even if things aren't fully ready. They may take chances, which would increase the possibility of them making a mistake."

Tamara's cell ring disrupted the conversation. She rummaged in her purse and opened the phone.

"Yes, this is Tamara Smith." Covering the speaker with one hand she said to Duncan, "It's from the Prime Minister's office. He wants to talk to me in person." Tamara waited awhile, avoiding Duncan's curious look. When the call came in, she answered without hesitation. "Yes, sir. I am aware of the danger involved. I'm ready to do whatever is required of me."

Slowly, Tamara closed her phone. "He wanted to be sure I volunteered for the operation, in case Romano remains in charge of it. Apparently one of the objections the military had raised was the use of an untrained civilian for the drop-off."

"That's really a concern for us, too. We don't know what you'll find once you board that strange boat."

****

Duncan, Mark, Ron, Tamara and Dale were having a late snack when the call from the Prime Minister arrived. Romano was to remain in charge of operations.

An American submarine had been dispatched to the area and would reach the coast of Maine in two days. Its primary role would be backup support, but it would keep in constant communication with the task unit.

Everyone breathed a collective sigh of relief.

Romano's energy seemed to double instantly. He made a few calls and synchronized the activities that would take place early the following morning. A chopper would take Tamara and Romano to

London airport. Aboard a military plane they would reach the Atlantic coast, where a CH-124 Sea King was ready for action. "A gem in its class", Romano explained, "the Sea King could land on small decks as well as on water and serve as a surveillance station or a combat unit. Equipped to fly in the dark, the aircraft was ideal for the action that was going to unfold."

****

Zaccaria took a plate with a tuna sandwich and a few carrots to Dianne Templeton. He deposited the dish on her stomach and took off the gag that covered her mouth. To his great relief she didn't scream. He untied her hands and quickly stepped back to avoid being scratched. Fortunately her ankles were solidly fastened to the footboard of the bed.

"Your friend Tamara Smith will be here pretty soon. She'll bring the ransom and you'll be free."

Dianne didn't make a sound and didn't look at him. She devoured her meagre meal.

"Drink," she said.

"You can drink all you want when I let you go to the washroom; the water is potable," he said, "or close to it," he added with a smirk, and left.

Having the woman as a prisoner had been a pain. For the first few days she had screamed every time her mouth was free — evidently hoping to attract attention. Fortunately, two days ago she had realized that she was detained on a boat. That had quieted her down, to the great relief of everybody aboard.

With a set of binoculars in his hand, Zaccaria climbed up on deck and explored his surroundings. There was a marvellous stillness, hardly interrupted by the noise of the waves breaking against the hull. Zaccaria opened his arms in an attempt to embrace the immensity of it all. The vibrations of his phone called him back to reality. It was Frank.

"Did they pay the ransom?" Frank asked.

"Not yet. I gave them another 24 hours."

"And why was that? Once they know your whereabouts, things get dangerous!"

Zaccaria roared with laughter. "What else can they do, but pay? They have no choice!"

"They may attempt a coup," Frank said, his voice carrying a subdued tone.

"And leave the country at the mercy of a terrible disease? No, I don't think so!"

There was a pause, and then Frank said, "Should I go ahead with the dissemination of our…our samples? We need time for the jars, since we decided to ship them."

"Are you talking about the beauty creams?"

"Yes."

"Go ahead with those."

"Okay then, free samples to the spa's customers. I'll ship those by mail. We're close to Christmas; they won't raise any suspicion." He paused. "The others?"

"Let's wait 24 hours. I'm convinced that they won't play tricks. You have the map of the designated locations, right?"

"Yes, everything is ready, even the messages to provincial and federal agencies, to be emailed concurrently to the major TV stations. The full blast, in case they hesitate to pay."

"Great. Let's see how it works out," Zaccaria said, and shut his phone off.

The noise of an approaching chopper filled the air. Zaccaria felt energized. Finally, it was showdown time.

The Blackpox Threat

****

"Are you okay, Tamara?" Romano asked her, his voice barely audible because of the noise of the rotor blades.

"I'm fine, Dale. We can see the boat. I'll check up on Dianne and only if she's okay I'll surrender the diamonds. I'll try to get pictures of what's under the boat's awning, as you told me."

"Great."

Claude Price, the pilot of the Sea King, was frantically switching on and off a couple of switches. "Dr. Romano?" he said in the direction of the phone.

Tamara put the phone close to the pilot's mouth. "Dr. Romano, the equipment for subsurface acoustic detection isn't working," Price said. "Do you want me to abort the mission?"

There was no immediate answer, so the pilot repeated the question.

"No, go ahead. I don't think that particular feature is very important at this stage of the game."

"Roger," Claude said, and the communication was over. Within a few minutes the helicopter was circling over the boat.

"Are you ready, Ms. Smith?" Price added.

"Ready as I will ever be."

With a smooth manoeuvre Claude set down the Sea King near the prow of *The Master of Masters*. Nobody was on deck.

As instructed, Tamara stepped out of the chopper and stood close to the aircraft, her left arm close to her body. In her left hand she held her special cellular, set to take one photograph after the other. She clicked and clicked while observing what was under the dark tarp. There was an enormous baggy pillow made of orange and blue wedges.

Finally a tall man, cloaked in a black mantel and with a mask around his eyes, appeared, holding a kicking Dianne by the waist.

"Here she is," he hollered, and lifted Dianne above the ground. "Throw the bag with the diamonds to my feet!"

"Tamara! Help me! This man is a monster!"

Tamara exchanged the cellular for the bag that she pulled from inside the chopper.

"Romano knows Dianne is alive?" she asked Claude, trying to surpass the compound noise of the vanes and Dianne's shrills.

Claude nodded.

Tamara waived the bag she held in her hands. "I have the diamonds. Set Dianne down," she screamed, pointing to the floor. "I want to talk to her."

There was a moment of hesitation, then a whistle. Near the starboard gunwale two people appeared like magic: one, in a yellow outfit was pointing an assault weapon toward Tamara; the other, dressed in green, was aiming at the chopper. The cloaked man let Dianne down, restraining her by her arms.

"Come over," he ordered Tamara.

Walking slowly, Tamara moved closer, the hand with the bag extended toward the man.

"Get the chopper's engine off and throw the bag!" he commanded. He gestured to one of the men to hold Dianne.

Tamara signalled the pilot to turn off the engine and then slid the bag toward the man's feet.

"Let me talk to Dianne," she said, and neared her with secure strides.

The man in black looked into the bag and examined the gems. "Fine for the time being," he declared, and turned toward the man who was holding Dianne. "Let Tamara talk to her, but hold onto our prisoner."

Tamara embraced Dianne, who exploded in tears. Between one

sob and the next Tamara murmured into Dianne's ear. "Jump overboard as soon as the commotion starts."

The remote noise of an aircraft attracted the attention of everybody on the boat. "What the heck?" the man in the black mantel exclaimed, looking into the sky. Then he shouted, "On with phase two!"

****

Riding in a second chopper, Romano and his crew had followed the events, as information and images were transferred from the Sea King onto his aircraft. "Abandon the helicopter and the ship!" he ordered Claude Price. "Now!"

To the combat and rescue units he broadcasted a clear command. "Bullfrog-o-two. Go ahead. Full force."

Chapter 55

Mayhem broke out aboard *The Master*. One armed man shot at the chopper blades while the man cloaked in black fiddled with the colourful object that lay under the tarp. A second accomplice ran across the deck, tripped on a cluster of ropes, then struggled to get untangled. A fourth individual pointed his rifle toward the approaching naval unit. For a split second the man who was holding Dianne relinquished his grip. It was enough for Tamara to grab her friend. Her adrenaline kicking in, she swiftly lifted Dianne up and threw her overboard. She pushed herself onto the gunwale and was ready to plunge into the ocean when she felt the clamp of hands onto her legs. Using her elbows she managed to repeatedly poke at her assailant until he lost his grip and fell to the ground. They both ended on top of the colourful object that was being inflated.

On board his helicopter Romano scrutinized and evaluated the scene. The HMCS Kingston 700, a vessel of the Coastal Defence, released a launch for the rescue of Dianne and the Sea King pilot who were battling the frigid waters; the Sea King transmitted data on the position of the boat and meteorological information that wasn't useful anymore; on *The Master* there was frantic action, but now only one man, armed with an assault weapon, was in firing position.

All of a sudden a discharge of bullets hit close to the launch, forcing its pilot to turn around and stay out of range. Romano focused his binoculars onto the boat, trying to see Tamara. She was out of sight, but the man in green, who had captured her minutes ago, was now working on a web of ropes.

One of the options Romano had was to give orders to torpedo the boat, but he excluded it on two counts: Tamara was on it, and capturing the people on *The Master* would spread light on the ramifications that the criminal ring might have. Also, there was no assurance that the mastermind of this biological terrorism was aboard and therefore would be eliminated. He laid the binoculars on his lap, took off his glasses and rubbed his eyes.

He ordered his chopper to circle around the boat once more, staying out of firing range.

"Somebody is jumping off the boat!" his pilot screamed. "It's a woman!"

Quickly, Romano took a look. Tamara, who wore a slim life jacket underneath her jogging suit, was beating a fast crawl. In no time she reached Dianne. She helped her to lie in a supine position and began dragging her.

Intent on following what was happening to the people in the water, and attracted by the new attempt that the launch was making to rescue the swimmers, Romano didn't notice that the people on deck of *The Master* had disappeared.

In a flash the tarp that covered a large portion of the boat rolled down and a balloon sprang out, taking for the sky.

Romano was flabbergasted. What was the meaning of the

balloon? Somebody was trying to escape in that fashion? How far would they think of going? Or it was just a diversion?

"To all units with a vision system: try to detect if anybody or anything is aboard the balloon."

"Why don't we shoot it down?" the pilot asked.

"In a moment."

The inflated balloon was defining its own course, taken astray by the wind. Soon it would be out of reach. Romano waited a few minutes, hoping to get some information about the content of the balloon. None came.

A burst of machine-gun fire filled the air and the basket plunged into the water, followed by pieces of the colourful gores.

Romano entered in contact with the vessel of the Coastal Defence. "Can you take care of what remains of the balloon? Every single piece could be of importance."

He didn't want to spend much time on what was clearly a diversion. The most urgent thing was to find out what was happening on the boat, which now had a spectral look.

To the small unit in charge of bomb defusing he ordered, "Drop your weights on deck. See if the boat is set to explode on contact." Romano relaxed his back against the seat. "Take me to the Kingston unit," he ordered the pilot. "I want to talk to Dianne and Tamara."

Isolated in a stateroom reserved for patients with infectious diseases, Dianne had asked for scrambled eggs, ham, potatoes and a pot of fresh coffee. She was demolishing a set of toast when Romano approached the room's transparent divider. They would communicate by phone.

Romano introduced himself and asked her to tell him all she had gathered about her abductor.

"I remembered little about that night at the hospital. Somebody walked in and put a cloth on my mouth. When I woke up I was tied to a bed in a dark bedroom. A man came to bring me food — very little each time — and beat me if I screamed." She took a long swig of coffee. "He drugged me when we moved to his boat. For a while I was seasick, then the sea calmed down enough that I recovered." She stopped and looked straight into Romano's eyes. "I hope you catch the bastard who did it and make him pay."

"We intend to. Did you ever hear anybody talk about a bomb?"

"No. I was segregated all the time. I didn't see or hear anybody else talking."

"I see. Any special features that you noticed about the man who kidnapped you?"

"He talked funny, an accent, I mean; the grammar was okay."

"Physical aspect?"

"Tall. Slim. Actually gaunt. He wore a silver mask that covered half his face. His lips were thin; his mouth was like a cut in the lower part of his face." Dianne shivered at the memory. "He was scary, I tell you."

"Thank you, Ms. Templeton," Romano said. "We may talk again later on."

Soon Dianne would be airlifted to the Montreal General Hospital for observation — in case she carried the blackpox virus.

On the way to see Tamara, Romano met Claude Price. The man was still shaking because of the cold dip, and was mourning the loss of his beloved aircraft.

"Anything you can tell me?" He had been in constant communication with the pilot of the Sea King during the first phase of the mission and therefore Romano didn't expect any big news.

Claude shook his head. "The man in the black mantel moved like a cat: with agility, swiftness and power. That's all I can add."

Romano thanked him and proceeded to see Tamara.

Tamara was wrapped in a blanket with a man rubbing her back.

"Hi Dale," she said, and smiled. "We got Dianne out, right?"

"Yes, you did. How come you're still shivering?" He sat at the small table across from her.

"I think it's because of exhaustion, but this nurse who's taking care of me thinks it's because of too much coffee."

"Did you eat something?"

Tamara shook her head, her hair still wet. "My stomach isn't ready, yet. Maybe later."

"What can you tell me about the people who were on the boat?"

"The man in the cloaked outfit — the one that looked like a huge, nasty bat — is the one in charge. Then there are four militants; they take orders well and speak little English. When I rolled down after one of them grabbed me, we ended up amidst something that was ready to be inflated. With helium, I managed to notice."

"They launched a balloon."

"Oh. That went fast."

"Any idea, I mean, did you hear anything about their plans?"

"No. I was there only a few minutes. My captor got tangled up and I crouched under the balloon, still folded in layers, to emerge on the other side. I made a beeline for the rail and jumped out."

"Good girl. Anything else you can tell us?"

"Not really. The equipment on the Sea King filmed everything that happened before it was shot at, right?"

"Yes. I wanted to know if, by any chance, you had an idea about their next move. The boat, now, looks deserted."

"A trap?"

"Could be that they're waiting for us. We'll soon find out." Romano rose and stroked Tamara's shoulder. "Good work, *Agent Smith.*"

A tray with all sorts of snacks appeared on the table. Tamara took a glass of milk and held it up in a toast.

"To the success of Operation Bullfrog!"

Chapter 56

Small tables, juxtaposed to form a long contiguous surface, and chairs of all kinds accommodated the members of the task force aboard the Kingston 700. Romano had had a long call with the Prime Minister and spent an hour briefing his crew on the events of the morning. Duncan worked on wireless routers to provide the same computer facilities that he and Romano were accustomed to.

Romano turned off the sound on his cell.

"Questions?" he asked.

"The Sea King had sonar aboard," Ron Brenner said. "Did it capture any underwater images?"

"No, that equipment was out of order."

"The boat didn't explode when weights were dropped on the deck," Mark Farin said. "Should we attempt to climb on it?"

"Dangerous; there still could be a time-bomb."

"Is the boat going adrift?" Brenner asked.

"No. It's fighting a strong current. The engine is running; a course is clearly set."

"I volunteer to go aboard," Claude said. "The Sea King is damaged, but it could fly again with a pair of new blades."

"There is more damage than you think. The signal acquisition centre is out of order. Probably other navigation features are in need of repair."

Duncan tapped Romano on the shoulder. "For you," he said, and gave him a sheet of paper.

Romano looked at it and his face brightened up. "Got something important. *The Master of Masters* received a call yesterday and CSE intercepted it. It's from our elusive Frank Milton." He looked at it again. "It appears that Frank is the man in charge of distributing the vials which can cause the epidemic of blackpox. The call came from a cell in London." He turned toward Duncan. "Read aloud the content of this paper while I make a phone call."

Exhilaration was still in the air when Romano re-entered the room.

"RCMP, OPP and London Police are going to hunt down our man. Once they catch him, I'm sure they'll use some effective methods of persuasion to make him talk and give us all the locations of the containers with blackpox."

"Do you think there could be another...another distributor, so to speak?" a member asked.

"Don't know. Let's not minimize what we have done so far. We've broken the criminal ring." Romano paused and gratefully accepted the steaming coffee that a sailor had put in front of him. "For one day, we've achieved a lot. Rescued a hostage and got an important breakthrough." He sipped his drink. "Now, let's take a break. When we come back we'll put our brains to work and decide what we should be doing with that ghost boat. It holds secrets, I can feel it, but how can we get at them without risking anybody's life?"

The Blackpox Threat

****

Around 21:00 the task force met again.

"Just a short meeting before calling it a day," Romano said. He looked refreshed, as if more ready to go to battle than to retire for the night. "Anything anybody wants to say or ask?"

"Did they catch Frank Milton?" a member asked.

"Not yet. They're actively patrolling the city."

"I think we should go aboard that boat and see what it is all about," Ron Brenner said. "The navigation lights are on now."

"There is no rush. The boat has entered territorial waters. We're following it at a safe distance. Whatever they plan to do, we're prepared."

"We need an aquatic robot equipped with CT acquisition," a young member stated. As everybody looked quizzically at him, he added, "Sorry. I saw it at work in a computer game."

"We have a robot. It doesn't swim and has no CT scan, however. It can manoeuvre fairly well in clogged places, and takes pictures as it walks around. It operates in two modes: autonomously, as it senses obstacles, or by remote control. But it can't go down the stairs, unfortunately. And it's what is in the belly of that boat that worries me." Romano paused.

"Useless, then. A pair of binoculars is all that we need to look at what's on deck," the young member said.

"Right on the dot. The other solution is to make use of sniffing dogs. I've requested three from our canine unit. It's being airlifted by 0800 hours tomorrow morning."

"There could be other dangers hidden on the boat — even if there aren't explosives," Mark Farin said.

"That's right. But our rescue unit is prepared for those contingencies. That's what we specialize in."

"They've fished out most of the remains of the air balloon. Any discovery of importance?"

"No, although that's not a great surprise. The balloon was simply a diversion." Romano looked around. "I see a lot of tired faces and red eyes," he said. "Let's stop here and reconvene tomorrow morning at eight o'clock."

Romano had one more chore to do. He descended to the lower deck and knocked at the door of a stateroom.

"Tamara?"

A sailor came by. "She's probably asleep," he said. "She was an hour ago when I checked up on her." He opened the door and let Romano in.

"Tamara," Romano called, and shook her by the arm that lay on top of the blanket.

"Eh, what?" Tamara rubbed her eyes. "Oh, it's you. What happened?"

"We got word from our team that the credit card Nekton used had been stolen. Considering that sometimes criminals declare a card stolen and use it later on to purchase weapons, we've checked on the card's owner. The name is Thomas Sarcin, and he's connected with the Modano Company."

Tamara perked up and sat straight. "Thomas?"

Romano nodded. "I thought you might know him. That's why I'm here."

Tamara sighed. "He's a difficult character to assess. After I met him the first time, I asked Brad Wilson to do some checking. He told me he'd done it and that nothing suspicious had transpired — of course, his statement has no value, right?"

"None whatsoever. Actually, it only confirms the suspicion that he could be involved."

"The next few times I met him, I changed my mind somewhat.

He seemed on the level. He was interested in a partnership with Charles Modano, who found the shipment part of his business too demanding."

"Hmm. From what we can gather, the Modano Company was only marginally involved in the shipment of the virus. The shipments went around the company's main office, not through it. I'm inclined to think that Charles Modano and his company have nothing to do with biological terrorism." He paused. "However, we never know…I'll put the word out to bring Thomas Sarcin in, and I'd like you to be present. We could fly you back to London tomorrow morning."

"Sure," Tamara said, and smiled. "I'd be happy to go home. Justin is waiting for me."

"Justin is a lucky man," Romano said, and wished Tamara good night.

****

Frank Milton couldn't believe his eyes. They were towing away his car!

The driver of the tow truck was ready to climb into his seat.

"Stop, stop!" Frank shouted with all the wind he had in his lungs. He ran toward the truck and knocked on the side window. "You're taking away my car!"

The driver lowered the pane. "Sorry, sir. The sign states clearly that you can park for a maximum of 10 minutes. Your car has been sitting there for almost an hour." He gave Frank a card. "You can come and claim your vehicle at this address."

"But it's crazy! It was the post office's fault! I lined up for 45 minutes. Look, look inside, see how many people are there! Look at the line!"

The Blackpox Threat

The driver rolled up the window, put his truck in motion and drove away.

That was all he needed, to be deprived of his car, which still contained vials with the blackpox. He imprecated aloud. It was all Stan Glover's fault. He had disappeared from sight. It would have been Stan's job to go around mailing and depositing the containers in the pre-arranged locations.

Frank drove to the closest station of taxicabs and gave the driver the card he had just received.

Chapter 57

Romano bent forward, intent on looking at the dogs and their trainer, Peggy Alberton. Crouched among the dogs, Peggy didn't stop petting them and fondling their ears. It was getting late and Romano was anxious to start the new phase of Operation Bullfrog, Bullfrog-o-three, that would reveal if explosives were aboard *The Master of Masters*.

Peggy murmured something in one of the dogs' ear. When she caught Romano's puzzled look, she said, "Nescia — she's a Belgian Malinois — is the best I've trained. She'd jump in the fire for me." She petted the dog one more time.

"Let's go," Romano said.

Together they walked to the Kingston 700's deck. He hoped nothing would happen to the dogs — clearly they were very dear to Peggy. He could only hope, though.

Once on deck, Romano imparted the latest instructions to the helicopter's pilot.

"You make three rounds on top of the boat, one for each dog.

The automatic release of the animal should work. Don't worry about the dogs. If one falls into the water, we'll rescue it."

"But the camera they carry around their necks will be damaged."

"Never mind. We have plenty of those. Be concerned about being directly above the boat for the least amount of time possible."

"Yes, sir. I understand, the concern is that boat could contain explosives."

Romano nodded. He saluted the pilot and took several steps away from the aircraft. He watched as it lifted itself up and flew toward the location where the ghost boat was. He joined the captain of the Kingston 700 on the upper deck; together they would follow the canine enterprise.

"Are you confident the dogs will be useful?" the captain asked.

"Yes, I am. The camera they carry transmits both sound and images. We'll get a better idea of what is on the ship as the dogs freely roam; if they smell explosives, they will sit in front of the bomb. They're trained for passive response." He paused. "If there're people aboard, most likely they'll kill the dogs and destroy the camera. That'd be useful information, too."

"You mean there's a lot more to gain, than to lose?"

"Right. Although there is concern that some of the dogs could get injured when the chopper releases them on deck. Their handler is here. She may get sick if that happens, she's very attached to the dogs. When a trainer works long hours with an animal, an intangible, yet strong bond is established between the two. It happens also with machines, especially if your life depends on them. Look at Claude; he's still depressed because of the loss of his beloved Sea King."

For the next half hour they watched the helicopter fly over the ghost boat, as the pilot assessed the proper time and height to release the dog. The first attempt failed, and the dog ended up in the water.

"Two more to go," the captain said.

The second attempt was more precise, but too rough for the dog's slender legs. It cried, limped for a stretch and then lay down. Clearly, it was injured.

"Does the pilot have any experience in what he's doing?" the captain asked.

Romano didn't answer, as his concentration was focused on the third dog, Nescia.

The captain repeated the question, and Romano answered.

"Sure; he has done it two times. The first he was off target, the second he wasn't low enough. Now he has experience, so he should make it."

And in fact he did. The dog, startled at first, began moving around.

"I'm going downstairs," Romano said to the captain. He joined Duncan in what had become their temporary meeting room. "Ready with your gadgets?" Three screens were lined up on the table, one for each dog. Two were blank.

"I resent you calling these sophisticated pieces of equipment gadgets," Duncan said, jokingly.

They both sat in front of a monitor where the images captured by the dog's camera were continually projected. Nescia was sniffing high and low. Almost immediately the dog took for the stairs, moving fast from one place to another, discarding each place as uninteresting.

"No plastic so far," Duncan said.

"Are you sure you're storing the video? I may want look at it again, with calm."

"Of course."

"Good. Nescia, that dog, moves so fast it's impossible to have an idea of the boat's blueprints."

"We'll reconstruct the boat's setting later," Duncan said. "Nescia is going one more floor down."

"That boat is a labyrinth!"

"Maybe not. The dog moves its head very quickly. That's a problem with capturing images this way."

"It goes down one more set of stairs!"

The images were dark, and Duncan adjusted the monitor's brightness to better follow the dog's movements.

Nescia circled a large, round object at the bottom.

"It's a hatch!" Romano shouted. "Like those you find in a submarine. See that red handle? That's for opening it; the hatch can be locked in place from the chamber underneath."

Nescia was ready to move away when she hit the lever.

All at once they heard a splash. The screen registered a spurt of water and then went fuzzy.

"What the heck — " Duncan said.

"Got it!" Romano said. "Our friends escaped with a bathyscaphe. It was connected to the boat. Now we know. Come, Duncan, quick; let's go give the news to the captain. They may be able to do something about it."

****

For the last hour there was frantic action around *The Master of Masters* as two divers alternated in reaching deep into the boat with the hope of closing the hatch. Unfortunately, one hinge was damaged and underwater repairs would take time they didn't have. When the prow tilted upward, the last diver abandoned the boat.

Slowly but inexorably, the ghost boat sank and disappeared in a final vortex, taking all its dark secrets with it.

There was disappointment aboard the coastal vessel, but also satisfaction for the attempt.

As a gesture of camaraderie, the captain of the Kingston 700 had invited the members of the task force to sit side-by-side with the navy officers. There was celebration for Dianne's rescue and the action on the boat. At the long table all members of either branch were present, except the dogs' handler.

Nescia was dead. She hadn't managed to emerge from under the huge bottom of the ghost boat. She was only three years old and the most effective sniffing dog of the unit. It would be very hard to replace her, the trainer had stated as the paramedics assisted the other dog, the one whose leg had been injured in the rough drop-off. The congratulations that Romano had offered her for a mission well accomplished hadn't been enough to ease her sadness.

Immersed in his thoughts, Romano hadn't immediately realized that his phone was vibrating. He flipped it open. The call was from CSIS. Discreetly Romano walked out of the room.

"You said it was a distressing fact. What's distressing?" he asked CSIS' assistant director of operations.

"We just heard from London Police. They impounded Frank Milton's car — the Chrysler 300 Touring — and let Milton drive away with it."

"How was that possible? We circulated the car's picture and its licence all over the country!"

"Well, a mistake, I believe. You see, the vehicle was towed away because of a parking violation in front of a post office. Milton followed the tow truck to the compound, paid the fine before the car was even unloaded and...well, drove away with it."

Romano pondered the situation for a few seconds. "A parking violation in front of a post office?"

"Yes, he claimed he had to mail a few packages and the place was very busy."

"You have the address of that post office, right? Get a court order to block the shipping. Those packages may very well contain samples of blackpox."

"Oh my God…we'll get at it right away."

Chapter 58

Justin was waiting for Tamara at London Airport.

"Am I happy to see you!" He gave her a big and lasting hug. "On the phone you told me that you were on a mission." Hand in hand they walked to Justin's Audi. "Can you tell me anything about it?"

"You knew that Dianne had been kidnapped, didn't you?"

"Yes, you left a message for me before leaving. Is she free?"

"Yes. That was part of my mission. Help rescue poor Dianne."

"Is she okay?"

"It looks like it, but she'll be at Montreal General for a few days. For observation."

Justin opened the car door for Tamara and tossed her bag onto the back seat.

"Where would you like to go?"

"Take me home, Justin. I need to be in a familiar environment for a while. And I wonder about my fish."

"Your fish have been taken care of. I'm a very conscientious housewife." He stretched his arm and caressed her hair. "Am I considered part of a familiar environment?" He put his Audi in gear and began driving.

"Very much so, Justin."

"Nice to hear. Any duty for tomorrow or can we spend some time together?"

"Unfortunately I have to report to headquarters."

"Well, we'll have a few hours together tonight. I have a couple of my father's recipes with me. I can cook dinner while you relax. I've stocked your new bar with plenty of bottles."

"Great idea. I can sure use a drink."

****

Once more, morning came too early for Tamara. The flight on the helicopter, the landing on the boat, the rescue of Dianne, the fear for her own life and the final plunge into the icy waters were taking their toll. She hoped Operation Bullfrog would soon come to an end. She didn't have the makeup of an agent. She was made for a peaceful life. She needed to hang onto something that didn't present urgency or danger all the time. Never so much as in the last weeks had she felt the desire for a steady companion, the need to have somebody she could depend on, the need for a stable family life.

She rose and wandered into the living room where Justin was sleeping on the leather couch, serene as a baby.

The cellular phone, that nasty invention that could reach you anywhere, anytime, rang. She answered it. The meeting with Thomas Sarcin was cancelled as the man was nowhere to be found. A break, Tamara thought with relief. She made breakfast and was ready to wake Justin, when he appeared in the kitchen, still dressed as the night before.

"Good morning," she said. "I don't have to go in right away. The meeting has been postponed."

"Great, but do you have to be on call?" He neared her and smacked a kiss on her neck.

"Yes, unfortunately."

"I thought so." He sniffed the air. "Smells wonderful," he said, and sat at the table.

"One of my specialties: omelette with mushrooms, onions, spinach, grated cheese and tomatoes." She placed a carton with milk and one with orange juice on the table. "Dig in," she said. "Coffee will be ready in a minute."

For a while they enjoyed their food in silence.

"Do you know Thomas Sarcin, a rich fellow who used to build safes?" Tamara asked. "The family is from Toronto, but he had recently moved to London."

"Never heard of him, but if he's rich, my father may know him."

Tamara laughed. "Does he know all the wealthy people in the area?"

"He makes an effort to. He caters to the rich and vain."

"Vain?"

"Those who want to build a past of glory that doesn't exist. You should see his albums of portraits: kings, princes, presidents, governor — generals, celebrities. They serve as models to create portraits of non-existing ancestors."

"Does he make money?"

"A lot of it. The actual work is done by Barbara's students for very little."

"You too must know a lot of wealthy people."

"Me? No way! I escape when they come to the house. That was

one of the reasons I didn't follow in my father's footsteps." He stopped talking to drink some milk. "He says there's nothing wrong with letting people pay for their vanity."

"Do you agree?" Tamara asked.

Justin shrugged. "I guess I do. But it's not a job for me. I like to be around people who don't pretend to be what they aren't."

The coffee machine gurgled and Tamara rose to fill two mugs. She took them to the table.

"Thanks." Justin looked at his wristwatch and hurried to finish the last piece of omelette that was on his plate. "Now that I remember, I have to go home. I promised Father to run a few tests on an old oil he'd like to buy." He rose and kissed Tamara. "Give me a shout if you're still at home after lunch. I'll come down."

Justin was just out the door when Tamara called Charles at his office.

"Oh, glad you called, Tamara. The police were here, looking for Thomas."

"Do you know where he is? That's the very same reason I called."

"No. Well, he was here this morning. We had a chat about remodeling the offices. He was cheerful as usual. Then…" Charles cleared his throat. "Something happened. He picked up the newspaper and went to his office. Soon after, he stormed out of it without saying a word."

"What newspaper?"

"*The London Free Press.*"

"Thank you, Charles."

"Wait, wait. Any news of Dianne? She isn't at UH anymore."

"No. She's been transferred. But she's okay." Tamara didn't want to mention any details about Dianne and the recent events. "You'll see her pretty soon. I have to go, Charles. I'll come to the office tomorrow."

Tamara stepped outside to get her copy of the local newspaper. She skimmed through the large headings on the front page and turned page after page. Before the classified started there was one picture with four frames, clearly shot from far away. They showed the Kingston 700, *The Master of Masters* twirling as it sank, a launch with dogs aboard and a helicopter in the process of landing on the coastal vessel. The caption read, "Is Canada at war?" There was no other comment.

Did those pictures trigger Thomas' stomping out of his office? If so, he was definitely connected to the blackmailing ring.

More than ever it was imperative to find him and learn more about him.

Chapter 59

Duncan Brown didn't answer the phone, so Tamara left a message that was purposely ambiguous. She had some files she would like to read, but she didn't have the proper software. Would Duncan come by the house and help her out?

She didn't want to send the material she had illegally downloaded from Thomas Sarcin's laptop to headquarters. Maybe Duncan would decipher them without asking questions. Recently, the young man had been less antagonistic than at the beginning of Operation Bullfrog.

Duncan called back a couple hours later, sounding pretty annoyed. "Tell me the system those files were written in and maybe I can email you what you need."

The files were protected by a password. No system would do the trick, but he, Duncan, could. "Well, I can't really tell," Tamara said.

"Tamara: what are the files all about? Messages by old lovers you'd like to revive?"

Duncan hadn't changed. The man would always belong to that particular ancestral culture, according to which a man thinks of rising to greatness in a woman's eyes by belittling her. She hesitated.

"Well? Speak up, I don't have all day!"

"It's something strange. Some I can easily read; others I can't."

"Where did you get those files?"

"That's nothing of your concern. I'll find somebody else to give me a hand." She considered Duncan a peer to her. He wasn't her boss. She closed her cell.

Duncan called back right away. "I'll come by your place. Give me half an hour."

****

"We have to strike a deal," Duncan said, and deposited his laptop on Tamara's kitchen table. "I'll help with whatever files you have on the condition that their content be disclosed."

"I have no problem with that as long as I can read them."

Duncan gave her a strange look. He transferred Thomas Sarcin's directories onto his computer.

"Most of these directories are password-protected! That's why you couldn't access them."

"Oh." Tamara faked ignorance. She looked at the screen of his computer. It was black now, and strange symbols appeared and disappeared at fast speed. "I opened Hannibal and Old-Addresses. The first contains a lot of sentences that made absolutely no sense, but the second had the address of the house where my parents lived and died — killed, actually. That's the main reason I want to see what the other files are all about."

Duncan looked at her from above his glasses. "Sorry. Now I get it. Romano told me you were concerned with any material that might pertain to your parents' murder."

"That's right. The official dossier CSIS had forwarded me contained no new information."

An hour later all directories were readable. One contained the correspondence between Thomas Sarcin and his lawyer; another, between Thomas and his old customers; a third one, emails received in the previous and current years; the fourth and oldest contained a huge amount of emails, all dated before 2005.

"Can you please transfer those onto my computer? I'm interested in all, but particularly in the oldest directory."

"Sure," Duncan said, and connected the two computers using an USB cable. "Romano may be interested in poking into Thomas Sarcin's secrets. But he'll be even more interested to find out how you got all these files."

"Maybe," Tamara replied.

Romano had gained the trust of superiors for his intelligence, knowledge and rectitude; but Romano also thrived on the cooperation of the people working with him — he might ask about the origin of those files, but as tactfully as anybody could.

"I'll take that chance. Thank you for coming." Tamara meant it.

****

Alone in her house Tamara went through the old list of emails Thomas had received. After two hours the only information of interest she had extracted was the name of the company that built safes, the *Impenetrable*. In spite of pain in her shoulders and neck, Tamara kept going, eager to see if she could solve the mystery of her parents' address in Thomas' files.

By night time she came across an invoice issued to Mr. Joseph

Smith for a wall safe.

Now she remembered.

It was again that terrible night of 13 years ago...

Her parents were lying in a pool of blood, her mother with a slashed throat, her father with multiple wounds in his chest. Tamara had run down the stairs to call the police. As she waited for their arrival, she had noticed the dark footprints that stained the living room's carpet. They concentrated underneath a reproduction of a famous painting of the Hermitage Museum, the Benois Madonna, behind which a safe was hidden. Her father and mother had decided to write their memoirs, from their growing up in Russia to current time. It was a dangerous undertaking, and they were well aware that a number of people were still active in hunting them down and making them pay for their defection. Their memoirs would add insult to injury. So they had bought a safe to safeguard their writing until the time for publication arrived.

Her father had opened the safe and given the killer what he wanted, the police had concluded. But that hadn't avoided the carnage that followed.

Tamara put her Lenovo on Stand By and pushed away the keyboard. She reclined her head on the table — raw, renewed hurt in her heart.

Chapter 60

London, Ontario
End of October 2007

Tamara knew she was late, very late. She waved her ID in front of the sentry, almost brushing her nose with her plastic card. She tiptoed into the conference room on Vanneck Street and hoped nobody had noticed her absence. The meeting was ending.

"The freeing of Ms. Templeton, the sinking of the blackmailer's boat and the confiscation of the jars containing blackpox at the post office completed operation Bullfrog-o-three," Romano said. "We're now entering Bullfrog-o-four. Objectives: capturing Frank Milton, sequestering all the vials with the deadly virus, arresting Nekton and his accomplices."

"There's going to be a Bullfrog-o-five?" Ron Brenner asked, his voice carrying a tone of annoyance mixed with tiredness.

"It depends on the success of o-four. If it's successful, there will be no follow-ups."

"Strategy?" Ron asked.

Romano shrugged. "Follow the leads we have."

"No warning to the public?" Mark Farin asked.

"Not yet. It's our belief that the dissemination of the virus has been halted."

"Based on — ?"

"No new threat. We hold off until Nekton's next move."

"Any information on his whereabouts?" a member asked.

"He escaped with a bathysphere that ended up on the shores of New Brunswick. The wreck is currently being examined for clues. We assume Nekton is hiding somewhere in eastern Canada."

A member chuckled. "A small place!"

"How many leads do we have?" was the next question.

"Two. Boris Youkenoff, the man suspected of having created this new variety of blackpox while hiding in a cave in the Carpathian Mountains, has been detained by Swiss police." Romano sighed. "He was carrying a bag with vials, which, at first analysis, seemed to contain a vaccine. The cooperation is slow and minimal. We suggested letting Boris free to meet his contact, who probably carries the money for the vaccine. They didn't go along. Swiss authorities are very sensitive to the issues of independence and sovereignty. So we discount the chance of catching Boris's contact, whoever he or she might be."

"Don't they understand the need to cooperate?" Ron Brenner asked.

"The Prime Minister tried. They promised to consider the matter. However, every day that passes decreases the chance to catch the accomplices Boris might have."

"The other lead?" a member asked.

"We're ready to contact Mr. Thomas Sarcin, whose credit card, supposedly stolen, was used to acquire Nekton's most recent satellite phone."

"Very weak leads," was the comment of another member.

"Well, there is also Frank Milton. A few days ago he was in London, as we all know. We're patrolling the airport, the bus and railway stations. If he rides on the big roads, we'll catch him. I'm confident that it's only a question of hours and our man will fall in our hands."

There were no more questions and Romano quickly moved to adjourn.

Tamara approached Romano and apologized for having missed the meeting.

"When I went to work this morning Charles was in a talkative mood," she said. "So I listened and asked a few questions of my own." She waved a piece of paper. "I wrote down what he said about Thomas Sarcin. He was a mechanical engineer, who worked for his father and desperately tried to get along with his older brother, Zaccaria — at least that's one of the many names under which his brother is known. Things didn't pan out. Zaccaria, according to Thomas, was an unstable individual, a fanatic activist for an equalitarian society, with a strong will and a humongous ego. He wanted to run the company even though he had zero knowledge in the field. Zaccaria's degree is in classical studies. Things went so bad that Thomas sold the company. Zaccaria joined activist groups, and for a while he stayed in Australia with his uncle. Later on, both brothers inherited from this uncle. A pile of money. Zaccaria dreamed of grandiose enterprises, enterprises that Thomas dismissed as chimeras, foolish and childish fantasies." Tamara deposited the paper on the table.

"Interesting,' Romano said. "Anything else?"

Tamara alternated balancing her weight between her feet. She still was uneasy about an action she'd taken that she felt was somewhat underhanded. "I called Thomas at home and left a message that I'd like to see him."

"Oh. Do you think he'll call back? We couldn't get hold of him."

"He already did." Tamara paused. "He's invited me for supper this coming Saturday. He'll pick me up and take me to his place. He wanted to show me his collection of miniature safes. From all makes."

Romano gave her a piercing look. "A personal matter, I assume?" Tamara nodded. "Hmm...it's risky."

"I know."

"Does he live in a house?"

"Yes." Tamara pointed to a picture at the end of the sheet she had given him. "I was sure you knew of the place, but I thought maybe CSIS hadn't had time to get a picture. It's in Delaware. I looped around it before coming here. Beautiful, but isolated."

"Hold on. I have to decide whether it's more suitable knocking on his door and asking him about the credit card or let you find out much more by accepting his date. I'll let you know. We may do some checking and see if we can hide in the neighbourhood."

****

Feelings of insecurity and anxiety troubled Frank Milton as he looked at the trophies hanging on the wall of his cottage. It must be terrible to be hunted, he thought. He hoped it would never happen to him.

His cottage was a good hideout. He had bought it from an old local who had been hunting deer, moose and wild turkey for most of his life. It was about 10 kilometres from Wasaga Beach, immersed in deep woods and accessible only through a rough trail.

The Blackpox Threat

It was an ideal retreat, away from the commotion of the city.

Frank began pacing the rustic living room, which was sparely furnished. There was still no news from Boris Youkenoff or Stan Glover. What happened to them? And why had Zaccaria not given him the green light for the dissemination of the vials? The blackpox wouldn't be active much longer. It was true that even an inactive virus would work to create panic among the population. What should he do now? After all, he shouldn't discount the money that the last phase of the operation would produce: another 30 million! Maybe he should try to call Zaccaria again. For the last three days Zaccaria hadn't answered his calls.

The noise of a motor vehicle resounded among the trees and stopped at his door. Stan, Frank thought, hopefully. Stan was back!

He rushed to the door.

Zaccaria was getting out of a jeep, dust all over his black suit.

"You? What are you doing here?"

"We have to alter our plans," Zaccaria said, and with resolute strides he walked inside, almost pushing Frank against the wall. He towered Frank by more than half a foot.

"What went wrong?"

"Get me a drink. It's been a rough drive." He slumped in the only leather chair in the room.

Frank didn't move. "Why are you here?"

"Because there's been a change of plans."

Frank crossed his arms. "What change, and why?"

"First the drink, then the explanation."

Reluctantly, Frank went to the kitchen and came back with a whisky and coke. "Now, speak up."

Zaccaria took a long swig of his drink. "I lost my boat and my men took off on me." He laughed. "They didn't like to be locked up in that sardine tin that was my bathysphere." He paused. "Now it's not only a question of power and money. I want revenge. They tried to engage me in a deal, when all they had in mind was to free my prisoner and launch an attack. You should have seen the display of forces: two helicopters and a combat unit. It was supposed to be a friendly encounter…"

"Friendly? Come on, Zaccaria, you were blackmailing them!"

Zaccaria held his glass high. "Hail, hail! Hail Zaccaria! I can still do it!" He finished his drink, and said, "Refill."

Frank hesitated a moment, then walked to the kitchen and returned with another whisky and coke.

"What about the diamonds?" Frank asked. "Did you get them?"

"Just a quarter million."

"What do they know about our involvement?"

"Close to nothing. They don't know who we are or where we hide the virus or vaccine. We can still go ahead with our operation, but we can't count on anybody else."

"You're kidding! By now they know the person under whose name *The Master of Masters* is registered."

"Still under my uncle's name. It'll take time to link it to me. That's the reason we have to act soon. Starting today!"

Frank remained pensive for a few seconds. First, Zaccaria wanted to proceed slowly, now, he was in a hurry. The man wasn't emotionally stable. He regretted going into business with him and felt that withdrawing would be the best.

"It's dangerous," Frank said firmly. "Our primitive scheme was simple. They had to drop off the diamonds, and after 24 hours we'd tell them where to find the vials with the blackpox. Your boat was in international waters and we could count on secrecy, as we assumed that the government wouldn't want to alarm people."

"Secrecy is still in effect. Not a word of what happened has transpired."

Frank paced back and forth. "But we lost the most important factor, the element of surprise."

Zaccaria waved off his concern. "Power is still on our side."

"We need an extra person for sending the threatening messages all over the country. This person has to disappear soon after, since by then they'd be ready to flock to the spot where the messages originated."

"I have that person. It's you. You disseminate the vials, send the messages and then disappear."

Frank shook his head. "If I send the messages from this cottage I would have to abandon it soon after. Where would I hide? This is my hideout! We need a different spot for broadcasting the messages."

Zaccaria finished his drink. "Go to my new house on Lake Huron. Nobody suspects any of my activities over there." He tossed a card to Frank.

"What is this for?"

"It contains the code to open the main door."

Frank looked at the card and pocketed it. He stood in front of Zaccaria, his fists in his pockets.

"We have another problem," he said. "Where would the drop for the ransom take place? We need a safe location."

"Don't worry. I have a place in mind." Zaccaria rose, his tall figure spreading a dark shadow in the small living room. "Let's go. We can't lose another minute."

Chapter 61

Tamara didn't know what to do. Catherine Ferreiro had shown up at the condominium gate, saying she had great news. Tamara, who was in the midst of getting ready for her date with Thomas, had little time to spare. But Catherine was still her best friend. She invited her in and offered a soft drink as she continued her beauty preparation.

"Wow! Look at you! New fancy hairdo and makeup! Even mascara! He must be important!"

"Catherine, don't make a big deal out of it." Tamara was in her robe, still undecided on the outfit she should wear. "Rather, tell me the big news!"

"We're moving to London. My husband is taking over the outlet my family has here."

"That's splendid! When?"

"After the baby is born. Today I went to see a few houses. But I wanted to come here in person to give you the good news. We'll be able to jog together again." She giggled. "Maybe while I'll be pushing the buggy with the baby. I missed you so much you can't believe it." She hugged Tamara as close as her pregnancy allowed. "But now it's up to you to say something. Who is he?"

"A client of the company I work for."

"Is he handsome?"

"I'd say, yes, he is."

Catherine's eyes sparkled. "Money?"

Tamara hesitated. She didn't want to lie to her friend, but she didn't want to say much about her date. After all, she was on a mission.

"Come on, Tamara! We used to have no secrets!"

It was true. And now she had only secrets for her.

"I don't know much about him," she said at length. "But why don't you come to the bedroom and help me choose the outfit?"

On the bed she spread the pale blue silk pantsuit and the green cocktail dress she'd gotten from Stephanie's shop. "Which one?"

Catherine feathered the fabric of both outfits. "Silk. So soft. They're both fabulous." She glanced at Tamara. "It's an important date, I can tell, so I'd choose the dress."

"Dress it is," Tamara said, and retreated into the bathroom. She had to hurry up. Thomas would pick her up in half an hour. She had to find an excuse to get rid of Catherine.

The bell rang.

It could be Thomas. She had told the superintendent that she was expecting a Mr. Thomas Sarcin, and to let him in. She got out of the bathroom and set the bedroom door ajar so that she could listen in.

Catherine had opened the door.

It was Thomas. "Sorry," he was saying, "I must have the wrong address."

"No, no," Catherine said. "Tamara is here. I'm just passing by."

Tamara slipped on the dress and came out to meet her date.

"Hi Thomas," she said, and shook his hand. She made the presentations, and emphasized that Catherine had a long drive ahead of her.

"I'm early," Thomas said. "I can come back later."

"Oh no, I was almost ready. Just give me a couple of minutes. Catherine, can you play hostess?"

"Sure. I can entertain your date for a few minutes." She turned to Thomas. "Drink?" she asked.

Tamara went back to her bedroom. Even if she didn't have a real reason, she felt nervous. There was no harm in Catherine meeting Thomas. And her friend would be on her way soon.

She chose a pair of sandals of a golden shade and freed her big purse of everything that wasn't necessary for a dinner party — everything except her faithful handgun and her special cell.

When she returned to the living room she had a big surprise. Catherine and Thomas were seated side by side, clearly involved in pleasant conversation.

Catherine's eyes were sparkling. "Guess what? Thomas has ordered the food from the Ferreiro's shop in town." She paused and winked. "I asked him if I could stop by his place and do some sampling. To check on the quality, I mean."

Tamara was dismayed and made a big effort not to show her reaction. "Well, I don't know…"

Her dear friend — a good soul, but curious as a groundhog — had managed to intrude in a delicate situation. Tamara didn't know what she would find in Thomas' house; what action might be developing there; they were still in the middle of a covert operation…pregnant Catherine would be in the middle — and as big as only a woman two weeks before the due date can be.

"You don't have to come," she said. "I'll promise you to taste each dish and report to you. Faithfully and objectively." Maybe Catherine would get the message.

She glanced at Thomas, who was flickering his eyes between the two women, clearly amused by the struggle for control.

After a few seconds of silence, Thomas broke the impasse. He rose and said, amiably, "I was told that pregnant women have special cravings. Maybe Catherine's are of different kinds, but equally important." He helped Catherine rise, took her left arm and Tamara's right. "Should we be going?"

****

"Justin, try to understand." Romano, crouched underneath a small tent, spoke in whispers. "Tamara is on duty tonight. Stay out of it. I know you can't reach her, but things are under control."

He had set camp at the fringes of Thomas Sarcin's property, protected by a copse of pine trees and evergreen shrubs. With him he had Serge Patton, a sniper, Alan Johnson, a rookie from Public Safety and Duncan Brown, who was operating his laptop under the mini tent. A CBRNE van was parked only a kilometre away.

"Easy for you to say. I don't like you a bit. You send a civilian to do the job that your agents should do."

"This was — and is — an extraordinary circumstance. Tamara was the only person who could manoeuvre with a legitimate reason in a web full of suspects. We didn't have anybody else who could play that role. The safety of the country was compromised. It was an emergency, Justin, believe me."

"She risks her life for you and your cause. And I bet you wouldn't even feel remorse if something happened to her."

"Justin, you're upset and don't know what you're saying. I care very much for all the people who work with me."

"You have no feelings. Work is all you have. No ties, no family. You don't know what love means."

He didn't need to be tangled in Justin's emotional problems; he had enough of his own.

"Justin: listen to me, and listen well. One, I have a wife and three kids. Two, I'm in the middle of an operation that requires all my attention. Three, if you don't stop whining I'll get you arrested." He closed his cell.

He'd been present when, after the briefing, Tamara had tried to call Justin. He'd heard her leave a short message in his voicemail, that she was on assignment and not to contact her. That's what probably had worried Justin. Romano sympathized with the man, but at the moment he had to concentrate on the ongoing operation.

"Anything new?" he whispered to Duncan.

"No. No calls recorded going to Thomas' phone."

Close to Duncan was an E-Gem generator that could supply power to his computer for hours; Duncan was prone, and supported himself with his elbows when he clicked on his laptop.

Since the four-man team had setup camp the only action around Thomas' house had been the delivery of food trays, set on the entrance steps.

Romano got out of the mini tent and leaned against the trunk of a tree, his mind wandering to his home and family. He hadn't been home once in the last three weeks, and in the months before he had spent only a few days there. How was Milena doing? She was holding the fort, he was sure. She was probably even skinnier, busy chasing after their pre-school kids. Added to that was their beloved no-pedigree dog, and now not one but two house cats. He had to use all his authority to stop the sheltering of animals that mysteriously appeared on their doorsteps. How a desert turtle had found its way to the backyard was still a mystery; fortunately it hibernated for a full six months. He smiled inwardly. Milena, he suspected, was probably as guilty as the kids in rescuing injured or abused pets. His wife was a warm, kind human being, who considered each day they spent together an occasion for celebration...

The noise of two cars approaching interrupted his musings. They stopped in the driveway which, brushing one side of the house, was in the team's line of sight. Darkness, however, forbade any guessing about the make of the cars. The sniper came close to Romano and pointed his night-vision scope at the newcomers.

"One woman, pregnant — oh, boy, is she big — is coming out of a van; a couple is getting out of a sedan."

"Who can the woman be?" Romano asked aloud.

"She surely doesn't look dangerous," the sniper said, and chuckled.

"Probably a friend of Tamara's," Romano said. "We just have to wait."

"We came here in force," said Duncan, who had come out from under the tent and was doing stretching exercises. "Almost certainly for nothing."

"It may be a quiet dinner party. You may be right. After all, the checking we've done on Thomas Sarcin points to no trouble at all."

"Yeah. Just the kind of social gatherings Ms. Smith likes. And we're here in the cold, freezing our butts."

Chapter 62

"Don't be so upset!" Michael said to his son. "You weren't available when Tamara called, and she left a message that she was going to be busy for the evening. Stop worrying."

"She said she was going on a mission. That's the word I don't like: *mission*! Do you know what that is? A euphemism for a life-threatening situation!" Justin threw his cell down. "She's risked her life three times already."

Michael rose from his upholstered chair and tapped his son on the shoulder. "You can't help it. Let's get busy. McKenzie should be back by now. Come with me to the lodge and find out if they know anything about him. I've insured the Delft pottery only until tonight. I'm anxious to deliver it."

"Okay, let's go. But I'm not finished with that Romano."

"Are you jealous, by any chance?" Michael shot him a teasing look.

"Hmm, a bit maybe. I think Tamara likes him. He's handsome, you know, tall and slim, with dark hair and blue eyes." He recovered his cell. "I do feel better now that I know he's married."

Together they carefully loaded the big box containing the precious pottery in Justin's Audi and drove to the lodge. It was situated on a gravel road that, a few kilometres farther, terminated at the entrance to the McKenzie property.

"Nice to see somebody is stopping by," the innkeeper said, and welcomed Michael. "It gets pretty lonely this time of year."

"Hi, Lesley." Michael said. "We're wondering if you have seen Mr. McKenzie recently."

"Well, I saw a motorcycle rushing by half an hour ago. Dust all over. That man sure has money to spare. He owns a Jaguar and a jeep. The motorcycle could be one of his new toys."

"Oh, great; thanks," Michael said. "We'll go there. Maybe we can catch him." He swiftly joined Justin in the car.

"He's in," he said to his son. "Let's go."

The gate was open and a dim light was shining in a far corner of the mansion. Slowly, Justin drove up to the entrance. Parked near the side door was a rather familiar looking Harley-Davidson. Justin put a hand on Michael's arm.

"Let's be quiet," he said, and turned off the engine and car lights. "Let me check the licence of that motorcycle."

He took a flashlight out of the glove compartment and both stepped out of the car. After having examined the plate, Justin unhooked his cell from his belt and clicked on voice-recording, where he usually stored all the important information. The licence number coincided with that of the motorcycle that had followed Tamara, Heather Motta and Brad Wilson to Fanshawe Park. He frantically dialled the number of Bill Hartwart, his friend at the London Police Service. He wasn't in, so he left a message giving the vehicle's licence and location. He had just closed his cell when a call came in.

It was Bill. "Be careful! That motorcycle belongs to Frank Milton. There's an All-Points-Bulletin over all North America. An OPP unit will be there in minutes. Don't take any actions."

"What is he wanted for?"

"Can't say. It's an issue of national security." And the call ended.

"What was that all about?" Michael asked.

"That motorcycle belongs to a criminal chased all over the country. The police will be here shortly."

"But if Karl is inside he may be in trouble. We should do something."

"That's true. But this Frank Milton could be armed." They stood quietly for a couple of minutes, then Justin said, "Let's sabotage his vehicle. At least he won't be able to escape."

They had finished draining the fuel out of the motorcycle when Michael bumped into a metal box attached to the wall.

"Give me some light," he said. He opened the box's door. "Well, well, well...we can spook this dangerous fellow out of the house. I'm going to turn the power off."

****

Thomas unlocked the door and picked up the containers with the take-out food. He gestured toward a big living room and turned on the chandelier.

"Wow!" Catherine said, her nose up in the air. "Look at those crystals, how they sparkle!" She then glanced at the cartons Tamara and Thomas had deposited on the dinner table. Pasted on top were instructions on how each item should be warmed up. "I'll take these to warm up," Catherine said. She then whispered to Tamara, "I'll do a little food sampling and then be out of your way." She winked.

"I've seen enough." She neared Thomas. "The kitchen?"

"Farther down, under the arch and then to the right." Thomas gestured toward the far end of the room. "The kitchen opens onto the patio. It's a nice feature I use a lot, in the summer, of course." He moved toward a counter. "Would you like a drink?" he asked Tamara.

"Oh, yes." Tamara hung her purse on the back of a chair and moved close to the bar where Thomas was standing. "I see you have Kahlua. I'll have a Black Russian, then."

Thomas poured two of the same. He held his glass high and said, "To our future together!"

Tamara tinkled her glass with his. "To your new business venture!"

They had just had the first sip, when a soft singsong resounded in the house.

"Oh my God, my brother is here!" Thomas said. "That's the lullaby our nanny used to sing!" He looked at the back of the room where the noise was coming from.

Zaccaria appeared, a gun in one end, a rope in the other. "I see you brought a nice girl with you. An old acquaintance of mine." He threw the rope onto Thomas' face. "Tie her up," he ordered.

Thomas didn't budge. "Zac, please, stop this nonsense. I know you lost your boat. I saw the pictures in the newspaper. I can help you buy a new one."

"A new boat? I want much more!"

Tamara was trying to assess the situation, and mentally counted the number of steps that separated her from the Smith & Wesson she had in her purse. Even if she managed to get at it, she couldn't match Zaccaria's firing power. He held an MP-5 that could discharge 30 bullets in no time flat.

Pointing his gun at Tamara, Zaccaria inched up to Thomas.

The Blackpox Threat

"Tie her up or I kill her right now," he said.

Thomas took the rope, made Tamara sit on a high back chair and put the rope around her.

"Tighter, tighter! I want to see the rope cut into her flesh."

Thomas complied, pain in his eyes.

"I'll kill the girl, but later. After I get my ransom it'll be a pleasure to finish the job I was hired to do a long time ago."

"What are you blathering about?" Thomas asked.

"I killed her parents — I was ordered to finish off the family, but the girl was out fucking. I missed her that night. That's why she's still alive." He laughed. "Not for long. At most 24 hours."

Thomas stood in front of Zaccaria. "Can we sit down and talk? I mean, you say a lot of things, none of which I understand." He gestured Zaccaria to a seat.

Tamara appreciated Thomas's calm demeanour. Clearly, he had experience in dealing with his brother and tried to find a way to gain control of the situation.

Zaccaria, however, swayed his gun up and down; his eyes, blinking incessantly, nervously scouted the room.

"Oh, no. You always want to talk. And that's bad for me. You convince me that I'm wrong, when actually I'm right." He held his chin up in defiance. "Tonight is the night. Turn on the TV, on the CBC. In a few minutes you'll hear my message."

The noise of wheels surprised everybody.

"Food is ready, nice and warm," Catherine said with her cheerful, high-pitched voice. She was pushing a cart. As she passed under the arch she was startled. "What the heck?" She recovered quickly and thrust the cart against Zaccaria.

For a moment Zaccaria lost his balance and hit the bar, but held the gun firmly in his hand. He then recovered, turned and went after Catherine.

"Come back here!" he shouted, but Catherine had disappeared into the corridor. As he rushed after her, he fired a shot.

Thomas bent over Tamara and started to untie her.

"I have a gun in my purse," she murmured.

"What?" Surprised, Thomas stopped loosening the rope.

"Quick, quick, before that madman comes back!"

Thomas freed her of all twine.

"Hide in the den and lock yourself in."

"I can't. Catherine's in trouble."

Tamara got her gun out and moved into the corridor, brushing the wall, her gun at the ready.

Chapter 63

Romano had received a call from headquarters saying that Frank Milton had been captured. As Serge Patton was the higher in command, Romano had put him in charge of the on-going operation, and had swiftly left, anxious to interrogate the man who had eluded the authorities for so long. For a while Serge Patton, Duncan Brown and Alan Johnson stood outside, curious to see what was happening inside Thomas Sarcin's house.

When Serge Patton heard a gunshot, he said, "We move in." He turned to Duncan. "You're the communications man. You can stay or come; your choice."

Patton and the rookie approached the house cautiously; Duncan walked a good few feet behind them.

At the back of the house a door opened wide and a woman rushed out of it. "Help, help! There's a crazy man with a gun inside. He shot at me." She stopped to take a long, big breath.

"Only one man?" the sniper asked.

"Yes, and two of my friends are inside. Hurry, hurry."

The two agents sprinted toward the house.

"Are we going to use a flash-bang?" the rookie asked.

"Only if we can't do otherwise," Serge Patton replied. "Let's see if we can assess the situation a bit better before making everybody deaf and blind."

"Ohmygod!" Catherine screamed. She leaned onto Duncan who had walked up to that spot. "Help me," she said, and leaned against him.

"What's the problem?" He turned on his flashlight.

"My water broke. I'm going to have a baby." She let herself slide down but held onto Duncan's trousers.

A panicky Duncan reached for his cell and called for an ambulance. He tried to shake off the woman.

"Don't go away." Catherine huffed. "Help me…help me get rid of my clothes."

Duncan kneeled first and then fell on the ground.

****

In the corridor Zaccaria was holding Thomas at gunpoint.

"Where is Tamara?" he asked.

"I don't know. She was probably scared and hid somewhere."

"Hmm…it could be." He gestured Thomas toward the living room. "Let's watch the news. Tonight I *am* the news. Tomorrow I'll be the news, and so on for a few days. Turn it on the National."

"Too early. It doesn't come on for another couple of hours."

Zaccaria glanced at the clock over the fireplace mantel. "The news about my enterprise is important enough to have crossed the border. Turn on CNN, then."

Slowly Thomas complied.

Zaccaria made Thomas lie on the floor near the TV set; he sat in front of it. For a few minutes the TV screen was filled with a beautiful woman who announced a number of important events, quickly followed by station identification and a few commercials; no breaking news carrying Zaccaria's name.

"What did you do this time?" Thomas asked, the tone of his voice soothing. "Something important, you said. What is it?"

"Something to talk about for ages. I have in my possession a valuable product. I put it on the market for a handful of diamonds. A good bargain, I tell you."

The noise of the television had muffled Tamara's footsteps. She walked toward the couch where Zaccaria was seated and stood behind him. She brushed his neck with her Smith & Wesson.

"Drop your gun, or I'll shoot you," she said. "Now!"

"What?"

For a few seconds Zaccaria remained still. Then, with a swift and agile move he turned sidewise, brandishing his MP-5 in the air.

A wave of sound and blinding light knocked down Thomas, Tamara and Zaccaria, making them scream from the excruciating pain. Serge Patton had released the flash-bang as soon as he recognized the type of gun Zaccaria was holding.

"You can take your earplugs off," Serge Patton said to the rookie. "It's a bang, a one-time deal."

He cuffed Zaccaria and took the guns that lay on the floor.

****

In the headquarters on Vanneck Road Frank Milton shook his head one more time. He had given his name and address and then asked for a lawyer. He hadn't answered one single question. Romano, exhausted, was ready to take a break, when a call came in. He moved into the corridor and listened attentively.

The Blackpox Threat

When he re-entered the room, he felt totally refreshed. He sat down.

"Days ago, the Swiss authorities arrested your partner, Boris Youkenoff, and sequestered 12 containers and sent them to WHO in Geneva for analysis. The results just came in. They have found dead samples of smallpox. Confronted with this fact, and the threat of extradition, your partner agreed to cooperate." He paused. "We're very much aware of the role you played in importing the virus with the intent of blackmailing the world." He paused once more. "Ready to have a little conversation?"

Frank Milton put his arms on the table and reclined his head on top of them.

****

No matter what the situation turned out to be, he shouldn't talk. As far as he knew, they hadn't found the vials with blackpox hidden in his car.

After Zaccaria had left his cottage, Frank had decided to play it safe. There was no time to take care of the vials' distribution, send the threatening messages and then return to his cottage. He had simplified the plan of action, especially because the effect of the virus, according to Boris, was now close to nil.

He had hidden his green Chrysler, which still contained all of the blackpox vials, under a grove of pine trees at the back of the cottage. The grove was so thick that it would be almost impossible to discern the shape of the car lying underneath. He had taken the CD with all the addresses of influential people who were to be sent the email messages and rushed to Zaccaria's house — to that mansion on the shores of Lake Huron known as the residence of respectable millionaire Karl McKenzie. He had driven his motorcycle, the whipping wind giving him an invigorating sensation.

Then things had started to go wrong. He was sitting in front of Zaccaria's desktop, ready to hook up to the Internet, when the power had gone off. With no light, and in an unfamiliar setting, he had been totally lost. He had waited a good 10 minutes, hoping for the power to resume but when that hadn't happened, he had decided to give up on his mission and return home.

He had walked outside the house and mounted his powerful motorbike. Within a couple of kilometres the engine had stopped — the gasoline gauge mysteriously on empty. Immediately after, two police cars had surrounded him.

How had all this happened? Who had informed them of his presence at his buddy's house? What did the police know about him for certain? Clearly Romano was aware of his involvement in the blackpox scare, but he had not much proof of it. He was fishing.

The best thing to do was hide under *The Charter of Rights and Freedoms*.

Chapter 64

Two cones of bright light, spread by the CBRNE van, almost blinded Catherine. The van, stationed nearby, had arrived in place long before the ambulance Duncan Brown had called for. Catherine lay on the ground of Thomas Sarcin's backyard. Bereft of any privacy, Catherine was giving birth, her hand squeezing Tamara's hard.

"Good girl, you're almost through," said Tamara, who guessed, but couldn't see, that a newborn was on its way.

Finally the ambulance arrived. Two paramedics opened the rear door and got a gurney out. One man, a big bag in his hand, kneeled near Catherine.

"Oh, we're a bit late for the big event," he said. "You've done it all by yourself."

He opened his bag, rummaged inside it, and swiftly cut the umbilical cord. The other paramedic came with a big blanket and wrapped up a very vocal baby.

"Is she okay?' Catherine asked, her voice a high pitch.

"She looks great."

Silently the paramedics lifted Catherine onto the gurney and then inside the ambulance.

Tamara was ready to jump in to keep her friend company, when she realized that Duncan Brown was still lying on the ground.

"What about him?" she asked.

"We're taking him with us," one of the CBRNE agents said. "We can give him first aid if necessary. Feel free to go with your friend."

****

At St. Joseph's Hospital Catherine was lying in a soft, comfortable bed, speaking to her baby. "You're in a hurry, eh?" She tickled her under the chin. She turned toward Tamara. "You should go home. My hubby will be here shortly and in a moment they'll take the baby back to the nursery. I'll have a nap." She chuckled and winkled at Tamara. "No wonder I missed you so much when you left. There's always action when you're around. Being with you makes me feel alive, ready to tackle the world."

A nurse tiptoed into the room and took the baby away as Catherine's eyelids slowly dropped closed.

"I'll leave you," Tamara murmured. "See you tomorrow."

Catherine nodded.

Tamara stepped out of St. Joseph's Hospital to use her cell. She was ready to call a cab when a voice behind her said, "Looking for transportation?"

The voice had an unmistakable pitch. She would recognize it among thousands. Tamara turned and threw her arms around Justin.

"Always close when I need you," she said. "What would I do without you?"

"I hope you need me for more than a ride." He kissed her and held her tightly in his arms. "I heard from Romano that everything went well. It was very kind of him to call and let me know how great you've been. And, most important, that you were safe."

"It seems that Operation Bullfrog came to an end today. Fortunately. The day after tomorrow we're having our last meeting."

"A meeting on Saturday?"

"It'll be informal, more of a get together, Romano assured me."

****

Tamara wondered if the CSIS conference room on Vanneck Road was the same place where so many dramatic events had been unfolding week after week. That was the past this is the present, she thought as she absorbed the changes around her. The longer counter sported bottles with real glasses; on the table lay three huge trays with pastry, sandwiches and canapés of different shapes and kinds, all compliments of the Ferreiro's shop; the dozen members attending were vociferous, speaking to each other and across the table. And the clothing — wow — everybody, except for the uniformed sentry, wore casual shirts and bright colours.

They had greeted her warmly as she entered, and Duncan had given her a friendly smile. For a moment she hadn't recognized him, with his beard and hair drastically trimmed. And there was no laptop in front of him!

Tamara sat close to Peggy, the dog trainer who had come to London to get a young German shepherd.

"Nice dog there." Tamara pointed to the dog, which sat on his hunches, his snout on Peggy's lap.

"I got him today out of the kennel. He's six months old; he's a bit shy yet." She petted the dog and whispered something in his ear.

"He's sure beautiful." Tamara looked around. "Romano not in?"

"No. We're all waiting."

There was a big applause as Romano appeared, dressed in jeans and a Senators' sweatshirt. He carried a case of Labatt's lager that he slid over the table.

"A short briefing and then...party time!" He sat down. "Our office is finalizing the charges against Karl McKenzie, aka Nekton, and Frank Milton. Through the registration of Milton's motorcycle we traced his refuge in the woods, and found the much hunted Chrysler. In a large insulating container we found vials. They're being analysed as we speak. Probably dosages of blackpox."

"Any news of Boris Youkenoff's contact?"

"Oh, yes, and good news. His name is Stan Glover, and he's been arrested."

"On what ground?" Mark Farin asked.

"Oh, that was another of Nekton's tricks. He gave Stan money to pay Boris for manufacturing the virus, but it was counterfeit. Stan couldn't find Boris, who was in custody since he couldn't pay a 20-frank fine. Stan was arrested when he took the fake five million euros to a bank." Romano grinned. "It's incredible how at times people get trapped because of their own vices. Boris' weakness was gambling. He was stuck on Swiss territory without a cent and couldn't pay a fine for having fed pigeons in a public park." Romano laughed. "The Swiss authorities impounded his truck — and found the famous containers with the vaccine."

"Did anybody sing?" Ron Brenner asked.

"Not Frank, but our friend Nekton has given us all the details we need to know. We have already recovered the diamonds."

"News of Dianne?" Duncan asked.

"Still in the hospital, but all tests were negative."

Romano paused and eyed the trays in the middle of the table. "Next week I'll file my report. It'll be lengthy, I am afraid." He smiled a broad, satisfied smile. "After that, I'll get all my back vacation. A full month." He grinned. "The right time to take off, since the Prime Minister will be busy answering the ton of questions the media are going to throw at him."

He threw his cap up. "Let's party!"

****

Comfortably seated on the chesterfield of her living room Tamara asked Justin, "Anything in particular you'd like to do?"

Justin gave her a lopsided and teasing look. "Do you need to ask?"

Tamara threw her head back and laughed. "I was thinking long term."

"Spend time together. I think we're made for each other." He neared the couch and kneeled close to her. "Let's find out if it's true."

The End

Made in the USA
Charleston, SC
18 January 2013